TOWER HAMLETS

91 000 004 826 66 5

D1092960

SECRET

CA

LONDON'S MOST ELIGIBLE DOCTOR

BY
ANNIE O'NEIL

idea

Library Learning Information

To renew this item call:

0333 370 4700

(Local rate call)

or visit
www.ideastore.co.uk

TOWER HAMLETS
Created and managed by Tower Hamlets Council

Carol Marinelli recently filled in a form asking for her job title. Thrilled to be able to put down her answer, she put 'writer'. Then it asked what Carol did for relaxation and she put down the truth—'writing'. The third question asked for her hobbies. Well, not wanting to look obsessed, she crossed the fingers on her left hand and answered 'swimming'. But, given that the chlorine in the pool does terrible things to her highlights, I'm sure you can guess the real answer.

Annie O'Neil spent most of her childhood with her leg draped over the family rocking chair and a book in her hand. Novels, baking and writing too much teenage angst poetry ate up most of her youth. Now Annie splits her time between corralling her husband into helping her with their cows, baking, reading, barrel racing (not really) and spending some very happy hours at her computer, writing.

THE SOCIALITE'S SECRET

BY
CAROL MARINELLI

TOWER HAMLETS LIBRARIES	
91000004826665	
Bertrams	19/02/2016
ROM	£5.99
THCUB	TH15001856

WITHDRAWN

All rights reserved including the right of reproduction in whole or in part in any form. This edition is published by arrangement with Harlequin Books S.A.

This is a work of fiction. Names, characters, places, locations and incidents are purely fictional and bear no relationship to any real life individuals, living or dead, or to any actual places, business establishments, locations, events or incidents. Any resemblance is entirely coincidental.

This book is sold subject to the condition that it shall not, by way of trade or otherwise, be lent, resold, hired out or otherwise circulated without the prior consent of the publisher in any form of binding or cover other than that in which it is published and without a similar condition including this condition being imposed on the subsequent purchaser.

® and TM are trademarks owned and used by the trademark owner and/or its licensee. Trademarks marked with ® are registered with the United Kingdom Patent Office and/or the Office for Harmonisation in the Internal Market and in other countries.

Published in Great Britain 2016
By Mills & Boon, an imprint of HarperCollins*Publishers*
1 London Bridge Street, London, SE1 9GF

© 2016 Carol Marinelli

ISBN: 978-0-263-25434-1

Our policy is to use papers that are natural, renewable and recyclable products and made from wood grown in sustainable forests. The logging and manufacturing processes conform to the legal environmental regulations of the country of origin.

Printed and bound in Spain
by CPI, Barcelona

Dear Reader,

Luke and Scarlet surprised me all the time as I wrote their story.

Sometimes I wondered how they would get to their happy ending. This couple had so much to work through, and yet every time I doubted they could Luke stepped in and reassured me that he knew where they were headed.

I love a hero who is one step ahead—not just of the heroine but also the author!—and Luke has the calm assuredness that I felt Scarlet needed. I *do* believe in love at first sight, and their story confirmed that for me.

Happy reading!

Carol x

Books by Carol Marinelli

Mills & Boon Medical Romance

London's Most Desirable Docs

Unwrapping Her Italian Doc
Playing the Playboy's Sweetheart

Bayside Hospital Heartbreakers!

Tempted by Dr Morales
The Accidental Romeo

Dr Dark and Far Too Delicious
NYC Angels: Redeeming the Playboy
200 Harley Street: Surgeon in a Tux
Baby Twins to Bind Them
Just One Night?
The Baby of Their Dreams

Visit the Author Profile page at
millsandboon.co.uk for more titles.

**Praise for
Carol Marinelli**

'A compelling, sensual, sexy, emotionally packed,
drama-filled read that will leave you begging for
more!'

—*Contemporary Romance Reviews* on
NYC Angels: Redeeming the Playboy

CHAPTER ONE

NO NEWS WASN'T always good news.

It was just the tiniest of diversions from Luke Edwards's usual morning routine but, having poured a glass of grapefruit juice, Luke turned the television on and listened to the news as he got ready for work.

It was just after 5:00 a.m. on Monday.

There was the usual stuff that should make mankind weep, yet it was immediately followed by the news that Anya's Saturday night performance at the O2, the last in her sell-out world tour, had been amazing and she would be heading back to the States today. The reporter moved to the next piece of celebrity gossip—a football star's wife who was rumoured to have had buttock implants.

He changed channels and found that it was just more of the same.

Luke flicked the television off and, though he still had half an hour to kill, he was restless so he decided to head into work. He went upstairs and selected a tie, which he put in his jacket pocket. As he came back down he grabbed his keys and glanced in the mirror, wondering if he really ought to shave.

No.

His straight dark hair needed a cut too but that could wait for next week.

It was still dark outside as his garage door opened and Luke headed out into a cold and wet November morning. He drove through the practically deserted, sleepy, leafy village, where he lived, towards the heart of London. He had recently been promoted to Consultant in a busy accident and emergency department at a major teaching hospital.

People sometimes said that he was crazy to live so far out but he also had a flat at the hospital for the times when he was on call or held back at work.

Luke liked it that where he lived was between Oxford, where his family were, and London, where he worked. The very distinct separation between his work and home life suited him well. The village was friendly but not overly so. He had been living there for close to a year now and was getting to know the locals at his own pace. Luke knew that, despite what others might think, he had made the right choice.

Or not.

It all depended on today.

It was a long, slow drive but he was more than used to it. Often he listened to music or a lecture he had heard about, but this morning he turned on the radio.

He needed to know if there was any news.

For the last four days Luke had been on edge and hypervigilant while doing all he could not to show it.

The traffic was terrible, he was told.

Thanks for that, Luke thought as he glanced at the time.

There was a huge snarl-up on the M25.

Luke was in the middle of it.

Finally, just before 7:00 a.m., the sun was coming up, the hospital was in sight and a new day had dawned.

He drove towards the underground car park, where he had a spot reserved, and was just about to flick off the radio, as reception was disappearing, when there was a break in a song.

'Unconfirmed reports are starting to come in that Anya...' the newsreader said, and Luke sat, blocking the traffic and listening to the brief report, before he drove into the basement. He parked but, instead of heading straight into work, Luke sat for an essential moment to collect himself.

His instincts had been right.

Today was the day, just not for the reasons he'd hoped.

Luke got out of the car and went up the elevator and made his way through the hospital.

Security guards were starting to race towards the accident and emergency entrance but Luke refused to rush. The only concession that his skills might be immediately required was that, as he walked along the corridor, he put on his tie.

'Morning,' Luke said to Geoff, one of the security guards, as he raced past him.

Not 'good morning'.

They weren't any more.

'Have you heard who's coming in?' Geoff answered by way of response, though he did slow down and fall into step with Luke.

'I have.' Luke nodded. 'It just came on the news. Can you call for backup and start setting up the security screens? How long until she gets here?'

'Ten minutes.'

Luke nodded his thanks and walked into the department.

'Thank God you're here early.' Paul, his registrar, came straight over.

Yes, Paul was very glad that his boss was here. Luke Edwards epitomised the calm that the department would be needing today—Luke never got ruffled and simply dealt with what was. 'Anya is on her way in,' Paul explained. 'She's in full cardiac arrest. The place is going to blow.'

Luke disagreed with Paul's assessment. Yes, drama was about to hit but the place would not blow.

Not while he was in charge.

'What do we know?' Luke asked as they walked into the resuscitation area where the nursing staff were already setting up.

'Just what I told you,' Paul answered.

'Have you called for an anaesthetist?'

'The first on call is in Theatre. The second on is David. He's coming just as soon as he can but he's with a sick child on PICU,' Paul answered, as Luke started checking and labelling the drugs that Barbara, a very experienced senior nurse, was pulling up. 'I was about to see if Switch could do a ring around...'

'It's fine.' Luke shook his head before Paul could suggest otherwise. 'We'll more than manage until David gets here.'

'Do you even know who Anya is?' Paul checked, because Luke looked completely unruffled by the news of who was on their way into the department and the fact that the anaesthetist wasn't there.

'Yes.'

Oh, Luke knew.

Better than most.

Anya had been famous for forty of her fifty years of life and would, after today, be even more so.

Especially if she died.

'You'd better let the director of nursing know,' Luke said.

Paul gave a worried nod. 'I already have.'

'Good. I'll go and make sure the screens are up out-side.' As he went to go out, Heather, the director of nurs-ing, was running down the corridor towards him.

'Do we know what she's taken?' was the first thing that Heather asked when she caught up with Luke.

'We don't know that she's taken anything.' Luke's re-sponse was tart and Heather flushed as Luke continued to speak. 'Let's just make sure that the screens are up and no cameras can get a shot of her.'

The media were already starting to gather. He could hear the sound of a helicopter hovering overhead but thankfully the ambulance bay was covered.

Right now it was about affording Anya some privacy.

Whether she would want it or not.

Paul came outside and briefed them further. 'Ambu-lance Control has just called. It's an unspecified drug overdose…'

'Well, that was never going to happen.' Heather's re-sponse was sarcastic.

'If you want to help—' Luke had heard enough innu-endo and the patient hadn't even arrived. He turned and faced Heather and made his feelings on the subject very clear. '—then cast judgement aside. If you can't manage that—leave.'

He meant it.

Luke had long ago learnt not to judge and to keep his own feelings very much in check, and it would take ev-erything he had in him to maintain that today.

'I was just—' Heather attempted.

'Well, please don't,' Luke interrupted.

Heather looked over at Paul and they shared a glance. Luke had worked at the Royal for just over two years now. He was never the sunniest of people but he rarely snapped and his mood seemed particularly dark today.

The ambulance arrived and as Luke opened the doors he saw that Anya was being given cardiac massage by a paramedic and that a sun-tanned man was shouting orders in a strong Californian accent. He informed Luke, only when asked, that his name was Vince and that he was Anya's private physician.

Luke already knew.

And he hated that man more than anyone could possibly imagine.

'What's the story?' Luke asked him, as the paramedics worked skilfully on the unconscious woman while they wheeled her in and Luke pulled on a gown and gloves.

'She must have taken some sleeping tablets,' Vince said.

It was a vague response but, with time of the essence, for now Luke ignored him. Instead, he listened to Albert, one of the paramedics, who relayed far more information than the private physician seemed willing to give.

'She was found unconscious by her daughter at six a.m.,' Albert said, as they moved Anya over to the resuscitation bed.

'Semiconscious,' Vince corrected.

'The daughter, Scarlet, is hysterical,' Albert said. 'It was hard to get any information out of her. Apparently Anya was given an opiate reversal but then vomited and went into respiratory and then cardiac arrest.'

'What has she taken?' Luke asked Vince, but any clear information remained unforthcoming.

'We're not sure.'

Albert gave Luke a wide-eyed look, which he took as meaning that the paramedics had had as much trouble extracting details.

Paul took over the cardiac massage as Albert relayed

the rest of what he knew. 'There were no bottles or syringes and she had been intubated before we arrived.'

Oh, so they'd had a little tidy up, Luke thought, and he looked over to Vince as he listened to Anya's chest. 'What medication is she on?' Luke asked.

Vince gave Luke a short list that consisted of antianxiety medications and some light sleeping tablets.

'So why are there no bottles or packets to be found?' Luke pushed.

'I give Anya her medication,' Vince answered coolly. 'I also have her on a strict regime of nutrients…'

'We'll get to them later,' Luke snapped, as he started delivering vital drugs that might reverse anything Anya could have taken. 'Any opiates?'

'Only when her back injury is exacerbated.'

It would take pliers to extract any useful information from him, Luke was sure. 'Get a toxicology screen,' Luke said to Barbara, who was pulling blood as he listened to Anya's chest.

'Her chest sounds terrible.' Luke was very concerned that the tube might be somewhat blocked. 'I want to replace the tube.' He wasn't happy that the right size had been inserted or that, given Anya had vomited, the tube was clear, so he decided to reintubate her.

'Watch the vocal cords!' Vince warned.

The billion-dollar vocal cords!

Luke did not look up but Heather swallowed as she watched Luke's jaw clamp down as he was delivered an unnecessary order.

Luke did not pause in his treatment plan, he just carried on with the procedure and then secured the tube, but he offered two words in response to a very unwelcome guest in his resuscitation room.

'Get out.'

The celebrity physician did not.

Luke repeated his command, but added a couple of expletives this time, and everyone startled because Luke rarely showed emotion. He never really swore or raised his voice. He didn't need to assert himself angrily. He just chose to now.

No one present could even guess at Luke's true loathing for this man.

Luke listened to Anya's chest again and, happy that the tube was in the correct position and that her air entry was better, he pulled off his stethoscope and asked Vince to repeat whatever it was he had just mumbled.

'I'm not leaving Anya,' he said.

'Oh, but you are,' Luke responded. 'Unless you can tell me, right now, exactly what Anya has taken, and why it took so long for you to get her here, you are to leave my area now.'

Foolishly he did not.

David, the anaesthetist, arrived then and took over the care of Anya's airway. Luke called for more anti-opiate and inserted that into Anya's IV line and then awaited its effect.

'Can we can call for Security?' Luke said.

'Security?' Heather checked, knowing that they were busy outside and wondering why they might be needed in here.

'I want him out,' Luke responded, and as he did so he briefly turned to the unhelpful and unwelcome visitor in his emergency room who was diverting his concentration yet still refused to move.

Luke kicked at a silver metal trolley. It clattered into a wall and the implication was clear—Anya's private physician would be leaving by any method that Luke saw fit to use.

Paul's assessment had been right after all—the place was about to blow, only not for the reasons anyone had been expecting!

What the hell was going on with Luke?

'You make me sick!' Luke shouted, and, wisely perhaps, Vince chose to leave.

Everyone glanced at each other but Luke made no comment. He simply did all he could to focus his attention fully on Anya, who was on the very brink of death.

It was a long and lengthy resuscitation.

The drugs were reversed and her heart started beating but she had aspirated too. It was more than an hour before they had Anya under control. Then it was another fifteen minutes before she started to rouse and began gagging at the tube.

'It's okay, Anya,' Luke said, and then blew out a long breath because for a while there he hadn't thought that it would be. 'You're in hospital.'

Anya was fighting and confused, which were good signs—all her limbs were moving and her terrified eyes briefly met Luke's before David put Anya into an induced coma.

'I want her up on ICU,' David said, and looked over at Heather, who was just returning from a lengthy phone call with Admin. 'Can you call them and ask how long until they're ready and then arrange to clear the corridor?'

Heather nodded. 'I'll get onto it now. Luke, will you speak to the press?'

Luke hated how normal policy seemed to have been thrown out of the window. He was certain, quite certain, without checking, that the department would have seen several drug overdoses overnight. He just loathed how everything had changed simply because of who Anya was.

'I'll speak with Anya's family first,' Luke said in response to her request.

Even Heather had the grace to blush. 'I've put them all in the staffroom.'

'Who?' Luke checked.

'Her manager, the vocal coach, her doctor, her bodyguards. Scarlet's in there too.'

'Scarlet's her daughter,' Paul added, because unless it was rugby or medicine, no doubt Luke wouldn't have a clue who she was.

'Okay, I'll speak with her now,' Luke said, as he binned his gloves and gown.

He walked out and although the department had grown busy in the hour or so that he had been working on Anya, all eyes were on Luke as he walked past. Everyone wanted to know what was going on and how Anya was.

Luke didn't stop to enlighten them.

Instead, he walked around to the staffroom and saw that Anya's huge entourage were all there on their phones. As Luke went to go in and speak with the daughter, one of them had the nerve to ask for his ID.

'It's your ID that I need here,' Luke responded, and with that line he warned them how any dealings with him would be.

'How is she?' a frantic woman asked.

'We've been waiting for more than an hour for an update,' another person said.

Luke just ignored them and walked into the very full staffroom. 'I'm Luke Edwards, I've been taking care of Anya. I'd like to speak with the immediate family.'

And there, in the midst of it all, she was.

Scarlet.

Still beautiful, Luke thought.

She was sitting, trembling, with her head in her hands.

Even her cloud of black ringlets was shaking as her knees bobbed up and down. She seemed oblivious to her surroundings but then she suddenly looked up and her already pale face bleached further in recognition.

'Luke?'

'Luke Edwards,' he said, doing all he could to keep them anonymous, to not let everyone present know the agony this was. 'I've been treating your mother. Are there any other relatives?' Luke checked.

Scarlet shook her head and opened her mouth to speak but no words came out so she shook her head again but then managed two words. 'Just me.'

'Then I'd like to speak to you alone.'

'We need to know what's going on,' a woman said. 'I'm Sonia, Anya's manager.'

'I'm speaking now with her next of kin.'

Luke's stance was not one to be argued with. It wasn't just that he was tall and broad—after all, there were far more burly bodyguards than he. More it was his implacable expression and cool disdain that had the manager step back and the path cleared for him to leave.

Scarlet was seriously shaken; her legs felt as if they were made only of liquid.

She was about to be told that her mother was dead, Scarlet was quite sure of that.

'This way,' Luke said, and down another corridor they went, and when she needed him to take her arm, instead he walked on briskly.

Luke opened the door to his office and she could see his grim expression.

She was dead, Scarlet was sure.

Luke was here.

Scarlet was very used to feeling conflicted but it was immeasurable now.

She stepped into his office and the first thing that hit her was that it was so quiet.

So completely quiet and calm that after the chaos of that morning the stillness hit her like a wall.

For the first time since she had found her mother, there was, apart from her own rapid breathing, the sound of silence.

Stepping into her mother's hotel bedroom had been something she would never forget.

'Mom?'

She had crept in quietly and seen her mother lying in her bed, face down.

'Mom?'

She had tried to turn her over but Scarlet was of slight build and she hadn't been able to.

She had screamed for help and after a couple of moments a shocked butler had arrived.

From then on it had been chaos. Hotel staff had started to appear. Vince, her mother's physician, had arrived dressed, wearing trousers and a shirt, and Scarlet couldn't understand why he had taken a moment to get dressed.

She had stood back, sobbing, watching chaos unfold, and finally had picked up her cell phone and dialled the UK emergency number.

She shouldn't have rung it, she had been told.

There was already a private ambulance on the way.

Scarlet opened her mouth to ask the inevitable question—'Is she…?' But her throat had been dry and scratched from screaming and no words had come out.

Luke could see her confusion and anguish.

'Take a seat,' Luke said, and he turned the engaged

light on above his door that warned people he was not to be disturbed.

Still Scarlet stood there.

She was going to hell for all that she'd done, Scarlet knew. In fact, she was going to hell twice because, instead of asking how her mother was, instead of begging him to tell her the news, she blurted out what was now at the forefront on her mind.

'I'm sorry…'

'Just take a seat,' Luke said.

She went to take a seat, but the chair seemed a very long way off and Luke's hand went on her shoulder to guide her towards his desk, but then he changed his mind.

His hand slid from the nearest shoulder to the farthest arm and he turned her into him. Luke's arms wrapped around her and he pulled her right into his chest and he held her so tightly that for a moment nothing remained but them.

There was the scent she had missed, the body she had craved and the understanding that Scarlet had never known till him.

It was an embrace she had been absolutely sure she would never, ever feel again.

'I'm so, so sorry,' Scarlet wept.

'It's okay, Scarlet.' That lovely deep, calm voice hushed her. Luke's chest was such a wonderful place to lean. To feel his breath on her cheek and his hand stroke the back of her hair was a solace Scarlet had never thought she might know again. 'I think she's going to be okay,' Luke said.

He was talking about her mother.

While she was sobbing for them, for their beautiful, painful past and all that they had lost.

CHAPTER TWO

CALM, PROFESSIONAL AND DETACHED.

That was how Luke had intended to be with Scarlet as he updated her on her mother's condition. The entire walk from the staffroom, right the way to his office, Luke had been telling himself that he was more than capable of being just that.

Luke had learnt a long time ago to push emotions aside—with patients and their relatives, with his own relatives too.

He had just never quite mastered objectivity when Scarlet was around.

It was something he knew he had better start working on.

Just not today.

Now the very last thing Scarlet needed was calm, professional and detached, but more to the point the impact of actually seeing her again meant that Luke could be none of those things.

Just yet.

As he pulled her into his arms, the embrace was as necessary for Luke as it was for Scarlet. There was so much anger and pain inside both of them. Their traumatic past was perhaps insurmountable but he dealt with the present now.

She was here. Not by the method he would have preferred—Luke had hoped Scarlet would contact him before she'd left for America today—but, yes, she was here, and so Luke held her in his arms and smelt again her hair, fighting not to kiss her salty tears away.

How messed up was that? Luke thought to himself.

He'd had a few months to prepare for the possibility of seeing her again. Since Anya's UK tour had been announced late last year, the thought that their paths might cross had been constantly on his mind. Since Anya and her entourage had touched down in England he had been wondering if Scarlet would call, if their history meant as much to Scarlet as it did to him. And, since seven this morning, when the news had broken that Anya was in an ambulance, being blue-lighted towards the Royal, he had dealt with the knowledge that he'd face Scarlet today.

Every preconceived response to her that he'd had crumbled.

Yes, there was an awful lot that needed to be discussed but Luke knew that Anya wasn't the only vulnerable, critical casualty that had been bought into his department today. Scarlet was another and, at a very personal level, he cared about her so very much more. Luke didn't want to let her go because, when he did so, back to her world Scarlet would return and so Luke took another moment to hold her.

Scarlet held him too.

She didn't just lean on him, she had slipped her hands into his jacket and wrapped her arms around his solid waist and just breathed in the delicious scent of him. Tangy, musky, male. It was a scent that she had yearned for and never forgotten and one that had been made familiar again now.

How could it be that he felt the same to her hands?

After all that had gone on, how, on this day, could Luke's arms be the ones that were holding her up?

As she was in England she had hoped that they might meet, but she had expected harsh, accusing words to be hurled at her. Words that he had every right to deliver, but instead of that he held her and made the horrible world go away for a moment.

As she had sat in the staffroom, waiting for news, Scarlet had blocked out the sounds of the people around her. Vince had been trying to speak with her, telling her what to say, insisting that her version of events wasn't quite correct. Her mother's manager, Sonia, had demanded to know where Scarlet had got to yesterday and why she hadn't been there to see her mother go on stage.

None of them knew about the row she'd had with her mother in the early hours and Scarlet had sat revisiting that as she'd done the best to block everyone else out.

And then in the midst of the madness she had heard the calm deepness of Luke's voice.

Her frantic heart seemed to have stopped beating for a second.

Oh, she had known that Luke was a doctor but she hadn't known he worked in London. When they had met he had been here for an interview but had been unsure if he'd take the job.

It had never entered her head that Luke might be here in the hospital and be the doctor fighting to save her mother's life.

Yet he was.

When Scarlet had looked up she had felt the very same jolt that had run through her the night he had walked into the club and their worlds had changed for ever.

He'd been wearing a suit that night and he was wearing one now.

It was the little things she noticed and remembered.

The other stuff was way too insurmountable for now.

And, as Luke had the first night they had met, when she clung to him he pulled back.

'Tell me.' Scarlet held him tighter, not ready to let go. If the news was bad, and given the morning's events she expected it to be, it was like this she wanted to hear it.

'She's doing better.'

Scarlet held her breath.

'Your mother briefly opened her eyes,' Luke explained. 'And she was fighting the breathing tube. That's good. For now she's been placed in an induced coma.'

'Is she going to die?' Scarlet asked.

'I don't think so but she came very close.'

'I know,' Scarlet said. 'I called an ambulance.'

'That's good.'

'You told me the number.'

She took a splinter of their time and they both examined it for a moment. A little shard of conversation that, had it come from another, would have been swept away, never to be examined again, but both now recalled that tiny memory with absolute clarity.

Scarlet looked up but not into his eyes.

Never again, Scarlet knew, would she be able to meet that deep, chocolate-brown gaze. There was just too much regret and shame for that. Instead, she looked at that lovely unshaven jaw and the deep red of his mouth that had once delivered paradise.

And Luke, feeling her eyes scan his mouth, despite the circumstance of this meeting, wanted to lower his to meet hers.

It was as simple as that.

But those days were gone and so, because he had to,

he let her go. 'Have a seat,' Luke said in his best doctor's voice.

Calm, professional, detached.

If he was going to do this properly then he could be no other way.

Scarlet remained standing as Luke took off his jacket, threw it onto a chair and then went around the desk and sat down, waiting for her to do the same.

'Tell me what happened.' Luke kicked the interview off.

'I told you,' Scarlet said. 'I called an ambulance. Vince had called for backup but they were taking for ever and—'

'Scarlet,' Luke interrupted, 'we need to start at the beginning. Before this morning when did you last see your mother?'

'Last night,' Scarlet said, and watched as Luke picked up a pen and jotted something down. 'There was a party to celebrate the end of her tour and...' Scarlet shrugged but didn't finish.

'And how was she?' Luke asked.

'I didn't make it to the party,' Scarlet said. 'I saw her back at the hotel.'

'What time was that?'

'About midnight.'

'And how was she?'

'Tired.'

'Who was the last person to see her?'

'Me,' Scarlet said. 'I think.'

'Around midnight?'

'Around one. Can you stop taking notes?' Scarlet asked. 'I can't talk to you when you're writing things down.'

'Scarlet, these details are important,' Luke said, but he did put down his pen.

He'd been using it as a distraction.

Not a word of this conversation would he ever forget.

'You found her?' Luke checked, and Scarlet gave a tense nod.

'What time was that?'

'Just before six.'

'Were the two of you sharing a room?'

'No.' Scarlet frowned.

'Were you staying in the same suite?'

'No.'

'So why were you in your mother's room at six a.m.?'

'I just went in to check on her.'

'Why?' Luke persisted.

'Because I was worried about her.'

'Why?' Luke pushed, but Scarlet did not elaborate. 'Come on, Scarlet. I can't help if you don't tell me.'

'You can't help me.'

'I'm talking about your mother!' Luke's voice rose, just a fraction. It had to if they were going to stay on track. That little pull back served to remind not just Scarlet but himself that this was work. He watched her eyes fill with tears at the slight reprimand but he had to push through. When no further information was forthcoming he chose to be direct.

'Has your mother been depressed lately?'

'No, no.' Scarlet shook her head. 'It's nothing like that. She just took too much.'

'How, when her physician keeps her pills?'

'She keeps some on her,' Scarlet said.

Luke honestly didn't know if Scarlet was covering up for her mother or simply had no idea how serious the problem was.

'Scarlet.' Luke tried to meet her gaze. 'Why did you go in to check on your mum? I'm not going to write anything down. Just tell me.'

'I was worried.'

'More so than usual?' Luke checked, and she nodded. 'I need to know why.'

'We had a row.'

'About?'

'Please don't ask, Dr Edwards.' It was Scarlet now who rebuked him, just a little but enough for him to get what she meant—if there were lines that could not be crossed, if he wanted to keep this professional, then, right now, the answer to that question could not be discussed. 'We had an argument.'

'Okay.'

'They want my mother to be moved to another hospital,' Scarlet said.

Luke had guessed that they might. 'Well, as of now, the only place your mother is being moved to is Intensive Care. Here.'

'They think that she needs to be somewhere more used to dealing with…' Scarlet stopped what she had about been to say. Luke loathed the word 'celebrity'.

'She's in the best place and in no condition to be moved,' Luke said. 'As her daughter, you get to make that call.'

'I don't think so.' Scarlet gave a worried shake of her head.

'I know so,' Luke responded.

'But she has Vince. He deals with all that type of thing.'

'Yes, well, Vince is going to be a bit busy for the foreseeable future. After I've spoken with you, believe me, I'm going to be speaking with him and getting a far more accurate history than the one he gave me earlier. I may also be speaking with the police so trust me when I say that I'll back your call if you want your mother kept here.'

'Luke, please, don't bring the police into this.' Scarlet started to cry and not very quietly.

He sat and watched unmoved. *Those* tears did not move him and certainly he would not be swayed by hype and celebrity status when he made his decisions.

He just needed more facts but few were forthcoming.

His pager trilled and Luke checked it. Seeing that it was Heather, he made a phone call and rolled his eyes as she told him that the press were becoming more insistent. 'Just say no comment,' Luke responded tartly. 'How hard is it to say that?' He let out a tense breath. 'Unless there is a change in Anya's condition, or you need me for another patient, you're not to disturb me. I'm speaking with a relative now.'

He looked over and saw that in the couple of minutes it had taken to speak with Heather, Scarlet had stopped crying long enough to take out her phone. Luke watched with mounting irritation. They were speaking about her mother's near-death and yet Scarlet was checking the news reports and quickly scrolling through social media!

'What are you doing?' Luke asked.

'It's everywhere!' Scarlet said, but then she really started to cry and they weren't false tears this time. As she put the phone down on the desk, Luke saw an image, and he reached over and picked it up.

The photo that he saw was of Scarlet. She was dressed in a pair of red pyjamas and her feet were bare as she stood on the street beside the ambulance that her mother was being loaded into. Two bodyguards were restraining her from climbing in. Her black hair was a mop of wild curls, her usually pale skin was red from crying and there was a look of sheer terror on her face.

Luke looked up from Scarlet's phone and at the woman who now sat on the other side of his desk—she was the perfectly groomed star in crisis now! Scarlet was wearing tight leather leggings and a tight black top. Over that there was a large silver leather jacket that looked as if it had been thrown on at the last minute. Her black curls were now perfectly tousled. Luke knew, though, from very personal experience, that the photo was a truer portrayal of Scarlet's morning locks.

He pulled away from that memory; instead, he looked back at the phone and the image that had been captured by the press.

It showed a rare moment of reality in a very unrealistic world and this would be the photo that would dominate, Luke was sure.

Scarlet looking less than perfect.

It was the Scarlet he far preferred.

'It's going to be worse than ever now...' Scarlet could not stop crying. Yes, she was terrified for her mother, but she'd had so much hanging on today, so many plans in place. There wasn't a hope of escaping from the press now and, Scarlet knew, now more than ever her mother needed her to be near.

'They're going to make my life hell.'

'Don't feed them, then,' Luke said. Her head was in her hands, her fingers were scrunched in her hair, but she lifted her face and gave him a scornful look as he continued to speak. 'You don't have to respond to the press, just focus on your mother and yourself.'

'What would you know?' Scarlet scoffed.

'Oh, I know,' Luke said. It was pointless to sit and pretend that he could take a comprehensive history from Scarlet and leave the personal aside. 'David, the anaesthetist, will take a more thorough history once your mother has been transferred to ICU.' He handed her back her phone, and as he did so he looked at Scarlet's slender, manicured fingers and remembered hands that were as smooth as a kitten's paws.

No, anger at her spoiled, pampered life didn't now gnaw at him; instead, it saddened him that that funny, adventurous mind had been locked away for so long.

Yes, the world was supposedly Scarlet's oyster, but Luke knew that since the day she had been born, her life had been magnified by a lens.

'You're handing me over.'

'I'm handing your mother's care over,' Luke said. 'That's normal policy when a patient is moved. I need to get back out there, Scarlet. I have patients to see.'

'What about me?'

Typical, Luke thought, but, though he tried to generate anger, though he did his best to remind himself of the spoiled princess Scarlet was and the absolute diva she could be, he failed.

'What about us?' Scarlet said.

'There's no us,' Luke lied.

He *was* angry now as he recalled all she had done, but instead of standing to leave, he sat there.

And so did she.

They sat in the silence of his office and as the world carried on outside, both went back to a time when things had seemed so different.

When hope had arrived in both their hearts.

Even if it killed them to do so, both remembered.

CHAPTER THREE

'I'VE GOT A HEADACHE.' Anya closed her eyes and massaged her temples. 'I'm going to have to go back to the hotel and see Vince.'

Scarlet frowned in concern and said all the right things to her mother but inside all she felt was relief. All she wanted was to get away from the noise of the club and close her eyes and go to sleep. It was after midnight and Scarlet had been up since seven. She had given interviews and done a shoot at London Bridge, and the rest of the day had been spent propping up her mother, telling her that she could get through the show.

'We'll get you back,' Scarlet said, and nodded to her mother's bodyguard.

'What would I do without you?' Anya asked, and Scarlet felt the knot that had lived in her chest for more than ten years now tighten a notch. And then, because she was Anya, her mother changed her mind about leaving when a young guy came over to their table with a drink and told her how amazing her performance that night had been. 'I'll just stay for one more,' Anya said.

Scarlet moved over to give the young man room to sit next to her mother but then she stood up.

She saw the exit door and started to walk towards it.

Scarlet wanted fresh air.

More than that she wanted to run.

'Hey, Scarlet…' A hand was on her arm and she turned to the face of one of her mother's bodyguards. 'I'll send Troy outside with you.'

She didn't want Troy.

Scarlet didn't want anyone, she just wanted one day, one moment to be allowed out in the world alone.

She didn't want to be here in this club.

And then she looked up and saw a man who looked as if he didn't want to be there either.

He was taller than most and, unlike others, he was wearing a suit. His hair was dark and as he raked a hand through it, it remained a touch messy. He was smart yet dishevelled, present but unimpressed, and there was something about him that had Scarlet intrigued.

'We're all leaving now,' Troy suddenly informed her. 'Your mother's ready to go.'

'I'm going to stay on.'

It was a rare request.

An almost unheard-of request, in fact, and one that did not go down too well.

'I don't need your drama now, Scarlet,' Anya hissed. 'I've been working all night and my head feels as if it's about to explode…'

'Vince will sort that out,' Scarlet said.

It ended the conversation.

Scarlet had known that it would.

Anya could stay and argue for ten minutes with her daughter or head back to Vince.

How Scarlet loathed that man!

And so, as her mother left the building, Scarlet remained.

Not alone, of course. Three bodyguards were still present, but for now at least she was minus Mom.

* * *

Luke, even before they had arrived in the club, had had enough.

It was his younger brother's twenty-first birthday and Luke really didn't want to be here, but up until now he'd had no real choice.

He'd bought dinner and had done the cursory pub crawl and had decided that he'd buy the first round here, stay for a little while and then disappear.

It wasn't a regular nightclub. Marcus's friend knew someone and had got the boisterous group into some very trendy, exclusive basement club.

At twenty-eight years of age, Luke felt old.

He'd always been more sensible than most, more responsible than most, and this place tested that to the limit. Everyone was off their heads and the noise just ate at him.

Still, it was his brother's birthday so Luke had gone along with things till now. He had been down from Oxford anyway, in London for an interview, and at lunchtime he had checked into a hotel.

His interview had been scheduled for four, which should have given him plenty of time to meet his brother and friend at seven. Except the interview had gone really well. So well that not only had he been extensively shown through the department, his potential new boss had asked him to wait back so he could meet a colleague who was in Theatre. Of course Luke had agreed. This was a senior registrar's position with a junior consultancy at the end of it at the London Royal after all.

There hadn't been time to get back to the hotel to change so he had arrived half an hour late to meet his brother and had felt on the back foot ever since. Especially here. Everyone was dressed in far less than a suit and drinking bright cocktails and were high, if not on life, just high.

'Nice to be single again?' Marcus asked, as Luke bought the drinks.

'Actually, yes,' Luke said, though it was wasted here, he thought privately.

Marcus and his friends hit the dance floor, which actually consisted of most of the place, and Luke took a mouthful of his drink and leant against the bar. He thought about the day he'd just had.

He wanted the job.

And that might prove to be a problem.

It hadn't been a difficult break up.

A painless procedure might be the best description.

Luke and Angie had been going out for a couple of years and had been about to move in together. Angie worked at the Royal and had told him about the upcoming role. But within a week of Luke applying, their relationship had finally come undone.

There just wasn't the passion that should be there for a couple who were about to move in together. Added to that was Luke's refusal to, as Angie had annoying called it, share.

Only she hadn't been talking about the last chocolate in the box!

'I know they're in there,' Angie would insist.

'What?'

'Feelings.' Angie's response had been exasperated. 'Emotions.'

'We don't all have to ride the roller-coaster, Angie. Just because I don't…' Luke had bitten his tongue rather than admit that yes, there were hurts there. Angie would have far preferred that he rise to the bait but Luke had consistently refused to. 'I guess I'm not messed up enough for a psychiatrist to date,' Luke had offered.

Luke was straight down the line and dealt with whatever life threw in his path without fuss. He saw no need for prolonged discussions as to how the past had shaped today. He had no wish to come home from a long and difficult shift and to share how it felt to lose a four-year-old or whatever agony the day had brought.

How he felt was his concern, he'd regularly told Angie. Amicably they had agreed that opposites did not attract and had quietly broken up.

There was one thing, though, that Luke needed to do if he was going to take the role at the Royal—and Luke was quite sure that it was his. He needed to be sure, very sure that Angie would be okay having her ex working at the same hospital.

Luke took out his phone and saw that there was a text from Angie, asking how the interview had gone, but it had been sent three hours ago.

It was far too late to return it now.

They were exes after all.

'Well?'

A soft voice, very close to his ear, pulled Luke out of vague introspection and he caught the heady scent of summer in the midst of winter as he turned to the sight of a young woman.

She had long, black, curly hair and huge navy eyes. Her face was incredibly pale but those large navy eyes were alert and smiling. Her lips were full and she wore dark red lipstick and not much else, just a tiny, tight, red dress.

'Well, what?' Luke asked in answer.

'Aren't you going to buy me a drink?'

'No.' Luke shook his head and tried to gauge her age. He was usually good at it but with her it was an impossible ask. Her skin was smoother than any he had seen and yet her eyes were wise. 'Are you even old enough to be drinking?' Luke checked.

'Of course I am.' Scarlet frowned at the odd question. Everyone knew how old she was. A fortnight ago she had turned twenty-three and it had been a massive affair—Anya had bought her onto the stage in Paris and had sung 'Happy Birthday' to her.

'I'm Lucy,' Scarlet said, just to test his reaction and to make sure that this man really didn't know who she was.

'I'm Luke,' he responded. 'And I'm still not going to buy you a drink.' Luke had already decided that he was going back to the hotel.

The bartender came over. 'Hey, Scarlet! Can I get you anything?'

'Scarlet?' Luke frowned and watched a small blush spread up her neck and to her cheeks. 'What happened to Lucy?'

'That's my…' Scarlet didn't finish her sentence. She didn't want to tell him about the alias that she used for hotel bookings and things. There was a heady thrill that Luke really had no idea who she was.

It was unbelievably refreshing.

'I'll have a glass of champagne,' Scarlet said to the bartender, instead of answering Luke's question.

'Put it on mine,' Luke said.

'Thank you.'

'No problem.' Luke drained the last of his drink and turned to sort out the bill. 'See you,' he said.

'You're going?'

'God, yes,' Luke said as the music pumped.

'That's not very polite! You can't buy me a drink and then leave me alone.'

Luke conceded with a small smile. 'Drink fast, then.'

She took the tiniest sip.

'And another,' Luke said, and then he started to laugh as Lucy—or was it Scarlet?— pretended to take another tiny sip.

They were, it would seem, going to be here for a very long time.

'Who are you here with?' she asked.

'My brother and his friends,' Luke said. 'It's his twenty-first.'

'And why are you wearing a suit?' Scarlet asked, and then took another tiny, tiny sip.

'To ensure that I look like an idiot.'

'Well, I think that you look…' She looked over his body and then up to his pale face. He was clean-shaven but there was a dark shadow on his jaw, and his eyes, when she met them properly, were a very deep shade of brown. So dark that she couldn't see his pupils. 'I think you're beautiful.'

'I don't think I've been called that before,' Luke said, smiling at her Californian accent. 'Though I'm quite sure you've been called it many times.'

Now Luke looked at her properly, in the way he'd been wanting to since he had turned around to her voice.

That dress showed far too much pale skin and the red stilettos she wore looked a little too big for her skinny legs. His eyes moved to her face and she was way more than beautiful. That fluffy hair was at odds with her delicate features and her mouth was very full and red.

A little too full perhaps, Luke thought, wondering if she'd had fillers, but, God, she was surely way too young for all that sort of thing.

He wanted to kiss her.

That in itself was a rather bizarre thought for Luke. While he thought about sex for approximately fifty seconds of every minute, to want to reach over and kiss, simply kiss, a virtual stranger was something he had never felt before.

Luke checked his memory.

Nope, not once.

This was a new feeling indeed.

'So who are you here with?' he asked.

'A few people.' Scarlet shrugged but was saved from elaborating when one of his brother's friends came over. 'Hey, Doc,' he said, and picked up his drink, but then he gave Luke an odd, wide-eyed look and left them.

'Doc?' Scarlet checked.

'Doctor,' Luke said, and told her a little bit more about himself. 'Which is the reason I'm wearing a suit. I was at an interview earlier.'

'Doctor?' Scarlet frowned and, almost imperceptibly, screwed up her nose, as if he had said that he specialised in sewerage and had just dropped in for a drink midshift.

'What do you do?' Luke asked her.

Scarlet looked at the bubbles fizzing up in her still very full glass and it matched her veins because they seemed to be fizzing too with excitement. Luke really didn't know who she was, which meant she could be anything she wanted to be.

Anything at all.

But what?

And then she remembered her time in Africa and a very far-off dream, and she brought it to life but with a little slant.

'I'm an OB nurse,' Scarlet said.

'Where?' Luke asked, rather hoping it was at the Royal!

'Back in LA.'

'You'd be called a midwife here.'

'A midwife?' Scarlet checked. 'A what?'

'A midwife,' Luke said, and watched as she started to laugh.

He didn't get a chance to play with words and, oh, they wanted to play with words, but his brother was heading over and Luke had no intention of sticking around for a drunken conversation with him. 'I've got to go,' Luke said, and as he moved to his full height from leaning against the bar he realised just how tiny she was because even though she was wearing stilettos he towered over her.

'So,' she asked, 'where are you moving on to?'

'Moving on?' Luke checked, and then realised that she was asking him what club he was off to next. 'Bed.'

'Yum!'

She took another sip of her drink and met his eyes. Luke had never met anyone like her in his life and, leaving aside the flirty offer, he actually wanted to know her some more, but well away from this dive.

'I meant…' Luke said, then gave up trying to correct her. 'Can I *Call the Midwife*?'

Clearly she didn't get his little joke because she frowned at his invitation to get in touch.

'It doesn't matter,' Luke said. She was from another part of the globe after all and, yes, he was going back to the hotel, he decided, as an overly friendly Marcus joined them.

'Can I have a word?' Marcus asked, slapping him on the shoulder.

'Sure,' Luke agreed, knowing full well that Marcus would be asking for some more money to be put behind the bar before Luke left. Marcus was studying medicine and was perpetually broke. It annoyed Luke. He himself had worked all his way through med school but he chose to say nothing tonight as it was Marcus's birthday.

But as they pulled away from Scarlet, and Luke went

to get out his wallet, it turned out that Marcus had other things on his mind.

'How did you two get talking?' Marcus asked.

'What?' Luke frowned. 'Do you know her?' he checked, wondering if she was cutting one of Marcus's friend's lunch. 'Is she here with—'

'You don't know who she is, do you?' Marcus grinned. 'Do you ever come out from behind that stethoscope of yours? That's Scarlet.'

'I know that.'

'Anya's daughter.'

'Oh!'

Yes, Luke did know who Anya was. After all, she had been famous before he'd even been born, not that Luke paid much attention to such things, but he had seen Anya and her entourage leave the club. Now that he thought about it, he did recall that Anya had a daughter who went everywhere with her.

He glanced over and saw that Scarlet was trying to get away from some loud, obnoxious guy who was trying to drag her over to dance, and two burly men were moving in.

She was here with her own bodyguards, Luke realised, not the vague friends that she had alluded to. Now he understood Marcus's friend's odd look when he had come over.

Scarlet was a star.

'She seems nice.' Luke shrugged. She had. 'Anyway, I'm heading off. I'll go and settle the bar tab and put some more behind. You have a good night.'

As Luke went to the bar Scarlet came over.

'Dance?' she offered.

'I'm just leaving.'

'Just once dance,' Scarlet persisted, but he shook his head.

'Not with your bodyguards watching.'

'You know who I am now, don't you?'

'Not really,' Luke said. 'I know two of your names and I've heard of your mother. You're not a midwife, I take it?' She shook her head and Luke glanced down at the bill he had just been given. 'There should be champagne on there,' he said to the bartender.

'It's on the house,' the bartender said, and smiled at Scarlet as it dawned on Luke that she didn't have to pay.

Scarlet's presence in the club was more than enough.

It annoyed Luke.

Not that Scarlet had been playing him along—now that he understood why, it didn't annoy him in the least—but he wanted to have bought her that drink.

'Add it,' Luke said, and handed back the bill.

'Sure.' The bartender shrugged.

He turned around and Scarlet was still there. 'Take me with you,' she said. Her arms went around his neck and Luke went to peel them off but then he heard the desperation in her voice. 'Please.' Scarlet closed her eyes. She was so tired of the noise and no doubt drama would await her when she returned to the hotel. It felt like for ever that she had been trying to escape. She looked up at Luke and he was so calm and so slightly bored with it all, as was she, and she gazed into his beautiful eyes. 'I'll make it worth your while.'

'You don't need to offer sex, Scarlet.'

'I want to spend some time with you.'

'Why don't you ask me to take you for dinner?'

'Dinner?' Scarlet frowned.

'Well, it's nearly one, so I'm not sure where.' Luke

smiled but he let her hands remain around his neck and his hands moved to her hips. The urge to kiss her was back.

'I haven't eaten since breakfast,' Scarlet admitted.

It was almost that time again, Luke thought, but then he pushed that aside. Unlike most men, the thought of a one-night stand didn't thrill him—his father's perpetually roving eye meant that he'd lived with the fallout for long enough to learn from James Edwards's mistakes.

'You really want to take me for dinner?'

'I do.'

'I'm sorry I lied to you,' Scarlet said. 'I just wanted to see if you'd like me if I was normal.'

'You are normal,' Luke said.

As was his body's reaction to her.

There was a need, an absolute need to get her away from here, to just talk, to get to know her some more and, yes, to get to that mouth.

'Can you lose your bodyguards?' Luke asked. He couldn't stand the thought of them overseeing things. He wanted Scarlet away from the hype and he knew he would take good care of her. Judging by her previous offer to make it worth his while, they didn't take proper care of her either.

'I can't.' She shook her head. 'You don't get how it is—I can't go anywhere without them.'

Luke didn't play games.

Ever.

'Can you lose your bodyguards?' he asked again, and Scarlet heard the warning. If she said no, he'd be gone.

'They'll dial 911 if I disappear.'

'Well, they shan't get very far if they do,' Luke said, and he told her the UK emergency number. 'I'll take care of you but I'm not buying you dinner with an audience.'

He *wanted* to take her for dinner!

'I could go to the loo and try to…'

'Climb out of the window?' Luke scoffed at her plans. 'Why don't you simply tell them that you're having a night off?' But then he halted as he realised, for the first time, that life in her world wasn't that simple.

'Please take me for dinner,' she said.

'I'll go outside and wait down the back,' Luke offered. 'If you can't get out of the loo there will be an emergency exit. But,' he warned, 'if you tell your bodyguards what you're up to, if I even get a hint that they're around, I'll hand you back over to them. I'm not going to be playing your celebrity game, Scarlet.'

Luke meant it.

CHAPTER FOUR

WHAT THE HELL was he doing? Luke thought as he stood in a cold, dark, basement alley next to bins and looked up at the tiny windows.

She'd never get through them, Luke realised.

Maybe she had changed her mind, Luke decided, because it had surely been ten or so minutes that he had been waiting. He was just about to give in when he saw one red shoe poke out of a very small gap in a window, followed by one skinny, pale leg and then another.

'I've got you,' Luke said, as he guided her legs out and tried not to notice that her dress was bunching up. He moved his hands from her flesh and then held her by the hips and negotiated Scarlet's body out of the small opening. As he dropped her down to the ground he turned her around. She was breathless and Luke could see the exhilaration in her eyes.

Not just that she was free!

Scarlet's dress was ruched up from her rather undignified exit and she could still feel where his hands had made contact with her thighs. Now she faced Luke and, despite his very cool demeanour, Scarlet knew that he was as turned on as she was.

Her hands moved up back around his neck and she

moved into him for warmth and for confirmation of his arousal.

'Oh,' Scarlet said.

An odd remark perhaps but she could feel him on the length of her stomach and those hands on her hips let her rest there a moment. His voice when it came was a bit ragged.

'Come on.'

He got the 'Oh' comment. Luke was feeling it too.

That urge to kiss was there and a whole lot of other urges too but a stinking dark alley wasn't at the top of his wish list and her bodyguards would no doubt realise that she was missing some time very soon. So, rather than kiss her, Luke grabbed her hand and they ran up some metal stairs and out onto a seedy street and then turned into another.

Luke hailed a black cab and, a touch breathless, they both climbed in.

He gave the name of a restaurant that he knew stayed open late, which he had been to with friends a couple of times when he'd been in London. It was nice and low-key with booths where they could tuck themselves away and he could get to know her some more.

Luke wanted that.

He really did, but as the taxi took off, the driver glanced in the rear-view mirror and must have seen just who his fare was.

'Scarlet!' He turned and smiled and it annoyed Luke that Scarlet smiled back and that she and the driver started talking about Anya's performance. Was it possible to have a conversation that didn't include her mother?

'Just drop us here,' Luke said, as they reached a busier street. They walked into a different restaurant from the one he would have chosen but the reaction to her was the same there and they left.

'I told you…' Scarlet said.

It was impossible.

No, it wasn't.

Luke took off his jacket and put it around her and then he went into the pocket, took out a serviette and removed her trademark lipstick.

God, he wanted that mouth.

Luke saw a bus and pulled Scarlet onto it.

Instead of going up with the night riders, they sat downstairs for two stops.

'Someone will recognise me…' Scarlet said as they sat at the front.

'Not with my face over yours…' Luke had it all worked out.

He took her face in his hands and the shiver that went through Scarlet had nothing to do with the fact it had started to rain outside. He made her wait for first contact. She watched as he looked at her mouth and then back to her eyes and then their mouths met. She felt the first nudge of intimate flesh, a tiny precursor, a small tease, and then Scarlet found out that he *had* been holding back on her since they'd met because there was no tentativeness. He led this kiss, taking her lips between his and then parting them, only to expose bliss. It was a kiss of contrasts—his tongue was slow and tender and yet his jaw was rough and his hands kept her head steady, so there was nowhere to go but to taste and feel the bliss of Luke.

It felt like she'd never been properly kissed until now. They breathed together, their tongues mingled and probed and it took all Luke had to pull back as the bus jolted and to remember where they were.

He looked out at the dark, shiny streets and took her

hand and they stood. 'Come on…' As her hand, in his, moved up to ring the bell he halted her. 'Someone's already rung it.'

'I never have though.'

She pushed it and the driver moaned and she went to ring it again but Luke stopped her. The doors hissed open and they stepped out into the rain.

'Where are we?'

They were just a short walk from his hotel. 'We're going for that dinner I promised you!'

'And?'

'That dance we never had,' Luke said.

'And?' Scarlet asked, as she tried to keep up with his long strides, even though Luke wasn't walking particularly fast, but he halted then and turned her to face him.

'Let's see how those two go.'

He really didn't like one-night stands, they left him feeling like a user and he didn't ever want to use her.

Luke was quite sure she'd had enough of that in her life.

Not just with men.

The free drinks for the crowd she pulled, the circus that was her life.

And, perhaps more pointedly, he didn't have any condoms with him.

They walked to his hotel with his arm around her, passing through the foyer, and no one really noticed.

Without that exposed skin and red lips she didn't stand out so much and he had her pulled tight into him.

The elevator was empty and as she went to resume a kiss he pointed a finger and told her to stand back.

'Not here,' Luke said.

He was very confident and a bit bossy and she wasn't used to being refused.

'I like you,' Scarlet said, as she leant back against the elevator wall.

'Good,' Luke responded. 'I like you too.'

Up they went to his suite and as the door closed on them, for Scarlet it felt like home. It just did. There was a suit holder over the chair and an overnight bag on the bed, which was open.

She thought he'd resume their kiss now that they were alone but instead he picked up a menu.

'It's after midnight so it's just the night menu…'

'Are we eating?'

'You said that you were starving.'

'Oh.' Scarlet was very used to being starving.

She was starving all the time, in fact.

He handed her the menu and Scarlet instantly knew what she wanted. She usually stayed away from carbs but this was her night, her great escape. 'I want the club sandwich.' Then she changed her mind. 'Maybe the burger.'

She couldn't choose.

'Both,' Scarlet said, and Luke smiled and picked up the phone and placed their order. 'Twenty minutes.'

'Whatever will we do?' Scarlet smiled and Luke watched as lifted the hem of her dress and went to peel it off.

'Scarlet…' He stopped her. 'I hope we're going to take more than twenty minutes and I don't want interruptions.' Luke watched as she went over to the bed and lay back, sulking. 'They said that we should order breakfast now if we want it delivered in the morning.' He picked up the menu cards that would need to be hung outside the door. 'What?' he said when he saw that she was staring.

'I want a kiss.'

'Let's sort this out first. Tomato, pineapple or grapefruit juice…'

'Grapefruit.' Scarlet sighed, and he pulled a face. 'Don't you like it?'

'Too sharp,' Luke said, and he ticked pineapple for himself.

'Don't you like me?'

'Why do you ask that?' Luke asked. 'I don't need you on your knees within the hour to like you, Scarlet.'

He guessed she wasn't very used to that.

And he did like her and want her.

But it was more than that…

She picked up a wad of paper that was beside his overnight bag. 'What's this?'

'Just notes I made for my interview.'

'Were you nervous?'

'No,' Luke said, and then glanced up to see she was really reading his notes.

'What was it like?'

'It was an interview.' Luke shrugged but then thought about it and realised that, unless it was for the media, Scarlet wouldn't know so he amended his earlier response. 'I wasn't nervous because I was quite sure I wouldn't get the role. Now I am nervous because I want it.'

'Do you think you'll get it?'

'I think so.'

'So why be nervous?'

Luke usually left such conversations where he had first left this one—at a shrug. There was no point discussing it till he knew if the role was his, but Scarlet was curious rather than nosy and he forgot about breakfast for a moment and, to his own surprise, told her something that was on his mind.

'My ex works there,' Luke said. 'We only broke up last month. I need to speak to her about it.'

'Why?' Scarlet asked. 'Do you still fancy her?'

'No.'

'Does she still fancy you?'

'No.' Luke smiled. 'It was a long overdue break up.'

'No problem, then.' It was Scarlet who shrugged this time. 'I don't believe you, though.'

'Sorry?'

'Can you ever unfancy someone?'

'Actually, yes.' Right up to the moment the words left his mouth Luke had believed it, but in that split second he disbelieved it also.

Not when he looked at Scarlet, who had just kicked off her shoes and was still reading through his notes. Her knees were up and she rested on the pillow, holding the paper above her face, rather than sitting up to read. He could see the hollow of her stomach and the jut of her nipples through her dress and then she moved the papers so that she could see him and smiled.

And Luke doubted if he could, as Scarlet put it, ever unfancy her.

'Breakfast,' Luke said, and tried to take care of the morning.

'I don't eat breakfast,' Scarlet said. 'Just a coffee.'

And again, for Luke, everything changed. He wanted dinner over and done with, he wanted to dance, and then he wanted her naked and writhing in the bed.

'You're going to be starving in the morning, Scarlet,' Luke said.

Something in his voice had her throat tighten and she put down the paperwork.

'Then you'd better read me the menu.'

'Cereal, muesli?'

'Muesli.'

'Full cream or—'

'Full cream, I think,' Scarlet interrupted. 'Don't you?'

With each tick they got sexier.

'Toast?' He looked at Scarlet and she shook her head.
'Too many crumbs.'

She came over and stood in front of him and they read it together.

'Ooh, bacon,' Scarlet said. 'That's very forbidden.'

Hurry with that dinner, Luke thought, because he was pressing her bottom into him and his face was in her hair and he wanted to turn her around and have her against the wall.

And she wanted him so badly, in a way she never had. His hand pressed onto her stomach and now his mouth was on her neck and his kiss to her skin was so sexy and gentle.

'I was watching you from the moment you came in,' Scarlet said.

Luke turned her around and looked down at her. 'I wanted you from the moment I turned around.'

There was a knock at the door. He was tempted, so tempted to ignore it, to call to leave it outside, but, no, they should have dinner.

As the trolley was brought in, Scarlet turned on the television and found a music channel.

Luke paid the tip and as soon as the door closed they faced each other. Luke took off his shirt.

Then his shoes. And she watched as he stripped.

What a body.

Muscular, lean and very, very male, given she was used to men more waxed and bald than even she was.

'You have hairy legs.' Scarlet smiled.

'I wouldn't make it off the rugby field alive if I didn't.'

Scarlet peeled off her dress in one easy motion and Luke made no moved to stop her as she took off her tiny knickers and took her seat at the little table.

The burger was fantastic.

Fat, juicy, and when some onion fell on her breast, Luke kindly retrieved it for her with his fingers and they fed each other dinner.

It was the most amazing meal she had ever had because it came from his fingers.

He'd be laughed off the rugby field if they could see him because Scarlet was bringing food to his mouth and he didn't just suck on her fingers, he kissed her palm deeply. When the meal was over, Luke stood.

'Dance?' he said.

With just her shoes on, Scarlet stood.

She went into his arms and he pulled her right in.

Scarlet felt that chest naked against her cheek and her hands moved around his waist; she had never been any-where nicer in the world. Luke felt her sway against him and inhaled the scent of her hair and then lifted her face so he could again meet her lips, and then they danced like no one was watching.

CHAPTER FIVE

THAT WAS THEN.

And here they were now, sitting in his office, trapped in the fallout of that time.

It was too painful to think about that night with the other there in the room. Or rather it would be impossible to think about what had taken place in the morning and hope to hold a sensible conversation.

And sense was the one thing that he had to maintain today.

'I don't know what to do,' Scarlet said, though the words were said more to herself than to Luke.

Her head was back in her hands as she sat at his desk crying, not for effect, just because she honestly didn't know what to do.

She'd had plans.

Big ones.

She had told her mother some of them.

And now this had happened.

Luke looked again at the picture of her getting into the ambulance and pushed aside the anger he felt. Scarlet had found her mother unconscious and close to death after all.

For all her money and fame she couldn't buy the one thing she required most now. More than ever before, Scarlet not only needed space and peace, she deserved it.

'Why don't you go somewhere else and check in under Lucy…?' She had told him about that secret name when they had fed each other dinner and he had found out more about her life.

How her mother's fame had been declining but then Scarlet had been born and the beautiful baby Anya had worn on her hip had shot her back into stardom.

He had gleaned that Scarlet had been nothing more than a pretty accessory to wear along with her mother's designer gowns and had been far too precious to send to school.

Luke hadn't said that to her at the time, of course. Whatever he felt, he rarely shared.

'Check in under your alias,' Luke suggested.

'And that will buy me a couple of hours before someone tips them off,' Scarlet said. 'And what happens when I want to visit my mom? The press are everywhere, they'll be all over me.'

'Only because you'll arrive at the hospital with your bodyguards in tow,' Luke said. 'You could dress down and come in through the maternity entrance. Nobody would even know that you'd arrived. Security could take you straight up to ICU without anyone noticing. Visiting your mother doesn't have to be a big deal.'

Scarlet just couldn't buy it. 'I need the security now more than ever. The press are more interested these days in me than…' Scarlet stopped speaking then.

She couldn't tell anyone about the jealous row that she'd had with her mother last night.

'Luke, can you help me, please? I need to get away, I need space, peace.'

'We tried that once, remember?' Luke reminded her. 'And you blew it.'

'I won't this time.'

'I don't believe you, Scarlet.' Luke shook his head. 'I actually don't think you can help yourself. You crave attention…' Luke halted. He didn't want to add to her distress but, two years on, he was still hurting and angry and it was proving hard not to show it.

'I know that it might be a disruption for you if I came to stay…' Scarlet persisted, but Luke swiftly broke in.

'A friend coming to stay shouldn't be a disruption. It's only when that friend brings an entourage along…' He was struggling to hold on to his temper.

'Or is it because your partner wouldn't like it?'

Luke didn't respond. He didn't say he didn't have a partner, that really since two years ago every attempt at a relationship had ended not just because he was cold, arrogant and obsessed with work, but for another reason— guilt. He still thought about their one night together and since then nothing had matched up.

She took his silence the wrong way—that, unlike her, Luke had moved on with his life.

Scarlet stood. 'Can I see my mother?'

'Of course,' Luke said. 'We're just preparing to move her up to Intensive Care.'

'I'd better tell Sonia first.'

'Just have some time with your mother.' He reached for the phone and asked to be put through to the head of security, and Scarlet watched and listened.

'Hi, Geoff. How is it going with clearing the corridor?'

Whatever Geoff said, Luke rolled his eyes.

'I'm going to bring Anya's daughter to see her. Can you please have all her entourage move inside the staff-room and close the door? Tell them Scarlet will be in to speak with them when she's ready to.'

Luke spoke about logistics as she dug one hand into her

pocket and her fingers closed on a stone she had picked up on a faraway beach yesterday.

Oh, Scarlet had made plans. She thought about the little cottage she had found, the month she had planned where she might sort out her head space. There was no chance of that now, with her mother's life hanging in the balance.

Luke was right, though not in the way he had meant—she couldn't help herself.

He did his best to prepare her for what she was about to see but he knew that nothing really could.

They walked out of his office and a security guard stood outside the staffroom and gave Luke a nod.

'Thanks, Geoff.'

They walked down the corridor and through the department, past all the nudges and stares. Only Luke noticed them. Scarlet felt sick.

Luke parted the curtains. 'This is Barbara,' Luke said. 'And the anaesthetist, David. And this is Paul, he's a registrar…'

Scarlet didn't hear much else. All she could see was her mother's deathly white face and all the tubes, and all she knew was that this was her fault.

After all, she knew what she had said to her mother last night.

'Can she hear me?' Scarlet turned anguished eyes to the nurse.

'We don't know,' Barbara said. 'Try talking to her.'

Barbara put her arm around Scarlet's waist and Luke was relieved to step back as Barbara did the job she was very good at.

She answered all Scarlet's questions about the machines and why Anya's face was so swollen.

Luke stepped outside.

Scarlet wasn't his problem. If Anya hadn't done what she had, he wouldn't have even seen Scarlet.

He glanced at the time.

She'd have been on her way back to the States by now.

Then, through the curtain, he heard her voice and it tore at his heart.

'I'm sorry, Mom. I should never have said what I did…'

Luke took a breath to the sound of Scarlet completely breaking down and, after a couple of moments spent trying and failing to resist reaching out to her anguish, he stepped back in.

'Paul, could you please go and speak with her manager?' Luke said. 'Give as little information as you can. Just let them know that her condition is critical but stable.'

'They'll want to know more than that.'

'Of course they will,' Luke said. 'And if we let them, the press would be in here, taking photos.'

'Scarlet,' Luke went on, 'can I speak with you outside?'

He nodded to Barbara and David and then he took Scarlet into one of the relative interview rooms.

'Scarlet,' Luke asked, 'what happened last night?'

She couldn't tell him.

'We need to know if this was an accidental overdose or deliberate.'

'It was an accident.'

It had to be, Scarlet thought.

Please, let it be.

'You can tell me.'

She couldn't look at him; she wanted so badly to meet his eyes but she couldn't.

'Tell me,' Luke pushed gently. 'You said you had a row.'

She nodded.

'A big one?'

'I shouldn't have said what I did.'

'Which was?'

Scarlet shook her head. She was scared to go there, especially with Luke.

'Tell me.'

'I said that I wasn't going back to LA with her.'

'Okay.'

He held her hands then and she looked at his lovely long fingers entwined around hers. 'I said some terrible things.'

'Tell me.'

'I can't.'

'You can.'

'I said she was jealous of me… I said…' Scarlet stopped but then she made herself say it. 'I said something about our baby.'

Silence stretched as she voiced it.

Not all of it.

Just the part that rendered them lost or, worse, unsalvageable.

Wreckage that lay too deep for rescue.

It was surely time to pack up the equipment and head for home.

He sat silent for a moment and then dropped her hands and Scarlet sat staring at the floor as Luke got up and walked out.

She had guessed he would.

For two years every day had hurt but some days hurt more than others and that was today.

Scarlet sat in a room where she guessed people found out their loved ones had died and mourned her baby so badly, even if she didn't deserve to.

She had signed the consent form after all—crying

and shaking, unlike Vince who had calmly handed her the pen.

It had been the worst day of her life.

Even with her mother lying near death, it still was.

But on that day there had been one saving grace—a nurse who had sat with her afterwards and let Scarlet speak.

There could be no saving grace today.

She didn't look up as the door opened and Luke came back in.

'You've got two choices,' Luke said, and Scarlet blinked. She'd never had even one. 'I've got a flat here at the hospital you can stay in for a few days, but on several conditions.'

She stared up at his chin again. 'I can stay?'

'As long as you agree to my conditions.'

'Which are?'

'You lose the phone.'

'I need to know how my mother is—'

'I work here,' Luke interrupted. 'I'll be kept updated.'

'But I need to see her, to be with her.'

'She is in a coma,' Luke said. 'There will be plenty people keeping a vigil, I'm sure. I think right now you need some time to take care of yourself.'

'What are the other conditions?'

'This time you don't tell your bodyguards where you are.'

'How?'

His face darkened but, instead of stating the obvious—that she simply didn't tell them—he threw her blue theatre scrubs and a theatre cap, and wrapped up in them were some clogs.

'I'll give you directions...' But even as he said it, Luke knew it was hopeless. In the flat across the hall from him was one of the radiologists known for gossip. There were the domestics who came in and serviced it. So he told her the other choice. 'Or you can go to my home. It will be easier to keep things under wraps there.'

'Your home?'

'It's about an hour's drive from here,' Luke said.

'I can't leave her.'

'That's up to you. But if you do decide to go there, I mean it, Scarlet, if you call in the entourage, there'll be no time to give your excuses because I won't be listening. You'll be out.'

'Why do you hate them so much?'

'How do they protect you, Scarlet?'

'They keep the public back.'

'But when you wanted to make it worth my while when we met, they were fine with that?' Luke checked. 'A quick blow job and they look away?' He watched her cheeks go red. 'That's not protecting you, Scarlet. I can do all that.'

'What if something happens to her and I'm an hour away?' Scarlet asked. 'What if she dies?'

'Then I'll come home and tell you myself.' Luke didn't sugar-coat it and she sat there, absorbing his words.

She would want to hear it from him, Scarlet knew that much.

'You'll take me there?' Scarlet asked.

'No. I have to work. My car is in the underground car park. You go out of here and turn right and then follow the sign for the staff car park. I have a navy Audi. If you press the keys the lights will flash but you'll see it just as you come out the elevator. Can you drive?' Luke asked, but then checked himself. He knew the answer to that one—not very well, given all the little well-publicised prangs she'd had.

Scarlet nodded.

'On the opposite side of the road?' he checked.

Scarlet nodded again.

'What will you do for a car?'

'There are taxis.' He did the best not to sarcastically remind her of the last time they had got into one. 'I've got friends who can give me a lift too…'

It all sounded alien to her, Luke knew, but she either wanted the real world or she didn't. He wasn't going to handle her with kid gloves, he was way past all that.

'If I need to speak to you I'll ring three times and hang up. Pick up the phone the next time it rings.'

'Can't I call you? Can I page you?'

'No.' Luke shook his head. 'If I'm busy one of the nurses often answers my page. I'll call if I have to but, Scarlet, if I get even a sniff of your bodyguards, or the press find out where you are and it's your doing, you will be on your own.'

'But people will be looking for me.'

'Write a text now, explaining you're safe but you just need some time, and I'll hit Send once I know you're safely gone.'

'What about seeing my mother?'

'We can work out those details later. Right now I need to get back to work.' He handed her one of the large yellow garbage bags. 'Leave your clothes and phone in this.'

'I'll need my clothes to change into when I get there.'

'You'll stand out like a sore thumb where I live, wearing that.'

'Luke, I don't know.'

'Then decide. Go back out there and be with your people or you hit the sat-nav in my car and press Home. It's up to you.'

He refused to make decisions for others unless he was paid to.

'Will you be okay with me being in your home?' Scarlet asked.

Luke chose not to answer that. He was about to; he could almost feel the sneer of his lips as he went to ask when she had ever taken his feelings into any equation.

But today wasn't the day to row, he told himself.

'It's up to you,' Luke said again. 'You need to speak with David before you leave, though,' he added.

'And tell him what?'

'That you're staying with a friend.' He wrote down his home number and handed it to her. 'Tell him if he needs to reach you to leave a message on the answering machine and that you'll call straight back.'

And then Luke was gone.

David was thorough, going through all that Luke had and more.

'We'll talk again once I've got her settled into ICU,' he said.

'I shan't be here.'

Scarlet met David's solemn gaze.

'I'm going to be staying with a friend.' She waited for him to chide her.

'I think that's wise,' David said. 'Can I have contact details in case of an emergency?'

'Don't let—'

'I shan't.' David nodded and Scarlet handed him the phone number that Luke had given her.

'If you leave a message, I'll call straight back.'

'Of course.'

He left her then and once alone she took off her silver jacket and her leggings and top and her shoes and then slipped on the scrubs and the disgusting clogs Luke had brought her.

Her hair she tucked into a hat.

With shaking hands she wrote a text to her bodyguard but didn't hit Send and then she threw her phone in the bag.

But then she retrieved it.

She needed it. Her mother was desperately ill after all but, recalling his rules and knowing Luke always meant what he said, Scarlet threw it back in the yellow bag.

She walked out and followed his directions and it was slightly dizzying that no one really gave her a second glance.

Past the canteen she went and then she saw a sign for Maternity and beneath that an arrow that pointed to the staff car park elevator.

She stood beside a blonde woman, waited for the doors to open and then stepped in.

'Hi...' The blonde woman nodded to her in the elevator and Scarlet nodded back.

'Are you new?'

'I just started,' Scarlet said.

'Where?'

'I'm an OB...a midwife,' Scarlet replied.

She wished that she was. How she wished this was where she worked and that she had just come from meeting Luke.

Oh, she wanted that to be her life so very, very much.

The woman was waiting for her to give her name, Scarlet knew. 'I'm Lucy.'

'Angie.' She returned her name with a tight smile. 'You're supposed to always wear your ID, Lucy...?'

Scarlet could hear the question mark and the woman's demand for her full name and more information. 'Lucy Edwards.' Scarlet borrowed Luke's surname and gave Angie another smile and then almost folded in relief as the elevator door opened.

She pressed the key and a very dirty navy Audi flashed

its lights. Scarlet went to the wrong side of the car, of course, but then remembered and walked to the other side.

She was sweating and breathless, as if she'd been running, and that damn woman was watching her, Scarlet knew. She climbed in, turned on the engine and reversed out, and as she did so she glanced up and saw that Angie was *still* watching.

Angie thought she was an impostor, Scarlet was sure. She just hoped that she didn't call Security.

Any minute now the call that she was missing would go out, Scarlet knew.

And Luke knew it too.

It was already starting.

Scarlet had been gone for too long. Her bodyguards were walking down corridors and knocking on doors. Luke went into the interview room, picked up the yellow biohazard bag and walked through the department into his office. He turned on the engaged sign.

Luke opened the bag and took out her phone.

I've gone away with friends for a few days. I just need to get my head around things. Don't look for me.

Luke hit Send.

'I'm busy,' Luke called, when there was a knock at his door.

'It's Angie.'

Luke frowned. Angie rarely stopped by and she was the last person he knew to ignore an engaged sign.

He opened the door. 'What do you want?'

'Are you with someone?'

'No.'

'Then can I come in?'

Luke nodded.

They still got on.

Both had agreed they would never have worked and were now colleagues and very good friends.

'What the hell are you up to, Luke?'

'Nothing.'

'So should I call Security, then? Because a certain famous woman is pretending to be a midwife and driving your car.'

'Angie…'

'What the hell are you doing, getting involved with her again, Luke?'

A few weeks after they had broken up, Angie had seen the change in him and, knowing how lukewarm Luke had been about the break up, she'd been astute enough to know it hadn't been about her. Luke had always been a bit aloof but he was frantic now and had finally told her why.

Angie had held her tongue when she'd heard that he'd had a one-night stand.

That wasn't the Luke she'd known.

And then to find out that the said one-night stand was in LA and pregnant with his child had had her even more confused.

'Are you sure it's yours?'

Luke had always been so-o-o-o careful, it had made no sense.

'Very sure.'

And in the end, reluctantly he had told her, not just about that night but some of the things that had happened afterwards.

'She's trouble,' Angie now pointed out. 'She messed with your head big-time.'

'No,' Luke corrected. 'Scarlet's lifestyle messed with my head. When I was with her she actually cleared it. Anyway, I don't need you with your psychiatrist's hat on.'

'Luke, she had an abortion without even telling you.'

'Do you think I don't know that?' Luke's response was terse.

'Just be careful,' Angie warned.

'Oh, I intend to be.'

CHAPTER SIX

Scarlet could breathe.

For the first time in the longest time, as the garage door closed behind her, Scarlet sat in Luke's car and dragged in a long breath.

Apart from having taken a couple of bricks out of a very low wall as she had negotiated the narrow driveway to his home, the drive had been an easy one.

She had kept glancing in the mirror, checking that no one was behind. At first she had listened to the radio, but when they hadn't been talking about her mother they had been playing her songs. It had been too much for Scarlet so she had turned it off.

She'd made it, Scarlet thought as she got out of the car.

The garage was small and there was a door that she pushed open, stepping into a utility room and then walking through to the kitchen.

The kitchen was far smaller than any that she was used to.

Scarlet opened the fridge and there wasn't much in there—a loaf of bread, some eggs and bacon. Scarlet thought of the lovely breakfast they had been about to have two years ago but never had.

She couldn't think about that now so she quickly closed the fridge door and sat at the kitchen table, but all she could see was her mother and those awful words from the fight they'd had replaying in her head.

Scarlet was sorry, but not for what she had said but the way those words had been delivered and the effect they had had.

But she had meant them.

It felt odd to be here.

An unwelcome guest.

She walked down the hallway and looked at the phone, and saw that the answering machine was flashing. She hit Play.

'Hi, Luke, it's Emma. Just reminding you about Wednesday.'

Scarlet swallowed. Of course he had a life.

She held her breath as the next message played but it was some man called Trefor to say that training had been moved.

Yes, Luke had a life.

Still, there were no messages for her and that was a good thing so she moved through to the lounge.

There was an open fire and some logs beside it but building a fire wasn't exactly her forte so Scarlet sat shivering on the sofa, still dressed in theatre scrubs. She just stared at the wall and wondered whether, if it hadn't been for her mother, she would have ever seen this place.

Of course not.

He was a very decent man and he was helping her out, that was all.

Even though she was sure he would rather not have had to.

Dusk arrived and apart from a trip to his downstairs bathroom she didn't move, but then Scarlet realised just how hungry she was.

She hadn't eaten all day.

In fact, she'd had nothing since breakfast yesterday.

Yesterday she had driven for miles in a car the hotel had provided, planning her escape, too busy and excited for all that was to come to stop and eat.

There had been a welcome basket at the cottage when she had arrived and in there had been some snacks and local cheese and condiments, but she had been too nervous to do anything other than put them in the fridge.

Scarlet thought about the long walk on a pebbly beach that she had taken and the plans she had started to make that could never happen now.

Anya had made very sure of that.

She wanted the stone she had collected but it was in her jacket back at the hospital.

Scarlet turned on the television and it went straight to the news. Of course her mother was at the top of the hour but, sure enough, they flashed the image of a terrified Scarlet as often as they could.

'*Scarlet is holding a vigil at her mother's bedside,*' the press release said. '*At this difficult time she asks for your prayers.*'

Scarlet flicked off the news and wandered into the kitchen. She opened the fridge and took out a carton of eggs but then she saw a bottle of grapefruit juice in the door.

It was almost as if it had been left there for her. Scarlet knew, from their one night together, that Luke didn't like it—he had screwed up his face and told her it was too sharp.

The memory of an uncomplicated them made her smile and Scarlet poured a long drink and scrambled some eggs, even if that hadn't been her intention when she had first cracked them.

They were lovely, apart from the bits of shell that she had to crunch through.

Maybe her mother had been right when she'd said last night that Scarlet could never survive without her.

Now, as darkness came, she was ready to check out the house.

The lounge she knew, she'd been in there for a few hours after all, so she pushed open a door and saw a study. There were shelves and shelves of books and on closer examination she saw they were textbooks.

Scarlet pulled one down and opened it at a random page and, rather than being repulsed at the image she saw, it was actually quite fascinating. Still, she didn't have time to read about ligature marks and entrance and exit wounds from bullets so she closed the heavy book and put it back on the shelf.

It was a very masculine house, Scarlet thought as she headed up the stairs. There were no unnecessary pictures or flowers but she'd love to see it in spring, with a huge vase of something pretty in the hallway.

He must have been in the middle of decorating because there were ladders and tins of paint at the top of the stairs. Scarlet found the bathroom but didn't go in. Instead, she went down the hall and pushed open a door and guessed that this was supposed to be her bedroom tonight.

She didn't go in there either. Instead, she hurriedly closed the door and headed back down the hall and into Luke's bedroom.

There were dark green sheets on the bed topped by a dark green duvet, and the bed was all rumpled and un-made. It was a very low bed with low tables at either side. There was a phone on one and some books so she knew that was his side of the bed.

Yes, she was nosy.

Scarlet opened up his bedside drawer and there were some foreign banknotes and cash and a few tickets, and she felt her lips purse when she saw an open packet of condoms, with its contents spilling out.

She counted them.

Scarlet couldn't help herself.

Oh, so he used them now.

Bitterness, anger, jealousy all rose in her chest but she swallowed them down. It was very hard to be bitter about the memory of the love they had made.

It was any woman who had come after her that had Scarlet drop the condoms back into the drawer and slam it closed.

What did she expect? Scarlet asked herself.

That two years on he'd be as stagnant in his life as she was?

Oh, but it hurt, it really, really hurt, the thought of him with another woman.

She left his bedroom and headed back to the one that was presumably hers.

And that hurt even more.

It was why she had so quickly shut the door on it but Scarlet opened it now.

Would this have been their baby's room? she wondered, then answered her own question with the very next thought.

Of course not.

Scarlet would have had her baby back in LA and the baby would have been balanced on her hip and paraded for the cameras and dragged everywhere, just as her mother had done with her.

Luke would never have allowed it, though, and her mother had told her only too clearly the impossible odds she faced if she dared to leave.

'A one-night stand?' Anya had rammed it home again and again.

'It was more than that!'

'Oh, so you're going to be a doctor's wife!' Her mother had gone into peals of laughter and her manager, Sonia, had followed suit. 'I know I told you to dream big, but please…'

Now she stood in the door way and it felt as if her arms were being pulled in two direction as her body was torn apart.

Scarlet had cried so much today that she been quite sure that there were no tears left.

For a moment there were none.

Just a scream of rage that came out so loud and so raw that it had her sinking to her knees on the spare bedroom floor and she sobbed for her baby and, yes, she was going to hell. Not just for the terrible things she had done but right now, right this very minute, Scarlet wished that her mother was dead.

CHAPTER SEVEN

'Luke?'

It was close to ten and he just wanted home. It had been one of those days that never ended but just as he went to leave, Mary, the night charge nurse, called him back.

'I hate to ask…'

Mary did hate to ask, she could see how exhausted Luke was, but she also knew that he would prefer that she did.

'There's currently a two-hour wait but I've got a man here whose son is on ICU and all he needs is a sleeping tablet.'

Luke nodded.

'And a couple of headache tablets,' Mary added. 'His blood pressure's high and if I get Sahin…'

Sahin, the registrar on tonight, was thorough, extremely so, and he would run a battery of tests, Luke knew.

'Where is he?' Luke asked.

'I put him down in the interview room. If you need a cubicle, I can bring him into one.'

'The interview room is fine.'

Luke knocked on the door and went in. He saw a gentleman pacing and he introduced himself.

Evan Jones was doing everything he could to hold it together, Luke could tell.

'My son's not well.'

'I heard,' Luke said. 'I'm very sorry.'

'We just had some very bad news. The sister in charge suggested that I come down here. I haven't slept for a couple of nights. I really don't want to sleep…'

'You *have* to sleep,' Luke said.

No one really knew why, just that you did, and if you didn't, well, here was living proof that sleep was necessary. Evan's anxiety was through the roof and his blood pressure was high, as was his heart rate.

'Please, don't start suggesting I need to lose weight or investigations,' Evan snapped as Luke removed the blood-pressure cuff.

'I shan't but you do need to sleep,' Luke said. 'Seriously…'

Evan nodded.

'How long have you had the headache for?'

'Since they told me unless they get a liver in the next seventy-two hours that they were taking him off the list.'

'And when was that?'

'Sixty hours ago.'

Luke didn't make small talk and Evan didn't want it. All he needed now was rest and Luke wrote down his findings and wrote up a prescription. He then went and checked the script with Mary then dispensed it himself and went back to the interview room with a small cup of water.

'Take these now for the headache and the same again when you wake up. And here are some sleeping tablets. Take two tonight,' Luke said. 'Good luck with your son. I'm on in the morning. If you're not feeling better…' Luke amended his words. 'If there's no relief from the headache or if you get chest pain or any other symptoms just come straight back down. Mary will make sure you're seen straight away. I'll be on tomorrow—ask for me.'

'Thank you.'

'Are you walking up to ICU now?' Luke checked. 'I'm on my way there now.'

'I might just go and get some air.'

Usually Luke would just go back to the flat on a night like tonight as he was due in at eight tomorrow.

Luke even thought about doing just that.

But Scarlet was at home.

That gave him even more of a reason to stay at the flat, but it would be unfair to her, Luke knew. And so, before calling for a taxi to take him home, Luke headed up to Intensive Care.

There were a couple of waiting rooms outside the unit that he had to walk past. One was taken up entirely by Anya's team, the other contained the rest of the loved ones of patients on ICU.

It was injustice all the way, Luke thought, but then he hesitated for a moment before using his swipe card to get in as he realised he wasn't here for business reasons only.

He was rarely conflicted—he was here for both personal and professional reasons, though he couldn't really tell David that.

Or could he?

For now, Luke chose not to. He wasn't crossing any lines, he was merely here to catch up on a patient.

He would keep it at that, Luke decided, as he walked over to the vast station where various staff sat writing up notes and checking results as well as taking a quick break. All the patients had a nurse at their bedside and he asked Lorna, the ICU charge nurse, if David was still there.

'He's just in with a patient,' Lorna said. 'He shouldn't be too much longer.'

'How's your night been so far?' Luke asked, and Lorna gave an eye-roll.

'Better than it could have been.' Lorna sighed. 'Thankfully the day staff had the foresight to arrange an extra receptionist to cover tonight. We've got one phone ringing hot solely to enquire about Anya, and it's people using any guise…'

'Such as?'

'Her partner, her lover, a close friend, her aunt…' Lorna turned as someone called her name. 'It would seem that it's her daughter now,' Lorna said, and rolled her eyes once more. 'Again.'

Luke was proud of the staff at the hospital and how they guarded their patients' privacy so fiercely. After a brief pause, Lorna was back. 'You'd think they would get someone with a *real* American accent to call and pretend to be Scarlet.' Lorna gave a wry grin. 'Someone who at least knew their mother's real name.'

'Which is?' Luke asked, because he'd never actually got around to that.

'Anne Portland,' Lorna said. 'Are the press still at the entrance?'

'They are.' Luke nodded. 'Hopefully they'll get bored soon and go.'

'Not a chance,' Lorna said. 'They've just got wind that Scarlet isn't here. I don't know how they found out and I don't want to know either. It didn't come from my staff, that's all I can say.' She had seen it all before and on many occasions. 'Anyway, I've got other things on my mind right now.' She nodded out to the unit. 'Ashleigh— an eighteen-year-old waiting for a liver transplant. We're going to have to take him off the list soon.'

'I just saw his father.'

'Poor man. He's been holding it together for his wife but he's starting to lose it. And on the other hand I've got Anya's people moaning about the coffee and the lack of information.' She looked up as David came over. 'How is he?'

'One word or two?' David asked.

'One,' Lorna said.

'Gutted.'

Luke looked over to the young man they were discussing. He didn't need to be told that Ashleigh was in the third bed along. The young man was a sickly yellow colour and completely emaciated and exhausted, yet he managed to smile at his father as Evan walked back onto the unit.

Evan returned the smile.

God, life could be cruel.

'How are you, Luke?' David asked.

'I'm well,' Luke replied. 'I just thought I'd stop by and see how Anya was doing.' He felt as shallow as hell, especially when David rolled his eyes.

'I never thought you'd be one to jump on the bandwagon.'

'I'm just following up on a patient I thought I was going to lose this morning,' Luke answered.

'Sorry.' David gave a brief shake of his head. 'Long day,' he said, 'and it's going to be an even longer night.'

'You're on call?' Luke checked, and David nodded.

'I'm doing a double.' He got back to Anya. 'There's been no real change with her.' He pulled up Anya's notes on the computer and Luke read through the toxicology results that had come through so far. 'She ticks every box…'

'Yep.' Luke read it with a sinking feeling. It really was starting to look less and less like an accidental overdose, especially coupled with the row that she'd had with Scarlet last night.

'There was some discord with the daughter the night before,' Luke said.

'I saw it in your notes,' David said. 'Scarlet didn't mention it to me, just said she was going to stay with a friend.'

Luke said nothing. The fact there had been an argument was pertinent to Anya's care plan and that was the reason he had noted it.

Where Scarlet was staying wasn't pertinent.

'Thanks for that.' Luke stood, though knew he had to ask David for more than he usually would. 'David, can you call me if there is any change in Anya, either way?'

'Where on the list do you want to be?' David sighed as he headed away from the desk and towards another patient and there was a slightly sarcastic edge to his voice. 'Before or after her manager, the DON, the—'

'Can you call me first?' Luke interrupted.

David stopped walking and looked at Luke and frowned for a moment. It was a very unlikely request from a very unstarstruck Luke.

'I'm asking as a friend,' Luke said.

'Okay.'

'Don't ask any more than that,' Luke said.

'I shan't,' David agreed.

'But you will call me?' Luke checked.

'I shall.'

'And will you pass that on to whoever takes over from you in the morning?'

David nodded. 'I'm here on and off for most of the week. I'll be sure to keep you informed.'

'Thank you.'

Luke said goodnight and then he walked out, past the entourage and then down the corridor and there, walking just ahead of him, was Angie. When he called her name she turned around and, Luke thought, she looked just as tired as he felt.

'How come that you're still here?' Luke checked.

'Full moon,' she said. 'Do you need a lift?'

'I'll be fine. Anyway, I live ages away…'

'Which will give us plenty time to talk, and I promise not to lecture. I can listen, though.' Angie gave a wry smile.

Luke never said very much.

'So what are your plans?' Angie asked as they drove out of the car park.

'No plans really,' Luke admitted. 'I think it's just about giving Scarlet some space.'

'You won't get any space if they find out where she is.'

'We'll see.'

They drove in silence for a while.

'Why *do* you live so far away?' Angie asked when they hit the motorway.

'It's just nice to get away,' Luke answered.

That wasn't the full reason, but Luke kept that to himself.

'Have you spoken with her private physician?' Angie asked with a sarcastic edge.

'Not yet.' Luke's response was tart as he thought of Vince. 'He's *unavailable* at the moment.'

'I'll bet.'

They were silent for a while but for Luke it was an angry silence, not at Angie, but because all that had gone on in the past was now firing his mind in all directions.

'Did I tell you that Anya once offered me a job as her private doctor?'

'No.'

It still angered him now. 'That was Scarlet's solution, to put me on her mother's payroll and have me be a part of that circus.'

'I think that sounds more like Anya's solution,' Angie said. 'Anyway, she'd soon have fired you when she realised how tight you are with drugs.' Angie smiled. When she'd had her wisdom teeth out Luke had rationed all the decent stuff, but then she stopped smiling at the memory and was serious. 'The baby would have been a part of the circus too.'

'No.' Luke shook his head.

'Of course it would have, and so would you.'

Luke just stared at the road ahead. He'd thought about it, of course he had. Life as Scarlet's partner or ex, access visits played out with the media looking on.

And even if he could have somehow taken it, which he doubted, what about his own family? They had their own lives, their own secrets, their own issues, and he'd have been exposing them too.

No, he couldn't live that life and neither would he have wanted it for his child.

'I'd never have let it come to that,' Luke said.

'Do you really think you could have shielded Scarlet, a pregnant Scarlet at that, from the press?'

'I'd like to have at least had the chance to try.'

'Is this what this is about?' Angie asked as they pulled up at his home.

'No,' Luke said, but then he looked at his house, which felt very different with the knowledge that Scarlet was in there. 'Maybe. Or maybe I'm just trying to give her a break.'

'God knows, she must need one after twenty-five years of it. Her whole life played out in front of the cameras...'

Luke sat there as Angie spoke.

'Poor kid,' she said. 'She's never known anything different.'

'She wanted to, though.'

It was what he had admired so very much about her.

Scarlet had wanted to escape.

She had told him the morning they had made love.

Luke had always laughed at the very notion of love at first sight.

Not now.

But he could not let himself remember that morning if he wanted to get through tonight so he thanked Angie for the lift, got out of the car and said goodnight.

Scarlet was definitely here. Luke could tell from the missing bricks in the low wall of his driveway, which he guessed the car had clipped. The house was in darkness and he wondered if he'd have to knock but, no, the door opened and he stepped in and locked it behind him.

Her scent was there and there were his car keys on the hall table beside the theatre cap and the clogs he had given her to wear, which had been kicked off.

Luke walked through to the kitchen and, no, Scarlet hadn't done his breakfast dishes, he thought with a wry smile as he saw all the evidence of her scrambled eggs. The shells were on the bench; she hadn't even soaked the pan, though he could forgive that one because he always meant to soak his breakfast bowl but never did.

He poured himself a glass of grapefruit juice and sat there for a long moment before heading upstairs.

Luke walked straight past the spare room. He knew that she wouldn't be in there and he was right.

Luke turned on the lights to his bedroom and there Scarlet was, naked in his bed and asleep, but she stirred as he came in and then yelped as he whipped back the duvet.

'Bed,' he said.

'I'm in it.' Scarlet smiled, not remotely fazed that she was stark naked. 'How's Mom?'

'Same,' Luke said, and scooped her up in his arms and carried her down the hall towards the spare room.

'Luke, I want you...'

'No way,' Luke said.

She was trying to rain kisses on his face as her hands went behind his neck, and recall was instant—he was as hard as anything, feeling her all warm and squirming, but there was no way that he'd be sleeping with her.

'Bed.' He dropped her onto the spare one and wished he'd thought to pull back the sheet first because Scarlet lay naked, her arms above her head and every bit as beautiful as he remembered.

More so even.

She had filled out a little bit and there was a jet of pubic hair that hadn't been there last time.

It was now silky and tempting and taunting Luke in his peripheral vision as he tried to meet her gaze.

Still Scarlet refused to meet his eyes.

'How could you sleep with me when you can't even look at me?' Luke asked.

She didn't know how to answer that and she screwed her eyes closed in shame.

'There's no change with your mother.' Luke tried to keep his voice calm and even as he brought her up to date. He tried to be all professional and detached but with an aching hard-on and closer to tears than she could ever know. 'But she's stable.'

'When will we know more?'

'I'll be called if there's any change. Other than that, I'll check on her first thing in the morning. I'll be leaving early tomorrow. Don't answer the phone unless it's me.'

Scarlet nodded. 'Will you come in and see me before you go to work?'

'Why?'

'Because I don't want to have to wait till tomorrow night to see you again.'

There was so much to say, so many questions, but, no, he couldn't bear to go there just yet so he gave a brief nod instead.

'I'll pop in and say goodbye.' He could not stay a moment longer. 'Good night.'

'How can it be a good night?' Scarlet asked, as she looked at the man who was walking out the bedroom door.

It was the longest, loneliest night for both of them.

It simply felt wrong to be at opposite ends of the hallway but raw was the hurt that kept them apart.

And the hurt was still there the next morning as Luke had his breakfast then made her a coffee and braced himself to go up the stairs.

'Good morning,' Luke said, as she gave him a just-awake smile.

For both of them it was.

Oh, it was awful still, but better than yesterday's had been, and certainly better than the seven hundred and forty-eight that had come before.

She watched as he put her coffee down but then, suddenly embarrassed by her behaviour last night, she covered herself with the sheet as she sat up. 'I don't get why you're cross that I came on to you.'

'I'm not cross,' Luke said. 'Sex isn't going to fix things, Scarlet.'

'I wasn't intending to fix things, just...' She told him the truth. 'I don't want you to change your mind about me staying here and I thought—'

'I didn't bring you here for sex, Scarlet. Did you sleep?'

'I did!' Scarlett sounded surprised. 'Not at first,' she said.

'Nor me.'

'It's a nice room,' Scarlet said, and even if it wasn't the room she would prefer to be in, she looked around the little spare room, pulled open the curtain by the bed and peered into the dark outside and saw a lamppost and beneath it someone walking a dog.

'I'd love to go for a walk.'

'Then go,' Luke said.

'I haven't got any clothes.'

'I'll sort that out today. I know it's probably a bit boring, being cooped up.'

'Oh, I'm far from bored,' Scarlet said. 'I love your home.'

'Thank you,' Luke said. 'So do I.'

He sat down on the bed and she felt relief that he wasn't dashing off.

'How long have you lived here?'

'Nine months,' Luke said. 'It's a bit far out but I like it.'

'I can see why. It was a nice drive, even if I was terrified I was being followed at first.' She pulled a little face. 'I think I scratched your car. I didn't see the wall on your driveway.'

'That's okay.'

'It's quite a scratch actually,' Scarlet said.

'Yeah, and I'm missing a few bricks from my wall,' Luke said. 'I saw.'

'Sorry.'

'It's not a big deal. I did the same when I first moved in.'

And then, when he should have gotten up and left,

Luke did what he had to—as she went to reach for her coffee he halted her.

Not her arm. Instead, his hands went to her face.

Scarlet felt the heat of his palms caress her cheeks and then his mouth soft on hers and he kissed her. Oh, how their mouths needed each other's. It was a soft morning kiss and for it, Scarlet knew, she would float better through the day.

She kissed him back, feeling again the lips she'd missed, and so gentle and unexpected was he that Scarlet felt tears sting in her eyes.

It was just a kiss and neither pushed for more.

'Look at me,' Luke said, still holding her face, yet she still would not meet his eyes.

'I can't.'

'You can.'

But she couldn't.

'Have your coffee,' Luke said, and he let her go and handed her mug to her. 'I'll call once I get into work and I know how she's doing.'

Scarlet nodded and he got up off the bed and walked to the door.

'You'll never be able to forgive me, will you?' Scarlet said, and she waited for his terse response, for angry words, for reproach and to be shamed, but instead he turned around.

'Or you me,' Luke said.

He was Dr Responsible.

Boring, some said, not that he cared what others thought—only what she thought of him and his actions.

In something so basic he had let her down.

'That morning...' He watched the colour rise on her cheeks.

It hadn't been the night.

He had kissed her all over and made love to her with his mouth through the night and Scarlet had done the same to him but it wasn't the night they now remembered.

No, it had been just as dawn had arrived that things had changed and moved in ways he had never thought they would...

Luke couldn't think of that now so he turned and walked off.

She heard him go down the stairs and the closing of the front door, and Scarlet got out of bed and ran onto the landing, still holding her mug. She wanted to call out for him to come back.

But then came the sound of his car starting up and as he drove down the street Scarlet heard the automatic door to the garage close.

She looked down the hall to his bedroom and stood there, and despite the fact the house was cold, she felt warm as she headed into his bedroom.

Luke had left her alone with the memory of them.

CHAPTER EIGHT

'THANK YOU FOR a wonderful night...' Scarlet sat on Luke's stomach and looked down.

That shadow on his jaw was darker now, and his hair was messed up in a way that she liked.

She circled the bruise her mouth had made on his neck and then her fingers moved to the hairs on his chest and she toyed with them. 'It was the best night.'

'It's been great,' Luke agreed.

The lack of condoms hadn't been an issue. They'd found plenty to do without them and now he lay looking up at her as they chatted. 'You don't live in London?' she checked.

'No, I'm just here for an interview.'

'So where do you live?'

'Oxford.'

'With your family?'

'No.' He rolled his eyes at the very thought. 'I was out of there at eighteen.'

'Don't you get on?'

'We do.' He was dismissive and Scarlet frowned.

'Are your parents together?'

Luke nodded.

'How long have they been married?'

'They just had their thirtieth anniversary.'

'Wow!'

He saw her wide eyes as she pictured his perfect life.

'It's not all roses, Scarlet.'

'It sounds it to me.'

And so he let her think that.

Luke let everyone think that.

It wasn't his place to tell.

'So it was your brother's birthday last night?' Scarlet checked.

'Marcus.' Luke nodded. 'He just turned twenty-one.'

'Do you have any other brothers?' Scarlet asked. She wanted to know everything that she could about him.

Luke shook his head. 'I have a younger sister—' Luke started, but Scarlet jumped in.

'I'd love that,' Scarlet admitted. 'I'd give anything to have a sister.'

'It's just you?' Luke checked.

'My mom says we're like sisters.' Now it was she who rolled her eyes.

'Well…' He tried but he couldn't really grasp it. 'I could never see my mum in a nightclub with me.'

'It's embarrassing,' Scarlet admitted, and went a bit pink. 'She gets wasted and the guys chat her up…' She pulled a face that showed her distaste.

Luke thought about his own mother and her love affair with gin. It was bad enough seeing her that way at home—heaven forbid if he had to witness it when out.

'Then she sings,' Scarlet said, and it was the way she said it that had Luke smile.

'Can you sing?'

'Do you really think I'd even try?'

He looked up into shrewd eyes and he wasn't smiling now. This was a young woman who had learnt to never attempt to outshine her mother.

He looked right into her eyes and wondered about all she could be.

'Would you like to sing?' Luke asked.

'No.'

'What would you like to be?'

'To be?' Scarlet frowned. 'Without her, you mean?'

Luke nodded and he watched as the little pink blush that had receded now darkened.

'I've never thought about it,' Scarlet said.

He knew that she was lying and he didn't mind a bit. In fact, he was inordinately pleased that, given her circumstances, Scarlet *had* thought about it, even if she preferred not to reveal her thoughts. And who could blame her? There were secrets in that pretty head, Luke was sure, and no doubt the press would love to know them.

He glimpsed her life again—Scarlet could trust no one, not even the man she was in bed with.

She *could* trust him, Luke thought, even if she didn't know it.

'Do the two of you get on?'

He watched as her eyes narrowed, and he knew she was about to shoot him down, say that of course they did.

'This is just between us,' Luke clarified.

'Of course it is.' Her response was sarcastic and then she met those deep brown eyes and tempered her thoughts. Something about Luke had drawn her to him at the club— his calm disposition at first and then that he'd had no idea who she was had at first been refreshing. Now that he knew, and only wanted her, he made her feel safe.

It would be foolish to let her guard down, Scarlet warned herself. She'd been the victim of pillow talk in the past and yet she could no more imagine Luke selling his story than she could him suddenly sprouting horns.

She might live to regret this, Scarlet thought, but she took a tentative breath and spoke on.

'If I behave we get on.'

'If you don't?'

She shrugged but Luke persisted. 'What happens if you argue?'

'People don't tend to argue with Anya,' Scarlet said.

Luke stayed silent as she prevaricated. It was a survival mechanism, he knew, and it concerned him greatly. He knew she was seriously scarred.

'Ever?'

Scarlet shrugged. 'I choose my battles.' She gave him a smile and moved in for a kiss. 'You're going to be one of them...'

He halted their kiss, wanting to talk some more.

'When you say—'

'You ask too many questions,' Scarlet said. 'We're a one-night stand.'

'Are we?' Luke checked. 'It doesn't have to be.'

'Don't you have a girlfriend?'

Luke frowned. 'I wouldn't be here if I did. I told you we just broke up.'

'When?'

'A month or so ago.'

'That's ages!' Scarlet laughed. 'How long were you together?'

'Two years,' Luke answered. 'What's your longest relationship?'

'Oh, I'm too busy to have a relationship,' Scarlet said. 'Anyway, they only want me to get to my mom.'

'Not true,' he said. 'Scarlet...' He wanted to tell her that was utter lies she'd been fed. He wanted many things, not just for Scarlet but for both of them.

Scarlet's thighs gripped him, but her hands were relaxed to him rather than suggestive. His were the same, running over her slender ribs, positioning her a little bit farther back and just enjoying her as they spoke.

'Why did you break up?' Scarlet asked.

'We just did.'

And he was very glad that they had, or he'd have missed this.

He looked up at her smiling mouth. Her face was flushed and pink and her hair was tousled. Luke's eyes moved down over her body. There was a bruise on her left breast from him and her nipples were darker from his attentions.

He didn't answer her question; instead, he put one hand behind her head to pull her down and, with her body angled over his, he went for the other breast.

'I wish we…' Scarlet panted as he licked her breast and then took it deep in his mouth, but she didn't finish saying she wished they had condoms. He was hard against her thigh and she had never wanted someone inside her so badly.

Luke wanted her badly.

But then he remembered he was the sensible one and dragged her turned-on and wanting body to lay by his side. Scarlet felt as if she were floating, with only his arm pinning her down.

They kissed, a kiss that demanded more from both of them, one that had Luke deciding that soon he'd just get dressed and find an all-night store, but now it was Scarlet that halted them.

'Why *did* you break up?'

'Because,' Luke said.

Because he hadn't want to drag her on a bus and make out with her, because he hadn't had to fight not to pull her down onto his aching hardness.

He wanted all of that with Scarlet.

'When you say this doesn't have to be a one-night stand, does that mean you'll call me?' Scarlet asked.

'Of course.'

'When?'

He reached over and handed her his phone and she tapped in her number and then took a photo of herself lying in his arms. 'Send that to me.'

'Okay.'

He did so and Scarlet heard her phone buzz across the room and smiled.

'Do you want to go out tonight?' Luke asked. He was more than happy to miss checkout and spend the day in bed and then take her out but Scarlet shook her head.

'I can't tonight. Anya's performing.'

'So you can't go out because your mother's working?' Luke checked. 'I don't get it.'

'She needs me there when she goes on and all the build-up beforehand,' Scarlet explained. At first she had said it as fact but, resting her head on his chest, the madness of her world was all the clearer for her short six hours away from it.

'Maybe we *could* go out?' Scarlet said. 'Or we could stay in again.'

'Sounds good.'

She thought of telling her mother that she wouldn't be there today, or tonight, and the hell that would break out. And then she thought of the worst scenario—being there for her.

Again.

And again and again.

Panic was starting to hit and she tried to deny it, to just lie there and keep her breathing calm and not ruin what had been a wonderful night.

Feeling the sudden tension in her, Luke pulled her in.

His hand stroked her arm and that, just that, had Scarlet feeling a little better.

It was the nicest sensation she had ever felt, just these soft yet firm strokes and the thud of his heart, and, despite her best attempts to stem them, silent tears started coming out of her eyes.

'Scarlet?' Luke checked, and lifted her chin. And it was then, for Scarlet, that panic truly hit as she revealed a truth she had never dared to.

'I don't want to go back...'

Tears never usually moved him but hers did. He could almost feel her desperation and she turned in his arms and released herself and lay on her back, panting as if she'd just run a race.

'What do you mean?' He came over her and started kissing her tears, and they were talking in whispers as she revealed her secret.

'I don't want to go back to my life. I've been trying to work out for years how I can get away,' she admitted, and then closed her eyes. 'Sorry, too much...'

'No, no,' Luke said, when usually he'd be thinking, *What the hell?*

'I don't know how to, though,' Scarlet admitted. 'Everyone I speak to is employed by her.'

'What about friends?' Luke asked.'

'All of my friends are hers first.'

She lay there rigid beneath him. His legs were on the outside of hers and Luke was up on his elbows, looking down at her, and a more lonely world he could not imagine.

Oh, his family had their own issues, but nothing like this.

And he had friends that went way back.

There were people he could turn to if he chose to.

That he chose not to was his own issue.

'I've run away before but I never get very far,' Scarlet said.

'What do you want?' Luke asked.

'I want,' Scarlet said, 'this.'

He got it that she wasn't talking about them at that point, just normality, and on a cold, wet morning, in a very warm hotel room, it didn't seem an awful lot to ask.

'We'll make it so, then.'

And then she was more honest than Scarlet had ever dared to be. 'I want you.'

'Good,' Luke said, 'because I want you too.'

Those dark brown eyes looked right into hers.

'It will be okay.'

She believed him.

'It will.' His mouth was on her lips and they tasted of hope and his words were so assured. 'I'm here now.'

His kiss deepened and it was like he had opened a tap in her heart and kept filling it.

She had lain there rigid but now she just moved beneath him. Like curling ribbon, her limbs wrapped around him and her lips were in thrall to kisses that were deeper and edgier than last night.

His skin was rough and she craved it. Her tongue matched his and her breasts, which had already had more than due attention, were needy and sore as his thumb tweaked one so expertly that her hips arched as if he had touched her between her legs.

The covers were too hot and heavy but the weight didn't feel like a burden, it just cocooned them. As her hips arched she felt the thick length of him pressed to her groin and stomach and then he moved back so he was between her thighs and she squeezed them tight and he moved into their vice.

She was damp, he was too, and there was an ache for more that rushed between them and her hands went to his buttocks and dug in.

'I want you.' Scarlet had never heard her own voice in that tone. It was determined, it was assured, it was desperate, though.

He moved and she could feel him thick at her entrance and she felt dizzy at the brief feel of him parting her, but as he pulled back she moaned and pressed her fingers tighter into taut muscle and begged him in.

He entered just a little way and those small thrusts had their breathing halting, because if they dared to take in air they might lose the giddy sensation.

Common sense, where was it? Luke wondered, because he had been overtaken by sheer want. She was swollen and aroused and sore for him and when Scarlet sobbed, 'Please,' he drove in hard.

'Oh...' Scarlet was frenzied. She had never been made love to like this, nowhere even close.

He offered the brief lie that he would stop soon and took her over and over, and it felt as if he were exploring her deep inside because knots of nerves awakened and he addressed each one.

He kissed her cheek and there were no more tears as he moved down from his forearms so more of his weight was on her and he scooped his arms under her. Her body was shaking and taut beneath his and he felt the intimate pull of her—she wanted more.

She was coming and claiming him with her thighs wrapping around his waist, and she sobbed out as he drove in harder and she met each thrust.

It wasn't pretty but it felt divine.

The bed was banging, both could hear it, and Luke, who never lost his head, quite simply did.

The feel of her was intense, the sound of them was volatile, like a drive-by shooting was taking place as they exploded one into the other.

Bang.

Bang.

Bang, bang, bang.

Bang, bang, bang, *bang*.

And Luke, who always held back a part of himself, was moaning and shouting and coming deep into her.

The hotel room rattled to their tune, and they were still going.

She came again, just on the tail end of his, and Luke groaned and shot out a final release, and then they collapsed into a void of silence and breaths and hot kisses and promises that made no sense because they'd been together for just a few hours.

Her hair was wild and damp and it felt as if they'd made love in a sauna.

It was hot, sticky sex with no end in sight because he was still inside her.

He moved to pull out but Scarlet gripped him. She gave him no rest, just a slow kiss to recover, and then a deeper kiss as he started to grow within her. But then came a knock on the door.

'Damn.' Luke laughed. 'Breakfast.'

She had no idea in that moment that the knock on the door heralded the end of them.

Scarlet opened her eyes as if someone had just knocked on the door to Luke's bedroom.

Her face was red in his pillow, her sex still twitching

as it had that morning, and still she wondered what would have happened if breakfast hadn't come then.

Sometimes she lost herself to her imaginings of how their worlds might have been had they not been disturbed, but not today. Instead, she remembered how he had climbed from the warm bed, semihard, and had pulled a towel around his hips.

She'd heard the door open and then, after a moment, it had closed and, suddenly remembering what she had done, Scarlet had closed her eyes in regret.

Scarlet could almost hear the rattle of the tray and Luke's tense breathing as he'd slammed it down on a table.

'Scarlet…' His voice was clipped and she could feel his contained fury. 'There are three security guards outside the door…'

It had been the end of them.

The beginning of a very rapid ending and now, two years later, she lay alone in his room.

Last night, Scarlet had thought she had no more tears left to cry over them.

But of course she did.

CHAPTER NINE

THERE WERE DIVERSION signs in place as Luke drove into the hospital.

'What's going on?' Luke asked, winding down his window and speaking with Geoff.

'One of the news vans broke down at the entrance to the staff car park,' Geoff said. 'At least, that's what they've said has happened. I think they're trying for a view of ICU.'

'Call the police,' Luke said. 'Get them moved.'

Instead of parking in his usual spot underground, Luke took for ever to find a space.

The press were still outside the foyer and security and other staff who were arriving for their shifts were looking very unimpressed with it all.

As was Luke.

Instead of heading straight into A and E, Luke headed up to ICU to catch David before he started handover.

Anya's people were still there but their numbers had thinned down.

In the other waiting room he saw Ashleigh's parents. Evan was sitting with his head in his hands as the mother paced.

When Luke stepped into the unit he found out why.

The space where Ashleigh's bed had been was empty

and Luke walked over to Lorna, who was just coming off the phone.

'Did he get a liver?'

'He did.' Lorna nodded. 'He just went to Theatre.'

He saw that Lorna, who was possibly the toughest of the tough, was on the edge of tears.

'Ashleigh's been in and out of here for the last six months. It's wonderful to see him get this chance.' Lorna shook her head. 'I'm not going to be able to sleep.'

'Well, you need to,' Luke said, 'so you can be back here tonight to look after him.'

'Please, God,' Lorna said.

He glanced over at Anya. 'How has she been?' Luke asked.

'She's had a stable night, apart from a spike in her temperature, but we were anticipating that. David's going to be a while. He took Ashleigh down to Theatre, just to see him put under. He's not staying for the op, though. He should be back soon.'

'That's fine,' Luke said.

He'd call back in on his way home, Luke decided, but for now he made his way down to his own department and worked through his list. But at ten, just before he started the fracture clinic, he called Scarlet.

Luke wasn't sure if she'd be up but he didn't know when he would get a chance to call again so he rang three times and hung up then called again.

Scarlet had spent a long time crying and her eyes were still watery as she lay in his bed and stared at the ringing phone at the bedside.

It rang off on the third ring and then rang again and she picked up the phone.

'Is that you?'

'It is,' Luke said. 'How are you?'

'How's Mom?' Scarlet asked, by way of answer.

'She's stable. There's no real change.'

'Is that good or bad?'

'It's good for now,' Luke said. 'Have you been crying?'

'A bit,' she admitted.

'Well, your mum's doing as well as can be expected and…'

Scarlet listened to his soothing words. She could let Luke think she was crying about her mother.

Later on she might be.

Just not now and she told him so.

'Luke, I wasn't crying about my mom. Seeing you, being in your home, well, it's kind of brought it all back. Not that it ever went away. I'm sorry for what I did—'

'Scarlet,' Luke interrupted. 'Let's not do this over the phone.'

'When, then?'

He didn't answer.

She lay in his bed when she should be sitting by her mother's.

'Do you think I should come in and see her?'

'That's up to you.'

'I know it is, I'm just asking for your take.'

'Okay, then, I think you need some time.' Luke was honest with his answer. He had seen Anya's lab results and it was looking less and less like the accidental overdose the spin doctors were trying to say it had been.

'What if she wakes up and I'm not there?' Scarlet asked.

'Yeah, well, I know how bad that feels,' Luke said, and it was the first real glimpse of his temper weighted against them because he abruptly rang off.

Luke stared at the phone.

He told himself to pick it up and pretend that he'd been cut off.

But as he sat there staring, he was reliving it too.

Not the nice part before, just the hell of afterwards, when he had walked back into the hotel room.

'What are they doing out there?' he'd demanded.

There had been three guys standing right outside the door and he'd recognised a couple of them from the club!

Scarlet hadn't fully understood his anger. 'I texted them to let them know where I was.'

'You. Did. What?'

Each word was an accusation in itself and Scarlet rose in the bed to her own defence. 'I didn't want people worrying.'

'So while we were…' His anger was mounting at the thought that her bodyguards had been standing outside and would have heard the noise they'd made. Worse, that Scarlet thought this completely normal incensed him. 'You told me that you wanted a night away from it all.'

'And I did, but I didn't want to make trouble.'

'You said—'

'You have no idea what my life is like,' Scarlet shouted.

'I'm trying to understand.'

'Well, you can't!' Scarlet could not take it in that he was angry at her. It spun her into a panic and she started crying. There was a knock on the door and then another, and, despite Luke telling her to leave it, Scarlet opened the door to say that she was okay. But, given she was crying, her bodyguards came in.

'What the hell…?' Luke exploded at the intrusion. He was furious at the insult their coming in inferred—as if he might have been about to hurt her.

'So you'll stand outside while she's having sex and then interrupt a discussion?' Luke shouted at the burliest one, and what had him raging was that Scarlet was standing there naked.

'Get back in the bed,' Luke shouted. He wanted her covered, he wanted this audience gone, but she misread his anger and dressed instead and within moments she was gone.

And now, two years later, he sat staring at the phone.

Scarlet couldn't deal with anger or arguments, and no wonder. He could see that now, he just hadn't been able to then.

Today was the second time in their history that he had hung up on her.

He didn't want to discuss the other time but knew that soon they'd have to.

Luke didn't take the easy way out now.

He picked up the phone and called her back.

CHAPTER TEN

THE PHONE RANG again and she didn't wait for three rings but picked it up straight away.

Had he missed her for all of these two years?

Was that what he'd just said?

The brusque tone of his voice gave her no clue.

And if he was angry, why was he calling her back?

'Sorry about that,' Luke said.

'Did you just hang up on me?' Scarlet asked.

'Yep,' he admitted, rather than saying they had been cut off, which was what he would normally have done. Luke had never known anyone like Scarlet, or the feelings she evoked in him. He couldn't remember hanging up the phone on anyone before. He was so obstinate at times that it was usually the other way around. 'I'm back now.'

Scarlet smiled. 'I'm glad.'

'We'll talk properly later,' Luke said. 'I know we have to but not over the phone…'

'I get it,' Scarlet said.

He got back to the subject of her mother. The reason for his call.

'She's not going to be waking up today. They're keeping her under for a day or two more at least and when she does wake up she'll be drowsy,' Luke rather more patiently explained. 'We'll cross that bridge when we come to it.'

'Okay,' Scarlet said, and then she said the nicest thing, Luke thought, when there must be so much on her mind. 'How are you?'

Fine, he was about to say. 'A bit tired,' Luke admitted. 'I'm going to finish up early today.'

'That's good.'

'What are you doing now?' Luke asked.

'I'm still in bed,' Scarlet said. She just omitted to mention whose bed she was in! 'What about you?'

'I'm just about to start a clinic so I have to go. Do you need anything from the shops?'

Indeedy she did!

Luke finished at three and by four-thirty he was in the supermarket to purchase his fugitive's supplies.

Quinoa?

He'd never even walked down the health-food aisle.

Kale?

His mother used to put that in soup! No way.

And she could have button mushrooms, like the rest of the world, Luke decided.

He threw in some eggs but he did make a small concession and got the organic, free-range ones—he'd been meaning to switch to them for a while anyway.

Luke stopped by the meat section but then looked back at the list. Did Scarlet even eat meat?

Yes! Luke remembered the breakfast they had ordered and never eaten but memories like that were too risky to have right now so he moved through to the clothes section.

There wasn't much choice.

He tried to guess her size and guessed she'd be the smallest so he bought some leggings, a couple of baggy tops and a pair of jeans.

And, thinking of the boots she had been wearing,

which weren't really made for walking, he bought some slip-on shoes.

Then he headed over to the underwear section.

Maybe not, Luke thought as he stared at a pack of five-for-the-price-of-three knickers.

He paid and left the supermarket but instead of going to his car he walked down the main street of the village and into a small boutique, which was a first for Luke.

'It's my partner's birthday…'

Trefor's wife smiled.

Trefor was the local policeman and Luke could never remember his wife's name. It was one of those names he should know by now but it was a bit late in the day to ask.

'Oh, well, we'll have to get her something nice, then.'

'Not too nice,' Luke said.

'How have you been, Luke?'

'Very well,' Luke answered, embarrassed that she knew his name.

'What size is your partner?'

'I'm not sure,' Luke said. 'She's very slim.'

'Well, do you know her bust size?'

'Small,' Luke answered, glad that he at least he knew that!

'Do you know, Trefor was just saying the other day that I should put the store online. Apparently men don't like coming in.'

'No,' Luke agreed.

'These are nice,' Trefor's wife said, 'though not *too* nice, and they've got a bit of stretch in them.'

It was very possibly amongst the most uncomfortable twenty minutes of Luke's life but, having made his purchases and thanking her, Luke was just about to head for home when Trefor came through the door.

'Hi, Luke.'

'Hi, Trefor.' Luke was about to head out but then he thought better of it. 'Trefor, I've got a friend staying with me.' He told him who it was. 'I'm hoping—'

'No problem,' Trefor said. 'I'll keep an eye out. Thanks for letting me know.'

Finally he was home.

The house felt nicer with Scarlet there. It wasn't just the warmth from the heater that changed things when Luke came in, it was Scarlet coming out of the lounge, wearing one of his shirts and also a smile.

'I missed you,' Scarlet said.

'Well, I'm here now.'

'How is she?'

'Much the same,' Luke said, and he looked at her worried expression. 'Do you want me to take you in to see her?'

'I don't know,' Scarlet admitted. She could see that Luke was exhausted but that wasn't the real reason she was holding back.

Here she could think.

Beside her mother's bedside she couldn't.

'No rush,' Luke said, sensing her quandary. 'She's stable.'

'I should be there, though.'

He didn't know what to say because his truth was that he didn't want her near that woman, but he held back from saying so.

'I'm going to go and get changed,' Luke said.

He went upstairs and put the underwear he had bought her in his wardrobe, pulled on some jeans and a jumper and then came back downstairs, carrying a mug, and not in the best of moods.

Scarlet had gone and the shopping still stood in the hallway.

'Scarlet!' he called, and she came out of the lounge.

'What?'

'I don't have servants and I've been at work all day.' He gestured to the bags and then held up a mug. 'What's a half-empty mug of coffee doing by my bed?'

'Maybe you were in a rush and didn't finish it?'

'I don't drink coffee.'

'Oh.'

'Were you in my bed this morning?'

It annoyed him that she smiled and nodded. 'It's more comfortable.'

It concerned him that he was fighting not to smile back.

That's what Scarlet did to him, though.

'Don't do that again!' he warned as she picked up the bag that held the lettuce and other heavy goods and carried it through to the kitchen.

'What did you do today?' Luke asked.

'Not much. I read some of your textbooks,' she admitted.

He was putting away the shopping and he held up a bottle of wine and she nodded.

'Do you like your job?' Scarlet asked.

'I love it,' Luke told her. 'I can't imagine my life without it.' He looked over at her. 'Would you like to be a midwife?'

'I just said it that night for something to say.'

'You said it again when you spoke to Angie.'

'Angie?'

'She's a friend.'

'The woman in the elevator!' Scarlet laughed as she remembered the conversation. 'I thought she was about to call Security on me for being an impostor.'

'No, that's Angie just trying to work things out.' He turned and gave her a smile. 'Lucy Edwards.'

Her cheeks went pink and then she told him something.
'I've seen babies being born.'

'When?'

'In Africa,' Scarlet said. 'The first time I went they
gave me a private tour of the maternity ward. I didn't
want to leave.'

'Really?'

Scarlet nodded.

'I went back again last year.'

'I saw,' Luke said, but without malice. 'Did you visit
the maternity ward again?'

'I did, and I saw some babies being born. They'd told
me they needed a drug called oxytocin for the women and
we brought loads with us.'

'That's good.'

It was good and he turned and smiled.

'Here…' He tossed her a bag of clothes and he started
to make dinner as Scarlet went through them.

'I'm not wearing these…'

'I thought the intention was for you to blend in.'

'Supermarket jeans?' Scarlet pulled a disgusted face
and then she took out the shoes. 'These are men's shoes.'

'They're not.'

'If I wear these, people will think I'm a lesbian.'

Luke rolled his eyes and carried on chopping as Scarlet
brought the subject back to the one they'd been discussing.

'Anyway, I don't think I'd be a very good midwife.'

'Why not?'

'I just don't.'

'Well, there are plenty of other things…' He glanced
at her. He could see she was pensive and he could feel the
shift in the light-hearted mood and knew she was thinking about their baby.

He loathed it that he carried on with preparing dinner but he did.

That was him.

'I thought you hadn't called me,' Scarlet said, touching on the subject that had to be faced but not yet, Luke thought, not with so much other stuff going on.

'It was only when I tried to ring you. After...' Scarlet sat and looked at his tense back. 'That I realised they'd blocked your number. Till then I thought you hadn't tried to call.'

'Well, I did,' Luke said. 'Over and over and then, when I couldn't get through, I arranged for some time off.'

'I didn't know.'

Luke said nothing. He didn't know what to say so he threw the mushrooms in the wok. Then he glanced up at the kitchen window. It was already dark and he could see her strained features in her reflection.

He was so loath to discuss it, though he knew he had to at least try, and he took the less easy option for the second time that day.

'Why didn't *you* call *me*?' Luke asked, and turned around. 'Why didn't you at least try and call to discuss things with me?'

'Because I was being selfish to land this on you, apparently. Because you had your life planned out and it sure as hell didn't include me.'

'Is that what she said?'

Scarlet didn't immediately answer. 'I was reminded that in two months' time I was going to Africa again. It's my favourite place and I was reminded that I could do a lot more good there...'

'Your mother said that?'

'Everyone said it.'

And by everyone she meant everyone, Luke thought.

Every person Scarlet came into contact with was on her mother's payroll. He thought of his own confusion at the time. Everything that had seemed so simple in the bedroom, when it had just been the two of them, had been muddied beyond recognition.

He'd spoken to Angie about the pregnancy and had listened to her objective thoughts, then there had been a long conversation with a friend from rugby he'd gone to school with who had been through similar. He had given somewhat less than objective advice and had suggested that Scarlet was after a meal ticket.

Luke had omitted to mention Scarlet's name and her millions but those words had rattled.

It had been a one-night stand. He'd been aware at the start that they wouldn't last and he'd wondered if he had merely been an escape route.

Luke had looked at his parents' crap marriage, a couple who were together for the children and appearances' sake.

He'd had so many people and life experiences to draw on.

Scarlet had had Anya and her empire.

'Anyway,' Scarlet suddenly said, 'I couldn't do that to my child.'

'What?'

'Give it my life.'

'I wouldn't have let that happen!' Luke responded. 'All you had to do was pick up a phone or get on a plane…' He was trying to keep his voice from rising. Hell, there was a reason he hadn't wanted to discuss this now. It was too raw, and he was exhausted, not just from work but from the impact of having Scarlet back in his life.

He watched her stand.

'Don't walk off!' Luke warned.

'Oh, you can talk!'

'Meaning?'

'It's a shame we're not on the phone. You could just hang up!'

'Scarlet…' He didn't get to finish—the wok was spewing black smoke and he dragged it off the hob, but Scarlet wasn't sticking around to eat, or discuss, charred ruins.

'I don't want dinner,' Scarlet said. 'I'm going to bed.'

Yet there was no relief when she walked out of the room and up the stairs. Words needed to be said.

Dinner was stuffed so he poured a glass of wine and sat there, just staring out at the darkness, until the phone rang.

He took a call from his mother, reminding him about tomorrow and that they'd be there around four but couldn't stay for long.

Good.

He was in no mood for happy families and pretending that thirty-two years of marriage was anything to celebrate when he knew what a sham it was.

Not when he could hear Scarlet crying upstairs.

They were different tears. In fact, he couldn't hear them, just the pad of her feet and the turn of a loo roll and Scarlet blowing her nose once she was back in the spare room.

Luke had learnt to stay back, he'd been told to stay back, to hold in the important stuff and let people live their own lives.

This time he chose not to listen to that ingrained advice and a little while later he made a very long walk and knocked at her door.

'What?' Scarlet lay in bed, surrounded by balls of scrunched-up loo roll.

'I brought you some dinner.'

'I don't want it.'

'Come on,' he said, and then waited till she sat up and

put the tray down on her lap. She stared at mushrooms on toast and a glass of wine.

'Aren't you cross?'

'I'm not cross,' Luke said. 'Even if I was, I'm not going to…' He was about to make a joke about withholding food but stopped himself. He could remember her saying that no one won with Anya and he guessed Scarlet flouncing off to her room would have been the only protest she could make.

And he was quite sure they'd leave her there hungry.

'Do you want to talk?' he offered.

'So you can hate me some more?'

'I don't hate you,' Luke said.

'It's okay if you do.' Scarlet gave a tight shrug. 'I hate you too sometimes.'

'Because?'

'Because you've got it all together, because the only mistake you ever made was me.'

'I've made plenty of mistakes, Scarlet, and you weren't one of them.' He came and sat on the bed. 'But, yes, I should have been more careful.'

'Yes, you should have been and so should I,' Scarlet shouted. 'But you're careful now, aren't you?'

'Meaning?'

'How many women since me?'

And he could fudge numbers or say, *Oh, they meant nothing*, or just ride it out, but he answered with the truth. 'Too many,' he admitted, and then he made himself ask the same when usually he would tell himself it was none of his business and back off. 'How about you?'

'Are you serious?'

Very.

He'd seen the smiling photos, the tour of Africa, the red carpet with gleaming plastic men by her side, and he'd tried, God knew, he'd tried to get past the hype, but sometimes, yes, it had felt as if she'd simply carried on without a backward glance.

'You really think I just pulled my knickers back up and carried on…'

'Sometimes,' he admitted, and held his breath, not sure they were strong enough for voicing the truth.

'Well, you're wrong,' Scarlet said. 'You're the one who carried on.' She rose up in the bed and the tray came with her, but she just tossed it to the floor, furious. 'I called you, Luke, and when I told you what I'd done, what did you do, what did you say? Nothing!'

'I didn't want to say the wrong thing.'

'And so you said precisely nothing!' She rose up farther and she pushed on the chest that was so strong but so immovable. 'Believe me, Luke, there was nothing you could have said that I wasn't thinking about myself. I was twenty-three, a woman, I should have been able to know my own mind…'

There were times Luke regretted his inability to speak up, to voice the thoughts in his head or the feelings that ate at him, and one minute ago had been one of those times. Instead, he was glad now that he had held on because the floodgates opened and she beat at him, and raged at him, except it wasn't about him, and Luke knew that.

He had known when he'd walked in the door that her loathing was aimed at herself.

'I listened to them and I shouldn't have.' She raged and raged. 'I'd rather you'd called me a bitch than stay quiet.'

'Really?' Luke took her arms and then he took her chin and still she would not meet his eyes. 'If that's the sort of reaction you were hoping for, Scarlet, then you really are with the wrong guy.' Now she looked at him and she saw those lovely brown eyes she had trusted so much and still did, and she saw tears in them too. 'I didn't know what to think, let alone say,' Luke admitted. 'I was on the way to the airport when you called…'

She started to cry but it was on him this time.

And Luke said nothing, not because he didn't know what to say now but because all she wanted was to cry and be comforted without agenda. And when she'd finished, when there were many more little balls of loo roll added to her pile, it was Scarlet who admitted that she didn't want to talk.

'Fair enough,' Luke said. 'We'll try again when you're ready.'

She looked from his chest to the floor and saw the lovely second dinner he had made dressing the carpet.

'I'll get it,' Luke said.

Scarlet lay back on the pillow when he left quietly and then looked over at the massive wine stain on the carpet and thought about how she'd thrown the tray and shouted. She tried to work out how on earth she could face him tomorrow when there was a knock at the door.

'Third time lucky,' Luke said, and he came in with a tray.

It was completely unexpected and the nicest thing anyone had ever done for her because she really was starving.

No wine this time. Instead, there was a lovely mug of milk and cinnamon and lots of slices of buttery toast smothered in jam.

'Where are the mushrooms?' Scarlet asked.

She'd never ended a row on a smile.

CHAPTER ELEVEN

SOMETHING WAS WRONG.

Scarlet woke and opened the curtain and she looked out at the streetlight and then lay back on the pillow.

The house was cold, even with the heating on. She hadn't felt warm since she'd arrived in England.

She thought of her mother and their row, and whatever had gone on between them, Scarlet wanted to see her.

It wouldn't be fair to ask Luke. He'd had a couple of glasses of wine and was exhausted, she knew that.

She recalled his words—visiting her mother didn't have to be a big deal.

What if she did what he said, went in through the maternity entrance?

The clothes he had bought her really were awful but she put them on and wrote a note and left it on the hall table.

'Gone to see Mom.'

It was an easy drive. There were some roadworks but in less than an hour the hospital came into view. She bypassed the main entrance, indicated for Maternity and parked the car. As she got out Scarlet saw a couple walking towards the door, where they buzzed at the entrance. She walked over quickly.

'Here,' Scarlet said, and held the door open for them as the woman doubled over.

'Thanks.'

She was in.

Her heart was pounding but Scarlet told herself she was doing nothing wrong but then she saw a security guard walking towards her.

'Can I help you?'

'I'm here to see my mother.'

'You can't wander around the hospital at night.'

'The emergency consultant told me if I used the maternity entrance...'

'Scarlet?'

She nodded.

'Geoff.' He gave her a smile. 'Remember?'

Now she did.

'Just wait there,' Geoff said.

He made a phone call and then came back. 'This way.' They chatted as they walked. 'You've saved me a right old drama,' Geoff told her. 'The press have been awful. I've told the ICU staff and they said to bring you up in the theatre lift, which will take you straight onto the unit.'

He went with her but when Scarlet arrived on ICU it was like stepping into a spaceship, but then a woman came over and gave her a smile.

'I'm Lorna.'

'I just wanted some time with her.'

'Of course you do,' Lorna said. 'Did you want to speak with a doctor first?'

'No.' Scarlet shook her head. 'I just want to see her. Is anyone with her?'

'They're all outside,' Lorna said.

It was all very low-key. There were a few other relatives sitting with their loved ones. The curtains weren't drawn as it was break time and the staff were thinner on the ground, Lorna explained.

'I can close them if you need me to. I'll call Ellie back from her break.'

There was no need.

Scarlet sat there and held her mother's hand and was brought a plastic cup of hot chocolate and a packet with two biscuits in.

'Your mum?' a man sitting nearby asked, and Scarlet nodded.

'Who are you here with?'

'My son. He's been in Theatre all day. I've just got in to see him now. I'm Evan.'

'Scarlet.' She smiled.

'I know!' Evan rolled his eyes. 'They're all out there, trying to work out where you are. Good for you!' he said. 'Ashleigh, my son, likes you. He was very fed up that he never got to see you!'

Scarlet laughed.

They chatted.

Not a lot but about how nice the hot chocolate was, how good the staff were.

How scary it was to be here.

'My wife's just gone for a sleep. I had to get some sleeping tablets,' Evan admitted. 'Never taken anything in my life but they did the trick. I thought I was dreaming when I woke up and heard he had a liver.'

'How long has Ashleigh been sick?' Scarlet asked.

'Since he was born,' Evan told her. 'We had a few good years when he turned eleven, but the last year has been the toughest. What about your mum?'

And she was about to make her usual small talk, or smile and say just how wonderful everything was.

Here wasn't the place to, though.

Lies made no difference in the ICU, Scarlet guessed.

It wasn't just the patients who were exposed to serious diagnoses.

'She's been sick for a very long time too,' Scarlet admitted.

'It takes its toll, doesn't it?' Evan said, and she nodded.

'Hot chocolate helps,' Scarlet said. She just sipped on her warm drink and held her mum's hand and then, when the clock nudged three, guessing Luke might need the car early, she stood and gave her mum a kiss on the cheek.

'I love you.'

Scarlet did.

I love you not.

Sometimes.

She just had to love herself more.

'I hope he's improved in the morning,' Scarlet said to Evan.

'Thanks, love.'

And then she offered something stupid, something silly and fun for when Ashleigh woke up, but it made Evan smile.

God knew, he needed it.

The charge nurse called for Geoff to walk her back down and she nodded in the direction of Luke's car.

'I'm fine now,' Scarlet said. 'Thank you.'

'Next time, page the head of security. It's usually me at night,' Geoff said.

'Thanks.'

Scarlet drove home, or rather to Luke's home, feeling better.

Not brilliant but better.

A part of her wanted to turn off the motorway. To simply drive to the cottage that was supposed to have been her haven while she sorted out her head with the luxury of time that had been denied to her now.

How did she tell her mother now that she was still leaving her?

How could she face the impossible conversations that were to come with Luke? And then there were his parents coming later today. Maybe he'd welcome her disappearing?

Scarlet wanted to curl up into a ball and for the world to sort itself out before she came back.

It wasn't going to, though.

The garage door opened as she approached and, hell, England was cold, Scarlet thought. Even the garage was freezing.

The house felt only marginally warmer.

Her note was still there on the table and her midnight adventure had paid off.

She went up to her room and stripped off her clothes then looked at the bed and simply couldn't face getting in. She wanted Luke, not for anything other than who he was and because of where she'd just been.

Scarlet padded down the hall and pushed open the door and there was Luke, deeply asleep. He hadn't even noticed she'd gone, Scarlet knew.

She slipped into the bed and moved straight over to him.

'You're frozen,' Luke said, and pulled her in closer.

Just that.

He stroked her arm as he had once before, and it was as if it was normal that she lie in his arms.

It was.

Luke pulled the covers over her shoulders and went straight back to sleep.

A sleep so deep that Luke even struggled to wake to his alarm. Instead, it blurred into the sound of ambulances or IVs alarming, and then he prised his eyes open and felt Scarlet wrapped around him.

Where it felt she belonged.

CHAPTER TWELVE

HE TURNED OFF the alarm but didn't have the energy to tell her to get back to her own bed, and neither did he want her to get out.

He knew she was awake, he could feel her lashes blinking on his chest.

'Are you okay?' Luke asked.

'No,' Scarlet admitted, and then she said what she'd wanted to when they'd been in the kitchen, as if hours hadn't passed since then. 'I didn't know what to do, Luke.'

Hours might have passed but he knew what was on her mind. 'Tell me.'

'You have to go to work.'

'No.' He did but some things were more important.

'And we can't storm off to bed,' Luke pointed out, 'given we're in it, so maybe we can try and talk.' There were so many details missing, ones he had thought he'd prefer not to know. But that had been when he had thought her callous. 'What was your mother like when you told her?'

'Fine,' Scarlet said from the depths of his chest. 'At first. I had toothache once and she handled it in pretty much the same way—you'll be fine, Vince can take care of that for you. That's when I rang you. I knew we'd ended badly and that I shouldn't have told Troy where I was but—'

'Forget about that now.'

'When you said to come here, that we'd talk and work things out…' She felt stupid explaining it. 'I don't keep my own passport, Sonia does. I didn't know how to get on a plane unless it was my mother's jet. I wanted to, though. I told my mother that I wanted to keep the baby and that I was going to England to speak with you. She went crazy. I didn't get it. I pointed out that she was a single parent and at least I knew who the father was.'

'What did she say to that?'

'She slapped me and told me how ungrateful I was, that, yet again, she had to sort me out. They had a crisis meeting about me. That's when I called you again. She wanted you to come and work for her, alongside Vince.'

'Scarlet, I could never do that.' Luke was honest. 'I wanted to be with you and I wanted us to work out how. I could have accepted some attention and a change to my life but I could never work for your mother.'

'I understand that but when you just dismissed it out of hand…'

'Scarlet, medicine is important to me. I take it very seriously and I could never be paid to prescribe, ever.'

'It seemed like the only way.'

'We'd have worked on finding other ways.'

'And then you didn't call back.'

'I did,' Luke said. 'I was going crazy. I spoke to Angie, and to a friend whose girlfriend, well, his wife now, had got pregnant. I asked my boss if I could take a couple of weeks off. He didn't want to give it to me, given that I'd only been working there for a few days. I told him he could have my notice if he wouldn't give me time off. I was on my way to the airport when you called.'

He'd never forget it.

First there had been relief at hearing her voice when she'd finally called. *'I'm on my way,'* he had said.

'There's no need, it's been taken care of.'

He'd driven straight into the back of someone.

'I heard the other driver shouting,' Scarlet admitted. 'Then I listened while you moved the car and swapped details and then you came back to the phone.

'Are you still there?' he had asked.

'Still here,' Scarlet had replied, and then had come the agony of him ringing off.

'I'd just got back from the clinic.'

'Did anyone go with you?'

'Mom,' Scarlet said.

So no one helpful, then, Luke thought.

'She was all nice to me afterwards. I was a mess and she had Vince see me and he put me on antidepressants. I didn't take them. I think I was right to be sad.' Scarlet thought back to that very difficult year. 'I knew things had to change and I also knew they were watching me. I picked up a bit when I found out she was going on tour again and that we'd be coming here.'

'Were you going to call?'

She didn't answer straight away. How could she have landed on him not just herself but all her hopes and dreams? How could she have told him about the shiny, poised, together person she had hoped to be when next she saw him?

'I don't know,' Scarlet said instead.

It hurt to hear that. He'd spent the last few months wondering if she would get in touch and to now to hear that she hadn't made up her mind cut deep.

'What would you have done?' Scarlet asked. 'If I'd called?'

'I guess it would have depended how the conversation went,' Luke admitted. 'But…' He couldn't.

She *hadn't* called.

'Tell me.'

'No.' Luke shook his head.

They were nowhere near ready for that. They might never be.

'I hate it that you went through it on your own. I mean, I know you had your mum…' He tried to be polite but Scarlet gave a low mirthless laugh at his effort.

'She didn't come in. Actually, there was a really nice nurse. I thought they'd be horrible,' she admitted. 'I was a bit of a wreck but she really was lovely to me.'

'I would hope so.'

'She was.' Scarlet still sounded surprised. 'I got very upset afterwards. I knew I'd made a mistake and she spoke to me for ages. She said that one day I'd be able to move on and that I didn't have nothing, that I'd learn from it…'

And it killed him to hear her say she'd thought she had nothing and he was very glad of that nurse who had taken the time with her on such a difficult day.

'And I have,' Scarlet said. 'Which is why I blew up the other day at my mother.'

'Can you tell me about the row?' Luke asked, and Scarlet nodded.

'I told her that I was leaving and she laughed and said I wouldn't last five minutes without her.'

His hand was still stroking her hair.

'I said that I had you,' Scarlet admitted, and she started

to cry. 'I didn't know if I did, I guessed not, but I was just trying to get away…'

'I know that.'

'And she said you wouldn't want me, given all I'd done, and then I got angry,' Scarlet said. 'Really angry.'

Now his hand was on her arm, the way it had been that morning, stroking her arm gently and firmly, and there was nothing that she couldn't tell him.

'I said that she'd always been jealous of me and that the reason she didn't want me to keep my baby was because she didn't want the spotlight on me and the "Grandma Anya" headline.' Scarlet looked up at him. 'I'm just sorry it took me so long to work that out.'

'I'm amazed that you could work it out,' Luke said. 'Sometimes I think my family is complicated but…'

He stopped.

She was used to it.

Luke always held back.

'It's just as well that we'll never make it.' Scarlet smiled. 'You could hardly have me meet them.'

'They're coming this afternoon.' Luke sighed. 'It's their wedding anniversary so they're stopping by on their way down to London for a long weekend.'

'Do you want me hide in the bedroom?'

'I don't want to hide you, Scarlet,' Luke said. 'Don't you get that?'

She didn't.

CHAPTER THIRTEEN

LUKE WALKED INTO ICU and nodded to Evan and then he looked over to where Anya lay.

On the morning she had come into Emergency it had taken almost everything that Luke had in him to treat her as just another patient.

He wondered if he could do that if she came in now. He hoped so but right now he was so angry that he truly didn't know.

'We're going to try and rouse her later this afternoon.'

It was a different anaesthetist on this morning.

'Did David pass on my message?'

'He did,' Craig said. 'I'll call you with any changes.'

'Thanks.'

'Lorna spoke with daughter last night,' Craig added. 'She's aware of what's going on and—'

'She spoke with the daughter?' Luke was horrified at any leak in information and tried to sort it out. 'How did Lorna know it was her?'

'Because she came in.' Craig gave him a wide-eyed look. 'Lorna wouldn't speak to just anyone.'

'I know that.'

A nurse came past and started laughing. 'Go and ask Evan if you don't believe him.'

'Evan?'

'Over there.'

Luke looked over and there was Evan, doing his crossword. Luke made his way over to him. 'How are you doing?'

'A lot better than I was the last time I spoke to you,' Evan admitted, and he saw Luke go to open his mouth. 'I'll make an appointment with my GP about my blood pressure.'

'Good man,' Luke said. 'I hear that you had a visitor last night.'

'Don't tell that lot.' Evan winked and nodded towards the exit door behind which Anya's entourage sat. He took out his phone. 'Lovely lady…' He glanced at his son, who was asleep. 'Ashleigh laughed when I showed him this morning.'

Luke looked at Evan's phone and for all he hated this type of thing, now it made him smile.

There was Scarlet, looking very unlike Scarlet. Not a scrap of make-up and her hair was wild and she was wearing a very baggy jumper and one of his shirts and smiling with Evan into the camera.

'How long was she here?' Luke asked.

'A couple of hours.' And then he looked over at Anya and he said exactly the same as Angie had. 'Poor kid.'

Luke worked for a couple of hours and then he called home in the familiar style and she answered the phone.

'Sorry,' Scarlet said, peeling her eyes open. 'I was asleep.'

He thought of her driving through the night and then coming back to his bed but he didn't let on that he knew.

'Are you up to going out for a walk?'

'Of course.'

'My parents are dropping by about four. I'll be home before then but I need something…'

'What?'

'Biscuits.'

Scarlet frowned.

'Biscuits?' she checked, because where she was from you ate them for breakfast and with gravy. 'You're going to give them biscuits?'

And then Luke remembered there were so many differences between them.

'Cookies.'

'Why?'

'Because they'll want a cup of tea. We're polite like that,' Luke said with an edge.

'You want me to buy cookies for their anniversary?'

'If you've got time.'

'Ha-ha.'

'Do you have any money?' Luke asked.

'I do.'

'Because there's some in the drawer by my...' Luke hesitated. There were some other things he didn't want her to see in the drawer by his bed. It was too late for that, though.

'I've already found them,' Scarlet said. 'I snooped the first day I was here.'

'Well, beside them is some cash.'

'I'll treat you,' Scarlet said and, suddenly too angry for words, she rang off.

Luke called back.

'Did you just hang up on me?'

'I did.'

'Good for you.'

He liked it that she could argue, that she was starting to find her voice.

'I've got a present for you,' Luke said.

'Really?' Scarlet frowned. 'What?'

'Go and open my wardrobe.'

Scarlet got up and Luke sat there hearing her swear at how cold it was, even thought he'd left the heater on high, and trying not to imagine her streaking naked across his bedroom.

'Where?' she asked.

'There's a bag at the bottom.'

Scarlet peeled it open with delight and pulled out all the lovely knickers and bras. 'Are these for me?'

'Scarlet, if I'm hiding a bag of ladies' underwear in my wardrobe for myself, then we really do have a lot to discuss. Enjoy.'

'Talk to me,' Scarlet said. She was already pulling some knickers on.

'I've got to go, I really am busy.'

A running commentary about underwear with Scarlet he really did not need!

It felt odd to be out in the village. Scarlet had found a scarf and wrapped it around her head. Not so much to hide, but she didn't get why everyone was saying it was mild for November. She'd never felt more frozen in her life.

One thing the English did very well, though, Scarlet decided as she walked through the store, was cookies! Then she saw a recipe card for coffee-and-walnut cake and decided that she'd make that and bought the necessary ingredients. Happy with her purchases, she headed out of the shop but then caught sight of her reflection.

She looked like the Matchstick Girl in the clothes Luke had bought her so she walked into a small boutique and smiled at a woman behind the counter.

'Hi,' Scarlet said.

'Hello!'

She started to look through the racks of clothing. 'Are you looking for something special?' the woman asked.

'I'm looking for something not too special.' Scarlet sighed. 'I'm staying with a friend and I don't have much with me.'

Her name was Margaret and she was lovely and a happy hour was spent trying on various pieces of clothing. Scarlet had soon amassed quite a collection.

'Ooh, I haven't seen this one,' Margaret said, as Scarlet handed over her card to pay.

That card and the money on it was Scarlet's biggest achievement, not that Margaret could know. It had taken a year to get to this point. A year of squirrelling away cash, pretending she wanted to know what it felt like to go into a restaurant and pay. Setting up an account on an auction sight and selling signed photos. Just putting a little away with a dream in mind.

And maybe that dream had been a cottage on the beach to clear her head before she again faced Luke, but that hadn't quite worked out. Still, it felt brilliant to choose and buy her own clothes.

It was a very different house that Luke came home to—the scent of cake hit him as he came in and there was Scarlet looking like a Scarlet he had never seen.

Gone the celebrity, gone too the Matchstick Girl clothes he had inadvertently bought her.

She was wearing a huge chunky nutmeg jumper and thick black stockings and black velvet stilettos and, possibly, a skirt, but the jumper was a bit too big to tell.

'Wow,' Luke said.

'I know.' Scarlet grinned as she spread icing. 'It's my first cake.'

He wasn't talking about the cake but he made the

right noises, even if it did look like she was icing two burnt pancakes.

'How's Mom?'

'They're going to try and take off the ventilator later on today.'

'Should I be there?'

'She's going to be drowsy at first…'

'Luke, please, tell me what to do.'

'Whatever it is that you want to do,' Luke said. 'Scarlet…' He wanted her away from that woman, and to never have to see her again.

But it wasn't his place to say that.

She busied herself icing her cake.

'Coffee and walnut,' Scarlet explained.

They were pecan nuts but he chose not to say anything.

He put a finger in the icing mix and it was butter and not much else.

'It doesn't look like the picture.' Scarlet sighed.

'They never do.'

'I hope they like it.'

'Who?' Luke said, and then realised she had made it for his parents' visit. He'd actually forgotten they were coming. The whole drive home he'd been thinking about Scarlet and her mother, interspersed with Scarlet and what knickers she was wearing.

'Look, I know my being here might make things awkward for you, so if you don't want to have to explain me I can go for a walk.'

'I don't explain myself to my parents,' Luke said. 'The same way they don't have to explain themselves to me.'

'I just don't want to create tension.'

'Oh, there'll be tension,' Luke assured her, 'but I promise it has nothing to do with you. There's no need to be nervous.'

'Easy for you to say. Do they know about us, about…?'

Luke shook his head and gave a tense shrug. 'A bit.'

'How much?'

'Just that I met you a couple of years ago. Marcus wouldn't stop going on about it. They don't know the other stuff.'

'Do they work?'

Luke nodded. 'My father's a professor in cardiology.'

'Your mother?'

'She's a curator.'

He looked at her and could see she was daunted, so he came over and wrapped his arms around her waist. 'Just be yourself.'

'Sure.'

'Scarlet…' He looked right into her navy eyes and, yes, he loathed sharing but he loathed her unease with herself even more, so he said what he could to help her relax. 'My father screws around like you wouldn't believe. He has affair after affair. Some casual, which my mother ignores. Sometimes they get serious and my mother hits the gin when it does.'

Scarlet just looked at Luke as he gave a weary sigh and told her some more.

'Then he stops seeing his mistress, my mother stops drinking, everyone's happy and the cycle repeats itself. It's like living in the laundromat.'

Scarlet laughed. 'How do you know?'

'It's obvious. Well, it is to me but, with that said, Marcus and Emma don't have a clue…'

'Emma?'

'My sister.'

'Oh, I thought she was a lady friend.'

'You're my lady friend,' Luke said, and then he changed tack because his hands were moving southwards. 'Anyway, this weekend they're going to be celebrating thirty-two years of dysfunction, but I'm not allowed to say that.'

She frowned.

'I'll raise a cup of tea and we'll have some walnut cake that you very nicely made and they'll carry on their way. And no doubt by Sunday he'll be out with his latest and my mother will be passed out on the sofa.'

'Why are you telling me this?'

'Because I don't want you to feel intimated.' Luke let out a breath and Scarlet looked at this very deep man.

'Thank you.'

'For?'

'Telling me,' Scarlet said, and then she smiled. 'Some of it.'

He smiled back and then he stopped smiling as tears filled her eyes.

'I'm scared about my mom…'

'I know. Look, I've taken tomorrow off—' Luke started, then groaned when he heard a car in his drive-way. 'They're here.'

Oh, they were, and they were also very taken aback to find Scarlet in situ.

Thankfully, though, it would seem they cared less about the famous Anya than they did about their son. His mother ran a very disapproving eye over Scarlet's stockinged legs and the questionable presence of a skirt, and his father simply looked her up and down.

Oh, my God, Scarlet realised, James Edwards was seriously checking her out.

Scarlet actually wanted to laugh as she saw Luke's eyes briefly shutter.

'You made cake!' Rose Edwards spoke as if Scarlet had just come in from the fields and mastered the appliances.

Which she sort of had!

'Not too much,' Rose said, as Scarlet cut a very generous piece.

'So, do you work at the Royal?' James asked her legs as she handed him a plate.

'No.' Scarlet smiled. 'I'm taking a break at the moment.'

'Studying?' Rose checked.

'No.' Scarlet gave Luke a slice. 'I'm just—'

'Scarlet's just taking some time out,' Luke said, and watched his mother pull a noncomprehending face and give a little shrug in a way only Rose could.

'Luke didn't mention anything,' Rose said, and then she frowned. 'Scarlet? Weren't you two…?'

'Scarlet and I go back a couple of years.' Luke gave nothing away with his response. 'She's over from LA and has come to stay for a few days.'

The cake really was amazing! Burnt and unrisen and the butter cream was almost pure butter.

'You're not having any?' Rose said to Scarlet as they all chewed through hell.

'Oh, no.' Scarlet screwed up her nose. 'Full of carbs!'

Luke actually laughed and never had he been more grateful for poor cooking skills because when Scarlet went to offer more, his mother pointed out they had to be in London by seven.

'Can't count on the traffic,' James said.

Scarlet said her goodbyes but stayed in the kitchen because Rose was making frantic eye gestures to Luke to have a word outside.

'Has she moved in?' Rose demanded.

'Temporarily, yes,' Luke replied.

'Luke, she's…' Rose was all pursed lips. 'Just watch yourself.'

Luke stood as they drove off and his father took another brick out of his wall. He walked inside.

'Is that American hussy after your money?' Scarlet was sitting on the kitchen bench and grinned as he walked back into the kitchen.

'It would seem so.'

'Your father!' Scarlet started laughing. 'He spoke to my thighs.'

'I don't know what to say about that.' What could he say? 'Never let him give you a tour of the library.'

'Well, if I ever do get to see your home I'll bear that in mind.'

He came over and she wrapped her arms around his neck, and she could just feel his tension. She just looked at him and smiled.

'Are you adopted?' she teased, only because Luke was a younger version of his father but their personalities could not be more different.

'I wish.'

'Is he like that with all your...?' She hesitated. She wasn't really a girlfriend, she was just the hot mess that had landed at his door.

'Yep,' Luke said. 'So don't take it as a compliment.'

'I shan't.'

He looked at her and usually he found family occasions, particularly if there was a girlfriend present, excruciating, but this one had almost ended with a smile.

His father's actions reflected no more on him with Scarlet than Anya's did on her. Still, he was cross with them.

'I can't stand how she doesn't notice what he's up to, or pretends not to,' Luke said. 'And yet she nitpicks and judges everyone, what they wear, how they talk...'

'How they cook...' Scarlet smiled. 'Poor Luke, having to eat that awful cake!'

'I like it,' Luke said.

'Good, because it's dinner.'

Now she did make him smile. What he had said before about Scarlet clearing his head was true. It was as if the rest of the world was crazy when it was just the two of them.

'You look beautiful,' Luke said.

'I went shopping.'

'I can see.'

'And I *love* my presents.'

'I want to see.' He ran a hand over her bottom as she sat on the bench and they kissed. A kiss that both had been waiting for. Her hands pressed into his hair and Luke moved in between her thighs and she wrapped them around his waist.

His kiss deepened, as if making up for two years of none. A slow, deep kiss that she didn't want to end but it did.

Luke remembered how upset she had been just before his parents had arrived.

He didn't want this to be about distraction. Both knew that at any moment the phone would go and there would be news about her mother. And, though he wanted more than anything to take her up to bed, or even on the kitchen table, there was so much to sort out first.

'Do you want to go and visit your mum?'

'You don't want to drive all that way again…'

'Do you want to go in?' he offered again.

'I don't know.'

'That's an answer,' Luke said. 'It's okay not to know.'

They went through to the lounge and it was like waiting for a bomb to go off. Scarlet sat cross-legged, tapping one foot, and then came over and lay on the coach, in her favourite spot—her head on his lap.

'I can take you in tomorrow and I can stay with you while you speak with her.'

'There's no need for that.' Scarlet shook her head. 'I know you think she's awful but she's not all bad…'

'No one is,' Luke said. 'It would be so much easier if that were the case.'

'She can be so nice. I don't know how to tell her I'm leaving after she's been so ill.'

'Leaving's hard,' Luke said. 'Even when there's no real reason to. Especially when there's no real reason.' And he told her a bit about the demise of his relationships prior to her. 'It's hard to admit something's not working when there's nothing really wrong, but sometimes…'

'What?'

'Well, you should *want* to stay,' Luke offered, not just to Scarlet but to himself as he thought of the demise of too many okay-ish relationships. 'Not have to come up with reasons to.'

He picked up his phone to glance at the time and Scarlet took it as a sign he was about to get up so she turned in his lap. 'Don't go…' She ran a hand over him and her lips did the same. Luke took her hand as she went for his zipper.

'I wasn't going anywhere,' Luke said.

'Just making sure…'

'Scarlet, I don't need a blow job to stay on the couch with you.'

He watched her face redden and tears fill her eyes, but he wasn't shaming her, more those who had taught her that was the way to make someone stay.

'You don't want me.'

'I want *you*.'

'And I want you to hold me.'

Finally!

He lay down beside her and showed her how nice it was to be held for no reason other than that.

'You're hard,' Scarlet said a little while later.

'It'll pass.' Luke grinned. He was as turned on as hell but there was a reason he wasn't tearing her clothes off now and he stopped smiling. 'Is that how you get your affection, Scarlet?'

He'd guessed as much but it hurt when she nodded.

They needed to start from the beginning, and that was why they lay there, half talking then dozing, and he wished they could stay there, but time moved quickly when you didn't want it to and just as Scarlet dozed off he heard the buzz of his phone.

He took the phone call and then sat there quietly for a moment and looked down at Scarlet. He did not want to invade her peace.

But he had to.

'Scarlet…'

'Mmm…'

'That was Craig, the anaesthetist working this evening. It's okay…' He felt her tense. 'Your mum's doing better.'

'Is she asking for me?'

'Yes.'

He could feel her rapid breathing.

'It wasn't an accident…'

'It was,' Scarlet said. 'She just took too much.'

'No.'

'It was.' She started to cry and Luke just sat there, thinking that her intense pain would stop soon because very soon it would be made to.

An accident.

Whoops.

But that just dulled the pain, it wouldn't take it away.

'I need to see her.'

'She's very angry and upset,' he warned, but Scarlet was already pulling on her shoes and he had this awful feeling that back to her world she was going. Especially when she went upstairs and started filling her bag with her flats and the scarf she had pinched from him.

He stood in the doorway, watching her, and told himself that they had, from the moment they had met, been temporary.

'Can I have my clothes,' Scarlet said, 'and my phone?'

'Are you coming back here?' Luke asked.

She just looked at him. 'I don't know!'

Her honest answer felt like she'd thrown a knife.

Luke's eyes felt as if he'd been swimming underwater as he drove back in to work.

People were right—he should live closer.

Except, as he looked over at Scarlet, he wouldn't change where he lived for the world. At least she'd had some time away. He just wished he could have given some more.

He had called ahead before he'd left and had spoken with Lorna, who was back for her night shift.

'David should be in soon,' Lorna said.

'It's not David I'm ringing for,' Luke said. 'Lorna, I'm bringing Anya's daughter in. Could we use the direct theatre lift?'

There was a very long pause as Lorna resisted asking any questions. 'Of course,' she said. 'Do you know the code?'

'I do.'

'I'll see you shortly, then.'

His filthy Audi moved unnoticed into the car park and

they took the elevator up to the ground floor, where they headed straight to the central column.

There they took the service lift straight up to Theatre and then another up to ICU. Instead of arriving in the corridor, as the other elevators did, they stepped straight onto the ward.

To their credit, the staff there gave him no more than a slight wide-eyed look as Luke came over to the desk with Scarlet.

'Hi, Scarlet.' Lorna smiled. 'Your mom's been asking after you.'

'I know.'

'Why don't we go somewhere a little more private?' Lorna suggested, and glanced over at David, who nodded.

'I'll be there in a moment.'

'Do you want me to come with you?' Luke offered, but Scarlet shook her head so he stood there as Scarlet and Lorna headed off.

'I'm not sure what's going on between you two,' David said, 'and I don't need to know.'

'Thanks.

'You need to know this, though,' David said. 'She's about to walk into the lion's den.'

'I know she is.'

Scarlet sat and listened to Lorna, who explained that her mother was doing a lot better but was insisting that she be moved elsewhere. 'She's not being very cooperative,' Lorna explained gently. 'And she's also extremely angry.'

'With me?'

'With everyone,' David said as he walked in, and Lorna looked up and smiled. 'I want her to stay here and I've told her that but she wants to be moved. I've told her that can't happen yet.' He was honest with Scarlet. 'I've dragged out a couple of procedures and told her it wasn't possible till late tomorrow but I can't force her to stay.'

Scarlet nodded. 'I know.'

'She's very insistent that she leaves.'

'Anya can be exceptionally difficult,' Scarlet said. 'I'm very sorry—'

'Scarlet,' David interrupted, 'you have nothing to apologise for.'

And she took a breath because she knew he wasn't just telling her that she didn't need to apologise for her mother's behaviour tonight.

This wasn't her fault.

Scarlet told herself that as she stepped behind the curtains and saw her mother lying there.

Lorna stayed with her but it wasn't pretty.

It was her fault apparently, and basically Anya told her that if at first she didn't succeed then she would try and try and try again because she could not live without her daughter by her side.

Luke had always thought that he was the strong one.

It had been an assumption of his that was summarily squashed when, after a few minutes of Anya's ranting, he heard Scarlet's clear voice.

'I'm going to go now, Mom. I love you. Please, get well.'

Scarlet walked out and straight to the elevator then she turned as if she'd forgotten something and thanked David. 'And can you thank Lorna?'

'Of course,' David said. 'Are you happy for me to call Luke with any change?'

'Please,' Scarlet said.

And that was it.

They stood in the elevator and made their way back to

the underground car park, and Scarlet felt as if she might
jump out of her skin.

'Can I drive?' Scarlet said suddenly.

'Of course.' Luke handed her the keys and Scarlet
climbed into the driver's seat.

'She blames you,' Scarlet said, 'well, when she's not
blaming me.'

'I heard,' Luke said. He didn't really know what to say
here but he tried. 'I'm sorry if I've caused a rift…'

'A rift?' She gave him a very wide-eyed look that told
him he was a master of understatement and then turned
her head to look over her shoulder as she reversed out.
'And do you really think any of this is your fault?'

Wisely he said nothing.

'What?' Scarlet challenged the silence. 'Why do you
have to be responsible?'

'I'm not.'

'Why do I?'

'You're not.'

'No,' Scarlet said, and she briefly looked at him as
they waited for the barrier to lift. 'I was always going to
leave, Luke or no Luke.'

'It's left here,' Luke said, as she missed the exit.

'Not tonight it isn't.'

She drove out of the hospital as if they were being
chased by the paparazzi and then he found out that, despite several prangs in her past, Scarlet could actually
drive, and rather fast!

There was somewhere she needed to be. Scarlet had
known it the very second Luke had broken the news to her.

It had been the place she'd intended to run to that awful
morning and it was the place she was taking him now.

'Am I being kidnapped?' Luke grinned.

He didn't blame her in the least for wanting a drive.

'Yep.' She looked over at him. 'So go to sleep. I don't want to talk.'

CHAPTER FOURTEEN

IT WAS A long drive, a very long drive through the night and she liked it that he didn't question her about where they were going and that after a while he slept.

God knew, he hadn't all week, Scarlet realised.

She read the signs, and the roads were very narrow and hilly, more so than she remembered. The hedges and stone walls loomed close but finally they had arrived and she pulled into a small deserted lookout and stared out at a waning moon and an angry black ocean.

The water looked a lot like she felt, cold and churned up and too dangerous to explore, but she wanted the man who was stretching out beside her to know her some more.

And so badly she wanted to know what went on in his head too.

Luke was so closed off and it had taken meeting his parents to realise that his guarded nature didn't just apply to her.

'Where the hell…?' Luke asked as he opened his eyes. The wipers were going full pelt but were still battling against the rain and the windscreen was fogging up.

'Devon,' Scarlet said.

Luke looked at the dashboard clock. It was five in the morning and pitch-black. The wind was howling, the sea was rolling black and white.

'I've dreamt about being here for a very long time.'

'Was it warm and sunny when you did?' Luke asked.

Scarlet shook her head. 'Nope.' It really was the place of her dreams but she had never dared to hope that she would ever be here with Luke.

They got out and Scarlet went into her bag and put on the horrible flat shoes he had bought her and then she put the giant bag over her shoulder. 'Leave it in the car,' Luke suggested, but Scarlet shook her head.

They didn't walk down to the beach, more the wind blew them onto it, and they ran hand in hand along the pebbly shore beside the roaring water.

Scarlet was angry, more angry and upset and terrified for her mother than she knew how to be, and Luke got that. He had heard her mother's cruel words and had seen Scarlet's calm exit but knew she was bleeding on the inside.

'I hate her. I love her but I hate her,' Scarlet said.

'Did you tell her that the other night?'

Scarlet nodded.

'You are allowed to say how you feel. What she did with that information was her choice.'

'You're allowed to say how you feel too,' Scarlet said, 'but you don't.'

'I know.' He pulled her right into his jacket and held her.

'What if she dies because I don't go back?'

And there was the reason that, in this, he didn't offer his thoughts, because one day that might well happen and he did not want to have influenced her choice.

He did not want, years from now, for there to be another reason for deep regret that came between them.

'If you do go back, will it change things?'

It was all he could offer and Scarlet tried to picture

herself back home in LA and her mother well, simply because she was there by her side.

It hadn't worked so far.

For twenty-five years, being by her side hadn't worked.

'Do you know,' Luke said, and with his words he offered her no easy solution but acknowledged the hell her decision must be, 'with this wind, if you scream and face out to the water, no one will hear you?'

'Oh, they would,' Scarlet said, because the scream that she held inside was so loud it might split the channel they stared out at.

Luke shook his head. 'They won't.'

And so she did. Scarlet screamed and swore and kicked at the stones, and she was like the witches that she'd read flew over these parts, and it helped.

It really did.

And when her throat was as dry and as sore as it had been the morning she'd found her mother, the morning she had found Luke again, he took her in his arms and he held her.

They swayed to the sound of the waves and moved to their own tune, and against his chest the world felt better. With her in his arms, despite the darkness, the world seemed brighter.

And so they danced, and cared not if anyone was watching.

CHAPTER FIFTEEN

'LET'S GET BACK to the car,' Luke suggested.

Neither were dressed for the weather and both were frozen but Scarlet had other ideas and she took his hand and, shivering wet, gulping in cold air, she started walking along the beach.

With purpose.

They came to a small track and walked up it, arriving at a dark cottage. Luke frowned as she went into her bag and took out some keys. 'Scarlet?'

'I'm not breaking in.' Scarlet smiled through chattering lips. 'I want to show you something.' She pushed open the door and turned on a light, and Luke looked around and there, by the sofa, was a large bag.

'This is why I didn't get to see my mother go on stage that night.'

'What are you telling me, Scarlet?' Luke asked. 'Or, rather, what aren't you telling me?'

'A lot.'

There was a fire in the grate and she went to light a log with the matches provided, which didn't work, so he took some paper and scrunched it up beneath and kept feeding it till the log took.

And, because it was Scarlet, she stripped off, right down to her knickers, and Luke rolled his eyes but also stripped down. He couldn't be bothered to spread his clothes out so he threw them, suit and all, to shrink in the dryer and put a towel round his hips.

He didn't even bother to bring one for Scarlet.

She'd warmed some milk and made drinks and now sat by the fire. He went and sat beside her.

Luke was very used to asking patients their pain score from one to ten.

If there was such a thing as a want score, he'd be demanding knockout drugs now, because for all the times and opportunities they'd had to evade things with sex, this was the biggest challenge he'd met. But tomorrow her mother left and Scarlet might not be with her and he was here in the space she had fought for, in her terribly complex world.

She needed help, not his want.

'How long have you had this place?' Luke asked.

'I booked it a few weeks ago. I've been trying to leave for years,' Scarlet admitted. 'Since I was about fourteen. I just never knew how. I ran away when I was sixteen and I got as far as a bar.' She looked at him. 'I didn't know how to start, who to turn to,' Scarlet admitted. 'Then we had that night together and as terrible as things turned out I knew then that I had to do it. I started looking into ways when Mom said she was going back on tour. I've been squirrelling money away for this place. I've got it for a month. That's why I missed being there when she went on stage. I took a car the hotel provided and brought my stuff here.'

'Did your mum know?

'I told her that I wasn't going to be returning to America with her.'

'You could have got in touch with me, Scarlet. I'd have helped.'

'I know that you would have. I actually told Mom that I would be looking you up, I thought it might be a bit of a false lead…'

That hurt but, Luke conceded, not as much as she was hurting right now so he let it slide.

'Even though I know what might happen to her, I'm not going back with Mom,' Scarlet said. 'I'm not cutting her out of my life for ever, but…'

She'd made her decision and had made it by herself, and instead of it hurting that she didn't need him, he was proud of the strongest woman he knew.

'I can't live like it any more. I've got this knot in my chest that I thought was normal until the night I spent with you. I honestly thought that was how life felt. I'm twenty-five, Luke. It shouldn't be called running away but that's what I feel like I'm doing to her…'

And he'd always held back. Luke had known she had to come to her own decision but he knew what a difficult one it must be for a woman who had never known anything other than the twisted love she'd been shown.

'You're not responsible for…' he attempted, and by reflex he felt her shoulders stiffen beneath his fingers. 'I've never run away,' Luke said. 'But I did skip school once.'

'Rebel,' Scarlet said, and her eye-roll suggested, what would he know?

'It was for me.' Luke smiled at her sulky expression. 'We took a train to London and went to the movies.'

'Did you get caught?'

'Sort of,' Luke said. 'Well, I ended up telling my mother…'

'You confessed!' Scarlet grinned. 'You are so damn…' And then she stopped because he just looked at her and he had told her something very few knew.

Not his brother or sister.

Nor his friends.

And certainly not girlfriends, because Luke's parents had warned him about sharing the truth.

'On the train back we were all fooling around and I looked over and I saw my father with a woman, getting off…'

Scarlet frowned.

They spoke the same language but it was so open to miscommunication that even Luke smiled. 'Not getting off the train, getting off with each other. Making out.'

'Did they see you?'

'No.' Luke shook his head. 'I went to another carriage and my friends followed. They never knew why I moved. I said I thought I'd seen an aunt.'

'You never said anything?' Scarlet checked, but then she knew she had said the wrong thing.

'Not at first. The next weekend I told my father that I'd seen him and that if he didn't tell my mother, I would.'

'And did he?'

Luke nodded.

'There were some terrible rows and after a couple of days he moved out. Marcus was about seven and Emma was five so they didn't really see it, but in the evenings my mother fell apart. She hit the bottle, cried her eyes out. One night I told her that she needed to go to bed. Do you know what she said?'

Scarlet just looked.

'This is all your fault.'

'For making your father tell her?' Scarlet checked, and Luke nodded.

'I realised then she hadn't wanted to know. I thought I was doing the right thing. I'd want to know, wouldn't you?'

'Oh, I'd know!' Scarlet said.

'She blamed it all on me. He did too. If I'd just shut up, none of that would have happened. After that I just stayed back. People can blow up their lives, do what they want. I'll fix them as much as they want to be fixed but I don't give unsolicited advice. Never again.'

She trusted him.

For the first time ever, she absolutely trusted another person.

Not more than she trusted herself, though.

He wasn't her safety net but it made the tightrope that she walked just a touch more steady.

'Can I ask you what you think I should do?'

Luke had held back for all the right reasons and for much better reasons he stepped in now.

'It isn't your fault. No matter what she says. It isn't. Change what you can,' Luke said, 'nurture the things that make you feel better. Follow your dreams and if that means you head to Africa…' He watched the reddening of her cheeks as he had one very special morning, and he'd been right—there were secrets in that pretty head. 'For what it's worth, I think you would be a brilliant midwife.'

It was worth so much.

'How can I be?'

She didn't feel she deserved it, Luke realised.

'Do you remember that nurse who was there for you? Was she perfect? I'll bet she didn't just sit with you, Scarlet. She brought some of her life, her experience to the bedside, and you've got a whole load of that.'

'Is that what you do?' She didn't get it, she just couldn't imagine Luke talking with someone and spilling out his life.

'In my own way,' Luke said. 'I don't jump in, I don't judge. It doesn't suit all my patients but for the ones that it does, they'll wait to see me.'

'I'd wait to see you.' Scarlet smiled. 'I used to think you were all like Vince.'

'Is that why you screwed your nose up when I said I was a doctor?'

Scarlet nodded. 'I hate that man so much. I was so happy when I found out that he'd only come on board when I was three. I used to worry that he was my father.'

'Do you know who your father is?'

'No idea,' Scarlet said. 'Nor does she.'

'Does it hurt, not knowing?'

'It used to,' Scarlet said. 'I had this notion that one day he'd come looking for me. By the time I got a bit older I'd worked out that, given my mother had no idea who it was…'

'I'm over casual sex,' Luke said, and he looked at her.

They were naked by a fire, the scene was set, he could have her now, but then again, Luke knew, she'd been so starved of affection that a burger could have got him there with Scarlet.

Not now.

She gave him a smile, she sat naked and looked at the most beautiful man on earth and she felt on the edge of something, that love really was worth holding out for.

'And me.'

CHAPTER SIXTEEN

'I DON'T KNOW if I should try and speak with her one more time,' Scarlet said

Luke was driving, and they were near the turn off that decided if they headed for home or the hospital.

He was honest.

'I think you have to,' Luke said. Even if just for Scarlet's sake, maybe it was better that she try again, but Scarlet shook her head.

She knew just how poisonous her mother could be.

It had taken the time away to see it.

'I can speak with her if you want.'

'You?'

'Well, she did ask me to be her doctor once.'

'I thought you stayed back?'

'Not in this.'

There were press everywhere. News of Anya's impending transfer had leaked, but not by the staff at the hospital, Luke knew that.

He nodded to Geoff, who gave him the most bored shrug as he gestured Luke's car to turn to the right. And Luke would thank him later for not letting on that a valuable photo was sitting with her heavy head leaning against the window of his car.

He parked and, at Scarlet's request, he left her in the car. On his way to ICU he called Angie.

He gave sparse details. It was for Angie to make her own judgements and he did all he could not to cloud them.

'If you could be there when I speak with Anya...'

'What if she agrees that I take her on?' Angie checked. 'I'm serious, Luke. If she's my patient...'

'I'll never ask,' Luke said. 'And I'm not just talking professionally, I'd never jeopardise our friendship.'

Absolutely he knew the value of a real friend who wasn't paid for, one who didn't simply say the right thing because it might be easier to hear a lie than the truth.

'Well, make sure you don't,' Angie said. 'I'll meet you up there.'

'Anya's about to be transferred,' David said when Luke came into the ICU.

'To?' Luke checked, and was informed that Anya was being transferred to a very swish private hospital for a couple of days and then would be heading for home.

'She wants her daughter.' David rolled his eyes. 'And she's not used to not getting what she wants.' He glanced over at the close curtains. 'She's furious that she isn't in a private room. She has no concept of ICU.'

'Can I speak to her?'

'You know you can.' David nodded. 'Though I have to say I don't think a lecture from the doctor who resuscitated her is going to do much. Still, it's worth a try.'

'Oh, no.' Luke was honest. 'I'm not here for that. I was invited to be her private doctor once.'

'You!' David frowned and then grinned. 'You?' he checked again.

'Yep, me,' Luke said. 'And, as you've probably guessed, her daughter is staying with me.'

'We had kind of worked that out, long before you brought her up here.'

'How?' Luke asked, not worried that they had, just curious to know.

'Well, the car Scarlet arrived in, Geoff kind of recognised, so we checked her emergency contact phone number and it matched yours.' David grinned. 'Talk about a dark horse…' As Angie came over and joined them, David stopped smiling and shook his head. 'I can tell you now, Angie, that she's certainly not going to speak with you.'

'Well, let's just give Anya that choice,' Angie said, and Luke watched as his friend and ex-lover put her psychiatrist's hat on firmly.

'Are you going to come in?' Luke asked David. 'I'd prefer you to hear what's said.'

'Sure.'

They all walked over and Luke took a breath and then parted the curtain.

'Anya…' He gave her a thin smile. 'I'm Luke Edwards…'

Anya just stared.

'I was the consultant on duty in Emergency when you came in.'

'And I want to thank you.' Anya said.

'There's no need.'

'Oh, but there is.' She reached for his hands and, Luke thought, for all the agony she had caused her daughter, she didn't even remember his name.

'You invited me to be your private doctor a couple of years ago…'

'Excuse me?'

'Your daughter was pregnant and you wanted to put

me on your payroll,' Luke said, and he watched as Anya blinked. 'But I refused.'

'I don't want to talk about that time.'

'It's a very painful topic, I agree,' Luke said, 'and as difficult as it might be to do so, it's better that it's discussed.'

'Have you got my daughter?'

'*Got* your daughter?' Luke checked. 'Yes, Scarlet has been staying with me, and before you press that call bell, I want you to listen to me.'

'Well, I don't want to.'

'I'm going to say what I've come to and then I'm going to go.' He introduced Angie and said that she was a psychiatrist who specialised in addiction.

'Oh, please…' Anya said. 'Is this an intervention?'

'Minus the cameras.' Luke nodded. 'Anya, we're extremely concerned. You attempted to take your life and very nearly succeeded…'

'I told the nurse this morning that I was confused when I said that last night. It was an accident.'

'Anya.' Luke held out her drug screen but she refused to take it. 'I cannot see how this could be an accident but if it somehow was, then how that happened needs to be addressed.'

'Which is why I'm being transferred,' Anya said. 'Where's Scarlet?' she demanded, and started shouting for her daughter. 'You're to bring her to me.'

'I'm going to take care of your daughter for as long as she wants me to,' Luke said. 'Me. No bodyguards, no cameras, and if you tell your crew where she is, or it comes out, you are to tell them that they are not to come. If I see another car in the street or someone at my door, I'll move on with Scarlet for as long as she wants to. I will never live your life.'

'You regret it,' Anya sneered. 'If you'd been my doctor…'

'Oh, no,' Luke said. 'I look back on that time and, looking at your toxicology screen, I know for sure I could never have been your doctor. This woman should be,' Luke said, and Angie stepped forward. 'Stay here and work on yourself or go back to the world you've come from.'

'If she can leave her own mother,' Anya said, 'do you really think she's going to stick around with you and play the doctor's wife? She's using you.'

An escape route.

He'd thought about his friend's words at times.

And Scarlet had said herself that she'd used him as a false lead.

But his love was real.

And if that meant he was an escape route, Luke could live with that.

Scarlet's future was worth it.

'We're different people, Anya.' He looked down at her. 'I believe that when you love someone, their happiness becomes a priority. I don't want Scarlet trapped and miserable. She's not some toy for me to keep locked away in the hope she won't leave.' And once, just once, calm, professional and detached he could not be because he sneered at her. 'As you've found out, it doesn't work.' He headed for the curtain and then he turned around. 'There is one thing you don't have to worry about, though—whatever she needs, I'll always be there for Scarlet.'

CHAPTER SEVENTEEN

'WHAT DID SHE SAY?'

Luke sat in the car beside Scarlet and even as he'd climbed in, it felt as if her mother's shadow had got in with him.

'Not much,' Luke said. 'Angie's in with her now.'

She looked at him. 'I don't believe you,' Scarlet said, and saw the set of his jaw. 'Tell me what she said.'

'Just…' Anya's words buzzed in his head. They were a touch too close to home but he did his best to ignore them. 'She was never just going to lie back and let you go. It doesn't matter what she said.'

Scarlet sat there and was glad that Luke didn't turn on the engine but just let her sit with her thoughts.

'I can't just leave her.'

'Scarlet,' Luke said. 'I think that even if you go back with your mother, nothing will change. I don't think anything you do can alter that fact.'

'I know that.'

'But if you feel you have to go back, I get that.'

'What about us?'

It wasn't a selfish question and it was one Luke pondered for a moment before answering. They had been together again for only four days and before that it had been just one night.

'You've still got my phone number?' Luke checked.

Scarlet nodded.

'We're thirty-fifteen on hanging up on each other. It's your turn next.'

'We'll talk?'

'Every morning and every night, just as much as you want to,' Luke said. He hadn't been lying to Anya. He would be there for Scarlet for as long she needed him to be. 'And I've got leave I can take so I can get on a plane and so can you.'

'Are we just friends?'

'In this,' Luke answered carefully, 'I'm your *best* friend. I promise you that, Scarlet. You do what you have to do.'

He gave her the one thing she'd never had—options.

Precious, rare options that came with no strings attached.

No want, or need, to drag her back, no promise of all he could do for her, no safety net, yet he made her able to fly.

'I'm going to go and speak to her,' Scarlet said. Luke was right, for that she *needed* a friend. 'Can you come up with me?'

'Of course.'

Luke walked with her right up to the unit and then he saw Angie coming out from behind the curtains.

'Hi, Midwife Lucy.' Angie smiled and then, when Scarlet felt she might break, Angie gave her a hug. 'It's okay.' Angie gave Luke a smile and then dismissed him. 'I'm going to speak with Scarlet.'

Scarlet sat in another interview room, where she guessed that people were told their loved ones had died. But then she thought about Evan, finding out that his son had a stab at life, and this was a bittersweet room she found herself in, Scarlet decided as Angie went through things with her.

It was just more of the same.

'Your mum insists on leaving here tonight,' Angie concluded. 'She's coherent, she knows what she wants...'

'So do I,' Scarlet said. She did now. 'Can I see her?'

'Of course you can.' Angie nodded.

She had choices and so did her mom.

'Please, take the help that's being offered,' Scarlet said as she sat at her mother's bedside.

'I don't need their help. It was an accident.'

And back to lying and blackmailing Anya went. 'I was thinking, in a few weeks you could go to Africa. I know you love going there and maybe—'

'I'm not coming back with you, Mom.'

'You're going with him,' Anya sneered. 'Believe me, Scarlet, you're only as good as your last—'

'Don't you dare!' Scarlet stood. She just stood up then and she thought of a man who had said no to her frequent offers, and if it had confused her at times it all made beautiful sense now. She could look her mother in the eye and know absolutely that what she said was right. 'I count for so much more than that with him.'

'Please,' Anya sneered. 'Is that what he told you?'

'That's what he *showed* me,' Scarlet said, and tears filled her eyes because over and over, every step of the way, Luke had. 'You need help, Mom.'

'I don't need help.'

'Well, I do,' Scarlet said. 'I need friends, I need support and I need space. I want a career, Mom. You've got one...'

It was almost pointless, but not quite. She was allowed to have hope that one day her mum would be well.

Not yet, though.

She kissed her mum goodbye, even if it wasn't returned, and then walked out and said thanks to Angie, who was sitting at the desk with Luke.

'This way,' Scarlet said to him, and instead of leaving via the internal lift they headed towards the main exit.

There were many reasons to be proud of her, Luke thought, because as they passed Ashleigh's bed, where he lay with his headphones on, Ashleigh gave his father a nudge as Scarlet walked past.

'Not now,' Evan said to his son. Curtains were thin and he'd heard what had just gone on.

Yes, now, Scarlet thought.

And Luke saw first-hand the absolute star that Scarlet was.

'Hey!' Scarlet smiled at Ashleigh and went over. 'Wow! You are looking so much better.'

'I'm feeling it,' Ashleigh admitted. 'I'm going to a regular ward tomorrow.'

'That's brilliant.' Scarlet smiled. 'Do you want a photo of the two of us?'

'Are you sure?'

'Of course I am.'

They snapped a photo, one that caught Scarlet kissing him on the cheek, and Ashleigh grinned as he looked at it. 'I won't share it.'

'Go for it.' Scarlet smiled. 'Show the world how much better you're doing and that they need to watch out.'

She was speaking for both of them!

They didn't leave by the lifts; instead, they walked out the regular exit and Scarlet asked, in no uncertain terms, for Sonia to hand over her passport.

'It's back at the hotel.'

'Then go and fetch it,' Scarlet said, and took a seat. 'I'll wait.'

'Actually…'

Surprise, surprise, Sonia had it in her bag.

And that was it, she was free.

They drove home in silence at first and Scarlet rested her head on the window.

'Thank you,' Scarlet said.

'For what?'

For being the true friend she'd never had. 'All that you've done for me. I've completely messed up your week.'

Luke swallowed. She hadn't messed up his week, she had changed his entire life, but that might not be what she needed to hear now.

'Do you know what you want to do?'

'Do?' Scarlet frowned. 'I don't know. Maybe…' she took a breath '…go to the cottage perhaps, do what I planned to and get my head together.' She took a breath. 'You'll get sick of me soon…'

Luke frowned.

'Tired of my dramas.'

'That's what she said,' Luke pointed out, because, yes, curtains were thin.

Luke looked at the road ahead.

Ten minutes in that woman's company and Anya had watered the weeds of doubt in both of them.

He had never admired Scarlet more—she'd had a lifetime of it but instead of weeds the flowers had somehow thrived.

And the lunatics were not running the asylum, Luke decided.

He was.

If what he had to reveal to Scarlet was too much, too soon, and not what she needed or wanted, then so be it, he wouldn't crowd her.

But something told him that what he felt inside was

right. That his words were something that Scarlet, who had never properly been loved, maybe needed to hear.

Whatever she did with that knowledge was fine with Luke but she deserved to know just how very loved she was.

It was time to do what he avoided.

Tell another person just how he felt.

CHAPTER EIGHTEEN

THEY DIDN'T PULL into his house; instead, they pulled up outside the pub.

'What are we doing?'

'Well, I don't feel like cooking, do you?'

'No!' Scarlet admitted.

'So let's have dinner here.'

They walked in together and Scarlet was more nervous than she'd been when she'd stepped on stage in Paris and had had her mother sing to her, but Luke was calm and relaxed.

'Hi, Luke,' Von, the landlady, said.

As they sat down a young couple did a double take and when one of them picked up their phone and started to walk over, Trefor, who was in with his wife, stopped them and reminded them that her mother was terribly ill.

They sat back down and the phone went back on the table.

Scarlet gave them a wave. 'Hi, Margaret.'

'It's lovely to see you, Scarlet.'

They took a seat and Luke grinned.

'What?' Scarlet checked.

'She bought me a casserole the day I moved in. I was so taken aback I forgot her name and for months I've been trying to find it out, without admitting I don't know.'

'Margaret,' Scarlet said. 'The shop's not doing too well, she's thinking of making a web page.'

'You chatted?'

'She helped me choose my outfit,' Scarlet explained.

'And she chose your knickers too,' Luke pointed out.

'I thought you chose them.' Scarlet smiled but she was frowning a little because that little comment was so open to one of her more usual responses, and Luke didn't generally offer such openings.

'I thought it safer to leave it to her,' Luke admitted.

'Safer?' Scarlet checked.

'That you were dressed by Margaret.'

She wanted to be undressed by Luke, though.

'You're in an odd mood,' Scarlet commented.

'Doesn't feel odd to me,' Luke said, and she looked at him, grateful that now she could do just that.

He smiled at her, not a grin or a happy smile, just a knowing one that had her toes curl in her shoes because she wanted to reach over and tell him she was wearing the purple knickers.

She restrained herself.

The shadow that had followed them since they had been to the hospital had lifted but the clearer air between them slightly dizzied her.

She was nervous to provoke, worried she was misreading the edge they were on.

God! Scarlet just sat there and went bright red with recall at some of the offers she'd made so readily, assuming that was what it took to be a guest in his home.

Luke gestured to a chalkboard. 'What do you want to eat?'

Scarlet screwed up her noise as she read the choices.

'The steak and kidney pie is good here,' Luke suggested.

She made a gagging face.

'Really good,' Luke said, unimpressed.

'Fine, then,' Scarlet said, and looked around for someone to take their order. 'Where are you going?'

'To order.' Luke disappeared and she sat there as he did so.

And still she sat there as he went over and had a quick word with Margaret and Trefor and then after a while he came back with two little bottles and two glasses.

'What are these?'

'Grapefruit juice for you,' Luke said, as he poured them. 'And pineapple juice for me.'

And she went a bit pink and then asked a question. 'Why do you have grapefruit juice in your fridge when you don't like it?'

She was so clever, so astute, Luke thought, and he wondered about all she could be.

'I have it in my fridge because I drink it every morning and think of you for a couple of minutes.'

'Oh, so you drink something you don't like and think of me...'

'I love it now,' Luke said. 'That time in the morning that I spend thinking of you is both the worst and best part of my day.'

She just looked at him, into those beautiful eyes, and love hurt so much more than she had ever thought it might.

'You think about me every day?'

'All day,' Luke said.

'And the trouble I make?'

'I think about so much more than that.' He took a breath. 'You know that there have been others—'

'Luke,' Scarlet interrupted. 'I don't want to hear about them. I know we need to talk but I can't take it today.'

'Yes, you can,' Luke said. 'I want to tell you something, I want you to know that, while there might have been others, I've never had sex in the morning since you. And do you know what else? I don't even have breakfast in bed any more, and if I'm in a hotel I go down and eat at the buffet.'

'Why?'

'I want to have that breakfast in bed with you.'

He just stared at her and she said nothing and then their plates came and she picked out all the kidney and tackled the rest of the pie.

'It's yum,' she conceded, glad of the diversion because talking today was surely too hard. She tried to keep it light as she turned her attention to the pastry.

Once she had finished her pie, she reached out to pick at his. 'You see, Luke, we really shouldn't be together because I'd be the size—'

'And I'd still want you,' Luke said, 'and if you stopped putting that stuff in your lips I'd want you even more.'

Scarlet looked at him. 'You say that now.' Her head was all jumbled and rather than look at him Scarlet had a piece of the kidney she'd picked out.

It was nice.

So nice that she had another piece.

And then she had another because if she didn't then she might open her mouth and tell him how much she loved him and beg him not to send her away now that her mum had gone.

Scarlet knew that she needed to get her head together; she wanted to be so suave and calm when she told him how she felt. 'I want to go to the cottage,' Scarlet said suddenly.

'I'll take you.'

'I want a few weeks to get my head together and then…' He didn't rush in so she took a breath and told him what she'd been planning. 'I might call you once things are calmer. If that's okay?'

'Of course.'

'See how you're feeling about me then,' Scarlet said.

'It won't have changed,' Luke said. 'It hasn't in the two years that I've been hoping you might call.'

'You hoped I'd call?'

'Every day, and knowing you were in the country and hadn't...' Luke stopped, not wanting to lay a guilt trip on her. 'I can't see my feelings for you going away any time soon. At least, not in this lifetime. And if that's too much for you to handle, I get that...'

'Too much?' Scarlet checked. 'I thought you were just...'

'Just what?'

'Tolerating me.'

'I don't tolerate you, Scarlet, I love you.'

'What sort of love?' Scarlet checked. 'Like a sister?'

'I certainly hope not.'

'A fancy?'

'Much more than that,' Luke said. 'How about a real love, which, yes, I guess means I can tolerate anything if it helps you to get where you want to be. And if that means holing yourself up in a cottage, or flying off to Africa, or even going back to LA...'

'So long as there are no bodyguards?' Scarlet huffed.

'Scarlet, if you want to carry on as a celebrity, I'll work my way around it. I won't be giving tell-all interviews, though...' He smiled as she laughed at the very thought. 'And don't try sorting out my career for me again...'

'You'd come to LA?' Scarlet frowned. 'For me?'

'For us,' Luke corrected. 'You asked how the conversation would have been had you called, well...' He didn't finish; it still hurt that she hadn't.

It was Scarlet that spoke. 'I was going to call. I knew I'd made a mess of things last time and so I was going to try and work things out at the cottage. I wanted it all to be sorted and for me to be all…' She saw his smile. 'Well, a rather more sophisticated and together version of me was going to give you a call in a few weeks' time.'

She *had* been planning to call.

Their stars would have collided, Luke found out then, and he was no fool rushing in, this *was* love, he knew that now.

All the naysayers, all the doubters could leave now, please, Luke thought, because when it was just the two of them, all was right in the world.

He could tell her everything now.

'Come on,' Luke said.

As they walked out they stopped and chatted to *Margaret* and Trefor.

'I've got some new stock coming in next week,' Margaret said to Scarlet. 'You should come and have a look.'

'I shall,' Scarlet said.

As they walked out of the pub, Scarlet, a little distracted, holding Luke's words in her head and going over and over them, just so they wouldn't disappear, bumped into someone and turned.

And when she saw who it was Scarlet gaped.

'Come on, Scarlet,' Luke said, and grabbed her by the hand as she craned her neck for another look. 'It's rude to stare.'

'But isn't that…?' Oh, my God, she knew that couple—the whole world did.

'Yes,' Luke said. 'They're even more famous than you.'

They walked out of the pub and there was his car.

'I can take you to the cottage now,' Luke said, dangling his keys. 'You can go and get yourself all suave and sophisticated if you want to…' he offered, and she poked out her tongue.

'I can't leave yet.' Scarlet shook her head and they walked hand in hand towards his home. 'I said I'd go and help Margaret get her store online on Monday. Apparently men feel very awkward when they come in to buy things.'

'I don't think so.'

'And they're not very knowledgeable,' Scarlet said. 'I'm not a size *small*, Luke,' Scarlet said and she told him her size. 'Just for future reference.'

Their future was referenced and that made them both smile.

But then Scarlet stopped smiling and she thought of all that had been lost, all the damage done.

'Can we ever get past it?' Scarlet said, and they stopped walking and faced each other.

'We have to get through it,' Luke said. 'And we *can* get through it together.'

They shared a soft kiss that tasted of regret mingled with love as they shared the hurt and what could have been and what had been lost.

They would work through it together.

He smelt her hair and she just leant against him. It was gone.

Her shame.

His acceptance of her, good, bad and the middle bits, would not allow shame to reside in her.

They walked to the house that had a few missing bricks in the driveway wall and she waited for Luke to open the door.

'You've got a key,' Luke said. 'Scarlet, this is your home.'

'Mine.' She laughed at the very notion but then she found out just how much he loved her.

'This village is why I live so far from work. There are couples here who are just as high profile as you are, more so, and they get to live a very normal life on their days off. They might have to work at it, but when they do…'

'You chose this house with me in mind?'

'Everything has been with you in mind. And if that's too much…'

'Too much? No. Never.'

She could never get enough of his love.

'So open up and let us in,' Luke said.

Scarlet did. She turned the key to her home and they both stepped in, and they would keep opening up and keep letting the other in every day of their lives, both swore.

She stood in the hall and resisted the urge to snap a photo and post it and share her joy with the world, but she was very easily distracted by Luke.

'What are you doing?' Scarlet asked. He began to strip off her clothes. 'Luke…'

'What I've been wanting to do all along.'

CHAPTER NINETEEN

'I LOVE YOU.' Luke told her the truth and it came from the very bottom of his heart. 'I have loved you from the moment I saw you.'

It made perfect sense now.

Love had led them to now.

'I love you back,' Scarlet said, and she wasn't afraid to admit it now. Furthermore, there was no hope of being sophisticated and level-headed when Luke was close and holding her the way he was.

Two years after they'd found out that they did, they got to say it and could believe it now.

And this time when he carried her wriggling in his arms and she rained kisses on his face, he didn't deposit her on the spare bed but again Luke didn't pull back the sheets.

Deliberately this time.

He stared down at her as he undressed her in a way that had Scarlet squirm.

Off came that chunky jumper to reveal the very small purple bra. His hands went to unhook it and he removed it without a word.

Off came her shoes and that tiny, tiny skirt came down with her stockings.

'Luke…' Her hands reached out for him but he flicked them away.

He had waited, now so could she.

Scarlet lay as he peeled off her knickers so slowly that her breathing kept catching in her throat as she fought the temptation for haste. Then Luke stood and undressed himself and revealed that delicious male body again, though his eyes did not meet hers. He looked at that jet of hair that he'd tried so hard not to and his gaze burnt so much so that she just lay there and parted her legs.

Still he made her wait because he flipped her over onto her stomach and took her hands out from where they needed to be and placed them palms down beside her head.

He kissed her all over, from the nape of her neck to the soles of her feet. He kissed the small of her back and he kissed the cheek of her bottom so deeply that she started to sob with want. Then he turned her around and kissed her stomach with the same lavish attention. Her spine curved so that her hips lifted but Luke hadn't finished yet.

His fingers were inside her and stroking her as his mouth met her breast and tasted her again, and sucked and nipped till she was frenzied. When she could take it no more, he very abruptly removed his fingers, parted her legs and kissed inside her thighs, not tenderly but deep, bruising kisses that made her remember that a gentle lover he was not.

He tried to be.

But Luke forgot the gentleman he usually remembered to be when her scent hit him.

The silky black hair had not been there last time and Scarlet closed her eyes as his teeth nipped and tugged, and then came the heat his mouth delivered.

Every tear she had cried, all the pain of the days, the

months and years dissolved as Luke probed her with his tongue. His hands parted her thighs farther when they tried to close in on his head. He completely exposed her, laved her, tasted her; he drew out musk, he tasted her deep and when she came he held her down and tasted her more, so she screamed.

As she tried to catch her breath he didn't allow her to; instead, Luke pulled her limp body up so she knelt and leant on his chest to recover. Very soon she did, stroking his thickness, feeling him again in her hands, wanting him, as she always had.

She left the safe haven of his chest and found his neck, and she bruised him now with her mouth as she raised herself, wanting him to gather her, yet he reached for the drawer.

'I want your babies…' Scarlet begged, not wanting to stop or wanting to part for a second.

'Not yet,' Luke said.

His love was older and wiser now and they would wait till they could cope with their love before adding to something so big, so precious and so worth protecting.

He opened the drawer and took out a condom and she took it from him and knelt back on her heels, stroking him with one hand and cupping his balls in the other until it was Luke who was now impatient.

'Scarlet…'

With aching slowness, she slid it on.

Luke pulled her in and they kissed, a sexy kiss, and she felt his tongue still and the holding of his breath as she slid down his length.

He moved her legs and they wrapped around him, and the feel of him filling her, moving in her while kissing her was sublime. Her lips closed and tightened and he forced them apart, and when his teeth gritted she felt him swell that final time and they gave up with mouths and just locked in eye contact for that final second before they were lost to each other.

His body mocked the times she had thought he might not want her as he thrust into her, so deep, and ground her down so hard that it could never now be questioned.

And one would hope there were no bodyguards outside the door, because she didn't hold back from sobbing or shouting, and as she came, tight around him, all his restraint was rewarded as he shot hard and released deep inside her.

And then they were back to the other, with eyes that stared right to the very bottom of the other's soul.

'What are you thinking?' Scarlet said.

'You don't want to know.'

'I do,' she persisted. 'Tell me.'

'That was an amazing come. I want to go again.'

'Just that?'

'Yep.'

'What else?' Scarlet smiled.

'I think I'm ready to go again.'

Still rivers did not run deeper when she was hot in his arms.

Scarlet laughed as they lay upside down in his bed. She then climbed up onto his stomach and sat there, playing with the hairs on his chest and loving that she was back where she belonged.

That they could talk now.

And for ever.

Luke loved it too. He looked up at her and she was lost to her thoughts. There were secrets inside that pretty head, he knew. 'What are you thinking?'

'Lots of things.'

'Like?'

'Have you really loved me all that time?'

She knew that he had, it was just hard to take in.

He reached out and opened the drawer, reaching not for a condom this time but for a receipt, which he handed to her.

It was faded, a long bar bill, and on the end of it was a glass of champagne.

'I never keep mementos,' Luke said, 'but I just couldn't throw it out.'

And there was the hotel bill too and a serviette with faded lipstick, and he had loved her since then, absolutely she knew that.

'What else are you thinking?' Luke asked.

With his love, there were so many things to think about. 'All the things I can do.'

'Like?' He watched the blush on her cheeks.

'What you said about me being a midwife, did you mean it?'

'Absolutely,' Luke said. 'What else are you thinking?'

'That I want to get married.'

Both smiled.

'I would have got round to that,' Luke said.

'We'll be family then,' Scarlet said.

'You're my family now,' Luke told her, but he got her insecurity. 'We'll get married as quickly as I can arrange it.'

'I want a big ring,' Scarlet warned. 'I think it has to be a ruby, but a massive one.'

Luke rolled his eyes.

'And I want a church with bells and hymns and flowers…' Scarlet held nothing back with her demands. 'And I'm going to wear red and…' Then she looked at the most patient man in the world. 'I just want us there, though.'

'Oh, I think we can manage all that.' Luke smiled.

'Maybe Trefor and Margaret can be witnesses,' Scarlet mused.

'Perhaps a little drink back at the pub afterwards?' Luke suggested.

'And we could maybe have a teeny party there?' Scarlet checked. 'Just an impromptu one.'

'No wedding cake, then?' Luke checked.

'Oh, yes, I want cake.'

'You can have cake,' Luke said, 'just as long as you don't make it.'

'And I want wedding presents too.'

Ooh, it was going to take a lot of organising for their impromptu wedding!

His hands slid up from her waist to her breasts and she felt him nudging against the small of her back. She knew exactly what Luke was thinking now and it wasn't about weddings.

'I thought there was no hope for us,' Scarlet admitted.

'There's always hope.'

He believed that—all those years in Emergency had taught him.

Even when it seemed as if there was none.

It was almost impossible to fathom.

As she had been making her plans to escape, Luke had been creating a world she could run to.

And here she was.

In his bed, making love, planning weddings, getting on with their precious world.

That was love.

EPILOGUE

One year and eight months later

THIS WAS THE third birth she had witnessed as a student midwife.

Scarlet knew that she should, as the doctor had yesterday advised, be at home, putting her feet up, but she really wanted to finish this semester.

It was her second one and finally, after all these months of study, for two weeks she had been allowed in the maternity ward and these last two days had been spent in the delivery room.

'I can't do this,' Hannah said, and shook her head.

Hannah was eighteen and alone and terrified, and when she should really be down at the action end, instead Scarlet put her arms around the young woman's shoulders.

'You already are doing this,' Scarlet said.

They had a bond.

Scarlet's first day observing in the antenatal clinic had been Hannah's first visit some four months ago.

Hannah had asked loads of questions and Scarlet had admitted that it was her first day with a real patient and that soon the real midwife would be in and would answer those questions.

'Aren't you…?' Hannah had asked when she had read Scarlet's name tag.

It still happened.

The other day someone had said, 'Didn't you used to be Scarlet?'

'I'm still Scarlet…' she had smiled '…but, yes.'

And now here Hannah was, about to give birth.

Scarlet had arrived on the delivery ward that morning at eight.

A niggling back pain had woken her and had not relented as Luke had driven them into work.

By eight fifteen she had been about to make her excuses—her back had been killing her, the baby had felt as if it was between her thighs and she had known she was in labour. Scarlet had been about to go and find Luke when Hannah had said it.

'I want my mum.'

'I know that you do,' Scarlet said.

Sometimes, so too did Scarlet.

Yes, there had been terrible times but there had been happier ones too, and, as Luke had said, leaving was always hard.

Anya hadn't been able to make their not-very-low-key wedding.

It had been an amazing day. Luke's family had, of course, been invited, as well as David and Angie, who felt like her friends too.

And she had, of course, asked her mother.

Anya had said that she would come but had changed her mind at the last moment. She had called two days before the wedding and said that she was in the middle of recording and had people relying on her.

Scarlet had learnt not to.

Luke had tried to come up with a solution and had suggested that someone else give Scarlet away.

Only Scarlet didn't need anyone else.

'Who giveth this woman to marry this man?' the vicar had asked.

'I do,' Scarlet had said.

And on the day she had found out she was pregnant, she had sat on Luke's lap and cried both happy then sad tears. After a lot of thought she had decided not to call her mother just yet.

They had told no one for quite a while. Her pregnancy had been something that she and Luke had chosen not to share for as long as they had been able to keep it quiet.

They had held in their lovely secret and just taken their time to get their heads around it themselves.

Finally they would be parents.

Scarlet would soon be a mum, or a 'mom', as she called it.

Yes, sometimes you needed a mum or a mom but sometimes you had to make do, and for Hannah today that person was Scarlet.

'Don't leave me,' Hannah begged.

'I'm not going anywhere,' Scarlet replied.

'I can't do this,' Hannah said again.

'Yes, you can,' Scarlet promised, because when she looked down there was a head about to be delivered. 'Put your hands down,' Scarlet said, and guided them to the baby that was about to be born.

Scarlet was, as it turned out, very, very good with women at their most difficult and tumultuous times.

She'd had twenty-five years' experience with the most difficult of the lot, Scarlet had said when Beth, her mentor, had praised her on her ability to connect.

'One day it will be your turn,' Hannah shouted as she went to push again. 'Then you'll know how hard it is!'

Scarlet just held her shoulders and watched as Hannah's baby was delivered onto her stomach and all was quiet with the world except for the noise of a newborn's cries.

A beautiful little boy, who was actually a very big boy, Scarlet thought as she put a little name band on his fat wrists.

And then another contraction came.

Hannah was right. Soon *she* would know.

Very soon, Scarlet thought as her stomach tightened for what seemed a very long time. And, no, these were definitely not imaginary pains and neither were they going away.

'Are you okay, Scarlet?' Beth checked, after they had helped Hannah into a fresh bed and had settled her in.

'I'm bit tired,' Scarlet lied. 'I probably shouldn't have come in but I really wanted to finish up the placement.'

'Go home,' Beth said, and signed off her card. 'Do you have any questions?'

'No,' Scarlet said, when usually she had about a hundred and twenty of them. They could wait, her baby was refusing to. She really wanted to go and find Luke. 'I might go home actually, if that's okay.'

Beth nodded and Scarlet didn't bother to grab her bag, she just left the maternity unit to take the elevator to the ground floor, and as she got in there was Angie.

'Hi, Lucy Edwards.' Angie smiled.

It was a joke they shared now and then.

'Hi.' Scarlet smiled back.

'Where are you off to?'

'Coffee break,' Scarlet said. 'I am starving.'

She lied and Beth knew that she lied. The canteen wasn't that way!

But there were some things she didn't want to discuss with Angie, or Beth, or anyone else, except the man who was, Scarlet soon found out, elbow deep in something in Resus.

'Can you tell Luke I'm free for a coffee?' Scarlet said to Barbara, who was dashing back into Resus.

'He's a bit busy at the moment,' Barbara said, then she saw Scarlet's lips press together. 'I'll let him know you're here.'

Barbara went into Resus, where Luke was observing Sahin put in a chest drain. 'Scarlet's here,' Barbara said.

'Tell her to go for her break without me, I'm going to be a while.'

'Sure.' Barbara headed back outside. 'He said go ahead without him.' Barbara smiled.

'It's fine,' Scarlet said. 'I'll wait. I might go round to his office if that's okay?'

'Sure.' Barbara frowned and watched as Scarlet walked off.

At first Scarlet had been a bit of a shadow, coming down for lunch or coffee, but not lately, though.

She was tiny. From the back she didn't even look pregnant but then she stopped walking for long enough for Barbara to guess the real reason that Scarlet wanted to see Luke.

She went back into Resus. 'Scarlet said that she's going to wait in your office.'

'Fine.'

'Luke,' Barbara said, and Luke looked at her and into the eyes of a very experienced nurse.

'Yes?'

'I'm saying nothing,' Barbara said. 'Except that I think Sahin can take over from here.'

Sahin could. There was just the drain to be sutured

in so Sahin nodded and Luke stripped off his gown and gloves, washed his hands and headed through the department.

There were a few people staring. They'd seen Scarlet waddle around to his office and now a usually unruffled Luke was walking briskly.

He didn't stop to enlighten them!

Luke walked into his office and Scarlet stood there. As he had done many months ago, he saw her fear and turned on the engaged sign and never, ever would she take for granted the luxury of his arms and leaning against this chest and the bliss of the silence that he gave her when she needed it most.

Neither would Luke ever readily dismiss the scent of her hair and the knowledge that even as they stood still life was changing for ever.

Their baby kicked and Scarlet let go of the sob of fear that she'd been holding in for the last hour, just as Hannah had decided that she'd wanted Scarlet to stay close.

Luke felt her stomach tighten and his hand moved between them and he was surprised at the lack of noise from Scarlet because this was a long, deep contraction.

'How often are you getting them?'

'They're getting closer,' Scarlet said. 'I thought it took ages.'

'It might still,' Luke said, and he held her for a long moment but then changed his mind as she moaned into him and tried to bend at her knees. They weren't even two minutes apart!

'Do they know upstairs that you're in labour?' Luke checked.

'No.' Scarlet shook her head. Just as she had wanted to hear it from him if it had been bad news about her mother, she wanted to tell him when it was good.

'Isn't it too soon?'

She knew thirty-six weeks was a bit early but that the baby should be okay. However, she wanted to hear it from him.

'Scarlet, the baby will be just fine.'

He was always so calm.

'I'll call the labour ward and we can head up,' Luke suggested, reaching for the phone.

'I think I might need a chair.'

She had walked, almost run the whole way down to Emergency, holding her secret within her, but the thought of heading up that corridor now was daunting. Luke was, not that he'd show it, also feeling a bit daunted. Scarlet had her hands on his desk and her knees were bending again and she looked as if, at any second, she might squat.

'Barbara!' Luke buzzed around to the department and a few moments later Barbara came with a chair and a blanket.

'Can you call them again and tell them that I want an epidural?' Scarlet said rather urgently to Luke as she clung to the sides of the wheelchair, because it was starting to hurt seriously.

'I'll do that,' Barbara said, and shared a look with Luke. 'Maybe take Scarlet up now.'

'You will call ahead?' Scarlet checked, and thanked Barbara, who put the blanket over her knees.

It was the last time Scarlet remembered to be polite!

On the way to Maternity her waters broke and Scarlet had never been more grateful for the blanket, but by the time the lift got to Maternity she didn't even care about that any more.

'Scarlet!' Beth wasn't surprised to see her, Barbara had called ahead after all, but she was very surprised to see that Scarlet's toes were curling and that she was gripping the arms of the chair. 'Straight through,' Beth said.

'I want my epidural.'

'David's been held up,' Beth told her, rather than telling her that that they were way past that window.

'I don't want to hear it!'

Luke undressed her as Beth gave up trying to attach her to a monitor as Scarlet screamed out her demands.

'You will pull strings,' Scarlet demanded of Luke. 'You will call in favours…'

Scarlet was in full diva mode.

But today she was allowed to be.

'I'm not wearing that.' She just tossed the gown to the floor. 'Where's my epidural?'

'It's too late for that,' Beth soothed.

It didn't work.

'This is barbaric!' Scarlet screamed.

'I know, baby…' Luke too attempted to soothe her but he was quickly shot down.

'Don't tell me you know!'

'You're doing a fantastic job, Scarlet,' Beth said.

Oh, she was swaying, she was shouting, she was sucking on the green whistle, and she really was doing a fantastic job!

'I need to go to the restroom,' Scarlet begged.

'Scarlet,' Beth said patiently, 'you don't. That's your baby…'

And then Scarlet found out there was something she was very, very good at.

Pushing.

She just crouched down and grunted, and instinctively she knew what she needed to do.

'Okay…' David rushed in. 'I'm sorry it took so long to get here. Scarlet…?'

'Get out,' she shouted, and then got back to closing her eyes.

'I want to get on my knees,' she said.

'You can,' Beth said and massaged her back.

Luke knelt down and faced her.

'This is the worst…' Scarlet started to say, but then she stopped and they smiled because this was nowhere close to the worst. She looked right into his eyes and found herself lost there for the sweetest moment. She was exactly where she wanted to be. 'This is the best,' Scarlet said.

'You're the best,' Luke said, because staff were coming for a very rapid progression.

'Go, go, go…' Scarlet said to him, because her baby was coming, and Luke went around and out came a head. He watched it turn.

He saw the dark, cloudy hair and then two eyes opened and he knew even before she was out that he was a father to a little girl. Just as he acknowledged that fact, she was born into his hands.

He passed the baby up to her mother and she sat there, holding her and crying and kissing her little girl.

And there was another thing that Scarlet took easily to—breastfeeding.

She just sat on the cold floor and held and fed her little girl as the cord was cut and the placenta was delivered.

Even as they got her into bed, Scarlet could not let her go. They didn't have a name for her yet, so she was tagged Baby Edwards.

'I'm being selfish,' Scarlet said, because she knew she should let Luke hold her, but her naked skin was keeping the baby warm and Beth put a blanket over them.

'Be as selfish as you like,' Luke said.

He had made them wait for this moment. He had kept

that promise and even though they were rock solid he had insisted that they did not rush into parenthood.

Scarlet had wanted a career, she had just wanted a stab at the world, and he'd encouraged that. They'd celebrated when she'd been accepted to study midwifery and their lives had been happy and busy, but her want for a baby had remained.

And now, finally, their daughter was here.

He watched as the baby stopped feeding.

'She's a bit small,' Beth said, 'so she'll tire quickly.' Scarlet knew that she might need some top-up feeds and she looked at the warmer waiting for their baby, who might need a little bit of help too to regulate her temperature for the next few days. Scarlet rested back on the pillow, looking down at their tiny baby, and then she handed their daughter to Luke.

He lifted the tiny scrap that was lighter than he could comprehend, and weighted his heart with happiness to hold her.

She watched him look into his daughter's eyes and hold her tiny fingers, and for the second time ever she saw tears in his eyes.

They were happy ones now.

'She's beautiful.'

Absolutely she was. A shock of dark hair and navy eyes that might stay the same colour or turn to chocolate brown, and she had lips that were as perfect as Scarlet's now that she'd given up on fillers.

He pulled back the blanket and looked at slender pink feet and then wrapped them back up in the rug. Beth came and put a little yellow hat on her and he knew soon he would have to put her down.

'She's perfect,' Luke said. 'Like her mum.'

Scarlet was going to be an amazing mother, Luke

knew, and in turn he would give his daughter the child-hood that her mother had never had.

They'd got this, Luke thought, and then he handed her back to Scarlet.

'She needs to go under the warmer,' Beth said. 'Don't worry, she can stay beside you.' They watched as she slept and her perfect little mouth slipped into what looked like a sleepy smile as Beth got on with the paperwork.

'Have you thought of a name?' Beth checked.

Scarlet looked at Luke and he nodded.

'Emily,' Scarlet said. 'Emily Edwards.'

There would be a couple of hooks at school with the same name, no doubt, and that suited them both just fine.

'I'm starving,' Scarlet said, as, on the maternity ward, she climbed into bed and Beth plugged in the warmer so that Emily could stay with them.

Scarlet had walked round to the ward, rather than be wheeled there. Had he not seen her just give birth, he wouldn't have known she had.

Every day she surprised Luke more and more. Scarlet was so much tougher than she looked.

'I'm seriously starving,' Scarlet said, and looked at Luke. 'Can you get me a muffin?'

They were her favourite thing from the vending machine.

'You've earned more than a muffin,' Beth said. 'It's a bit early for the lunches to come round so I'll go and see if there are any breakfasts left.'

There were.

Toast, scrambled eggs, bacon and mushrooms.

No grapefruit juice, though.

Scarlet pouted.

'It's still pretty perfect,' Luke said, and got up on the bed by her side.

Oh, it was.

Breakfast in bed, with their baby by their side.

It was a very good morning.

They all were now!

* * * * *

LONDON'S MOST ELIGIBLE DOCTOR

BY

ANNIE O'NEIL

MILLS &
BOON

All rights reserved including the right of reproduction in whole
or in part in any form. This edition is published by arrangement with
Harlequin Books S.A.

This is a work of fiction. Names, characters, places, locations and
incidents are purely fictional and bear no relationship to any real
life individuals, living or dead, or to any actual places, business
establishments, locations, events or incidents. Any resemblance is
entirely coincidental.

This book is sold subject to the condition that it shall not, by way of
trade or otherwise, be lent, resold, hired out or otherwise circulated
without the prior consent of the publisher in any form of binding or
cover other than that in which it is published and without a similar
condition including this condition being imposed on the subsequent
purchaser.

® and TM are trademarks owned and used by the trademark owner
and/or its licensee. Trademarks marked with ® are registered with the
United Kingdom Patent Office and/or the Office for Harmonisation in
the Internal Market and in other countries.

Published in Great Britain 2016
By Mills & Boon, an imprint of HarperCollins*Publishers*
1 London Bridge Street, London, SE1 9GF

© 2016 Annie O'Neil

ISBN: 978-0-263-25434-1

Our policy is to use papers that are natural, renewable and recyclable
products and made from wood grown in sustainable forests.
The logging and manufacturing processes conform to the legal
environmental regulations of the country of origin.

Printed and bound in Spain
by CPI, Barcelona

Dear Reader,

I'm so glad you're here! And 'here', this time, is in my semi-adopted town of London. Both Lina and Cole—my hero and heroine—come from other countries and fall in love in London! I can say from experience it is a delight! Then again, falling in love just about anywhere is lovely, isn't it?

Sometimes I struggle with getting the names of my characters just right—but this time I had a double dose of inspiration.

There is a great physiotherapist character who is named after our WHSmith Competition Winner #WHSBookmarks Gemma Holland! It's such a great name, and it was easy to make her character just as fabulous. Gemma, I hope you enjoy your literary incarnation! I have my fingers crossed that this book will delight you.

My second splash of inspiration came from a most excellent friend—Michelle. All I had to do was turn her into a Polish ballerina and *voilà*! Lina Keminsky was born.

I hope you enjoy this journey of healing and new beginnings. Please do feel free to let me know what you think. I love to hear from readers. I can be reached on my website, annieoneilbooks.com, or via Twitter @AnnieONeilBooks.

*Annie O'*Xx

This book is a delight to dedicate!
The heroine—Lina Keminsky—is inspired by
one of my favourite people in the world. She is kind,
passionate, and a most excellent maker of strawberry
daiquiris! Thank you, Michelle Kem, for being the
flame of creativity behind this flame-haired heroine.

Books by Annie O'Neil

Mills & Boon Medical Romance

The Surgeon's Christmas Wish
The Firefighter to Heal Her Heart
Doctor…to Duchess?
One Night…with Her Boss

Visit the Author Profile page at
millsandboon.co.uk for more titles.

**Praise for
Annie O'Neil**

'A poignant and enjoyable romance that held me
spellbound from start to finish. Annie O'Neil writes
with plenty of humour, sensitivity and heart, and she
has penned a compelling tale that will touch your heart
and make you smile as well as shed a tear or two.'
—*CataRomance* on
The Surgeon's Christmas Wish

CHAPTER ONE

IT WAS OFFICIAL. This was Lina's worst ever nightmare in the history of nightmares. Who knew it would have such well-appointed surroundings? En Pointe's reception area was about as Zen and soothing as it got. Creams and sages and tactically placed throw pillows in accent colors just the right side of understated chic. The polar opposite of the way she felt.

Auditioning—no, scratch that—*interviewing* for a job where she'd have to face her demons every day from nine to five? Someone up there was really testing her. Or having a mighty fine belly laugh. If this was her ultimate low, she was well and truly looking forward to the high.

A dark twist of pain tightened in her stomach. She'd had her highs—as a prima ballerina for three glorious, unbelievably wonderful years. Yes, she'd had her highs.

When she'd received the call from her former dance captain that there was a job going here, her first instinct had been to refuse it. It didn't even sound real to her. Something officey at London's premier dance clinic? That was the *one* job going in the whole of the city? Not that anyone in the ballet owed her anything. Not now.

She scanned the room. Okay. Fair enough. From the lack of a human on Reception she could see it was not a pretend job they'd made up just to get her out of her flat, but *really*? The path from prima ballerina to phone answerer was a bitter pill to swallow and already it felt like she was choking.

"What do you want to rely on? Your good looks?"

The words of her former ballet director—the notorious Madame Tibold—rang in her head. Over and over and over. So, here she was, feeling the opposite of pretty and down-to-the-bottom-of-her-piggy-bank broke. In the interest of keeping her landlord—and the ballet director's haunting words—off her back, she was here. Seeing as she was out of the house she might even see what change she could rustle up for a visit to the Polish deli. A taste of home would be nice. Even if she could only afford a small one.

She looked around the waiting room and felt her face going into scrunched-up *don't want to be here* formation. She fought it and forced her expression to return to *rehearsal hall* neutral. The one that didn't show the pain.

When Lina was really being honest with herself, this job was a lifeline she needed to grab. There wasn't a chance in the world she would call her parents for money after the sacrifices they'd made in her quest to become a ballerina. A small-town teacher shelling out again and again for shoes, tutus, training, trainers, foot stretchers, arch blocks…the list was endless. She owed them her very soul and would never ever ask them for anything again.

The most precious thing she "owned" was her shiny new titanium hip joint, which would have been difficult to hawk, and—more to the point—there would be no more income from the pirouette and plié department from here on out so it was time to look elsewhere. Which turned out to be here—En Pointe—where London's hottest ballerinas came to be fixed. She might as well have left her pride on the coat hook when she'd come in.

But, hey! She was Eastern European. She could take it. Her hand automatically slipped down to massage her bionic hip as yet another nonlimping dancer swept past her out into the hubbub of early evening London. She could always tell dancers apart from…civilians…by their posture and physique. Lucky minx. If she was smart, she'd cherish every single moment she had as a ballerina. *She* certainly had.

All the doctors said she was supposed to have healed from the surgery by now, but she still wasn't a hundred percent. She shook her head, a wry smile playing across her lips as her fingers toyed with her cane. Who was she kidding? She'd never be a hundred percent again and the fear that came with embracing that fact was threatening to destroy her. Just the buzz of the clinic wrapping up a busy day of sewing ballerinas back together for another night onstage—a night she would never have again—was like being seared with a hot poker again and again. No wonder she rarely left her flat these days. The pain that went with it was too much.

"Michalina Keminsky? I'm Dr. Manning."

"Lina," she snapped automatically, before looking up to match the male voice to the man. Uh-oh… She wished she'd not resorted to her post-accident narkiness quite so quickly. She remembered when people used to describe her as the "nice one." From the frazzled look on the man's face, a big load of attitude was the last thing he needed. Not that he didn't look like he could handle it. He was tall. Six-foot-somethin'-somethin'. And fit. Not to mention a healthy dose of straight-up-her-*strasse* good looks, as well. His deep caramel-colored skin spoke to a mixed-race heritage. No stylized hairdo, just a smooth grade two from a not very talented barber, from the looks of things. Her fingers twitched, fighting a curious urge to reach out and run her hands along his head and then see what else happened.

Interesting.

She hadn't felt physically charged in "that department" in quite some time. And his eyes! Two of the bluest, love-liest, darkest-lashed eyes she thought she'd ever seen. An optimum combo of sexy and nice.

"You coming?" He looked up for a nanosecond from the chart he was holding. "I've not got all day."

Okay, fine. Not so nice, then. But at least he spoke in one of those American Southern drawly type accents. It took the edge off. She pushed up from the sofa, trying not to make it too obvious she favored one hip over the other. Even so, false sympathy made her cringe.

"You're the boss."

"Not yet." He shot back. And then smiled. A nice and easy American smile.

Hmm. The jury was still out on this one. Dr. Cole Man-ning. He had been running En Pointe for a year after a stint up north with a rugby club, so she'd never met him in her prima days. A bit of a nomad, from the sound of things.

From monster athletes to the most delicately tuned bal-lerinas. Interesting switcheroo. Rumor had it he'd taken over for the clinic's founder, trying to escape some de-mons of his own back in the US. Then again, the rumor mill in the dance world was about as sharp-tongued and *schadenfreude*-laden as one could get. One dancer down meant another dancer in. After a lifetime of dedication she was now getting the full glory of being the dancer down and it hurt. Big-time.

"After you." Still focused on his chart, Cole gestured that she should head down the corridor before him. Not her favorite position as it would mean he'd probably see her limp. Not that the cane she carried wasn't already a dead giveaway. But she wasn't here for an audition. Only something she'd never done before in her whole entire life: a job interview. Not that she'd bothered to dress up for it or anything. Her thick, out-of-control hair was stuffed into a couple of over-the-shoulder plaits and she hadn't even bothered borrowing something businesslike. Not when she was already perfectly at home in her favorite forest-green swishy rehearsal skirt. Never mind that it had become her favorite swishing-round-the-house skirt. It was still her favorite. And it swished. A girl had to grab her delights where she could.

A smile teased at Cole's lips as "the favor" swooshed past him. He'd heard Lina was still smarting after her hip injury but at least she didn't seem depressed. He believed anger was always better than the bleakness of despair and, from what he'd heard, Lina Keminsky had plenty to be upset about. Anger he could work with. It could be channeled into something productive. Something that made your world come alive again. Experience had taught him that time and again over the past five years. At least he was still able to do what he loved. In Lina's case? She was going to have to do some proper soul searching.

"I've spoken to the City of London Ballet…" He let the words travel along the corridor and saw her spine stiffen, but the speed of her gait remained unchanged. The dance company would've done its bit for her as long as she was on the roster of dancers—but the phone call he'd received from Madame Tibold had confirmed she'd been officially signed off a few weeks ago. It was now seven months since her accident. Long enough to be up and about. Long enough to be facing the truth.

Unexpectedly, Lina whirled round at the end of the

corridor, green eyes lit with sparks of passion. "I suppose they told you my performance as Giselle was an excellent career pathway to answering the telephone."

It wasn't often someone took his breath away and this was one of those *Whoa! Howdy! Take a look at what we have here* moments.

So. This woman was the "favor."

Huh. Well. In for a penny…

He went to respond and found himself bereft of words. Peculiar. It wasn't an affliction he usually suffered from. But what sort of human came close to having green eyes so…so *green*? Lina's strawberry blond hair accentuated the extraordinary shade of pale green that—at this particular juncture—was being cloaked by heavy-lidded suspicion. Just like a cat. The way she held her body, tilted her head at him, impatiently tapped her foot—they weren't having the off-putting effect on him they were meant to. Her soft Polish accent just added to the overall affect. Mesmerizing.

There was no mistaking the dancer in her. Even if she'd chosen something else to do, she would command the eye. Lina Keminsky oozed sensuality. And a healthy dose of get-the-hell-out-of-my-business. Which, strangely, made him feel right at home. He knew that feeling, too. It was why he'd thought working with a bunch of rugby players would suit him. A no-feelings zone. Turned out, no matter where he went, those better-off-forgotten memories insisted on clipping at his heels.

No. Lina wasn't emanating serenity—but she had showed up. It was something.

He could easily imagine how beautiful she would look with a smile peeling apart those tightly pursed lips of hers. Even they were a different hue than mere mortal lips. A pale pink rose color. And it was all natural. No lipstick or gloss. Not a speck of makeup anywhere and, from where he was standing, so much the better. Lina pulled the sides of her navy crossover cardigan in more snugly over her front. He'd caught a glimpse of her collarbones as she'd tugged it into place—a bit too prominent, he thought.

"We're looking for someone with your experience." The words were out of his mouth before he could stop them. He hadn't ever actually planned to hire her. Just do the interview. That had been as far with the favor as he'd been prepared to go for the director of City of London Ballet. They had a lot of former dancers on staff, but they couldn't take everyone. Particularly if they weren't willing.

"What experience would that be, then? In breaking their hip, destroying their life, or both?"

"Reception." Which she should've already known.

"And that involves…" Impatience ran across her face. *For heaven's sake! Who was interviewing who here anyway?* Despite his best efforts, Cole heard his crisp, officious voice come out. *"*We need someone capable on Reception. Someone who knows about dancers would be a perk." Depending, of course, upon the level of "perk" Lina would bring to the job.

"I guess that rules me out, then." Lina arched a brow, daring him to contest her.

Cole could feel the urge to rise to the challenge properly awaken within him. This woman didn't want a pushover. She wanted combat.

He turned his own accent up a notch. Having a mother who'd grown up a dyed-in-the-wool Southern belle had its advantages. It had been drilled into him for years. *The impression you make is everything. What you really feel doesn't matter a hoot.*

He gestured to his office door. It was time to get the

balance of this little tête-à-tête back in order. "This isn't normally how I conduct job interviews, Ms. Keminsky, so if you wouldn't mind—"

There was a whimper from a small willow basket just inside the doorway and they both looked down. Puppy was looking up at them with his mournful eyes.

Good thing he wasn't sentimental. The little tricolored ball of fur would already have a name if that were the case. His receptionist—*ex-receptionist*—had called it Fluffy and there was no chance Cole was going to run around the park calling out that name. Not that keeping it—him—was part of the plan. It was temporary. *Right, Puppy?* He gave the mutt a grudging nod of thanks. They could, at the very least, work as a team while they were stuck together.

"Right—so now you see why we need a receptionist."

He pointed at a chair across from his desk and scooped up Puppy's basket at the same time.

"Why?" Lina asked drolly, folding into the chair. "He no longer likes to answer the phones?"

"He's broken his leg so he finds the hours too long. On top of which he doesn't make a very nice cup of tea," Cole replied.

Lina maintained a neutral expression. She was clearly a woman who didn't fall for corny lines. As if to confirm his theory, she raised a dubious eyebrow at him, then moved her eyes to the puppy.

Interesting. Not someone who cooed straight off the bat. Now, *that* he liked. Not to mention being able to spar verbally with someone. Ballerinas…hmm…

Ballerinas had thick *and* thin skin and it was sometimes impossible to tell which tack to use. Lina definitely didn't seem as though she needed coddling. Quite the opposite, in fact. While she took in his hodgepodge attempt at a puppy carrier—hey, needs must and all that—Cole took another studied look at her.

She was hands-down beautiful. A bit too thin. Proud. Still had a slight limp after the hip surgery, which really shouldn't have been there if she'd been doing all the rehab. And obviously resented being here. To hire or not to hire?

His number one motto sprung to mind: It's up to you. And Lina Keminsky didn't look like a willing player. This wasn't a charity. It was a business. A frantically busy one even in the quiet times. And with her chip-on-the-shoulder attitude, he didn't know if he could offer her the post. Not without making more work for himself.

"Our receptionist found herself a flamenco dancer who could only get work in Spain. He asked her to elope the same day as she got Puppy here. I guess the lure of the Latin lover won out. All of which is to say there's an urgent need for a receptionist here at the clinic. Comes with a puppy."

Lina's fingers drummed along her collarbone, her expression impassive. She never liked to react to things straight away and she could tell Cole was assessing her. A twitch or a frown spotted by the ballet master could've knocked her off her career path so she had taught herself to smile or remain expressionless, then deal with the fallout in private. Just like she was trying to do right now. Except…

Right now? Right now it was all she could to keep her fingers from dancing the tarantella, let alone keep her pulse in line.

Her stream of visitors since the accident had gone from steady to trickle to nonexistent. She liked it that way. At least she thought she did.

But a blue-eyed, caramel-skinned and ridiculously

long-lashed Dr. Charming, complete with a fluffy puppy in a basket? *Unh-unh.* No. She hadn't banked on that.

She looked out the window to the sprawl of sky visible beyond the rooftops. Maybe this was some sort of heavenly intervention. A dark bank of clouds was hunkering in the distance. Hmm.

The day was morphing into something entirely unexpected. Did she wish she'd tamed her hair into something more sophisticated, washed her face, put on something other than her reliable skirt and navy wrap-over?

Yes.

Did she resent her former dance captain for needling her into coming out of her cozy fortress of a flat for a job she didn't want?

Yes.

Coming along had seemed to be the only way to get everyone off her back. Now that she had, she wasn't entirely sure she wanted to leave without learning a bit more about Cole Manning. And the puppy. It was cute. Mishmash mutt cute. One ear up, one ear down. Forlorn expression on its face. A little bit like looking in the mirror.

She narrowed her eyes at Cole. He was cute, too. But his ears matched. *Hmm.*

Nah. Nope. She wasn't going to do it. Now wasn't the time to open up. She hadn't even come close to sorting things out for herself and she'd vowed not to let anyone in—let alone renowned Dr. Fancy Dance Clinic Manning—until she could face the world, aka her family, with pride.

Her fingers stilled as her gaze slipped away from Dr. Charming's expectant gaze. She had been wrong to come. She wasn't ready. Not yet.

"I'm sorry," she mumbled, pressing herself up and out of the chair. "Maybe another time."

"Ah, but that's where you're wrong." Cole leaned back in his chair, hands lacing behind his head. "This is a limited-time-only offer."

She pressed a hand against the wall to stabilize herself as a hit of dizziness unbalanced her.

The sensation was growing familiar. Food shopping hadn't exactly been topping her list of things to do. Very little topped her list of things to do these days. What was the point when her entire life's ambition—not to mention her daily routine for the past twelve years—had disappeared at the end of a poorly executed *plié*?

A *plié*! Of all the ways to shatter your dreams into smithereens…

"So what's on offer, Dancing Doctor? Is this a job with benefits?" The words were out before she could stem them. *Oops.* She doubted they were printed on his business card. Not that he'd shown her one.

"I doubt anyone who has seen me dance would call me that."

Maybe not. But he didn't seem to mind.

His full lips opened into a broad smile. There was a little gap between his front teeth that was… Ooh, *mój boże*… It was sexy! Lina hadn't felt anything close to even a hint of desire for months—okay fine, longer—and now twice in the space of an hour? Her giddy nerve endings were fighting her very best poker face for supremacy.

What was he doing being all good-looking and thirty-something anyway? She'd thought Dr. Cole Manning would look more—more academic, have furrows in his brow and maybe some white hair. A big shock of it. Who had put that dimple on his cheek when he smiled? That thing was about as close to irresistible as it got. *And on top of that a puppy?* Life was testing her. Hard.

Lina stopped herself from chewing on her lip. And

ogling. It could come across as flirtatious. She didn't do relationships. Not now—and she certainly didn't do flirting. Particularly at job interviews.

"I hope you're not trying to find another project—another success story. No headlines to be made here, I'm afraid."

Did his jaw just twitch? Hard to tell. Maybe she'd hit a sore point. Well, too bad. This time of day was normally when she took a first-class nap. Then again, she'd been taking a few too many of those lately.

"Why's that? What's so bad about your story?" he challenged.

Uh. Apart from the totally obvious fact that she'd never dance again? She held her cane out between them. "It's a bit too late for a full recovery."

He let the words hang between them for a moment. She liked that he didn't offer her the over-sympathetic expressions she'd had from all of the hospital staff when she'd been in recovery. The piteous looks had made her blood boil. She wasn't someone to be pitied. She was someone who...

Who...

Well, that was as yet to be decided, wasn't it?

Lina shifted her position as the wind dropped out of her sails. She didn't exactly know who she was these days. All she knew for sure was what she wasn't—a ballerina.

"I don't think I'd be much good at delivering messages quickly for you."

"Lina, I'm pleased to inform you En Pointe is part of the modern era. We receive and deliver our messages by telephone—not foot messenger these days." And there came that slow smile again—like the sun coming out from beneath a cloud. Warming, wrapping round her like a protective blanket.

She considered him skeptically. Why was he doing this? Interviewing *her*—the least likely candidate for the job?

"And we have the latest in ergonomic chairs ready and waiting to be whirled in." He gave her a playful smile and showed off his chair's three-sixty spin. "If whirling in wheelie chairs between taking calls is your thing."

She lifted an eyebrow and gave him a "yeah, right" look.

"And, of course, a whole lot of other things you are familiar with." Cole's face turned serious as he began to rattle off the seemingly endless list of injuries a ballet dancer—any dancer—could come across on any given day, at any given moment. Just. Like. Her.

He rose and crossed to a table where coffee and tea supplies were in abundance. Was that how he fueled himself?

"You're Polish, right? So I presume you take coffee?"

She nodded.

"How do you take it?"

"White—no, black." Her eyes caught his as she heard herself say, "I like both."

She wasn't talking about coffee anymore.

Heat instantly began to sear Lina's cheeks and she forced herself to look away. Anywhere but at Cole. He was obviously mixed race and—*słodkie niebiosa*—he'd turned out perfectly. Not that she was attracted to him or anything. She was more used to being surrounded by gorgeous men at work than not. It had just…been a while.

She watched as he flicked the switch on the kettle before he opened a packet—definitely from a specialty shop—and poured a healthy pile of grounds directly into a waiting *cafetière*, grinned and gave her a wink. Measuring didn't seem to be his thing.

"I hope you like it strong."

Her tummy fluttered.

Er…what was *that*? She didn't have tummy flutters. She had—well, she wasn't quite sure what she had but she wasn't a schoolgirl with strings of pastel-colored butterflies dancing gaily around her insides. She was a woman on the verge of figuring out what to do with the whole rest of her entire life now that all her hopes and dreams had careened straight over the horizon.

"So, tell me more about this job. Nine to five and see you later, boss man?"

"Something like that. Here, have some biscuits." Cole tossed her the packet. Guess formality wasn't his thing, either. Refreshing after years of ballet where every breath she'd taken, every gesture she'd made, *everything* had been based on exacting tradition.

Cole settled himself back into his chair after handing her a mug of coffee. "It's pretty straightforward. Answering the phones, checking clients in…" He pointedly looked at his coffee. "Making sure the milkman has come."

"You have a milkman?" The information brought an unchecked smile to her lips. She'd grown up in a small village where the milkman, the baker and butcher had still been everyday sights. Everyday *jobs*.

"Sure do." Cole grinned back. "Why? Were you a milkmaid in your past?"

"No." The smile abruptly tightened into a grimace. Her best friend from school had followed in her mother's footsteps and milked her father's dairy herd. They made cheese and, on special occasions, ice cream—but mostly

it was delicious, creamy milk and very, very hard work
which, by all accounts, she still did.

Lina had led a different life. Her parents had scrimped
and saved and sacrificed so that their daughter could
pursue her dream of becoming a ballerina.

Which one of them was happier now? she wondered.

She saw Cole watching her intently. Best to keep on
track. Trips down memory lane weren't of any use now.
"The job?"

"Right. The job." Cole had to stop himself from physically shaking his head to put himself back in the moment. He'd been outright staring and was pretty sure
Lina had caught him at it. He doubted he'd disguised it
as an interested-physician look. It had been a bald and
outright I-wish-I-knew-more-about-you look. He cleared
his throat.

"As I said, it's pretty straightforward. It doesn't pay
a high salary, but if you're happy to have a trial run—a
week to start with to see if you're interested and then
three months before we sign a full contract—we open at
nine a.m. I'd expect you at eight." He named a figure and
noticed Lina's eyes widen ever so slightly. It wouldn't put
her in designer heels but it would pay her rent. The last
time he'd checked, box-office staff at the City of London
Ballet were receiving more an hour than members of the
corps de ballet. Everyone needed to make a living, and
fallen prima ballerinas were no different.

"So?"

Lina still hadn't said anything. She took a sip of her
coffee, her face unreadable.

"And if after one day I decide this isn't for me?"

"We hire someone else. Simple as…"

"Simple as what?"

Cole laughed. "I don't know. I heard someone cool

on television say it and thought I'd have a go. Clearly, I'm not down with the hipsters."

Lina took a bite of biscuit, hand curled protectively in front of her mouth as she chewed, rather than risk a reply. He didn't need to be in with any crowd. Cole Manning was in a class of his own. She closed her eyes as the sugary sweetness of the biscuit melted into nothing on her tongue. It tasted like home. The one place she couldn't go until she could show her parents she'd been worth the effort.

She looked at Cole again. He seemed genuine enough. As did the job offer.

A receptionist job. Well… She tried to keep her dejected sigh silent. At least she knew she was physically up to it. Talking to people—talking to *dancers*—all day might not come so easily.

She looked away from him, teasing at a pile of invisible flower petals on the floor. She didn't want him to see how much she needed the job. Her foot automatically shaped itself into an elegant turnout as it swiped the "petals" to the side of the room with a controlled semicircle of movement. That much she could do.

"Cole!" A woman appeared at the doorway and gave the frame a quick double knock. "We need you in Reception right away."

It was then that Lina tuned into the noises outside Cole's office. There was the sound of a young woman crying. Periodically broken by an occasional heated wail. She knew that feeling. She knew it down to her bones.

"All right, Lina? Are we good?" Cole rose quickly to his feet, moving the puppy's basket to the floor.

"So I already have the job?" She couldn't help but let

some cynicism sneak into her voice. This whole thing was sounding more and more like some sort of setup.

"Let me check what's happening out there and then see how we go, shall we?"

CHAPTER TWO

"IT HURTS!" THE teenager's face was a picture of pure unadulterated agony. She was on the floor, knees slightly bent, back hunched over, and a wash of tears wetting her cheeks.

"It looks like it hurts," Cole agreed. He was never one of these doctors who brushed away the pain. If it hurt it hurt. Plain as. Apart from which the poor girl's foot was already thick with heat and swelling. If he had to guess? A serious sprain—level two. A possible tear in the ATFL? Nothing life-altering, but it would certainly keep her out of pointe shoes for a couple of months, and for a young girl like this—thirteen or fourteen—it would feel like a lifetime. He looked up at the mother, who also had tears in her eyes. He raised his eyebrows in lieu of asking what had happened.

"I dropped her before we reached the sofa."

"You mean you carried her in here?" Cole was impressed. It was a bit of a hike from the pavement.

"We were just about there and…" Her hand flew to her mouth in horror.

"You did well. No additional harm done. Just a bit of ego bruising, from the looks of things." He nodded to the mother before quickly returning his attention to her daughter. "You're all right, darlin', aren't you?" The teen gave an unconvinced nod before Cole looked back at her mother. "Shall we get her up and into an exam room?"

"Please. I am so— The day's just been… I tried…"

Cole rose, put a hand on the woman's shoulder and gave her a reassuring smile. Parents were often more traumatized than their child. From the looks of the number pinned on her daughter's chest she'd been at the London Ballet Grand Prix. The biggest day on a young ballerina's calendar. There would be no scholarships or job offers for her this year.

"Let me help. Can I have your arm?"

Cole looked down at the sound of Lina's softly accented voice. She was totally focused on the girl.

"What piece were you doing?" Lina instinctively sought to distract the girl from her injury.

Cole moved round to help Lina raise the girl from the ground but watched curiously to see how she dealt with a traumatized dancer. They shared common ground. It could be useful.

"I was doing the 'Spring Concerto.'" The girl only just held back a sob.

"Vivaldi?" Lina's face lit up. "What a wonderful choice. And your contemporary piece?" She sat back on her heels and looked at the girl seriously. "You *did* have a contemporary piece, right?"

"It was 'Spiegel im Spiegel.'"

"Are you kidding? That's one of my favorites. I used to dance to that one a lot."

"Used to?" The girl swiped away some of her tears, missing Lina's microscopic wince.

"What's your name?" Lina asked.

"Vonnie."

"Beautiful." She tucked an arm around the girl's small waist and began to raise her into a wheelchair she must have brought in. Resourceful. Cole found himself beginning to rethink the "just a favor" part of his agreement. Maybe she would be a good hire.

"I'm Lina. Shall we get you to X-ray?"

It was all Cole could do not to laugh. Lina didn't have the slightest clue where X-ray was and how she'd magicked a wheelchair out of nowhere was impressive…a picture of confidence. And, more importantly, she'd engaged Vonnie enough to begin to stem the flow of tears. Impressive for someone who hadn't seemed keen to spend her day with working dancers.

"Actually, can you put any weight on it?" Cole was the doctor here. Probably wise to take charge of this scenario.

Vonnie wrapped an arm round Lina's shoulder and, with Cole's help, heaved herself up.

"Have you already put ice on it? Kept it elevated on the ride over here?"

"Yes," Vonnie snuffled. "As soon as it ha-ha-happened!"

Uh-oh. Those tears were back again.

"Lina, I'll take Vonnie to X-ray, all right?"

The young girl twisted round, her face wreathed in anxiety, one of Lina's hands clutched in her own. "No! Please don't make her go. She *understands* me."

Lina looked over at Cole and gave him the Polish version of a Gallic shrug.

"Fine. But you'll have to leave the room during the X-ray." Cole stepped away from the handles of the wheelchair and handed over steering duty to Lina. She wanted to work here? She could prove it. "I'll lead the way, shall I?"

Cole tipped his head from side to side as he took in the extent of the injury. Swelling could hide things, but X-rays didn't lie. He'd been right. It was a typical grade-two ballerina sprain—a tear of the anterior talofibular ligament with lateral swelling.

"So what do you say? Eight weeks until she dances again?"

"Mmm…something like that."

In the tiny dark room, with only the X-ray board spreading a low-grade wash of light, having Lina so close, Cole had to rethink how wise a move it would be to hire her. He was attracted to her. And not just your average gee-you're-good-looking sort of attraction. He was fighting a Class-A desire to spin her round, pull her into his arms and find out how she tasted, how she would respond to his touch. None of which would really be appropriate in a professional environment.

"It'll be hard for her to hear…on top of missing out at the Grand Prix."

"Believe me, I've delivered my share of bad news."

Lina noticed Cole's change of tone instantly. Almost felt it, they were so close. There was something deep-seated in his words. Grief? Rage? She couldn't quite tell which, but maybe the rumors about him fighting demons was true. Not such a lighthearted Southern gent after all.

"I'd better get out of your way so you can let her know."

"Yes, that'd be great." Cole batted away the words, "I mean, I need to do this with the patient… Protocol," he added, as if it were necessary. She knew the drill. She wasn't a doctor so why should she have access to Vonnie's appointment? It was for her mother to be there for her, and from the sound of approaching voices she would shortly be with her.

"Okay, well…it was nice to meet you. I guess I'll wait to hear from you?"

She turned to give him a goodbye grin and got as far as turning. Right down to her very toes she felt the impact of the aquamarine of his eyes. A shame it would be the last time she was going to see them. A shame about a lot of things.

"How long has it been?" Cole's voice broke into the quiet, indicating she should follow him to his office.

"Since what?"

"Since you've had a proper meal?"

Lina stiffened.

A while.

But not because of— *Oof. Honestly?* She balled up her jacket and protectively clutched it to her tummy. As if that would stop the jig-jag of emotions bouncing around in there. She liked eating as much as the next person. She just hadn't been able to get it together and money was tight. Supertight. Things she most certainly wasn't going to admit to Mr. Doesn't-Like-to-Poke-His-Nose-Into-Other-People's-Business. Ha! That'd be about right.

"I'm fine."

"I didn't say otherwise." The puppy whined. Cole pulled the wicker basket up from the floor to have a peek and give the pooch's muzzle a little rub. Not that he was growing fond of the thing.

"Look." He gave Lina a pointed look. "This guy needs some grub and so do I. Why don't you join us for dinner? My treat."

"No, thank you. I'm not hungry."

Lina's tummy rumbled. Loudly.

Cole grabbed a couple of charts and a prescription pad from his desk before squaring himself to her. "After I finish with Vonnie, join me. Us. I know a little place down the road. Go have a nosy around Reception while you're waiting. See what you think. Consider it part two of your interview. You don't have the job yet."

Er… "Okay." Lina said the word to his back as he

headed out of the office but got a thumbs-up as he disappeared round the corner. Hmm...

The puppy whimpered again and Lina found herself gently extracting him·from his willow basket nest.

Poor little thing had a splint on his tiny back leg and looked terrifically sorry for himself. She gave an appreciative snort. "We all have our moments. Don't we, Puppy?" Now, to see what the future had in store...

A good nosy around and Lina felt none the wiser. Actually, it hadn't been much of a snoop session. She'd just gone into the reception area, plopped herself and Puppy down on one of the—very nice—sofas and thumbed through a magazine or two. Sitting behind the reception desk would have seemed too much like interest. It would have been akin to acknowledging how much she really needed the job. So reading magazines and enjoying the serene atmosphere, now that most of the practitioners had gone for the day, was what she did, happily enjoying the latest celebrity gossip and fashion mags... And then she hit *Dance Monthly*.

The cover story nearly sent her running for the hills: "Down and Out: Are the Fallen Forgotten?"

Against her will, tears sprang to her eyes. They may as well have put her face on the cover. Talk about cruel! She fought the growing tickle in her throat and nose, tightened her eyes, scrunched her forehead as much as she could, willing the pain to go away. Would there ever come a day when things wouldn't hurt this much? It was hard to believe. Impossible even.

"Dr. Manning said you were still here!" A tearstained but smiling Vonnie appeared in Reception with a pair of crutches and her leg done up in a pneumatic walker. Lina jumped to her feet and shook away the remains of her own tears. She didn't know why, but having helped Vonnie, for even a few moments earlier, had given her a boost. It would hardly do for the teen to find her blubbing on her own.

"Remember not to put any weight on that for three weeks!"

Cole appeared beside Vonnie with a bag of what she assumed to be treatment aids. Cooling gels, compression wraps, anti-inflammatories. She knew the drill.

"I know." Vonnie sighed melodramatically, and rolled her eyes in Lina's direction before singsonging, "RICE, RICE, RICE, RICE, RICE!"

"That's right, young lady," Cole replied in a stentorian tone Lina hadn't heard from him before. "And what does it stand for?"

"OMG, I practically came out of the womb knowing what that stood for!"

Cole crossed his arms and gave her a very good "I'm waiting" face. Lina could easily see him being a parent, willing to wait as long as it took for the child to clean their room, finish their homework, whatever... She wondered what— No, she didn't. She didn't wonder that at all!

"Rest, ice, compression and elevation. Are you happy?" Vonnie's tone was more teasing than truculent so whatever they'd discussed in the exam room had put her in a better mood. Her mother emerged with coats and handbags and a couple of tutus Lina hadn't noticed before.

"Ooh, look at these—they are wonderful!" Lina couldn't help herself.

"Do you really think so?" Vonnie's mum flushed with pleasure as Lina nodded emphatically. "I made them."

"They're amazing." Lina meant it. From the very bottom of her heart. Her own mother, to save money on the countless tutus she'd required, had stitched and stitched and stitched for her, as well. "You've got a wonderful mother, Vonnie." Lina gave the girl's shoulder a squeeze. "You make sure you let her know how much you appreciate her."

"I will!" Vonnie replied, working her way across Reception and out the door. She might, mused Lina. Or she might not. Lina hoped she had done the latter, but was never sure it had been enough. One day...she would let her mother know just how heartfelt her gratitude was. One day.

"So, I guess that's us! Just another day at En Pointe!" Cole shrugged on a wool blazer, scooped up the puppy in his basket from the sofa and gestured with his head toward the front door with a smile. "Are you ready?"

Cole took about three seconds to examine the menu before offering the waitress a smile and his order.

"I'll have the spaghetti carbonara, a fresh salad, some garlic bread and—uh—Rover, here, will have a bit of plain chicken and some rice. In a bowl. Is that doable?"

"Not a problem."

It was easy enough for Lina to see that anything Cole or "Rover" asked for wouldn't be a problem for the waitress, who had plonked herself down in the spare chair between the two of them. Lina may as well have been invisible for all the attention the waitress was paying her. Not that she minded. Going along to a job interview she'd been cajoled into was one thing, but being dragged out—okay, well, being *blackmailed* into going out to dinner was another.

"Who's the little puppy?" The server had on her best baby-talk voice now. "You're the little puppy! You're the little puppy!"

So much for the restaurant's no-dogs policy.

The waitress had already made a puppy-exception rule,

and brought the little guy a bowl of water and a couple of itty-bitty raw carrots to gnaw on in case he was teething. Right now the pup's head was resting on the brim of the basket, lending him more supercute factor than anyone— or anything—should be allowed.

Cute factor or no, Lina was there for the sole purpose of securing the job. That was it.

"Lina?" Cole tipped his head in the waitress's direction. It was her turn to order. She'd scanned the prices and hadn't even bothered to look at the menu choices. One entrée was the equivalent of her weekly food budget.

"Don't worry." Cole reached across and covered her hand in his. "I'll take it out of your first paycheck."

Lina tugged her hand away and clenched it in her lap. She wasn't comfortable accepting help…but it had been ages since she'd had a well-made restaurant meal. Gone were the days of being feted by London's social elite.

"The gnocchi, please. And a rocket salad." They were the least expensive items, but with the added bonus of reminding her of *pierogi. Pierogi!* Her mouth watered at the thought of her mother's *pierogi.* One day…she'd go home one day. Lina pursed her lips and handed the waitress her menu, who gave her a cursory glance, scribbled something on her notepad, then whirled off with a smile expressly for Cole's benefit.

Lina focused her attention on the puppy. Neutral territory. That's what she needed. Cole's hand on hers had been too close to feeling something—wanting something. She hadn't realized how curative the simple touch of a hand could be.

"He doesn't look like a Rover."

"No?" Cole rubbed a finger along the little guy's head. "What does he look like?"

As if by design, they both crossed their arms, leaned

back and considered the puppy. He had a white muzzle that broadened into a wide stripe that led up to his forehead. Black took over from there. He had little brown arches over each eye, white paws and appeared slightly affronted at this very obvious inspection.

"Vladimir," Lina pronounced.

"Horace," Cole countered.

Lina shook her head. "No. He is not a Horace."

"How do you know he's not a Horace?"

"I just know." Lina gave Cole her best I-just-know look, then tipped her head to the left as if it would give her a different perspective. The puppy opened his eyes wider as if in anticipation of her coming out with the right name.

"Wojciech."

"I can't even pronounce that." Cole laughed. "How about Spot?"

"No!" Lina protested. "That's lazy. And look. Where do you see spots on this guy?" She lifted him up out of the basket. His back leg was in a little splint. She wanted to ask what had happened but felt herself already getting too involved with the puppy and with Cole. They both looked at her as if she held all the answers to the question at hand.

Despite herself, she couldn't help giving the puppy a little cuddle. It was impossible not to. She held him up again so that they were face-to-face. "What's your name, huh? *Jak masz na imię?*" The puppy scrunched his face into a mess of wrinkles before yawning widely in her face. Then he sneezed. Twice.

"Maybe he doesn't speak Polish."

"Maybe he doesn't speak American." She kept her gaze on the puppy.

Cole rearranged the cutlery at his place setting with a grin. "Go on, then, Polish puppy-whisperer. What's his name?"

Lina looked across at Cole once she had given the puppy a good long stare. "Igor."

"Igor," Cole repeated, as if he hadn't heard her correctly.

"Yes. Igor."

For the second time that day Lina's mood lifted as that smile of his peeled apart his lips and heated her insides as if he'd unleashed a swathe of warm sunlight.

"I like it. Looks like we've got ourselves a puppy name."

Lina handed Igor across to him, careful not to get his injured leg caught on anything. "No. *You* have yourself a puppy name. *And* a puppy."

Cole cradled the dog in the crook of his arm, careful to adjust the little splinted leg so it could lie along his forearm. "Didn't I tell you? Part of the new job is dog walking. Once his leg heals, of course. Only until I find him a new home, of course."

"Yes, of course," Lina replied dubiously. Then the cogs started to whirl in a direction she didn't like. She could feel the smile on her lips press into a thin line. Part of her physio was to take regular walks. Longer and longer. She should be doing at least two or three kilometers a day by now. Cole would know that. And, having watched her walk to the restaurant, he would probably have assessed that she hadn't been taking as many walks as she had been advised to. She'd done countless laps of her flat but going out there—out *here*—where everyone could see her, judge her…she just hadn't been up to it. Igor pricked up his ears and gave her an expectant look. Her eyes shifted to Cole's face and he looked virtually the same—minus the furry muzzle. She couldn't help but laugh.

"Does anyone ever say no to you, Dr. Manning?"

The smile disappeared entirely from his eyes. "Oh, you'd be surprised."

When Lina excused herself to go to the ladies' room, Cole waited for the waitress to take away their empty plates and give a farewell coo to Igor before pulling his coat on. He was pretty sure he knew the server's life story by now but could honestly say he would leave the restaurant being none the wiser about the private life of Lina Keminsky. Not that prying had been his intention. They'd stuck to neutral topics when their food had arrived. And as much as Cole knew about how Reception worked, which, as it had turned out, wasn't all that much. He'd taken over the practice about a year ago from an old medical school friend who had run off to get married—a recurring theme at En Pointe—and things had been running like a well-oiled ship up until now. Not that the past hour with Lina hadn't lent a certain softening round the edges to the day.

It was pretty easy to tell she didn't like to talk about herself and she'd quickly sussed out the same was true for him—or perhaps she simply wasn't interested, which made a nice change. At home, or at least back in the United States, in the town where he'd grown up everyone knew everything about him. Back home everyone knew he'd had a fiancée—*had* being the crucial word. At twenty-six she'd been too young to die. Far too young. And her family was never going to let him forget it. So the fact that people generally kept themselves to themselves in London suited him to a T.

If what had happened to Lina had happened back home in North Carolina? There would've been a line of people at the door to her apartment, hands filled with bowls of potato salad, a platter of Grandma's best fried chicken, a warm, tea-towel-wrapped plate filled with buttery collard greens, someone's Great-Auntie Kay's to-die-for double-decker chocolate cake with the cherry filling people talked about so much at the church socials, and so on and so on until before you knew it the whole thing would turn into an Item of Interest in the "What's the Buzz" column of Maple Cove's local gazette. There was no escaping the caring embrace of a community like that one. Especially when your African-American father and Irish mother were pillars of the community. The local judge and the most sought-after doula? There was no surprise when the couple's son became a doctor engaged to the town's most promising lawyer! A smile twitched on his lips, then tightened.

He wasn't part of that community anymore.

He felt his teeth dig into his lower lip. It wasn't worth it. Opening that particular can of worms. His parents were good folk. They were just ambitious. For themselves and for him. So what if they hadn't been a huggy-kissy family? He'd made it, hadn't he? Decorum, status, success. They were paramount in the Manning household. And now that he was a doctor running one of Britain's most elite specialist clinics?

Nothing. None of it mattered.

The straight As at school, the letterman's jacket weighed down with athletic achievements, the Ivy League education, the long-awaited proposal…none of the graft he'd put in to win an approving smile or a hug had meant a bean after the accident. His parents had made that more than clear.

The flash of grief tugged his mouth downward.

So, no. He didn't like howdy-do-and-what-about-you? chitchat. Big-city anonymity had been suiting him just fine up to now.

But when it came to Lina? There was something telling him she might be worth breaking unwritten rules for.

She'd deftly managed to unearth his dry sense of humor and, as it had turned out, she had Eastern European drollness down to a T. Her impersonation of the waitress going all googly-eyed over the puppy had had him in stitches. Not that he hadn't tried to hide it from her. He was going to be her boss after all and there were boundaries. Not that he'd managed to wrangle a "yes" out of her. If she did take the job, he'd have to remember that would be the extent of their relationship. A working one. He didn't do personal. And he definitely didn't do personal at work.

So why on earth had he invited her out to dinner? Not to mention let her name his puppy! Correction—*the* puppy. The puppy he was going to find a home for as soon as humanly possible.

He gave his head a scrub and snorted at the results. He'd given himself a grade-two once-over with his electric shaver that morning and wasn't so sure even could be an accurate description. Yet another thing to add to the list of things that had turned his day into a catalog of disasters. Maybe he'd just wanted a bit of company for dinner. Someone who plainly didn't want anything from him. No answers, no advice, no decisions. That suited him perfectly. If he could just shake off his attraction to her, he could go back to being cool, calm and collected Cole. The one who left his emotions at home. His parents, he thought with a bitter twist, would've been proud. At last! He was now just like them.

"You look like a snake bit you in the face."

"Thanks and you look—" Cole stopped himself. He'd been about to say beautiful. "You look ready for a break from Igor and me."

Cole automatically reached for her coat and helped her slip into it. His mother had drilled that into him. "Manners don't make a man sexist, they make a man polite, and no one ever had a quibble about 'polite.'"

"You're too kind."

If only she knew. Cruel to be kind was more like it.

As Lina slipped her arms into the sleeves and shrugged the coat over her shoulders, Cole was struck by how fragile her neck looked. Before they'd gone out she'd swept her hair up into some sort of semitamed twist, and a few tendrils had come loose and were brushing along the length of her neck, her shoulders. It was taking some serious control to stop himself from reaching forward and letting the pad of his thumb or the length of his finger draw down the length of her neck. He could just as easily imagine fastening a set of pearls round her neck, then dipping his lips to kiss the bare, pale swoop of skin between her neck and shoulder—

Lina turned around abruptly, and their noses nearly collided. Cole instinctively grabbed hold of her so she could steady herself but in that moment—and it was just a moment—with her face within kissing distance, her eyes caught with his, Cole knew he'd have to channel his deepest powers of control to ensure he only saw Lina for what she was—a potential candidate for the reception job. A job she hadn't even committed to accepting. Hey! Maybe she wouldn't take it. It'd probably be for the best.

She blinked. He hadn't noticed the light color of her lashes before. He'd been too busy exploring the soft green hue of her— *Hold your fire, there, soldier!* No one's going down that road just yet. Or at all.

"Right. I'd better get Igor back to get some snuggly time. Or something like that." He regrouped and made his voice more doctorly. "Sleep. Puppies need sleep. Lots of it." Cole took a broad step away from Lina and scooped up the basket where—up until that very moment—Igor had actually been sleeping quite contentedly. The puppy quirked a sleepy eyebrow at him. Lina shot him a similar look for good measure. Fine. He felt like an idiot. *Could we all just get a move on now?*

"Okay. I'll see you at eight o'clock tomorrow morning, then?" She shifted her feet nervously.

Cole didn't bat an eyelid.

So, she *was* taking the job. Bang went that solution.

Maybe she'd hate it and this little frisson—or whatever it was that was going on between them—would be short-lived.

"Yes. Perfect. See you then."

Lina bent to give Igor a little scratch on the head. *"Do-branoc kochanie, Igor. Tu jest nic!"*

"What's that?"

Sweet nothings for the pooch? Or something about their near miss in the kissing department? He scrubbed his hand along his chin. *Terrific.* Now paranoia had set in. His former receptionist had better be having one hell of an elopement!

"Nothing." She tightened her coat round her slim frame and gave him a cursory farewell wave. "See you in the morning."

"You bet. With bells on!"

She didn't turn around. Which was for the best.

With bells on?

This wasn't going to just be a trial period. It was going to be a trial by fire. And Cole knew he'd be the one racing across the burning coals.

It was cold enough in the flat that Lina wasn't going to risk taking her hand out from underneath the downy duvet to give herself a good old conk on the head. What had she been thinking? Accepting the job at En Pointe? Pure unadulterated crazy.

She'd heard Cole worked miracles with his patients—but getting her to break her months-long hibernation? He hadn't pushed her, but there was definitely a won't-take-no aura about him. If she believed in that sort of thing. From what she'd gathered—and it wasn't that much—he was more of a take-it-or-leave-it type. He'd seen and done a lot in his lifetime. It was impressive. And he hadn't got where he was from sitting in his flat, moping. The train he was driving? It was ready to leave the station. If you wanted to be on the Manning Express, jump on fast!

So she'd jumped.

It was a matter of necessity after all. But that didn't stop her stomach from churning. Or the odd butterfly from taking a teasing swoop and whoosh around her tummy.

The tick-tick of the clock suddenly seemed louder than Big Ben's bongs.

In a matter of hours she was going from seeing no one but the postman—or his hand, at least—to answering the phone and sitting on Reception at Britain's finest dance injury clinic.

She chanced sticking a finger out of the duvet to give her cold nose a scratch. Once she got her first paycheck she could get the heat turned back on. Oh, to be warm! She scrunched her eyes tightly against the streetlight conveniently beaming directly into her bedroom and let herself—just for a moment—picture summertime in her childhood village. There might not have been much money coming into the homes there but it was undoubt-edly a rural idyll. Vast wildflower meadows sprawling up into the foothills of the mountains. Snow-capped peaks diminishing with the heat of the summer sun. A broad river teeming with shoals of fish and a seemingly endless array of birds. Maybe when his leg healed, she, Cole and Igor could find a park somewhere…

Maybe she, Cole and Igor *nothing*.

It was work. A job. They were not a magic trio. Cole was her boss. Igor was a—a patient? And she was going to answer the telephone. That was it. Working at En Pointe was a way to pay the rent and dig herself out of this ridiculous hole of unpaid bills she'd gotten herself into. Then, *maybe*, she could think about what to do next. There was no point in getting attached to anything because one thing life had taught her for certain was that nothing lasted forever.

But even as the thought crossed her mind, Lina couldn't help a smile from tugging at her lips—or stop the small burst of pride she felt for having said yes to the job. It was a baby step. But it was a step. Her smile broadened as an image of Cole leaning against his office desk flitted across her mind's eye. He looked all casual, relaxed and in control at the same time. Someone who was comfortable in his skin. Maybe he was a miracle worker. For the first time in a long time, apart from feeling scared out of her wits, she felt—just a teensy tiny bit—as if she just might be looking forward to a brand-new day.

CHAPTER THREE

"YOU DON'T REALLY know what you're talking about, do you?"

"Don't be ridiculous. Of course, I…" Cole tried to look affronted and then realized it was pointless. Apart from the fact that Lina's office look was about as pencil-skirt-tastic as a woman could get, he didn't have a clue how the phone system worked.

"Sorry, Lina. I'm newfangled. Just give me one of these…" he pulled the latest model mobile phone from his pocket "…and I'm fine. One of these?" He eyed the multiline reception system like it had just flown in from outer space and waved his hand dismissively at it. "All Greek. Or should I say Polish?" He gave her a wink chased up by a meaningful look. It was meant to convey confidence. Or a boss-like jocularity. Lina frowned in response.

"Dr. Manning, you're paying me to answer the phone—so I will answer the phone. Now, step aside, please, and go do your doctor thing." Lina sat down decisively in her very nice chair and shooed him out from behind the reception area. This was her turf now. Not to mention the fact it was a bit too cozy having the two of them behind the desk. Very cozy. He'd been there long enough for her to divine that Cole's mysterious, exotic man scent was not the coffee, the dog or anything else—it was *eau de Cole*.

Olfactory heaven. And strictly off the menu! She might have to mouth-breathe in future to resist the urge to bury her face in his chest and just inhale. And resist she would.

This was a chance for her to get a grip on her life— not play googly-eyes with the scrumptious doctor. She shot him her best "scoot" look, more for herself than for him—but it worked. Which was satisfying.

"Don't blame me for being all addlepated this morning. It's entirely Igor's fault. He kept me up most of the night with his crying."

"You didn't stick him in one of those horrible cages, did you?" Lina blurted. She couldn't help it. She had a soft spot for Igor. And Cole.

No. Just Igor. Not Cole. He was an ogre. Well, not an ogre exactly…

He raised up his hands with an irascible twist to his lips. "Guilty as charged." Then his expression softened. "That is, until about twenty minutes later when I couldn't stand it anymore and brought him into my room. He stole my pillow."

Lina couldn't help but smile at the picture Cole painted. So he was a softie at heart. A bit different from the pull-your-own-socks-up portrait he'd painted of himself last night.

Cole abruptly pulled out a thick stack of colored sticky notes from his pocket and plonked them on her desk before hightailing it to his office. He'd already given Lina enough office supplies to last a month. She hardly needed more! Not to mention the tour of the clinic, each and every one of the therapy rooms, the changings rooms—separate for staff and patients—the sauna, the steam room, the water-therapy center and the staff kitchen—complete with a tour of the contents of the fridge-freezer. "Best to put your names on things if you really want to eat them." Talk about a worrywart!

She eyed the phone system warily. Then again…

Okay. Release the breath you've been holding for the past twenty minutes. Three. Two. One. Fresh breath in… She watched as Cole turned the corner into his office, where he'd already stashed Igor in his basket… *And now you're on your own.*

The telltale tremble began in her hands. She shook them. Hard. It always worked before she went onstage, so why not here?

So what if telling Cole she knew how it all worked had been bravura? At least it had been effective enough to get him out of her hair. Her well-groomed and twisted-into-a-French-knot hair, thank you very much indeed. Sleeping hadn't really worked out so well the previous night, so a bit of overdue grooming had taken up the dawn hours. Not to mention the fact she was wearing her Sunday—and Monday through Saturday—best. She had one office-appropriate outfit and until she got a bit of money in the bank it would have to do. Not that she was planning on doing this forever. Not by a long shot. She was just playing a role—Tragic Receptionist. She'd even worn her old reading glasses from school for good measure.

Truthfully? Lina needed all the exterior armor she could get her hands on if she was going to convince herself, let alone everyone she would have to come into contact with, that she could do this job. And do it well. Turned out there was a lot more to it than picking up the phone and saying hello.

Answering the phones, greeting patients, pulling up medical records, making appointments, ordering flowers, milk, fruit, office supplies, updating staff schedules—*erp!*

She forced herself to take another deep breath in lieu

of short-circuiting. Cole had left a lot of details out when he'd offered her the position. The only thing she'd really cared about had been the paycheck. Served her right. It was all she could do not to run out the door and go back to her bed and curl up in a protective little ball. It was too much all at once. If she tried to remember every single bit of information she'd have to learn in the next five minutes, her mind could just…very possibly…explode. Not to mention the torture of having to smile and offer warm greetings to working ballerinas all day long. The clinic, it seemed, mostly worked with dancers who could make a full recovery. It explained why her dance company hadn't really pushed for the clinic to take her on as a patient. Not that she would've been able to foot what she imagined would be a very large bill.

The air whooshed across her lips in a panicky sigh. She sucked in a fresh breath of air and forced herself to think of the plus side of her conundrum. She needed to regain the control she knew she could impose on herself.

Once she had a bit of money in the bank she would be able to move on. Who knew what might be out there, waiting for her, apart from a big black void of nothingness? There might be rainbows and daffodils…and unicorns and horses that flew with wax wings that melted at the first sign of spring.

Okay, Lina. Get a grip.

Right now there was no money in the bank and nowhere to move on to. So, that being the case, she was stuck here pretending she knew how to be a receptionist. A blinking light on the phone caught her eye. She glanced at the wall clock. Nine on the dot. She poised her finger over the button, popped on the headset, blew out another steadying breath and here went nothing!

Lina pressed the button and greeted the caller as she'd been instructed, "En Pointe, this is Lina. May I help you?"

Silence.

She pressed the button again. "En Pointe, this is Lina. May I help you?"

Nothing.

Despite her best efforts, her mouth went dry. Just a little. Then another light started to blink. Panic started to set in. Another line lit up. The front door opened and a woman wearing bright purple scrubs entered and gave Lina a broad smile.

"Hi! Are you the new Scarlet?"

"Who?"

"Scarlet—the eloping receptionist," she explained, extending a hand across the high reception counter. "I'm Gemma Holland, one of the physios. Sports massage by day, aspiring osteopath by night."

Lina went to shake her hand but then thought she'd better try and answer the three calls coming in, and in swinging her hand back round she managed to get tangled in the headset wire and pull it free from the phone.

"Isn't it annoying?" Gemma smiled, unfazed as Lina's discombobulation grew. "I worked on the desk for a year and Cole still hasn't understood the importance of a wireless headset."

"You worked on Reception?" Lina couldn't hide her surprise.

"Yeah. A few of us have—before we qualified. Here…" She walked round the counter, plugged in the headset, popped it on, quickly and efficiently took the three calls and then turned to Lina with a mischievous expression. "Did Cole give you your 'training'?"

"If you call pointing at it and saying, 'That's the beast' as training."

"That's what I thought. Don't worry. I'll give you a quick run-through before my first patient arrives. Cole's useless. He doesn't do front of house."

Lina smiled at the term generally reserved for the theatre. She wondered if Gemma had been a dancer. She certainly had the figure for it. Had she been injured, too? There was a part of her that would love to have someone to confide in, make the world feel a bit less lonely.

Gemma quickly talked her through the system, which turned out not to be so complicated after all. "Just flick this switch here on the side and then punch the blinking light…" By the time Gemma had wished her luck and disappeared down the corridor, Lina felt a tiny bit more grounded.

Answering the phones? Check! She turned as the front door opened again. More staff and, from the look of the girl using crutches, the first patient of the day. Now all she needed to do was figure out how to do the four thousand other things the En Pointe receptionist was responsible for and everything would be fine.

Cole gave Igor a little scratch under the chin. It was five o'clock and about the ninety-thousandth time he'd checked his watch. He'd been itching to go out and check on Lina all day, but had thought she'd shy away from any sort of special treatment. He liked to be thrown in at the deep end and something told him—on that front—they were cut from the same cloth.

She'd need to find out on her own if she was cut out for the job. Not that he would've been much help anyhow. At least with the technical side of things. Yes, he could've introduced her to everyone—but a quick interoffice memo did the same thing, and more efficiently. So, yes, it was throwing Lina in at the deep end, but he wasn't in the business of coddling. So he'd done it surreptitiously. A handful of the therapists at EP had been in her shoes over the course of the years. Ballerinas, modern dancers, even circus performers who had, through either catastrophic injury or prescient decision-making, opted for a life in health care rather than completely destroy their bodies. Not everyone stayed. Not everyone left. He had to admit he hoped Lina would at least see through the week—and after that the three-month trial. At the very least, it would get her back out in the world and give her a bit of money in the bank. Not to mention buy her some time to think about her options, her future. As if it was any of his business and he cared at all. Which he did not.

Igor stretched out on his desk, paying little regard to the files Cole had been trying to read.

"Thanks for the respect, pal."

A light knock on Cole's door brought the puppy upright with a small yelp.

"Sorry, Igor. How's the little bitty pooch-pooch?" Gemma crooned, all eyes for the puppy and none for Cole, whose office she normally wouldn't have entered without an invitation. He obviously had some sort of invisible force field around him, screaming *Give me my space*, and it usually worked. Puppies apparently rendered it useless.

"Do you want him? Comes free with basket?" Cole asked, semihopefully.

"No way. He's cute, but I don't have the lifestyle for a dog." Gemma smiled. "Besides, my boss is a real whipcracker. He wouldn't let me bring him to work."

Cole smirked. "Yeah. I hear he's a real hard-ass." They both considered Igor, now shifting Cole's paperwork about to make a more comfortable bed for himself.

"How do you think it happened?" Gemma pointed to the splint still weighing down Igor's leg.

"Scarlet said he'd been rescued from a violent home, along with five brothers and sisters."

"Ooh! He must be missing them, poor little thing. Are you sad to be all alone in the world?" Gemma gave Igor's ears little single-fingered sympathy strokes.

"Hmm." Cole couldn't help but think of his family and how much he missed them. Not to mention his fiancée. Deaths from car crashes had just been one in a sea of medical statistics until it had hit home. His home. His heart. He rubbed at his chin. A change of topic would be good about now.

"Hey—where'd you find Lina?"

Not that topic!

"Oh, her name cropped up when…"

"When?" Gemma not so helpfully prodded a finger, teasing the shorter ends of her freeform hairdo into little spikes.

Technically, the answer wasn't confidential, but he didn't think it would be appropriate to tell her about the telephone call from the head of the ballet. Then again, he'd been very clear to them he wasn't taking Lina on as a patient. Not that he'd actually planned on making her an employee. The whole thing was meant to have been a meaningless favor. What a mess!

He scribbled a couple of doodles on the side of his notebook to buy time. Feeling so protective about someone he hardly knew was a new experience. It was instinctive, not wanting the staff to know any more than Lina wanted them to know until she was good and ready to share. He knew firsthand that was one of the biggest steps forward in healing—a step he hadn't exactly taken in his own life.

"Her name came up when I was at the rehearsal hall

the other day," he fibbed. "She seemed like she'd know her way round our specialist jargon."

"Wasn't she the one who shattered the ball in her hip joint?"

Cole sat up sharply. Lina obviously valued her privacy and he didn't want to "out" her before she'd had a chance to settle in, know that she was in safe territory.

"It was in the *Dance Monthly*," Gemma continued, oblivious to the internal battle Cole was having. "Apparently she out-*Giselle*d the best of them. Before the accident. I thought she looked familiar. It was a hard article to read. I hope she didn't see it."

Public figures equaled public domain. Just as it had been when the local rag had got hold of the news he had been the one to switch off his fiancée's life-support system. They hadn't cared about Katie's living will or the absolute, straight-through-to-the-marrow heartbreak it had taken to see her wishes through. All they'd said was that one of Maple Cove's brightest lights had been switched off by her own fiancé. And with that one headline all of the trust his patients had had in him had evaporated like a thin mist.

"What can I do for you, Gemma? Apart from offering some puppy therapy?"

His colleague grinned at him, perched on the side of his desk and scooped up the dog for a proper cuddle. "You know the sports massage therapy course I've been giving over at the continuing education center?"

"Yes. That's been going well for you?"

"Brilliantly. But I've reached the point where my students need some guinea pigs."

"And?" Cole warily asked.

"And…I was wondering if I could use the staff here at the clinic one day after work. Like a treat! On a Tuesday or Wednesday evening perhaps? When you— I mean, no one has anything going on socially."

"Speak for yourself, Gemma."

The physio didn't even try to contain her laughter. "Since when did you start going out on the razzle, Manning?"

"That's Dr. Manning to you." Cole tried to put on his best stentorian tone, but he and Gemma were the same age so it was ridiculous to try and come across as her older, wiser boss. They'd just had different career paths. His had involved tunnel vision and hers had been more circuitous—including having a life outside work. Going with the flow.

He stemmed an ironic bark of laughter. His specialty had been—was—rheumatology, loosely translated as the study of going with the flow. It was probably time he started practicing what he preached. "Fine. When do you want to start experimenting?"

"A week Tuesday." Gemma clapped her hands excitedly. "Brilliant! You won't regret it. I promise."

"You're not including me in on this, are you?"

"You bet! You're top of the list. Look at your shoulders—tense as anything! Tension like that could lead to all sorts of spinal prob—"

Cole's phone rang and as he went to answer it he gave her an assenting nod. Of course he'd go. If it helped his clinicians it helped the clinic—which helped the patients. Gemma put the puppy down with a grin, melodramatically tiptoeing out of the office while mouthing an exaggerated "thank you".

He gave her a smile and a wave. She deserved it. Gemma was one of the clinic's true success stories. Originally a modern dancer, she had ripped just about everything you could in a knee and had come back fighting.

Then had done it all over again. After a few dark months she'd rebounded, channeling the same passion she'd had for dance into dance rehabilitation and massage. She was looking at ticking osteopathy off her list if the word in the staffroom was anything to go by.

The phone rang again.

"Dr. Manning."

"Madame Tibold on the line for you." Cole smiled at the sound of Lina's voice and just as quickly shifted into work mode. He rarely had calls from the City of London Ballet's director, and now twice in one week? He'd done the favor and she wasn't one to make thank-you calls. Madame Tibold on the phone usually meant an injury. A big one.

"Thank you, Lina. Put her through, please."

Lina clicked off the line, her hand visibly shaking. She wondered if Madame Tibold had recognized her voice. The last words she had heard from the matriarch of the ballet corps had been, "It's a hard life and you gave it your best. Good luck in life, Lina. You'll need it."

The words had lacerated her heart. She had forsaken friendships, time with her family, schoolgirl crushes—everything a normal girl would've done with her free time—so that she could rehearse. Rehearse and take classes and train and stretch her feet and increase her arches. Everything! All she had worked toward her entire life had been that handful of lead roles, and at her darkest moment she'd been dismissed as if she'd been a pretender all along. At least, that was how it had felt. Particularly when the visits from her "friends" at the ballet had dried up pretty quickly after she'd left hospital.

That had been when she had realized just how alone she was. She'd all but trained her parents not to call.

"I'm too busy. Rehearsal."

"I can't even think about a visit for a few months, class is really intense right now."

She had let the few childhood friendships she'd had fall by the wayside, and as for friends in the ballet corps it was obvious now she hadn't really gone there. Her focus on getting to the top had been too intense. Maybe that's what Madame had been saying. *You've made your own crosses to bear—now let's see how you go about carrying them.*

It was the only way she had thought she could be the best. And now it was the only way she knew she could survive. Keeping her heart locked up tight.

"Lina, sorry to do this, but can you look after Igor for a bit?" Cole appeared in front of her desk, sending a ripple of goose pimples surging along her arms. Those blue eyes of his were mesmerizing. Best not to look into them too closely. Cole might be her knight in shining armor on the finance front—but that was as far as things would go. Now, as for the puppy… She reached out her arms and took hold of the furry critter.

"Of course." She glanced up at the wall clock. The clinic shut at six—looking after Igor until then shouldn't be too much of a bother. Never mind the fact that the only thing she'd vaguely mastered that day had been the telephone system. Turned out office work didn't come as naturally as she'd hoped.

"I'm not exactly sure when I'll be back—one of the guys has blown his knee out—but I'll ring you with an update." Cole shot her an apologetic grimace, then winked. "See you later?"

"Yes, of course, Dr. Manning."

What was up with the winking?

Her stomach did a flip-flop.

And what was up with the funny tummy? She didn't do flirting.

Did she?

"Thanks, Lina. And it's Cole when the patients aren't around, all right? See you later. The rest of Igor's things are in my office." Cole was out the door before she had a chance to stop him. She and Igor eyed one another. Dog-sitter hadn't really been part of the deal. Or had it? Good thing he was cute. The dog, that was. Not Cole. Well…

Lina scrunched one hand through her hair and stared into the puppy's eyes. There had to be an easier way to get herself out of debt, didn't there?

"OMG! You've got puppy time!" Gemma skidded to a halt in front of Lina's desk. She grinned. If that girl did anything in a speed other than double time, Lina would be amazed.

"Yes, well, Dr. Manning had to rush off and asked me to look after him until he was finished."

"Ooh, special treatment, eh?"

"If you consider pooper-scooper duty as special." Lina couldn't help but smile back. Gemma's positivity was contagious—and catching a bit of that sunny attitude would be good for her. She'd spent so much of her life being focused she didn't know if she'd ever been giddy outside performances. It was the only thing that had made her feel truly alive.

"Good point. He says he's going to give him up for adoption, but I doubt it. There's a big old heart lurking beneath that supermodel exterior." Gemma nodded her multicolored coif decisively, before abruptly changing her expression. "Hey, you wouldn't be interested in getting a free sports massage, would you?"

Lina stiffened instantly. She had only agreed to take the position here to get some money. Being "investigated" on a physical level was a whole other kettle of fish she didn't want to get into. On the other hand, she couldn't afford any massages and knew treatment could break down scar tissue, increase her flexibility and help her with a diminishing range of movement. But asking for help? She just wasn't there yet.

Gemma put her hands into the "pretty please" temple and pushed out her lower lip to make a sad clown face. "You'd be helping me heaps if you could come. Did I mention they were *free*? There will be a tiny bit of interaction between the other volunteers but nothing horrible. I super cross my heart promise!" And she did it for good measure.

Well. Gemma *had* shown her how to use the phones. One good turn and all that. Besides, what was the worst that could happen?

"It's gone."

"The whole thing?" Madame Tibold crossed her arms and gave Cole her famed wide-eyed stare. The one that brought the world's most famous ballerinas to tears.

"Do you want to tell him or shall I?"

Cole didn't even blink. After losing Katie, he'd had to plumb a huge reserve of professional cool he hadn't known he'd had. These days, he could take telling just about anyone anything. They were just facts. And you had to deal with them. How people dealt with them? That wasn't up to him.

"But he's had surgery before on the other knee. Surely, another would be easy enough—"

"I'm going to stop you there, Madame." Cole held up a hand. "Yes, Marc's had reconstructive surgery on the other knee and we can fix the cruciate ligament—but with both knees not entirely stable, it should be his choice how to proceed."

"Dancing is his life." Madame's ring-bedecked fingers moved to her hips.

"That's for him to say."

"He will choose to dance."

"Given half a chance, I'm sure Lina would've done the same."

Both Cole and Madame looked surprised to hear her name mentioned. Neither more so than Cole.

"Lina had an injury that wouldn't let her dance again. It was different." Madame's eyes betrayed a microwince of guilt.

"That's right. She didn't have a choice. Marc does. Let him make it."

Madame went to interject, but Cole raised a hand and calmly continued.

"There are numerous surgeries for a burst cruciate ligament. Shunts, supports, surgical tissue grafts. Auto- or allograft. We might need to use some of the hamstring, which would have a lead-on effect. Those are just a few of a number of excellent options *for a normal lifestyle*— but for a dancer? They're not the same as the real deal. I'm not trying to rain on your parade, or Marc's…but to dance again full-time? He has to be aware that he could destroy one or both of his knees permanently."

The pair of them stood there, arms crossed, each committed to their own stance. A tension of grudging respect crackled between them. To Cole it was a no-brainer. Choose life. Marc was young enough to make a career change now if he wanted.

Something inside him shifted. What if your life meant nothing without your true passion? Without your first love?

"Um…hello?" He turned at a tap on his shoulder.

"Lina! You found us. Excellent. Apologies." Cole

scrubbed a hand along his head, his telltale time-buyer. "Thanks for coming over."

"Lina, how lovely to see you."

Cole watched as Lina's body went rigid and an expression of terror ripped across her face. Seeing Madame, it appeared, wasn't quite as lovely. It hadn't even crossed his mind to say that Madame Tibold would be at the hospital when he'd rung to see if Lina could bring Igor over.

"Bonsoir, madame." Lina's face was a picture of elegant restraint. Her greeting included a light smile and a curtsy, of course. Some habits were obviously hard to break.

Madame Tibold would be right at home at his parents' country club, from the looks of things. A place where charm and etiquette were far more important than the truth.

"Let me ask you." Madame Tibold wasted next to no time with niceties, fixing her dark eyes on Lina. "Do you think it's right that a renowned practitioner of dance rehabilitation would counsel a patient that they shouldn't dance again?"

"I—" Lina's eyes shot to Cole.

"I didn't say that," Cole interjected. He wouldn't be played. Not now. Not ever again. "I said it was Marc's *choice*. I can offer him the facts and the facts are—" He stopped himself, aware he'd been about to breach patient-doctor confidentiality.

"No, do go ahead," Madame intoned. "I am his legal guardian. Have been for some time. You may speak freely."

"I don't need to be involved." Lina waved away any responsibility but found her arm restrained by Madame's aging fingers. From the look on Lina's face, it had happened before and had been just as unpleasant. Cole watched as the light drained from Lina's eyes.

"I just came to tell Dr. Manning that Gemma came over with me and is waiting outside with Igor. No dogs—even puppies—allowed in hospital, remember, Dr. Manning?"

"Do stay, dear. It'd be interesting to hear what someone with no career has to say about a doctor destroying a professional's future."

"No one is destroying anyone's future, Madame." Cole's eyes spit fire while his voice held caged restraint. "Marc's injuries are serious."

"And there are surgeries that can be done." The determined woman held her ground.

Cole shifted his feet and adopted a neutral tone. "Madame Tibold, I am going to have to ask you, respectfully, that we leave all decisions up to Marc. It's his body. It's his life and he's only seventeen. What he chooses now will impact his entire future." Cole's face was all business now. Any Southern charm he might have been using had turned into granite resolve. He knew how hard it was to accept someone's decision—even if it wasn't the same as his own—but he had taken an oath. And there wasn't a ballet director in the world who would get him to veer from it.

"Either way, he will be off stage *and* out of the rehearsal studio for many, many months. If he does his rehab and *if* he feels happy to continue, it should be left entirely up to him."

"I agree with Dr. Manning." Lina's voice broke into the strained atmosphere. "A dancer is also a person, Madame. And that person should be allowed to make a choice. Of course you know that I didn't have one."

"Lina. I didn't mean—"

"Yes, I think you did. If you'll excuse me?" It was less

of a question and more of an announcement. At which point Lina turned on her heel and left as swiftly as she'd arrived. Cole was impressed. He couldn't imagine how much courage it had taken Lina to speak to Madame in that way. Perhaps knowing she would—could—never go back? She obviously didn't know Madame had made the initial call for Lina to be given an interview. Neither, thanks to her secrecy, would Lina ever know.

"So?" Madame gave Cole an approving once-over. "You got her to come out of hiding."

"That was her choice, Madame. Not mine."

"Oh…' Madame ran her eyes up and down him another time. "It seems to me when you want to be, you can be very persuasive. Too bad you don't choose to exercise that skill with your patients. Let's go and speak with Marc, shall we? Explain to him his options."

The elegant woman, who had clearly been a beauty in her day, hooked her thin hand into the crook of Cole's arm and gave him the go-ahead nod. They would do it Cole's way. This time.

CHAPTER FOUR

"How strong are the meds they have you on?"

From the dip and swoop of his eyelids, it was pretty clear that Marc was heavily loaded.

"Not strong enough," the young dancer muttered, clenching his eyes tightly against the pain.

Lina knew well enough how he felt. The pain wasn't just physical. He was living through his biggest fear. A time when it was impossible to believe there was any light at the end of the tunnel. She felt her own breath become restricted as she took in the scene. She didn't even dare look up at the ceiling. How many nights had she stared at a hospital ceiling? Too many. Too many to remember.

"Have they spoken with you yet?"

"Dr. Manning did for a bit," Marc answered, eyes still closed.

"And Madame did for a lot longer?" Lina guessed. Madame hadn't even come to hospital when she had shattered her ball joint. Just being here, smelling the weave of scents of the hospital, was beginning to twist and tighten her gut. The fact that Madame had been here meant there was hope for Marc. At least for a while. And Madame was renowned for getting the most from her "investments."

"Will it get any better? Not dancing?"

"Is that what they told you?" Lina sat bolt upright on

her vinyl hospital chair. She wouldn't have wished what she'd been through on anyone.

"Not so much. But Dr. Manning just droned on and on about the facts."

"I think he wants you to know everything you can about your injury. There are so many different surgeries you need to choose from."

Was she standing up for Cole? Madame may not have been in the room, but speaking against her was akin to treason!

"So I should just get the surgery and dance as long as I can? *Dance! Dance!*" Emulating the melodramatic tones of Madame Tibold.

"But isn't that just obeying Madame Tibold?"

They eyed each other warily, then burst out into silent giggles, tears eventually popping into Lina's eyes she was laughing so hard. Madame Tibold could appear at any minute and hysterical laughter was hardly the thing they wanted her to hear.

"Stop! *Arrête!* Please, I can't shake my knee so much. I think I've invented new ways of destroying it."

Lina sobered in an instant. "I'm so sorry, Marc."

"It's not over, is it?" He looked all man, but sounded like a frightened boy. Dancing was what he had done since he was three and now he was looking at, very possibly, a series of reconstructive surgeries that may or may not leave him able to dance again.

"No." Lina shook her head slowly. "It's not all over. Dr. Manning is excellent and works with an incredible pool of rehab specialists. Listen to them. I didn't and I'm paying the price." She shook her head at her own foolishness. "I know it's hard to believe, but it seems there is this thing called life."

"*Dancing* is my life!" A tremble hit his voice at the end of his words.

"It was mine, too. And I know it doesn't feel like it…" Lina had to stop for a moment. Her voice had gone as wobbly as Marc's. The tears of laughter were now charged with sorrow and were threatening to flood her eyes. "You have a choice. I guess you have to decide how you want to live. How you would like your body to be. Just take some time to imagine what you would do if—if you absolutely couldn't dance again." Lina felt the wall she'd tried so hard to build in front of her feelings crumble. "If I can see the light at the end of the tunnel…I think anyone can."

"Really?" Marc's eyes filled with hope.

"Just… Oh… What do I know, Marc? Just don't let anyone tell you what to do. Dr. Manning is on your side whatever you choose, and Madame… You have to get the surgeries anyway, so…'

"So… I just wait and see." He gave a dissatisfied shrug.

"You have a choice," Lina pressed. It was more than she'd had. "You have a choice."

"And how do you do today, sir? What can we help you with?" Lina studied her patient for a moment, arms crossed, glasses balanced atop her pile of curls, her face the absolute picture of concentration.

"Oh? Is it your leg? No. Wait a minute. *Co można nazwać legbone?* Femur? Femur. Is it your femur that is troubling you today, sir? Or should I say Master Igor?"

Cole couldn't hold back any longer. "Technically, it's a greenstick fracture—and, as you will no doubt discover, it's an injury more common in our younger patients. The more mature ones tend to just go all out for a full break—but a compound? Thankfully, those are rare in our line."

"Oh! Dr. Manning, I didn't hear you." Color flooded

Lina's pale cheeks. She clapped her hands over them for good measure.

"Not to worry. And it's Cole!" He sat himself down on the bench where Lina had been giving Igor his "treatment" and gave the puppy a little scratch under the chin. When he turned to look at her again he was struck by her eyes, rimmed red.

His gut told him that was his fault. That he needed to fix it. Fold Lina into his arms and apologize for asking her to meet him here at the hospital. Not to mention the fact that the "rare" compounds he'd just mentioned were exactly what had taken her off the stage forever. Talk about open mouth, insert foot!

Still. He had to hand it to her. She was still at the hospital—albeit outside the building—and talking shop with Igor to boot. A lesser person would have fled the scene. He had and it would eat away at him until the day he died.

"I think it's brilliant—what you're doing. I wish all our staff showed such dedication."

"Well, I— It's not too late, really, and it wasn't exactly as if I could just leave. Gemma couldn't hang around any longer and you did leave me in charge of Igor after all."

"Yes, but it wasn't meant to be for so long. After you left him I went in to see Marc again. He is going to take some time to weigh his options, *despite* Madame's look." He tried to mimic the look and eked just the hint of a smile from Lina.

"Madame will speak with him. She will win." A shadow crossed her face. Seeing her former employer had obviously had a bitter sting to it.

"Maybe. Maybe not. He's got me in his corner. And whatever you said clearly resonated with him."

Lina's lips pushed out into a frowny moue. "I didn't say much."

"You danced together, he said. And he respected you. Respects you," he corrected, waiting for the words to sink in. "You have perspective."

"And this is why you were so long in coming to collect your dear, beloved Igor?" Lina redirected the conversation abruptly. From the look on her face, she didn't want to go there. Fair enough. He had plenty of things he never wanted to speak with anyone about. Ever.

"Yes, sorry. I guess I'm not used to being responsible for anyone else." As the words came out of his mouth he felt the irony. *He'd had responsibility for another life all right. And when the life-support system had been switched off, life as he'd known it had changed forever.*

He cleared his throat roughly and pointed at the dog to clarify—but as his hand fell back to his side, he knew he didn't just mean Igor. By bringing Lina into the En Pointe fold he had accepted responsibility for her, as well. Only this time his feelings weren't altogether...*professional*.

What was it he was going to do—practice going with the flow? Bend with the willow and all that?

"I wasn't going to leave." Her words were defensive.

"No, no. Of course not." He drummed the bench next to him with his fingertips. "What do you say I make up for it in the form of a walk in the park for Igor and a killer ice-cream cone for you? There's an amazing Italian guy who's got a stand just at the edge of the park across from here."

Lina eyed him warily, which was only fair. He had already imposed on her evening. Well, her life really. She could always say no. But he really hoped she didn't.

"Or overtime. I owe you that. At the very least."

Lina took her time considering her options. Her brows crinkled together and her lips did a little wiggle back and forth as she thought. And then it hit him. He didn't want to say goodbye. Not just yet.

"How amazing is this ice cream?"

"Depends upon how much you like double chocolate gelato or salted caramel...'

"All right, Dr. Manning. Please may I have my overtime in the form of ice cream?"

"*Pyszne!* Delicious,' Lina translated.

Cole made a stab at pronouncing the Polish word and it was all Lina could do not to choke on her ice cream. He may have English covered—but the man had a mountain to climb before he'd be bilingual.

"I think you'd better stick to medicine." She gave him a wry look, slipping her fingers into the gaps between the slats of the park bench to stop herself from giving him a playful swat.

"Stick with what you know and all that, right?"

"Something like that." Lina fell silent. She knew ballet and sticking with that was impossible now. She felt Cole's hand cover and squeeze hers but she didn't dare risk looking at him. The sting of tears was teasing at her nose and she'd already cried enough today. Cried enough for a lifetime.

"Poor choice of expression." He released her hand. "Do you want to talk about it?"

"Not particularly."

"Fair enough."

Lina snuck a glance at him. He wasn't pressing. It was nice. When she'd been in hospital it had seemed as though everyone—the doctors, nurses, visitors, her parents for the short time they'd been able to visit—had all pushed and prodded. How did she feel? Was she sad? Did she think she needed medication for any depression she might be having? Did she want to talk to anyone professional? No, no, no, no, *no*!

She hadn't wanted any of these things. She'd just wanted to dance. The impact of her injury had been so profound that when she'd finally walked—*hobbled* was more like it—out of the hospital, she had been completely and utterly numb.

She wouldn't tell him, but this job had brought her back from teetering on the edge of the abyss. It was hard to believe she had sunk so low she had nearly been homeless rather than go home to her parents. She just couldn't do that to them. So it was time to start listening to some of her own advice. Because of the job, she now had a choice. But how did you start your whole entire life over when the first twenty-seven years had been focused on one very specific thing?

"How'd you get on today?" Cole broke the silence.

"Fine."

"No hitches with the phone system thingy?"

Lina had to smile. Without Gemma's help she doubted she would've taken a single call the entire day. As it was, she'd been busy from start to finish, felt utterly exhausted, but had come out the other end. Just in time to see Madame Tibold. The last person she'd expected to see ever again. And the very same woman who'd steered her on the intense career trajectory to center stage.

Had her nerves jingled and jangled today? Most assuredly. But she'd faced the day and Madame. Proudly. Answering the phone was hardly on a par with brain surgery—but from the perspective of someone trying to leave the all-encompassing shroud of darkness behind, getting through a day of work felt good.

"I did all right."

"Modest."

"It's pretty easy to pick up." *Some of it. Definitely not all of it.*

"And you're finding interacting with the patients okay?"

Easier than she'd thought. It was less "them" and more "I know what you're going through." That had surprised her.

"Yes, of course."

"The chair?"

"Comfy. Now stop interrogating me!" She took a lick of her ice-cream cone and settled back onto the bench. The park was nice. She'd never been there before. Dogs, it turned out, were an excellent means of discovering a city's green spots. Honestly? She didn't know if she'd ever just sat in the park before. With an ice-cream cone.

And a man whose mere presence made her a little closer to behaving like a giggly girlie than she'd care to admit.

"How was your day at work?" She only just stopped herself from adding a "dear" to the end of her question.

"Ah—I see what you're doing. Turning the tables?"

"I am merely showing an interest in the clinic's clients."

Cole laughed good-naturedly. "Well, that's good, then. I'm pleased we haven't put you off. I was nervous it was your way of getting me to talk about myself."

"Why? What's so bad about you?"

"Other than my inability to keep time, lumber people with puppies they didn't ask for and a weakness for ice cream?"

"The last thing isn't so bad." She took a dramatic lick of her cone and ended up with some on the tip of her nose.

"Don't they teach you how to eat ice cream cones in Poland?" Cole dabbed away the smear with a serviette and paused for just a moment, his eyes locking with hers.

Lina's breath caught in her throat. Was Cole going to

kiss her? She felt her body go hot and cold all at once. *What am I going to do now?*

"I hear they have much more practice of ice-cream cones in America." Could he hear the wobble in her voice?

"What? You're not going down the route of saying all Americans have some weight to lose, are you?"

Lina stopped herself from making a lingering appraisal of him.

"I'm not saying that at all. But since life in America is supposed to be so nice, why did you come here?"

"Oh—you know… I needed…change."

"What? From your secret life as an ice-cream critic?"

"Something like that."

And that's when she saw it. The hit of grief shadowing the bright blue of his eyes. It surprised her how much it affected her to see him in pain. He'd been nothing but a lift to her and to see him struggling with something of his own? It was hard to imagine anything that would get Cole Manning down.

Cole finished his cone with a flourish and smiling widely, pressed his hands down onto the bench, raising his lower body off the bench planks whilst lifting his legs into a half pike. *Interesting.* He wasn't bulky, but he surely had to work out to exercise that sort of muscle control. He must have abs to die for! Running a finger or two along those would be— *Uh, whoopsy! Stop the bus!*

Lina realigned her gaze to the remains of her dark-chocolate-and-salted-caramel double-scoop cone. Visually undressing Cole wasn't part of the plan. Not that there was a plan.

"I know I said I'd give you a week to figure out if you wanted to stay, but is it too soon to ask if you're up for a three-month trial period?"

Lina turned to face Cole, who had just scooped Igor up

into his lap. The two of them looked at her expectantly. Igor's ears were pricked up and Cole's blue eyes were… *Mmm…* She might be imagining things, but Cole's eyes seemed to hold the promise of kindness, a gentle touch when it came to confronting her demons… He wouldn't push her, his eyes said. He'd just be there. And right now that seemed good enough. Good enough to stay awhile.

It was the biggest room in En Pointe and already it was full to bursting. Lina casually sidled toward the door. Gemma obviously had enough guinea pigs for her massage night—it would be easy enough to slip out with no one being any the wiser.

"And where do you think you're going?" A familiar chest blocked the doorway. If she looked straight up she knew she'd be looking directly into the blue eyes she'd been tactically avoiding for the past fortnight.

"Nowhere?" Lina hadn't meant for it to be a question, or for it to be addressed to his chest, but Cole's presence played havoc with any cool or calm she had shored up— so best to go with it. She widened her eyes for effect and shrugged her shoulders up tight round her ears.

"Exactly right. If I'm stuck, you're stuck."

"Oh, I think there are enough—"

"Uh-uh! No, you don't." Cole blocked the doorway with his arms and nodded toward the far end of the room where Gemma was clambering onto a chair. Lina turned around, grateful for the respite from those eyes. And his freckles. She'd never noticed before that he had a little smattering of freckles. Cute.

No!

Not cute. Definitely not cute. Authoritative. Well…and we're back to cute. *Turn around!*

"Okay, everyone, it turns out we've had more of you

show up for massages than we have trainee masseurs, so what we're going to do is teach you all to massage each other! Yippee! Today is all about shoulders." Gemma's ability to control a group with a grin and a brisk clap of the hands was admirable. "Everybody pick a partner!"

Lina stiffened. She couldn't help it. Coming along to the sports massage session was a big enough step for her but today had been a particularly active one and she really could have done with going home and having a good soak complete with a fluffy cloud of bubbles floating up to the rim of her bath. The pepper-scented kind that gave her hip the illusion of feeling better. Healing. It'd been two weeks since she'd started at En Pointe, but the learning curve was still steep and she was nowhere near crossing the emotional bridge into the comfort zone.

"Guess that leaves you and me, Lina. It seems no one wants to feel my healing touch." Cole appeared at Lina's side with a self-effacing smile. "Feeling up to kneading the knots out of my shoulders?"

Uh…not even remotely!

"Sure. Why not? You look stiff as a plank."

"I guess that's better than being as thick as two short ones." Cole threw back his head and laughed.

Little speckles of heat tickled at her cheeks. Her English must've failed her again. Cole seemed to be having that effect on her.

"Lina! Cole! You two are over here on the floor, I'm afraid. We're out of massage chairs."

"We seem to be drawing all the short straws today, eh, Lina?"

"Thanks a lot."

"I didn't mean you, Polly Pigtails!" Cole's mock-pained expression brought a smile to her face as her hands flew to clutch her two thick plaits protectively. She drew them up into little U shapes and put on her best bucktoothed smile.

Her smile broadened with his. She couldn't help it. Hadn't been able to for the past two weeks now. Cole in the room meant a smile on her face. It was almost as though she'd been frozen for the months following her accident and his warm demeanor was bringing about a longed-for thaw. It was easier to think it had been his puppy—which he still hadn't managed to rehome—but Igor was nowhere in sight and here she was, grinning from ear to ear.

"Me first!" Cole dropped to his knees in front of her. "I've been up to my eyeballs in paperwork today and sources say I could do with a good old shoulder rub." He threw her another one of those over-the-shoulder winks of his. She'd seen him do it to other people—an upward shift of the chin, the casual descent of his eyelid, just briefly eclipsing the pure sky blue of his eyes... Not that she'd paid that much attention. Not really. He did it all the time, right? So, it was obvious that being on the receiving end of one wasn't special—but it had been harder to stem the rush of butterflies each of those leisurely winks unleashed. And now she was going to have to massage him? *Niebo mi pomoc.* And just how, exactly, could heaven help her?

"Shirts on or off?"

Lina's stomach lurched. Then did a cartwheel. Then lurched again. Cole was her boss. She didn't need to be rubbing his well-oiled, seminaked body in front of—

"On, you cad! This is a place of work! The boss doesn't stand for silly talk!" Gemma's words brought a wash of emotion to Lina's throat. *Mixed feelings? That would be one way to put it.* She needed this job. Big-time. It had only been a couple of weeks but already it was giving her some longed-for structure, purpose and, in truth, opening her eyes to a whole series of physio and treatment therapies she hadn't known existed. Maybe one day she'd see if someone could help her with her hip. Perhaps even take up Cole on his offer to go over her file. One day. But not today and definitely not now with that please-help-me-I-need-you look on his face.

Giving Cole a massage would move their working relationship—which was about as hands-off as you could get—to a whole different terrain. Intimate terrain. And with his shirt off? She could only just imagine the—

"Is something wrong?" Cole's face looked as though she'd just sprouted a moustache.

"What? No. Why?" The words tumbled out as heat began to crawl along her cheeks again.

"Because you look like you're poised to attack a huge, smelly pile of pumpernickel dough, not give your boss a little life-affirming shoulder rub."

"How dare you compare yourself to pumpernickel? It's delicious!" Not to mention the dough being a near match to the warm caramel color of his skin.

"And I'm not?" Cole's eyes sparked, his chin upright, expectant as he waited for an answer. "Wait. No. I take that back. Don't answer on the grounds it might incriminate you. Or both of us."

The space between them seemed to disappear—as if the air were actively binding them together. Lina knew in an instant what she felt for Cole was more than the gratitude of someone who needed a job. From the moment she'd first laid eyes on him it was as if he'd waved a magic wand and turned her world from black and white to Technicolor. With him, she felt safe, like she was in a Cole-and-Lina-sized superbubble of protection. But was she trapping herself in another fantasy?

Pouring herself into something wasn't new. Giving herself entirely to the ballet had yielded nothing but heartbreak. Would giving herself to the dream of a bright future—one with Cole in it—be just as foolish?

"Right, everyone." Gemma clapped her hands sharply, instantly breaking the fizzing connection between them. "If the person giving the massage could just rub their hands together briskly so as not to put icy digits onto their partner's necks."

Lina followed the instructions in a daze. If she treated this like a rehearsal, the rehearsal of a woman pretending she wasn't the least bit affected by placing her hands along the neck of her lover— *Aaaaiiiiieeee! Where did that come from?* She and Cole had barely breached the friendship zone, let alone something that intimate. And yet…she became aware of her hands fluidly massaging the length of Cole's neck, shifting down along the curve toward his shoulders, fingers pressing into muscle—some tight, some not—and she watched as Cole responded to her touch, his body pressing into the rhythmic cadence of her hands…

"All right, everybody! Looks as though some of you have your groove on. Sorry to bust it up, but it's time to switch places!"

Lina rose in synchronicity with Cole and as he turned she felt his hand brush against hers—their eyes meeting simultaneously. Did he feel the same electric connection she did? Was his heart pounding as rapidly as her own? Would she ever tire of even just a glimpse of his unbearably blue eyes?

Sitting down and facing the wall seemed to be the best way to quell the ricocheting emotions turning her insides into a pinball machine. She crossed her legs, took in a deep breath and smiled a little as she heard him do the same. Just maybe he had felt the same complex rush of response to her touch.

And then Cole's hands were on her shoulders. The warmth they transmitted merged into her skin like a yearned-for tonic. His fingers smoothed along her neck, each hand—one by one—shifting her plaits to the front of her shoulders. A hand cupping the side of her head as his fingers soothed the length of her neck into something long and fluid. Her body responded to him as it would have if they had been dancing. One touch eliciting another movement, each connecting to the other as if they had known the choreography all along. Her breath quickened as Cole increased the intensity of pressure he had been using. An impulse to turn around and kiss him, taste his lips, touch his skin, even caress him threatened to overwhelm her.

Abruptly, Lina grabbed her jumper from the floor and pushed herself up to standing.

"I'm sorry. I—I just remembered, I am late for something."

"What? Lina, what's going on?" Cole was straight behind her as she sought refuge in the corridor.

"No, it's just…" Her hands moved automatically to her shoulders, giving warmth to the area his hands had just left. She couldn't do it. Not here. Not in front of everyone. Cole's touch elicited too much raw feeling.

"It was a shoulder massage, Lina." Cole reached out and gave her arm a quick squeeze. "Nothing more."

"I know." She was holding back tears now. Tears of embarrassment, shame, confusion. She just needed to get out of there. Away from Cole and all the feelings he seemed to be able to tap into like some sort of emotion diviner.

"It's been a while, hasn't it?" He dipped his head down so they were eye to eye. It was near impossible not to look away.

"Since what?"

"Since you've let yourself be touched. Held."

How did eyes carry so much *compassion* in them? Biting the insides of her cheeks only just kept the tears from spilling over.

Lacing his fingers through hers, he silently led her to his office. As the door shut behind them, she was aware of nothing but being folded into Cole's arms. Her forehead pressed against his chest and her hands pushed. Hard. But he held her to him until the fight in her began to ebb away. And that's when the tears began to flow in earnest. The logjam of emotion she had been holding back for months, if not years, had broken. The heartbreak, the pain of the surgeries, the bleeding feet, all of the missed birthdays, anniversaries, quiet moments with her family. The debt of time, money, sheer devotion she owed her parents, the endless flow of wishes that she had the ability to pay them back for an infinity of kindness—the fathomless depth of their love and belief in her… All of it whooshed up and poured out of her in a heated wash of tears, all of them cleansing.

And he stayed with her. Listened to her sob, let her use his shirt as a tissue over and over as each time she thought she was done and she looked up into those blue eyes of his, the tears began anew.

This wasn't new for Cole. Something in treatment giving a patient release. But the churn of emotion he was experiencing was new. More than anything, he wanted Lina to know she would be safe. Safe, right here in his arms. He looked up to the ceiling and gave it a wry smile. For now.

He had nothing to offer her long-term. Or short-term, for that matter. He had nothing to offer her.

Even so, just having his arms around her, holding her close to him, was one of the most natural things he had ever experienced. There wasn't a person in the world she'd felt she could go to and—after a bit of a fight—she'd stayed with him, opened the door just one small crack. Would it be fair to try and get her to open it a bit further?

Cole let his chin rest on Lina's head as her sobs slowed into deep, hiccupy breaths.

"Better?"

"Mmm." The murmur came from where she'd nestled into his chest. He turned his head so that his cheek rested on her head. If anyone were to walk in right now they would assume they were lovers. Soul mates. He pushed the thought aside and forced himself to focus on her.

"Anything you want to talk about?"

It's still too painful to talk about.

"No."

Surprise, surprise.

"I am a doctor, you know."

"Not my doctor."

"True, but if you want, I can help." He laughed good-naturedly. "Don't look at me so dubiously! I worked long and hard to get my medical degree. My parents made sure of it." He pulled back a bit and his voice turned sober. "I wasn't offering to be your shrink, but if there's anything I can do for you—take a look at your records or anything…"

"I don't want a doctor." She looked up at him, her green eyes still glassy with tears.

What was she saying exactly? Did she want *him*? Cole minus the protective medical accolades and folksy charm? Plain old Cole who made bad choices? Cole Manning who'd pulled the plug on his fiancée despite the heartbreak, not just for him but for both his and her parents? He didn't know if that Cole would be worth much to Lina. It hadn't been to his parents. Or Katie's. Or the rest of his hometown for that matter. Folk stuck together when they thought a wrong had been done. Obeying a DNR apparently didn't fall into the "right' category. And who could blame them? It had been the hardest thing he'd ever done.

"Well… I guess that puts us at a bit of an impasse."

Her brow lifted a fraction.

"You don't like to accept help and I don't like to interfere in other people's lives." He held her out at arm's length, making a show of sizing her up. "Maybe it's perfect. We were made for each other!" He flashed her his best cheesy salesman smile. It was the best he could muster after the dredging up of the past.

"That attitude doesn't sound very generous for a doctor." Lina wriggled out of his arms as if to punctuate her point, and he couldn't help feel the sting of disappointment.

"That's not true." He hadn't meant for his tone to be sharp, but if anyone had done some deep soul-searching, it was him. And he knew exactly how he stood as a doctor. "I give every patient one hundred percent. They get the best advice I can possibly offer—but at the end of the day that's all it is. The work, the passion, the commitment? I can't give them that. That's got to come from within."

"Don't you think you're the reason patients work hard?"

"No. Why should I?" He led her over to the small sofa tucked into his office's bay window and handed her a box of tissues just in case. "I'm not the one who has the work ahead of me. What if I were to sit here and say to you, you know—having this accident could have been the best thing that ever happened to you."

She pulled a face. Then reconsidered.

I never would have met you.

"I can see you're not persuaded."

Cole checked an urge to give Lina's shoulder a gentle knead. Being the boss meant reining in any attraction he felt. So squelch it down he did.

"Look. I have no idea what you're going through and I can see how working here—with the dancers, the therapists, the injuries—has got to be taking a bit of a toll. You've gone from what I understand was a lot of alone time to full immersion back into the 'real world.' It's got to be tough and—believe me—I take my hat off to you. Not everyone could be as cheerful in the face of adversity."

A tear snaked down her cheek.

"Well. Mostly cheerful." He used the pad of his thumb to wipe it away, resisting the temptation to cup her face in his hand, run the backs of his fingers along her cheek. "Have you considered going home at all? To Poland?"

"No."

The sharpness of her response startled them both.

She hurriedly continued, "I mean, obviously, I love my parents—"

"But—what am I missing?"

"I will not go home. Not now." Her jaw set so tightly he saw a nerve twitch.

"Is there a 'when' lurking out there anywhere?" Even his best smile couldn't elicit a hint of the same from Lina.

"What do you want from me?" Every defense she'd let down was re-erected in an instant. Walls double-thick this time.

"Well, I…" Cole stopped. This was not one of those moments to mess up. He thought of how proud he'd hoped his parents would be of their doctor son—and how he'd only brought them sorrow. Logical or not, he hadn't been able to stick around burdened by so much shame.

Could she feel the same?

Lina's face was creased with worry, upper teeth

steadily catching her lower lip again and again, turning it a deep raspberry red. Did she only see him as another person to add to the list of people to disappoint?

"I wondered if you would consider going halves with me in taking Igor to puppy classes."

"I'm sorry?" She swiped at her tearstained face and grabbed her plaits, as if for comfort.

"Igor. I can't seem to find him a new home…" He stopped, gave a self-effacing grimace and corrected himself. "I'm finding it hard to say goodbye to the little fellow and now that his leg is better the very least I can do is send him to comportment classes. The thing is, the only one I can find that starts straight away is on a Wednesday and I can't make the first half-hour because of commitments at the hospital. If I were to give you overtime, would you be willing to take him? It's not far from here. Just the other side of the park, actually."

"No ice-cream payments?"

Was that the hint of a smile?

"That could always be arranged." He crossed his arms, giving her his best studied look. "Pending, of course, your success—and Igor's—at class."

Lina pushed herself up out the corner of the sofa, already tying on the mantle of a new challenge. "You're not suggesting Igor and I will let you down?"

"Far from it."

Far from it indeed. Cole actually felt her smile touch his heart this time. He couldn't put his finger on what barrier they'd broken through, but whatever emotional journey they seemed to be on, they were doing it together. And for the first time in an awfully long time it felt right—*real*—to have someone he could tuck protectively under his wing—even if only for a while.

CHAPTER FIVE

"AND THE PRIZE goes to…Igor and Lina!"

Lina knew she shouldn't, but the whoop was out of her mouth before she could stop it, hands clapping along with sheer glee. She hadn't felt this proud in ages. Proud of Igor, of course, but proud of herself, as well. They had focused and practiced and now they were at the head of the class! So what if it was for best sitting? She was well trained in the art of posture and could assert with absolutely assurance that Igor was following in her footsteps. His posture was immaculate. Nureyev would've been proud.

"Someone looks happy!" The voice she'd come to think of as Hot Chocolate Deluxe swirled along her spine. The expected bolt of heat detonated in her chest as she turned and met that bright blue set of eyes. She felt intimate and shy all at once. But mostly proud.

"Igor's been amazing today. He has real panache."

"So you two'll be showing off at Crufts next year?"

Lina swatted away the compliment. "Igor maybe. You won't get me running around a ring in front of thousands of people." The words were out almost before she'd thought them. It had been weeks since she'd used her cane. She wondered if running was out of the picture. It would be nice to start getting some proper exercise. Break a sweat and feel the afterglow of endorphins a good work-out brought with it.

"I don't see why not. It'd be a lovely sight." Cole was scooping up Igor but finished up his pronouncement with his eyes fully locked with hers.

A little thrill of pleasure made her heart hitch. Gemma had egged her into coming along for a couple of gratis sports massages from her trainee students and she was definitely feeling better. Professional ballet might be off the agenda, but cycling? Running? They were all pos-sibilities.

"Ice cream o'clock?"

"Yes, of course." Lina picked up her sweater and hand-bag, suddenly aware of a hit of nostalgia as her mind reeled through the well-studied menu. "The Italian fla-vors are lovely but, you know, it's really too bad they don't have beetroot with poppy seeds. And a sour-cream swirl. Ooh!" She couldn't stop herself from giving a twirl at the thought. "It's so good."

"Now, I can get you on the sour-cream front, but beets? I'm not buying it, Keminsky."

"It's very popular in Poland."

Cole's face registered disbelief.

"Well. Polish people eat it anyway. Lots. I am sure they have it at the Polski center."

"Where's that?"

"Near the river in Hammersmith. I used to go there—" She stopped, on the brink of admitting she'd felt more than a little homesick lately. After The Great Weep she was definitely feeling she could speak more freely to Cole—but "the home-run topics," as he liked to call them? Still too fresh.

"Why don't we go there now? We can jump in a cab."

Cole was already heading toward the curb, arm raised as traffic approached.

"No. No—it's not necessary. I was just dreaming a little."

"I think after today's impressive show at puppy class you deserve to have a dream come true." He raised his arm again, this time bringing a taxi to a halt. "Where was it you said we were going?"

"Polskie Centrum Kultury—the Polish Cultural Centre," she said to the driver along with the address. He signaled for them to hop in the back of the black cab.

Settling into the seat, Lina couldn't stop a big grin from forming. One of her favorite things in Britain was the classic black cab and one of her favorite things from Poland was beetroot ice cream. She didn't feel ready to go home yet—but being at the cultural center always felt like stepping into a little section of Poland. Cole reached over and gave her hand a squeeze, then wrapped his fingers through hers.

"You look about five years old."

"I feel about five years old!" She squeezed his hand back and, despite her best intentions, kept her fingers laced through his. "Ice cream from home!"

They rode like that, in silence. Two people holding hands, heading off for some ice cream with their prize-winning pooch. It was amazing to feel so *happy*. An uncomplicated happy. Just good old-fashioned happy. Not to mention the little ideas that kept popping into her head. Maybe she could run. Maybe she could ride a bike. Maybe what she'd needed all along was not even a push, but the suggestion of a push. Perhaps what she'd needed all along was a certain someone who gave her the strength to believe in herself again.

She stole a glance at Cole, who was busy examining

Igor's new prize. It was the third time he'd won Top Puppy and his toy collection was becoming enviable. Her gaze shifted along Cole's face. The long-lashed blue eyes, caramel skin darkening as the spring months became more summery... How could a man with such an open heart be so very single? He worked a lot and, if office gossip was anything to go by, dated but had never been known to have a girlfriend. Which was crazy. He was definitely a catch. If the way he made her feel was anything to go by, someone would be a very lucky woman someday.

He was very rigid about how he treated patients. They could take his advice or leave it. He was adamant that it wasn't up to him to make a patient's decision about their health. Some people may have found that off-putting. Too scientific. But she liked it. He was right. If you didn't accept responsibility for yourself, who would?

She smiled down at their hands, still lightly clasped. Had she ever had anything near a normal boyfriend-girlfriend relationship before? She thought this was what it must be like. Feeling content. Light. Free.

Cole had passed the point of being able to hide his true feelings. Beetroot ice cream wasn't for him. Not by a long shot.

"They got any other flavors in there?"

"Honey and garlic?"

"You're joking, right?"

Lina shook her head in slow motion. It looked like nothing in the world would take the smile off her face, and he felt a tug of pride at having been a part of it. "I think they have the names in English somewhere—but I'm pretty sure there is sweet fish."

Cole looked appalled.

"No? Okay—watermelon?"

"Watermelon! Finally, something I can recognize. You Poles definitely have a—er—more refined palate than I do." A thought took hold and he nodded his head decisively. "One of these nights I'm taking you to a Southern food restaurant. I'd love to see how you get on with grits and blackened catfish."

"Why would you put black on a catfish?"

"Ha! Don't curl your lip like that! It's the seasoning—it turns the fish black when it's cooked. Barbecued is best. With collard greens and a side of po'boys? Delicious!" He smacked his lips at the thought. His father made a mean blackened catfish on the grill and with a serving of his mother's fried green tomatoes? "It's delicious, you'll see." Cole didn't even think. He just swung his arm round the back of the bench and pulled Lina close to him for a quick squeeze. He only just managed to stop himself from giving her a peck on the cheek, opting to plop his arm on the back of the bench instead, not quite ready to take it away. Not just yet, because what was happening between Lina and him felt…good…regular, but in the absolute best way. He hadn't had "good" or "regular" in he didn't know how long. It had always been cotillions or daughters of couples from the country club, or the rotary club, or— It just didn't matter because the whole town had always seemed to know whom Justin and Jenna Manning's son had had on his arm because they'd organized to get her there. Until "that night" with their best friend's daughter. He tightened his lips and flinched it away.

Right now? He was just a regular guy on a regular date with his girl and their dog. Except it wasn't a date and the only thing that was "his" was the dog.

"Hey, look, they are setting up a band." Lina nodded to the opposite corner of the quadrangle at the heart of the community center. Several older gentlemen—wearing suit

jackets and ties despite the warmth of the early evening—
were putting stools into place. One had an accordion, another a fiddle, a third was lugging a double bass into place.

"What's that?" Cole pointed toward a man carrying
an unfamiliar instrument, noticing Lina's eyes brighten
at his arrival.

"Ah—the *dudy* or *koza*. I am not sure exactly which
one—they are regional—but it is like your Scottish bagpipes."

"They aren't *my* bagpipes!" Cole snorted. "I'm American, remember? Apple pie and electric guitars and all
that?"

"Yes, but…" Lina paused, her face a picture of concentration.

"What?" Cole gave her a little poke with Igor's paw to
speed up her response.

"It's funny. I was just thinking how I always consider myself as the only one who is away from home in
London—but I guess I'm not so alone in being alone,
am I?"

"No," Cole answered easily, then, as their eyes met,
he felt his response shift. There was more there. Something weighted with meaning. "No, you're not alone." He
searched her pale green eyes, hoping more than anything
that Lina knew he'd do what he could to stem any loneliness she felt. He'd actively sought the anonymity of big-
city life, but he knew exactly what she was saying.

Sometimes it felt as though he was a natural part of
the place, easily absorbed into the fray of the capital's
population, just one of the millions of Londoners going
about his business… And other days? Other days it felt
like everything "foreign" about Britain was there to actively remind him he didn't have a home. He didn't have

a place—people—he could go to when he was hurting. He didn't have a "someone."

But being part of a person's life—laying himself open to all the hurt and anguish that went with loving them— he wasn't even close to being there yet. Might never be. If he'd been a man who prayed, right now he'd be sending a stream of prayers straight to heaven in the hopes Lina could see he was trying his best to do what he could. He stole a glimpse at her and smiled. She pushed herself to the edge of the bench, fingers curled round the edge of the seat, eyes bright with anticipation.

How could he not at least try? Spending time with Lina was evolving into something beyond a work relationship for him—but how much more? Shaking his head, he looked away. Answering that question was somewhere he couldn't go. Not by a long shot. Never mind the fact it wasn't fair on Lina. She was an employee, which made her strictly off-limits in the first place, and she was obviously busy battling her own demons. He pulled his hand back to his lap, where Igor was settling in for a nap. He'd be better sticking with "man's best friend."

The musicians began to play and couples drifted to the center of the square and with a touch of the hand, or a fleeting caress on the cheek, they separated into individual lines of men and women, then began to dance. Their movements reminded him of the dances his parents used to drag him to where—despite himself—he'd usually ended up having a great time. It had been about family, community, not just swirling in long-rehearsed circles round one another. From the smiles on everyone's faces they, too, were reminded of better times at home.

"What is this?"

"The *kujawiak*. It's a national dance of Poland." Lina smiled at a private memory. "The first dance I learned.

You learn it at school, you learn it in your village square, in your grandmother's kitchen. No matter what, if you are Polish you cannot escape the *kujawiak*."

"Show me?" Cole held out a hand. Just because she was an employee it didn't mean they couldn't share a dance.

"Hmm." Lina began shaking her head, her hand automatically reaching for her cane.

"No way. You can't use that as an excuse." Cole waved it away. "I've been watching you the past few weeks and you've hardly used it. I'm not even sure why you bring that thing with you anymore, to be honest."

"Yes, but I am not so sure…with the dancing."

Ah.

"Lina, look at these people. Everyone out there is about fifty years older than either of us and they're doing fine." He shifted Igor to the ground and swiftly fastened his lead to the bench. "C'mon, I bet there are at least four or five hip replacements out there." He tipped his head toward the dancers, who were slowly circling one another to the rhythm of the music.

Lina gave him a wary look but he could tell she was wavering. "Please? Would you do me the honor of dancing the *kujawiak* with me?" Lina stifled a giggle. "At the very least you can teach me the dance as we both know I'll never be able to pronounce it properly!"

"Go on, dear." An older woman good-naturedly nudged Lina with her elbow, speaking in Polish. "Don't turn down such a handsome fellow! You're obviously mad about each other. I'll look after your dog while I rest."

Lina rose, cheeks coloring as she did. She hadn't thought the looks she'd shared with Cole had been so obvious. Then again…did that mean her feelings weren't one-sided?

Before she could reconsider, the woman slipped into

her spot on the bench and tipped her head back into the final rays of the evening sun, eyes closed against the light. Lina couldn't help noticing that the woman looked a bit pale—but everyone in England looked a bit pale this time of year. It was probably nothing.

Cole offered her his hand. As she slipped her fingers across his palm it was all but impossible to hide her body's response to him. An overwhelming urge to arch in toward him took hold of her. She wanted to feel his chest against her own. Rise up on tiptoe and see if his lips tasted as nice as they looked. He clasped her hand in his and gave her arm a little tug, for which he received a shy smile as they moved into the square of dancers. If only he knew the saucy thoughts dancing round her head…with some fairy-tale thoughts latched on for good measure.

Everything about the evening felt like a first date. The ice cream, the hand squeezes, the short but, oh, so lovely moment when he'd slipped his arm across her shoulders. Even when Cole had moved it away to the back of the bench she'd still been able to feel the heated dance of goose pimples tickle their way up and down her spine. It would have been more than easy to snuggle right up, scoop Igor onto her lap and watch the dancers. Just a couple of young lovers— *Eek!*

Stop. Thinking. That. Word!

"So…where should I put my hands?"

Don't answer honestly!

"Just hold my right hand up like this and then…" Lina had to stop, it was too flustering, which was rich coming from a lifelong dancer. This was what she had done all day, every day for her entire adult life but right here, right now, with a man she could so easily imagine kissing that it suddenly seemed impossible.

"Don't you remember?" Cole laughed.

"Of course, it's just—it's been a while." She turned in a semicircle, ending up with her back to him, in sync with the other dancers. *See? It was all there.* Just like getting back on a bike. She pulled one of Cole's hands over her shoulders so that their fingers just met and signaled to him to watch the other male dancers. It was a simple enough dance. She'd been doing it in the school playground to the discordant accompaniment of teenaged musicians from the age of five. But it had never felt sexy before.

As Cole watched and mimicked, his movements became more fluid, more confident, and it was impossible not to respond to his touch. He lifted the tips of Lina's fingers up in a high arc and she spun in a slow circle before coming round to face him. The music was slow and crept into her bloodstream like a warm tonic. It reminded her of everything that had been familiar to her as a young girl. Experiencing it whilst being held in Cole's arms— slowly drifting this way and that in union with the dozen or so other couples—was little short of magic.

Their eyes locked and it was all Lina could do to remember to breathe. She felt Cole's hand tug her in a bit closer at the waist, his other hand teasing hers toward his chest. He slipped her fingers from his palm and laid them against his chest, his heartbeat palpable through the thick cotton fabric of his shirt. It was all Lina could do not to press herself into that chest as she had done the day she'd wept in front of him, but this time revel in his scent, the solidness of him—in both character and physicality. She had no idea if there was a washboard stomach under there but, frankly, right now? He could have a potbelly for all she cared. Being with Cole mattered to her. Mattered in a way she hadn't experienced before. And dancing here at the Polish Centre with him felt so incredibly *personal*.

It was as if, through their time at the clinic, sharing

duties with Igor and now giving him this glimpse into her heritage, she was slowly opening the doors to plain old Lina. The Lina who had been inside her all along, but who she'd had to hide away so that she could focus on her career. She braved a glance up toward his face, happy to see a peaceful smile lazily playing on his lips. If Cole were to hold her like this, and they could sway back and forth to the music of her homeland forever? That would be enough. That would definitely be enough.

Abruptly Cole pulled back from their embrace.

"Lina, over on the bench, by Igor…"

Adrenaline racing, she whirled round to see the woman who had encouraged her to dance slumped on the bench, Igor anxiously patting at her with a paw.

Cole was by the woman's side in an instant, fingers on her pulse points, a cheek by her mouth to check for breathing. "She's breathing, but we've got find out why she fainted."

Vaguely aware of the music coming to a stop and the dancers gathering round, Lina fine-tuned her focus on Cole.

"Can you help me lay her on the ground, please?" He was all business, pure concentration. He threw his jacket on the ground but then, with a quick look at Lina and a glance at the other woman's more generous proportions, thought better of it and suggested, "Maybe you could ask a couple of people to help us?"

Lina found herself playing the role of translator as the crowd around them closed in. Most people spoke English, as well, but not all of the older ones and here, where she knew everyone but Cole would understand, it was much easier to use her native tongue.

She hadn't spoken Polish with others in so long that had it not been an emergency she would have reveled in the pleasure of it. But from the questions Cole was throwing to her to ask the crowd—Does anyone know this woman? Does she have a handbag? Can we check for any medication?—she knew time was of the essence. As they eased the woman to the ground, she came to, muttering a few words in Polish. She pressed her hands to the ground as if to get up, then began shaking, a thick patina of sweat appearing on her forehead.

"She says she needs something sweet."

Cole's eyes lit up with recognition.

"She must be diabetic. Can you ask someone to grab an ice cream or a chocolate bar—anything? She could be going into insulin shock." Lina nodded and rattled off the request.

The moments passed with excruciating slowness. Lina knelt on the ground, holding the woman in a semiupright position. Her eyes went wide as the woman began to twitch and spasm uncontrollably. Lina went with her gut instinct, wrapping her arms around the woman as tightly as she could manage.

"She's seizing. The brain's not getting enough glucose," Cole explained, quickly placing several rolled-up serviettes left over from their ice cream between the woman's teeth.

Lina called for someone to ring an ambulance just as a young man handed across a large green handbag that must have been on the far side of the bench. He grabbed hold of the woman's legs to help control her shaking as Cole unceremoniously dumped the contents of the woman's handbag onto the ground.

"It's too late for the ice cream. Let me see if she has any glucagon in here."

He raked through the usual items—coin purse, public transport pass, house keys, tissues—until he unearthed a small orange plastic box. Inside was a syringe and small glass bottle topped with an orange lid. The vial looked like it held a small disc of powder.

Cole bit off the lid of the syringe and as he injected the liquid from the syringe into the vial, Lina asked another man to hold the woman's legs, her eyes still trained on Cole. "What are you doing?"

"I'm hydrating the glucagon powder. It is a synthetic version of the natural hormone that our body makes to balance blood-sugar levels."

He expertly shook the vial until the powder was completely dissolved, then refilled the syringe with the liquid once it became clear.

"Does anyone know how old she is?"

Lina asked the crowd and received mixed responses.

"Somewhere between sixty and seventy. She is a *babcia*—a grandmother—here on a visit, they think."

"Good. And I'd guess she's around eighty-five kilos," he continued, almost to himself, as he filled the syringe with most of the liquid. "The good thing about this stuff is you can't put in too much. But if we can be as accurate as possible…" He stopped in midflow to flick the syringe a couple of times, squirt a tiny bit out and raise the woman's skirt until her upper leg was visible. "Hold her steady now." Holding the needle at a ninety-degree angle, he injected the contents into the outer edge of her thigh muscle. He sat back on his heels, pulling the woman's skirt back down over her knees as he did so, and watched as her jerky movements slowed.

"Would you two be all right helping me roll her into the recovery position? Just follow my lead." Cole looked between Lina and the young man who had helped her. They nodded and gently helped him turn her on her side, where someone else laid a knitted blanket over the woman's side.

As they waited, Lina could hear the group discuss the situation. Would Irina or Marja's blanket be softest? Should they get one of the pillows Mrs. Wojek had cross-stitched for the new settee? What about the ice cream? Who had made the ice cream that day and why had no one noticed this poor woman sitting on her own fainting like that, and, my goodness, who was the handsome doctor? He looked like a television star sweeping in like that from the dance floor.

Lina felt a smile tease at her lips, only trusting herself to keep her eyes on Cole's fingers as they tracked the woman's pulse.

After what felt like the most interminable wait, the woman's dark eyes flickered open.

A relieved smile lit up Cole's eyes. "Can we still get that chocolate? And maybe a meat sandwich or some crackers and cheese? There's no need to rush because the medication will make her feel nauseous for a while, but she may need something to nibble on if the ambulance gets stuck in traffic."

Lina rattled off the requests, even though she could see people already responding to Cole's questions, and asked the woman her name. It was Beatrycze, the same as one of her aunties. She smiled up at Cole, aware he'd have no idea of the coincidence but happy about it nonetheless. His quick thinking had potentially saved this woman's life. The sound of sirens began to infiltrate the air around them, abruptly wailing to a halt.

"Looks like you beat the emergency services to it." Lina couldn't keep the pride out of her voice. She knew she hadn't had anything to do with the woman's recovery—it had all been Cole—but she felt proud by proxy.

"My parents will be pleased all the tuition they spent

on medical school was put to use," he quipped, his face shifting seamlessly from bright to dark.

She'd seen that look before, the one that clouded over those bright blue eyes of his. Her heart ached for him. As their eyes met, it was all she could do not to reach out and touch him, hold him as he'd held her when it had all seemed too much. Not that she'd told him anything. She hadn't been ready to talk about the hurt that had virtually shredded her heart into worn threads. Seeing him now, like this, she knew she would be safe confiding in him. He had hurt as much as she had. She was not alone.

"Looks like someone's been busy. Whose handiwork is this?" A man in a paramedic uniform appeared with another man close behind, carrying a large first-aid kit.

Cole rose and rattled through what he'd done and what he suspected the situation to be.

"We'll take her to hospital and they can run through some tests."

"No." Beatrycze pushed herself up to a sitting position. "Please, no. I prefer to go to Polskie Centrum Zdrowia."

"This isn't a taxi service, love. It's an ambulance. We go to St. Andrew's Hospital or the Royal. Your choice."

Beatrycze turned to Lina, visibly distressed, and began speaking in Polish. "Please, I am new here—only visiting. I know the Polskie Centrum Zdrowia. I don't know enough English to go to the hospital. I am fine. I will just go to my son's." She tried pushing herself up to standing, but wobbled halfway up, was caught and steadied by the sea of hands lurching forward to help her back to the ground.

"She doesn't have to come with us if she doesn't want to," interjected the paramedic. "We can't force anyone to come with us. But if she was my nan I'd get her somewhere to be checked out."

"I think it might be best if you go see a doctor," Lina said to Beatrycze in Polish, then continued in English, her eyes trained on Cole. "Perhaps you will let me accompany you to the Polskie Centrum Zdrowia, if that would help."

He nodded with a smile. "Sounds like a good idea. Want me to come?"

Igor barked from the bench and Cole shot his gaze back and forth between the two of them. "You'll be all right on your own?"

Beatryzce gave Lina's hand a grateful squeeze. It was the first time in a long time Lina had been the one who'd been able to help. The wash of thankfulness it gave her surprised her.

"Yes." She nodded her confirmation to Cole, too full of emotion to trust her voice not to shake. "Yes, we'll be fine."

CHAPTER SIX

"YOUR USUAL?"

"Yes, please!" Cole realized he was using his "bright" voice. The one that tried to convey happiness when he wasn't feeling it naturally.

"You and your wife must love our ribs. You buy so many!"

"Oh, there's no wife." Cole felt himself go on the defensive. He always bought enough so he'd have leftovers. That was sensible, right? Or just something that a bachelor would do to avoid the "cooking for one" scenario he loathed.

"Why don't you have a wife?" The Chinese woman who always took his order wore an expression of pure mystification. "You're not ugly." She rocked back on her heels to study him. "You must have a good job to buy all these ribs…"

"Uh…yes. I'm a doctor." He hoped he didn't look as gormless as he felt.

"Then what's wrong with you?"

"Just busy with work, I guess."

"Then you work too hard. It's not smart to not have a wife. There's no balance. No harmony." She shook her head decisively, then disappeared into the back where he heard the rapid-fire cadence of Mandarin fill the kitchen.

Cole scrunched his shoulders up, then jigged them up and down a few times in a stab at relaxing the line of tension tightening his shoulders. He scanned the Chinese restaurant that, as far as he was concerned, made the most delicious ribs in the city. Not to mention some ridiculously divine garlic beans. And the place was never empty. He took in the couples murmuring quietly over plates of dumplings, greens, noodles. Children delighting in the turntables at the center of their family tables, sharing not just the great food but conversation, smiles, laughter.

He looked down at Igor, sitting obediently by his foot. "Guess it's just you and me, buddy. Eh? No danger of exchanging garlicky kisses with anyone tonight."

Igor's floppy ear perked up to meet the other as Cole knelt to give him a scratch. It went straight to Cole's heart every time Igor's ears collided at the top of his head. "So much for you going back to the shelter…" Igor opened his eyes wide, then leaped at Cole for a few slobbery licks. He couldn't help but laugh. A couple of months ago he wouldn't have dreamed of getting a dog, let alone hanging on to a goofy mutt abandoned by his moonstruck receptionist.

Where was she now? he wondered. Dancing beneath the Spanish skies? Dancing…like he and Lina had been.

Good grief.

Talk about moonstruck. If he didn't watch it, he knew he'd be as moonstruck as Scarlet and there was one strawberry blond, rose-lipped reason why. He had come so close to kissing Lina tonight. Ice-cream cones and visits to the Polish Centre, where a whole new side to her had come to light, were going to have to be stricken off the list if he was going to retain any sort of professionalism between them. He'd take it up as a mantra if necessary:

theirs was strictly a working relationship. Work, work, work, work, work and…not even a bit of play?

All right, fine. His day improved from the moment he lit eyes on her and went downhill before they'd even finished saying goodbye. Truthfully? He knew he was stage-managing as much time with her as he could. It would've been easy as pie to sort out different classes for Igor, but knowing he'd see Lina again after a full day's work took the edge off the growing emptiness of his self-imposed hermit-like life. But there was a reason he was alone—had to be alone. Not monk-like. He'd definitely dated women since Katie had had her car crash—but commit to one? Take on the responsibilities he'd had with Katie? Bear the weight of her family's grief and his own? Their pain? Their fury at the unfairness of life?

"No more dancing from here on out. It's going to be just us menfolk, Igor."

The puppy's brow furrowed in consternation.

Fair enough.

"Guess we'll both take some convincing, won't we, buddy?"

"Double order of ribs for *one*."

Cole took the takeaway bag, trying his best not to acknowledge the restaurateur's pointed look. Fine. Enough already. He was an unbalanced, off-key bachelor. When you'd made the set of bad decisions he had, that's what happened—and on days like this you just had to learn to suck it up.

"It isn't protocol."

"It *is* common sense." Lina stood her ground. Or, more accurately, kept her seat beside Bea—as the woman was now insisting she call her. "If she wants me to be in the room with her, then you should let me. Isn't the patient always right?"

"I think you mean the customer."

"This is a private clinic, isn't it? Bea will be paying you the same money as everyone else."

The women looked at each other and nodded in tandem.

The doctor gave Lina a pained expression. She felt for him. He was just doing his job, but so was she. Well. It wasn't really her job, but Bea needed someone to look after her. To help. And for the first time in a long time she was feeling properly...*useful*. "At least let me stay through the examination until her family arrive. We rang them on the way here."

The doctor's eyes darted between the pair of women before nodding his assent and proceeding with the examination. Lina could barely suppress the happy smile forming on her lips, then decided to just go for it. Why not? She was happy.

Sure, she felt helpful at the clinic, answering the phones, doing the files, greeting the patients and so forth—but here, helping Bea explain what had happened at the Polish Centre, detail what treatment Cole had given her, she felt like she was actually making a difference. More than just commiserating with a dancer over a bad landing or a *relevée* gone wrong.

Later, when Beatrycze's family came, overwhelming her with thanks and gratitude and a small bottle of cherry slivovitz, it really was impossible to keep the smile off her face. As she pushed the door open to leave the clinic, the doctor who had been treating Beatrycze approached her.

"Miss Keminsky?" Lina turned to him. "I'm glad I caught you."

"Did I leave something behind?" She did the obligatory pat of handbag and pockets to make sure she had everything she'd arrived with.

"I just wanted to say thank you."

"For what?" Now she was mystified. She'd done little more than sit with Bea—well, *insist* she sit with Bea.

"We normally don't get NHS translators coming along with the patient. Obviously, we speak Polish here, but it was useful having someone who'd been with her from the beginning of her situation. Usually, you lot are too busy to take the extra step."

Quizzical lines formed on her brow. "I don't work for the national health."

"Oh!" He looked surprised. "I just presumed. You seemed to have a good understanding of everything that had happened so I thought you were a medical translator. If that's not what you do, you should consider it. My understanding is that they always need people. Any other languages?"

"German and French." Lina answered on autopilot, and then quickly backtracked. "My German is a bit rusty."

"Well, if you want a career change I would check it out. It's always great for the patients when they know there's someone fighting for them."

Work as a translator? The idea had never occurred to her before but as she waved goodbye to the doctor and let the idea settle in….translator…the spring to her step grew a little bit lighter. She was halfway down the street before she realized she was heading in the wrong direction to get home. She had automatically aimed for the underground station that would take her to the clinic. Her intention had been clear. To share her news with Cole.

It hit her like a thunderbolt. She was falling in love with him—which was mad! She hadn't even kissed him yet. Not that that was part of the falling in love To-Do Checklist, but... But nothing. There were about a million things they hadn't done yet but even so, her heart squeezed tight, then burst into an interior fireworks display. She was falling in love with Cole!

She wanted him to know everything, hear everything, be her North Star, hold her when she was happy, sad, exhilarated, scared and...oh! Just everything. Not that they knew the slightest thing about each other.

That wasn't strictly true, either. Lina forced herself to focus. Cole knew a lot about her but she knew remarkably little about him. Was it enough? He was kind, smart, funny, made her a little weak-kneed. Well, very weak-kneed—particularly whenever he unleashed that slow-motion wink of his. He did seem to enjoy spending time with her—or was that just guilt because of how much she helped with Igor?

Or was it all in her head?

The questions whirled and whirled to the point she could almost feel herself spinning along with them. She squeezed her eyes tight to make the world solid again. Real. It all boiled down to one thing—was she worth falling in love with? If she didn't even feel she could face her parents, she could hardly be worthy of someone's love.

She stopped in front of a shop window and took a good long hard look at her reflection. This was serious. Life-changing. She saw her reflection's narrowed eyes. This was tough—and necessary. It was time to start asking questions. The hard ones.

Was it worth sacrificing a chance at genuine happiness and love to fall back into the familiar vortex of insecurity Cole had pulled her out of? Or had she reached a point in her recovery where she finally had it in her to fight?

She'd done something really good today. Something rewarding. And the doctor at the clinic had noticed. Perhaps if this was a new niche she could explore for herself, a new purpose…something that would help her rebuild a sense of worth…maybe then she could let herself begin to believe that whatever it was that was happening between Cole and her could be real. She crossed her fingers and gave a quick look up to the heavens for good measure.

Please, let it be real.

"Someone looks busy. What have we got here?"

"Oh, it's nothing." Lina swept the papers she'd been reading into a pile.

"That's not a job application, is it?" The displeasure in Cole's tone was unmistakable.

"No, of course not." Her mouth went dry and she felt a chill shoot along her spine. The guilty kind. She could hardly compromise the job she had for one she could never get.

Lina hurriedly stuffed all the paperwork she'd been going through into a drawer. "Just something I was doing for Gemma." She looked up and met Cole's gaze, her breath catching in her throat as it did nearly every time she permitted herself to enjoy the azure clarity of his eyes. Uh-oh. Was this what he looked like when his hackles were…?

"She's not getting you to do her work for you, is she? I'll have a word."

"No! No. Please, don't. It's fine." Lina hastily covered with a plastered-on smile. What a mess! Served her right for telling a white lie in the first place. Biting back the fact she'd been looking for medical interpreter jobs, she handed over a wodge of messages.

"You've got a tendinopathy case next and after that a spondylolytic back injury and two posterior decompensations of the torso. Both teenagers."

"Get you!"

"What?" Lina looked at him blankly.

"You and all your medical lingo. *Shebam!* You've settled right in."

Please don't look so impressed.

"Nothing I didn't hear in the rehearsal halls my whole life. Plus I like saying spondylolytic." Lina smirked, trying to look lighthearted without belittling the condition. A fracture to the back was no laughing matter. Neither was her predicament. She might know these things, but from the research she'd just done it wasn't enough to just magically become a medical translator.

On top of which, she didn't want to add to Cole's stresses. He'd been working crazy hours lately. Dancers across the capital seemed to be tearing tendons, axing their Achilles and destroying their knees like it was going out of style. Good for clinic business, but the light shadows under Cole's eyes betrayed the fatigue he must be feeling. His work was his life and this week it was easy to see the wear and tear that sort of commitment brought on. She longed to reach out and give his hand a comforting squeeze but holding back came more naturally.

Especially now.

An internal groan wouldn't hurt anyone, so she let one unfurl across her rib cage, then felt it land with a weighted *thunk* in her belly.

Why, oh, why was life so full of obstacles? Where she'd felt so hopeful and excited for the past few days, just daring to believe she might have found a new calling in life—*urgh!* The leaded weight of disappointment sat heavily in her belly, the familiar feelings of failure building up like storm clouds in her psyche.

She'd scoured the sites of five recruitment agencies online and speaking Polish and English wasn't nearly enough. Many of the posts preferred it if you were actually a medical professional as well as being bi- or tri-lingual. University in the UK was no longer free, not to mention the fact she was about a hundred years older than any of the other students would be—

"Hey, there." Cole's broke through the roar of thoughts drowning out any and all confidence she had gained lately. "Everything all right?"

"Of course. I am just thinking."

"Thinking pretty hard from the looks of things." Cole picked up another handful of messages she'd put in his cubbyhole and sifted through them whilst giving her a periodic glance as if she would suddenly open up and spill the beans.

Why couldn't she? Why couldn't she just tell him everything?

Because, you first-class fool, it's unprofessional. At least one of you should remember he's the boss.

"It's Igor, isn't it?" Cole's face was the picture of gravity.

"What is? Nothing's wrong with him, is there?"

"We-ell…" Cole teased out the word with agonizing slowness. Despite herself, Lina's hands clasped together over her racing heart. She couldn't bear anything to happen to Igor. "He's been missing you." Cole gave her a pointed look. "Have you been feeling the same way?"

The breath she'd been holding whooshed out of her chest. Was Cole giving her an out? A way to avoid talking about what was really troubling her? Her heart sunk.

Wait a minute. Maybe it was the other way round and—Wait another minute! Did she actually *want* to tell him?

That was new.

Baring her very soul wasn't really her style.

She looked up, almost surprised to see he was still there, patient as ever, an expectant smile playing on his full and far too kissable lips. Her heart shot back up into her throat. Maybe… No… She chanced another glance. Was Cole offering her an excuse to spend time with him? Making it possible for her to open up? Show him her heart?

She swirled a finger round an invisible dust heart on her desk. "I do miss seeing his little furry face around here. It's not the same without him."

"It seemed sensible to send him to puppy day care instead of keeping him in my office. Socialize him," Cole explained, long fingers scrubbing at his jawline as he spoke. His eyes went up to the ceiling and on a long journey around the reception area as he spoke again. "Maybe you'd like to come to dinner with the two of us?"

Lina didn't answer right away. Of course she would, but with the knock to her confidence she'd just had she wasn't so sure it was a good idea.

"I know a great place that has outside tables and killer catfish. Good old-fashioned American soul food." Cole's eyebrows did a little jig. "Remember? I said I'd have to pay you back for making me eat beetroot ice cream the other day."

"Hey." Lina swatted away his insult, laughing at the memory of the face he'd pulled. "I didn't *make* you do anything."

"Lina Keminsky, let me make this very clear. I don't think there's anyone in the world who could've coerced me into trying that purple swirly whatever it was apart from you." The air turned electric as their laughter shifted into a taut silence. Was he thinking of the moment he'd held her in his arms while dancing, looking into each other's eyes, when it would've have been so easy to go up onto tiptoe and kiss him? So perfectly easy. Her lips parted. She couldn't help it. Her entire body ached to be closer to him. Was this the risk she was meant to take? Being with Cole?

"Is that a yes?" He looked as transfixed as she felt. Lina only just managed a nod. Her entire insides had turned to jelly. It'd be a miracle if she managed to get out of her chair and walk anywhere, let alone to dinner.

"Any messages, Lina?" Gemma's cheerful voice cut through the thick atmosphere.

"Oh, yes, sorry. There are a couple." Lina shook her head, almost convinced Cole had hypnotized her into saying yes.

"Gemma," Cole interjected, his tone taking a decided swing into boss territory. "You're not getting Lina to do all your paperwork, are you?"

Gemma shot Lina a questioning look and received a rigorous *deny, deny, deny* micro-headshake in return.

"Yup—sorry. My bad!" Gemma chirped, giving Cole a smart salute. "Won't happen again, boss."

Cole looked between the pair of them and shook his head. *Women!* his face said. He grabbed a sticky note, scribbled something on it and stuck it to Lina's computer screen out of Gemma's sight as a woman with a neck brace came in the front door.

"Right. That's me back to work." He gave the girls a quick nod and, with a practiced smile, began to steer his patient toward an exam room.

"Ooh!" Gemma crowed. "Someone's in trouble!"

Cheeks burning, Lina pulled the sticky note off her computer and held it in her lap.

Eight p.m.—Uncle Sam's in Borough Market

Warm swirls of anticipation began to fog her mind. "What were you doing anyway?"

Lina started and stared at Gemma.

Apart from staring at Cole and wishing I was kissing him?

"Nothing."

"Yeah. And I'm a talking tiger. C'mon, Lina, I've seen the looks you two have been exchanging. Someone looks like they've got a crush on the boss!"

Heat crawled up from Lina's neck onto her cheeks as Gemma's singsong teasing rang through Reception. Had she been that obvious?

"Not that I blame you," Gemma continued, oblivious to her mortification. "Cole's hot. No getting away from that. If you're the one who can crack that veneer of charm and get to the amazing guy we all think is underneath there, more power to you!"

"I don't think—"

"Lina." Gemma leaned on the reception counter and gave her a studied look. "There is nothing wrong with fancying someone. I'm just saying be realistic. The guy is…" Gemma paused, choosing her words carefully.

What? What is the guy? Gorgeous? Charming? Kinder than anyone she'd ever met before?

Out of her league?

"The guy seems to be a keeper. In my book anyway," she qualified.

"Have you dated him?"

"Oh, blimey—no way. Not my type."

Lina couldn't stop her eyes from widening. As far as she was concerned, Cole was like a Hollywood star— someone with a mass appeal factor.

Gemma laughed good-naturedly. "For my sins, I love me a bit of Viking. Shaggy blond hair, blue eyes, big huge arms that look like they could wield a sword or throw a log at marauding somebody-or-others…"

Her gaze drifted off into the middle distance for a moment, clearly besotted with an invisible Viking in their midst before shaking herself back into action. She grinned then paused. "What was it you were trying to pass off as my work anyway?"

Lina gave a quick scan of the corridors leading to the exam rooms. No sign of Cole.

"It's nothing really, I was just looking at some jobs."

"What? You've not even been here three months yet. Are you not enjoying it?"

"No, no. It's nothing like that. It's just—"

"Just that you're a dancer who can't dance anymore and you're trying to find your place in the world?"

Lina's jaw dropped. Few people were that blunt with her. "Uh—something like that. Yes."

"Look. I was in the same shoes as you a few years ago. Remember your first day? You've got a much better chair, though! It took a lot of work and a lot of soul-searching, but when I kept finding myself following the patients into the physical therapy rooms to set them up for their appointments and then not leaving…well…" She gave a happy shrug. "I guess I found my place! If you've found something like that, go for it!"

"I don't think it's as easy as that."

"Nonsense. Nothing is harder than becoming a professional ballerina and you've already ticked that off your list. Tick!" Gemma made a huge mark in the air with a flourish of her hand. "I'm going to take a wild stab in the dark and imagine you've got self-discipline in spades. I took all the energy I used to pour into rehearsals into my training. I have zero doubt you can do the same. *Zero*," she added for good measure. "What you did at the ballet was amazing. How many dancers get to be a prima ballerina? And you've got to move on at some point, right?"

Lina managed a half shrug. Maybe? Yes? Could she really ever let it go?

Gemma's finger did a quick rat-a-tat-tat on the counter. "The fact that you're even here proves you've done the hard bit in moving on."

Lina's forehead went into crinkle mode. "What do you mean?"

"In comparison to the life of a dancer, *everything* is easy…" Gemma headed toward the staff room, then turned to give Lina a mischievous wink and giggle. "As easy as falling in love!"

Color flooded Lina's cheeks again as Gemma giggled her way out of Reception. Was it that easy? Just letting go of the years and years of intense rehearsals and classes and sacrifice? Heaven knew the release she felt when she'd wept in Cole's arms all those weeks ago had felt like mourning of sorts. As if she'd been saying goodbye. And now here she was, looking for a job she never would have dreamed of doing before. Maybe it was all just part of her journey through life, a bit less "one direction" than she'd thought but…

She looked down at the note she was still clutching in her lap and smiled.

There was hope there—and possibility. All she had to do was believe in herself. Believe if she set her mind to it she could get a job as a medical interpreter. Believe that Cole was asking her out on a real, honest-to-goodness date. Not out of pity but because she was worth it. Even if it was just for a night. Her fingers drummed along the phone console. A sudden urge to call her parents took hold of her. She tapped out the numbers before she could talk herself out of it. The ringtone sounded and she struggled against a gut instinct to hang up again, as she'd done so many times before. She could do this. Her parents had loved her before she'd been a ballerina, and now she had news—lots of it. She worked at an amazing clinic, she'd helped a woman she'd met at the Polish Centre and despite her very best intentions she was falling head over heels—

"*Słucham.*"

Lina couldn't stop the tears springing to her eyes at the sound of her mother's voice. It had been too long.

"*Mamo, to ja.* It's me, Mama." The words washed through her again and again as her mother laughed with sheer delight, then whooped and shouted for Lina's father to pick up the other line.

For the first time in years Lina believed her own words were finally true. *It's me. Lina.* Not Lina the dancer, the receptionist, the dog walker, the failure. She was none of those things and all of them at once and there was one man who had been key to helping her get to this point. She traced the words on Cole's note as she chatted with her parents. Would she be enough to meet his expectations whatever they might be?

From the happiness in her parents' voices, perhaps she could begin to believe "just Lina" was enough for them. And maybe, one day, they'd even have Lina the translator! The thought of how much lay ahead of her was simultaneously thrilling and daunting.

What did Cole expect or want from her? "Just Lina?" With the scars, the feet that would never look great in sandals, the steep, steep learning curve she still had to climb in life? Would she be enough?

She hoped so. With every pore in her body she hoped so.

CHAPTER SEVEN

"WHERE'S IGOR?"

"I thought he looked a bit tired—it's just me, I'm afraid."

"Oh."

Cole replayed the opening moments of their "date, not date" on a loop as he watched Lina disappear into the ladies' room. Talk about an unmitigated disaster. This was worse than he could've imagined. A cotillion filled to the brim with women of his mother's choosing would have been better than this! Seriously better. And that was saying a lot.

Lina's expression had been unreadable when he'd broken the news he was there on his own. Just a neutral expression, eyes refusing to make contact with his, the menu providing the only distraction.

Just dandy! She'd shown up to see the dog. And there was him thinking she'd agreed because she'd wanted to go out with him. Have "grown-up time" away from the dog, the clinic. This was the first date in years he'd gone out with expectation, with hope. And it was gnawing him apart. He began to rearrange all the condiments on the table to occupy his jangling nerves.

He'd never cared before what the women he'd gone out with had thought of him because he'd known he'd never tell them. Never let them know the real Cole. The guy who'd tried to please his parents by marrying the right girl and having it go about as wrong as it possible could. But Lina deserved more. Deserved to know the truth. But the truth would most likely destroy what had been growing between them, the growing flirtation… No. It was more than that. More than a flirtation. He had feelings for Lina, but with that came respect. Honesty.

Ha! Showed him. She'd probably agreed to come out tonight because he was the boss. He'd kept her late at work countless times before… For the love of Pete! Had he really misread the "ice-cream overtimes'" as romantic rather than what they most likely had been: plain old politeness? Years of practice at his parents' country club had obviously dulled his people-reading skills. Then again, he'd just presumed everyone there had been faking perfect lives. It's what everyone did. Right?

He looked up to the ceiling and offered it a silent howl. He should've just bailed there and then. *Why had he left the dog at home?*

"Could I please have some more water?" Cole signaled to the waiter. He'd already had several refills, but the glasses here were so dinky. Or were they? Was it more the case that he was feeling like the world's largest oaf and everything was out of perspective? He tried to size up his water glass. Properly. Objectively. Like he normally sized things up. Scientifically.

Hmm. Okay, *fine*. It wasn't really that small.

He was nervous, all right? He hadn't been out on a proper date in who knew how long. Not that this was a date. Lina had clearly met up with him to see Igor. Igor, the blameless, adorable, lovable puppy.

Talk about showing up with your heart on your sleeve.

Maybe his parents had been right. He'd never learn to truly play his cards close to his chest.

He folded and refolded the napkin, glancing toward the ladies' room as if she'd swoop right back out of it, all smiles and adoration.

He struck what he hoped looked like a relaxed position. He'd been tense all evening. As had she. He readjusted his pose. It wasn't as though he'd never been out with other women before—obviously! But usually it was a group thing, or— *Nah. Nope. C'mon, man! Quit with the excuses.* The truth was he was falling for Lina hook, line and sinker, and this so-called date was a first-class disaster. It wasn't going to work when he told her what she was getting into, who she was really with. A rudderless, banished doctor who had single-handedly torn the heart out of his hometown.

He scowled at the largely untouched plates.

Blackened catfish and cornbread weren't Lina's things. Not that she'd said as much—she was too kind for outright criticism—but the food on her plate hadn't been eaten, just rearranged, and as for the conversation? It had hardly been sparkling. He should've backed off and headed for the hills after the hush-puppy starters.

Maybe he should just be honest. Tell her everything. The first day they'd met his intentions had not been altogether altruistic. Madame Tibold had caught him at a weak moment. He had just been lumbered with a puppy, lost his receptionist and everything had just seemed to fall into place to give a girl down in the dumps a helping hand, which, in turn, would help a guy who was down in the dumps.

And then she had turned out to be…Lina.

It was hard to even think her name without superimposing it onto his psyche in huge glowing letters. He hadn't meant to fall for her. Seriously. He hadn't. Not now when so much was still up in the air in his own life. He let his head fall into his hands.

What would she think when she found out he'd pulled the plug on his own fiancée? They'd only just become engaged. The only saving grace was that no one knew his feelings for Katie hadn't been as strong as hers had been for him.

Not that it mattered in the long run. After her parents, his parents, and the community had effectively written him off he'd survived by convincing himself he didn't care what anyone else thought. But this time he cared what happened. Really, really cared. And it scared the daylights out of him. He wanted—no, he needed—Lina to know what she was getting into and the idea that the truth could send her running—

"Was I gone so long that you fell asleep?"

"What? No—not at all!" Cole half rose from his bench seat as Lina rejoined him in the booth.

"Sorry."

"Sorry." They spoke simultaneously, laughed, looked away and then looked back, eyes caught with each other's, and— *Ah!* There it was again. That electric connection he had convinced himself he'd fabricated. There was nothing imaginary about it now. It sizzled between them, alive with expectation. The only question that remained was what to do with it.

"Do you want to get out of here?"

"Yes."

Thank you, Eastern European directness. Lina rarely minced words and he liked that.

He signaled to the waiter for the check.

"Shall I take you home?"

He knew the words were in total opposition to what he wanted, but this was up to Lina…choosing him.

She shook her head. The movement was so small at first he thought he'd imagined it. When he saw her lips begin to curl up into a smile, a hint of pink warming up her cheeks, Cole felt a surge of energy charge through him—something more powerful than he'd ever felt before. He wanted Lina. Had done from the moment he'd laid eyes on her. She deserved to know the truth about him. How and when he would tell her about the real Cole was yet to be decided—but he would tell her. Right now? Something more primal was at work. Something he couldn't ignore.

Cole quickly paid the bill and was up, helping Lina into her jacket, before either of them had a chance to re-consider. Was that a shiver of anticipation he detected in her? He slipped a protective arm across her shoulders. He would be careful with her. Gentle. Loving. He may have a past, but so did everyone—and not all of it was bad. Tonight it would just be the two of them, present in the here and now.

Just a guy on a date with a girl.

Lina could hardly keep a single thought straight as she and Cole made their way through the twists and turns that made up Borough Market until they reached the Thames. She'd been so nervous the entire date she was sure the only thing on Cole's mind had been how to get rid of her. Had their stilted conversation simply been because he was feeling the same way—jittery with anticipation? Riddled with nerves that they would be enough?

When they emerged on the broad esplanade they stopped for a moment as if neither of them had ever seen London before.

The riverside view was absolutely beautiful. Everything seemed crisper tonight. More…*real.* The air positively hummed with life. Tower Bridge, all lit up, fountains awash with light, street food vendors hawking delectables from every corner of the globe, and couples, just like them, strolling along the riverside, taking photos, holding hands…kissing. It was then that Lina realized she'd been tracing her lips with her fingers, first one then two taking a leisurely, slow slide across her lips.

Lina wondered if any of the other women felt the heated intensity of anticipation warming them from the inside out. They all looked so confident—so relaxed!

Did any of them feel the slightest teasing of fear—like she did—that she wouldn't be enough? That once Cole was with her, really saw her—the scars, the lack of experience, the long road of recovery she still had to traverse—would the disappointment in losing him be worth just one starlit night of kisses? Had that vital moment of connection they'd had in the restaurant been as real for Cole as it had been for her?

Insecurity threatened to overwhelm everything good about this moment—the "right nowness" being with Cole always seemed to elicit.

It would be so easy to just run away. Run back into her flat and curl into her well-worn nook of the beaten-up sofa, hiding away from the world, her fears. Easier to live with her own personal disillusionment than adding Cole's disappointment in her to the pile. But maybe…could they just have this one night? One night to see if what kept setting her body alight with desire was real?

She looked up at him and received a warm smile in return, a little squeeze on her shoulder and a nod out toward the river where a boat was going past, the deck filled with well-dressed revelers toasting a bride and groom.

Wait a minute. Was Cole showing her his intentions? No. That would be madness. Then again…

Running back to the flat suddenly didn't seem such a great idea after all. What was it her grandmother had always said to her when she'd dropped her off at her dance lessons as a little girl?

Serce nie kłamie. The heart sees further than the head.

The saying didn't extend to include a forecast as to how accurate the heart's vision was, but who cared? The very atmosphere of the spring evening was magical and, as if the Queen herself had just announced a decree, Lina knew it was time she stopped letting niggling doubts destroy the mood. She let herself snuggle a bit closer under the comforting weight of Cole's arm, peeped up at him and smiled. How could she not? She was a different person from the one he'd coerced out into the world.

Imagine that! A different person in just under three months. Or maybe she was simply allowing herself to become the woman she'd been all along?

"C'mere, I want to show you something." Cole slipped his arm off her shoulders, his fingers wrapping through hers with a little tug to run up the steps of Tower Bridge with him.

She pushed any reactions to the twinges she was feeling in her hip to the side. No pain, no gain—right? And just about everything that had led to this night was gain.

Her focus was so complete on matching his stride, feeling her fingers woven through his, the smile that might never leave her lips, she'd hardly noticed they had arrived at the center of the iconic bridge, festooned with lights and offering one of London's loveliest river views. Cole turned her toward the view and stood behind her, his hands shifting along her elbows until he'd folded his arms and hers into a cozy twist of limbs and hands. His and hers. She closed her eyes against the view for a moment and just let herself be completely and wholly absorbed by the sensations coming to her. She let her weight shift back into her heels so that her back met his chest—his body met hers.

For the first time in months she felt *feminine*. As each moment luxuriously unfolded, Lina became more and more aware of her own body in relation—in connection—to Cole's. Her back touching his chest elicited a warming in her breasts, a tightening she could feel against the lace of her bra. His arms, wrapped loosely around her, just grazed the sides of them and she nearly moaned with anticipation of more. The crowds around them seemed to thin—or perhaps it was just the awareness of Cole that made everything else fade to a luxurious blur... She tipped her head to the side, her cheek rubbing against the linen of his jacket, the scent of him making the world more complete. As if it were a dance they'd rehearsed in another time and place and had come back to as a longed-for memory, she slipped her hand out of the weave of arms and hands and softly, slowly caressed the side of his face as he lowered his lips to kiss her cheek.

Lina's body came alive in a way she had only ever felt onstage, but better. Nothing in the world mattered now but Cole. His touches, his caresses. Who was she kidding? All of it! Being in his arms, smelling him, feeling her fingers pressing into his arms, his lips moving along her cheek to her jawline, each microsecond was the fulfillment of a dream she'd hardly let herself believe could come true.

As if by design she turned and was instantly caught up in a tight embrace, their lips meeting in a searing synchronicity of movement, touch and exploration. How could something be so sweet and suggestive at the same time? A silent giggle tickled through her midriff when she realized she was actually weak-kneed. Thankfulness for the strength in Cole's arms flooded her as he held her close.

Kissing Cole, touching him, being held—upright!—by him felt like precious discoveries. A whole new world of hidden treasures. Joyful treasures she would let herself enjoy for tonight. She opened a far-off hidden door in the recesses of her mind and pushed and shoved all her insecurities inside and locked them away. Hadn't they earned a night together without her past weighing her down?

As Cole's kisses deepened, she felt the warmth in her heart begin to billow and flood her entire bloodstream. Through some unspoken message only their bodies knew, they simultaneously broke away from the slow, exploratory kisses—the feeling and intentions too intimate to carry on anymore in public.

Forehead to forehead, their breath intermingled as Lina traced her fingertips along the sides of Cole's face, delighting in the topography of his cheekbones, the spackle of shadow bringing further definition to his jawline, that sexy little gap between his teeth visible now that her finger had traced his lips into a smile. She chanced a look into his eyes and was relieved to see the same swirl of questions and answers, all of them bearing the bright sheen of expectation.

The silence that shrouded them as Cole took her hand and waved for a taxi was unsurprisingly taut with anticipation. The only words spoken on the short journey to his place was the address, as if saying anything more would break the spell.

Cole didn't trust himself to speak. The only words he could think of were meant for Lina's ears only—not those of the taxi driver, who appeared to be disappointed no chitchat was forthcoming. He had to smile. What a change to have some good news to share with someone in lieu of the usual exchanges over disappointing weather or snarled traffic. He pulled Lina in closer to him, pressing a light kiss onto her forehead as her hand slipped onto his thigh. He put his hand over hers and held it in place, far too aware of how his body would react if she were to shift her fingers toward the inner length of his leg. He was already feeling heated pulses of response below his belt, his tapping foot a sign of his growing need to be inside his house, the door closed solidly behind them so that they could explore this entirely new world they were creating. A Lina-and-Cole-centered world where even the lightest of kisses elicited volcanic surges of response.

The taxi driver was paid, and Cole held the front door open for Lina, hoping he would be distraction enough from his haphazard stab at decorating. Her eyes widened with delight as she dropped to her knees. *Interesting.* He didn't think the new wallpaper was that amazing.

"Igor!"

Ah. Of course.

Rather than let "puppy time" break the mood, Cole leaned against the corridor wall and smiled at the pair's happy reunion. It struck him how they'd both come into his life on the same day—each having an unexpected impact. A good one. Having the two of them in his house—everyone just enjoying *being*—made the place feel more like a home than it ever had.

"What do you say I pour us a glass of wine and we can take Igor out to the garden for a little run round?"

Lina's eyes shone with happiness as she pressed herself up from the floor. "You have a garden?"

He was on the brink of saying "of course," before remembering she only had a tiny flat and a dramatically different income. Another reminder to be more aware of all he *did* have in his life rather than what he didn't. Fo-

cusing on the empty holes in his life had been a bit of a
forte these past few years. Maybe it was time to start letting all of that go. What he had—right here and now—
was very good.

"Wow! It's beautiful." Lina's whispered response to
the sight of his garden brought Cole an unexpected swell
of pride. It certainly wasn't any near as big as the garden he'd had back in Carolina, but for London it was a
good size. Buckling down to pay off his medical-school
bills straight away had made this possible. A slate patio
stretched out from the back of the house, the handful of
pots he'd managed to fill earlier in the spring now coming to life with young flowers. A small lawn spread out
beyond the patio steps, easy enough to mow in five minutes, big enough to play catch with his pooch. A handful
of fruit trees ringed the garden. The former tenant had left
him some of the previous year's apple crop. On a particularly homesick day, he'd fixed a variation on his grandmother's apple cobbler—a bachelor's variation—and had
eaten the whole thing in lieu of supper.

Igor romped out onto the grass, throwing Cole a look,
and it was difficult not to interpret as one of gratitude.
The pup hadn't been a huge help in getting the garden up
to scratch, but his arrival had compelled Cole to work on
it a bit more. Invest some time and energy on filling the
empty flower pots, mulching the trees for the first time
since he'd arrived a year earlier.

He stood at the kitchen window, opening the bottle
of wine as he watched the pair of them. Funny how everything he'd wanted to rid himself of—attachments,
responsibilities—now held the promise of possibility.
Of family. He didn't want to be Lina's boss tonight. He
wanted more. Much more than might be possible, but
watching the two of them—Igor receiving a huge cuddle

before Lina pushed herself back up to enjoy the garden again—he was going to let himself believe for tonight. Believe in possibility.

Igor embarked on an exploratory trip, weaving in and out of the bushes and shrubs lining the garden fence, Cole and Lina no longer of interest to him. He had the neighbor's cat to sniff out, and city foxes to guard against. Cole set the glasses of wine on the patio table, not the least bit interested in whether it was a premium vintage or some mass-market plonk. He pulled Lina into his arms, keen to pick up where they'd pulled themselves to an unwelcome halt on the bridge.

Using a single finger, he swept first one then another thick coil of her honey-red hair behind her shoulders. Now that she was in his arms again, time was no longer a factor. The only thing he would make sure of was that he made the absolute best use of it.

Lina's breath caught in her throat as Cole's index finger skimmed along her hairline. She felt her head tip and move in harmony with his movements, her eyes completely engaged in absorbing each detail of his face as if trying to imprint it on her mind's eye.

He was so beautiful. Not a word she'd usually use for someone as divinely male as Cole was—but there simply wasn't a better word to describe him. Just his cornflower-blue eyes alone were enough to enchant a woman. She'd certainly fallen under their spell. She blinked, reopening her eyes in time to see him slowly lowering his face toward hers, lips parted in anticipation of meeting her own. The surge of emotion she felt joined forces with an overwhelming rush of physical desire. Before she could let another thought enter her head she was tasting him, kissing him, hands on his chest, then around his shoulders as she felt his hands shift from her waist up along her spine, before lightly tracing along the nape of her neck. The urge to become as one with him threatened to engulf her and for the briefest of moments she went completely still. Once she unleashed her full desire for him, she would no longer be able to hide anything from Cole. She loved him and after this? She would be his entirely.

What, for the smallest moment, seemed terrifying, shifted into the most natural decision she had ever made. Cole's every kiss spoke of an identical yearning. As their kisses deepened, Lina gave in to her body's need for him. Thoughts barely took shape as her hands continued their restless exploration of Cole's body. Her fingers slipped through gaps in his shirt. Buttons came undone, breath came more heavily. Her clothes—summer thin—suddenly felt too great a barrier between them.

"Be with me," Cole whispered in her ear, hand at the small of her back as she turned toward the patio doors, fairly certain she'd do just about anything for or with him if it was whispered in that soft Southern accent of his. Her eyes instinctively shot to the garden.

"Igor's fine," he added, reading her mind. How she even had a thought for the dog was beyond her as Cole's touch took over any common sense she might have left. They ran, tripped, crawled and laughed their way up the carpeted stairs, making it only as far as the landing where Cole slowly, luxuriously pinned her to the floor, his movements as graceful as a mountain lion's, his intentions as powerful. Her hands already pressed into the carpet, Lina moaned as her hips were pressed to the floor beneath Cole's, the slow sway and pressure of his movements sending shock waves of heat to her very core. She closed her eyes as her body arched into his, his fingers teasing away the buttons of her blouse. A whimper slipped between her lips as Cole shifted the fabric away from first her rib cage, then her breasts. His fingers traced along the lace of her bra, her small breasts pressing toward his hands as they glanced across her nipples. She hadn't known the ache of desire to ever feel as all-consuming as it did now.

"Please," she all but pleaded with him. "Please, let me be yours."

Time passed in a heated blur as clothes were dispensed of and skin finally touched skin. Their intentions united, Lina completely gave in to her longing for him.

Legs tangled together, fingers sought purchase, their lips met again and again to kiss deeply, urgently, as though this were both the first and last time they would ever be together. It was a thought she couldn't bear and as quickly as it had come into her mind she banished it, taking on instead the waves of desire she was experiencing as Cole rested the entire length of his unclothed body atop hers, taking most of his weight in his powerful arms and shoulders. She couldn't help but think it was as if she had been made for this very moment. The very pressure of him unlocked an even deeper hunger for more. She could hardly bear not having him inside her. Only then, when their bodies would move as one, when they shifted and pressed and cried out together, would she feel anything nearing satisfaction. Cole rolled them both over, swiftly lifting Lina up.

In a handful of steps they were in his bedroom, a ragged moan of need filling the room as he laid her on his bed, intensely aware that Lina was virtually aching with anticipation.

"Are you sure?" Cole asked, already raking through his bedside table drawer for protection. He knew this was a game-changer. It would shift their relationship forever and for the first time in years he knew he had to take that risk.

Nodding was all she was capable of. Lina wanted Cole

more than anything on earth. It surprised her to realize the thought didn't frighten her. Being with him wasn't playing on her insecurities the way she had thought it might. His hands on her body, his lips exploring and tasting her only made her feel stronger, more capable. More *real*.

Cole joined her on the bed, his caresses shifting from slow to urgent in sync with her response to his touch. When his lips touched first one nipple, then the other, Lina barely held back the cries of pleasure lying in constant wait in her throat. His fingers sought her hip bones, gently shifting along the soft curves and dips leading to her belly. As his hand slipped between her legs she was no longer able to stay silent.

"Now! Please, now!" She didn't care if it sounded like begging. Having Cole inside her was the only thing Lina wanted, the only thing that would satiate the longing she felt for him—and with a torturously slow descent he met her needs. Their movements took on the urgent syncopation of primal desire. Their bodies moved in union, each of them realizing the all-consuming ecstasy of the other's touch.

When at last their breathing slowed and steadied, Cole untangled himself, only to pull Lina securely into his arms, a finger occasionally swooping along the dip toward her waist, then along her hip before his hand came to a rest.

Lina felt sleep coming, as it was for Cole. His breathing slowed then deepened, playing softly upon the nape of her neck, and just as her eyes were about to close for the final time that night she first heard then saw a little canine figure standing in the doorway, tail wagging in a final confirmation that all was well that night in London, and—for now at least—nothing else mattered other than the simple fact that they were all together.

CHAPTER EIGHT

SUNLIGHT WAS THE first thing Cole was aware of. It played across his face with the gentle undulations of the curtain. He fuzzily remembered leaving the window open the night before. He pushed his feet into the beginnings of a full-bodied stretch— *The night before!* When Lina and he had— His hand moved to the other side of the bed. She wasn't there. Cole's eyes snapped open, his whole body on high alert.

Where was Lina?

He scanned the room as if it would offer him some answers, ear tipping upward so any auditory clues could more easily slip in. No Lina and no puppy. The house sounded deserted. Ah—maybe she'd taken Igor out for a morning walk.

"Lina?"

His call met with no response.

He was up and out of bed in an instant. Tugging on a T-shirt and a pair of boxers, he skidded down the stairs to the kitchen. A tour of the garden revealed nothing. A buzz started in his ears. Thoughts clashed against each other, drowning out logic. He'd made a mistake by bringing her here. Had he misread the situation? Had taking away the invisible boss-employee barrier pushed her away? Had she somehow found out about his past?

A little tap at the door made him come to. Impatiently, he pulled it open. Where on earth was—

"Lina!" A wash of guilty relief flooded him. His secret was safe, but the door to his heart, he now knew, was well and truly open to exposure.

"Sorry, sorry." She held up a paper sack from a nearby bakery, Igor's lead complete with dog in the other hand. "I was going to surprise you and then surprised myself by remembering that neither of us have keys."

"C'mere, you." Cole took the bag and Igor's lead off her hands, his main goal to pull her into his arms. Close. Too close. "I thought you'd gone and left me, too."

"Too?" Lina looked up at him, green eyes gone wide with curiosity.

"Oh, man." Cole gave Lina a kiss on the forehead, released her and scratched a hand across his head, buying himself time to answer. "I just… It's a long story and one I don't want to ruin our day with."

Lina wasn't so lovestruck she was willing to play the fool. Cole's distress had been plain as day. "So I'm free to blub like a baby in front of you, but you have to be Mr. Big Man and keep all the secrets of your life in your big head?"

Despite himself, Cole laughed, tipping his head toward the kitchen. "Is that one of your wise Polish sayings?"

"No." Lina laughed along, because she couldn't help it. Cole always unleashed the giggler in her. But he had stoked the fires of her curiosity. He had looked absolutely stricken when he'd opened the door.

Who else had left him? Whoever it was had made a big impact on his life.

"It's not exactly as if you've told me your life story, either, is it, Lina?" She heard the words coming from behind her and was relieved he couldn't see her face. He'd just served up a big, juicy touché.

Tell him absolutely everything?

She might be better, but being that open with someone wasn't how you survived. Was it time for a change?

"Hey." She swiveled, hands on hips and gave him a cheeky grin. "I don't suppose you have any *polski kawi*?"

The emotion-thick air relaxed a bit. They'd both dodged the truth bullet. For now.

"You want good coffee?" Cole accepted the challenge. "I will make you some good coffee! It might not be Polish but—just you wait!"

"Oh, yeah?" Lina looked dubious, even though she could already tell it would be great. From everything she'd seen, Cole didn't do so-so on anything. He poured his whole heart into things. She widened her eyes as he grinned at her. Would his whole heart be with her?

"Go put the kettle on and let the master work."

Hmm...hard to tell from that one.

"Wait, no." He laid a hand on her arm to stop her in mid-kettle-approach. "I have a better idea." He gave her a wink. The kind that sent her stomach on a whirly run of flashy-blinky carnival lights.

She pulled out a chair from the kitchen table and, after a whimper or two from Igor, relented to a cuddle on her lap. Not that it was a hardship. Cutest puppy in the world in the kitchen with the cutest guy in the world? This was a day she'd just have to enjoy. Put a lock on the door of the room of insecurities and just enjoy.

"I hope whatever you've got in that bag has the stamina to stand up to my coffee magic." Cole spoke over his shoulder, cupboard doors opening and closing with such speed she wondered if he was planning on making a four-course meal along with it.

"It's from the *boulangerie* down the road. You know— Chez Robert?"

"Ah! Very good! Pastries, I hope? You didn't go down the health-food route?"

"I don't really think the *boulangerie* is famed for its lettuce-leaf croissant."

Lina's droll tone brought a smile to Cole's lips. He didn't even need to see her face to know it would be one of raised eyebrows and rosy-red lips pressed forward in... not a pout exactly. What was it she did with those lips of hers? It was great, whatever it was.

"Fair enough."

"Chocolate, almond and plain croissants. Two of each. You must have done something to me overnight. I only had eyes for carbs." Cole's grin deepened as he spooned richly scented coffee grounds into the small sieve of his Italian coffee pot and deftly screwed the top into place, gas burner already on high. Must be nice for her, he thought, to be able to let go of the strict diet of an athlete, be-cause that's what the dancers were—incredibly fine-tuned athletes—and splurge on some buttery carbs.

Pulling a bottle of water from the refrigerator, Cole grabbed two glasses and turned his full attention to Lina. He'd been a bit jangly since she'd been back and needed to stop, just for a moment, and *be* with her.

"Just in case you also need to rehydrate." He handed her a full glass of water, condensation already damping up the sides of the glass.

Lina didn't say anything, but a light flush of color appeared on her cheeks. She took a sip, traced a squiggle or two along the edge of the glass, absorbed in her own thoughts.

"What do you say you be a tour guide today?"

"Tour guide?" Lina's green eyes met his, forehead crinkled.

"Yeah. I've lived in London over a year now and I still haven't seen most of the sights. Big Ben, the crown jewels, changing of the guard. Maybe you could show me around and we'll have a picnic in the park with Igor after. What do you think?"

"Oh, I'm afraid you've asked the wrong girl." She moved her toe in little arcs from parquet square to parquet square.

"Why's that? You've lived here for years!"

"Yes, but—" She stopped, lower teeth taking ahold of her upper lip, her concentration focused on tweaking the fur on Igor's forehead into a just-so quiff.

"What? You haven't been locked in a closet the whole time you've been here, have you?"

"No, but I was locked in a rehearsal room." She wished she hadn't sounded so defensive. But there it was. She'd said it. So much for the Cole-and-Lina bubble of perfection. She let her lip scrape out past her teeth. He might as well know what he was getting into—at least a little. Before the accident, before Cole, she hadn't had much of a life—any life—outside the ballet. He had done and seen so much more than she had and beyond the world of dance she was well out of her depth.

The high-pitched screech of the coffeepot gave them both a start. Her shoulders lowered, relieved Cole's attention wasn't solidly on her, watching the tendrils of the past trying to take hold of her, pull her out of the lovely, lovely place she was in when she was with him.

On a bare-bones level, her salary had never run to those

things. Jewels and palaces were for moneyed tourists or comfortably-off doctors. Not scrimping and scraping ballerinas who would be better off fine-tuning arabesques. Cole wasn't naive but he certainly didn't have a clue about her reality.

Her *passport* knew more of the world than she did. Paris, London, Sydney, New York? Rehearsal rooms were the same everywhere. Some a little warmer, some a little colder—it didn't matter as long as they were constantly perfecting, constantly sloughing away any of the rough edges, constantly on point. *En pointe.* Something she'd never be again and, no matter how hard she tried, it felt as though it would always hurt.

"Here you go. This should bring you back to the land of the living." Cole slid a mug of deliciously scented coffee and milk across the table toward her.

Lina shot him a sheepish smile of thanks, grateful he couldn't see the temper tantrum she'd been having in her head. She still wasn't there yet, in the place where she could let everything go, but for this moment, this day she would try.

"What do you say we both take in the sights of London, then? Let someone else do the work?"

"My paycheck might not stretch that far." She winced as the words came out. She hadn't meant them to be accusatory.

"I know." Cole took her words in stride. "I hear your boss is a tight-ass. What do you say you let me treat you? Me. The man you were naked with all of last night." His lips turned into a naughty smile as his eyebrows performed a hopeful set of press-ups. "Just a couple of tourists out in the big city? Wouldn't it be fun?"

She knew her smile was saying yes, but…but nothing! *Just say yes!*

"What do you have in mind?"

"Ever been on the red-bus tour?"

The sounds filtered in and out of reach. Cole pressed his ear to the wall again, where the guide had assured him he'd hear Lina standing on the other side of St Paul's whispering gallery. He thought he'd heard her, but there were so many other voices, whispering sweet nothings— *Hello... Hello-o... Hello-o-o-o-o-o*—all weaving through the beautiful tones of evensong rising from the church's choir below.

Had they been alone, Cole knew exactly what he would whisper. Hell! He knew what he would shout! *You're the most amazing woman I know, Lina Keminsky. Let's do this thing—whatever it is.* But they were words he couldn't trust himself to say despite the morning's near-confessional. He was wrong to have moved their relationship—such as it was—to this level, but his gut was working overtime on overriding his head and, last night, it had won. Every bit of him *wanted* to be with Lina. The only trouble was he just couldn't. Not for her sake. Not if he really wanted her to find true happiness.

"Are you hungry?"

The words came loud and clear in the voice he would recognize at one hundred paces. The dome echoed with his responding laugh.

"Always."

There was a pause as their eyes caught—some forty meters apart—but the effect was as strong as if she were next to him. Closer. Being held in his arms.

Cole could still hear an intermingling of voices and messages coming from across the gallery they'd tromped up over two hundred steps to reach. He noticed Lina occasionally stopping to rub her hip, but there was no evidence of a limp and, from where he stood, there on the opposite side of the dome, she looked nothing short of heaven-sent. Rays of sunlight filtered through the iconic dome, turning her hair from gold to flax to flames and back again. They'd popped by her flat after breakfast so she could change, and the simple sage-green wraparound dress she'd chosen... *Ay, caramba!* Any man would've struggled to keep his sanity. The sooner he could get her alone and start to tease away the fabric... Whispering at long distance didn't cut it anymore.

Eyes locked with hers, Cole quickly left the throng of tourists between them in his wake. The sooner he was holding her the better. No words were exchanged when he reached her. Just an understanding. Cole folded his arms around her, tourist map dangling from one hand, the other shifting along the small of her back. He felt her hands join together in a loose clasp around his waist and he all but sighed with gratitude when she let her cheek rest on his chest. They stood like that, just listening—the whispers, the music, the hushed footfalls wending their way around them. With Lina in his arms, Cole felt the world become complete again and it scared him.

What could he offer her? More running? Incomplete answers whenever she wanted to know about his past? None of it sat right and he knew he was going to have to be honest. He'd tell her everything. He would. And if she left? Well, it wouldn't be the first time.

He ran his thumb along her arm and felt a spray of goose pimples form despite the early summer warmth. He tipped up her chin and when their lips met?

Perfection.

No awkward bumping of noses, mismatched cadences or ill-judged approaches. Just one of those slow, beautiful, film kisses where—at the very end—each pair of lips is reluctant to part from the other. He wanted more. So much more. In the interest of keeping a very tenuous grip, Cole gave her a light kiss on her freckly forehead, and felt her head come to a rest on his chest again. And that was good, too.

For today? Today they were just Lina and Cole—two wide-eyed tourists in London Town. He grinned as his chin nestled among Lina's billow of hair. If only his main attraction wasn't the one he held in his arms, playing the role of tourist would be much easier.

"Do you want to get out of here?"

"Yes."

Thank you, Lina!

"This is much better, isn't it?"

"Only about a thousand million times!" Lina's eyes twinkled, her attention divided between a short-range game of catch with Igor and long, luxurious kisses with Cole as he plumbed his memory banks for the best way to start a barbecue. Each time he pulled Lina in for another proper make-out session he sent out a silent thank-you to the previous owners, who had put up high fences. Perhaps theirs had been a fledgling romance, as well.

"Not that a day of culture isn't worth its weight in gold."

"We've already had a day of my culture," Lina riposted as she sent the multicolored ball rolling across the lawn. "Now we will have a day of yours." She checked herself as Cole's expression was an instant reminder of their disaster at the American restaurant the night before. A disaster that had turned into something a little closer to heavenly. "*Another* day of yours." She waved at the glut of groceries they'd hauled home. Turned out kissing and shopping made for an incongruous set of ingredients.

"I wouldn't say this was anything my mother would've whipped up but—"

Lina crossed to him, a glass of wine outstretched in her hand.

"What would your mother have made for her little boy?" Her face was wreathed in smiles, her tone cajoling, warm…and it took everything in his power to hide the flinch that usually accompanied mention of his mother. He turned to the shiny, unused barbecue and shook in a few more briquettes. Sure, it looked like an Everest of coals but heat was important—right?

"What's wrong?"

"Nothing, I was just distracted."

"Didn't your mother cook for you?" Her tone was still light but he could hear a new twist of concern woven through it.

"Yes, of course she did!" *Oh, for the love of some sanity!* He hated the sound of his artificial happy voice. "Go on. You tell me yours and I'll tell you mine." He raised his glass for a quick chink and a peck in return for one of her full-beam smiles.

"Moja matka…" She drew the words out so slowly he could almost see the images of her childhood table flash before her eyes. "My mother was—*is*," she corrected herself, "a very good cook."

"And what did you eat when you were a little girl?"

"Ah. Well. As a little girl I was not even a tiny bit fussy. *Borscht*, buttery noodles, *gołąbki*—they are cabbage rolls with pork or mutton—vegetables, always. I would eat everything." She tipped her head back and laughed at a private memory. "You would always find me waiting at the table, fork and knife in hand, before my father had even arrived home from work—but I learned to wait very, very quietly."

"Why?"

Lina settled into one of the wooden chairs with the demeanor of an old woman, her voice mimicking the same. It was easy to see the performer in her. "'*Głodne brzuchy nie mają uszu,*' my grandmother would say again and again. 'Hungry bellies have no ears.' Of course she was talking about the leaner days when there was no food, during the Wars and lean days—these ears couldn't hear there wasn't any food. In my case, though, it was because I was a chatterbox."

Cole burst out laughing. "You? I would say you were the least likely candidate for a chatterbox I've ever met."

Lina pushed her lips out into a rose-colored moue and shook her head. "People change. I changed early."

History began to cloud the laughter in her eyes and Cole hated to see it go. "Go on," he prodded, enjoying that her accent thickened when she spoke of home. "We were talking about food."

"Yes, well, my grandmother said it was rude to interrupt someone's focus when they were cooking with unnecessary chatter. Then, of course, my mother said it too—but a bit more…hmm, how do you say…? *Child-friendly.*" She smirked, then switched voices. "In order to know when a dish was finished you must listen very carefully. It will tell you when it is done. The fish, for example—the Polish love fish. For the fish to taste good she must swim three times—in water, in butter and in wine. When the fish has had enough wine, it will sigh and then you will know it is done."

"I guess that's in line with what my father used to say about his grilled steak."

"What did he say?" Lina scooched to the edge of her seat expectantly, happy to have the spotlight removed from her.

"He said unless it was still mooing he didn't want to have anything to do with it."

"Then why did he bother cooking it and just eat steak tartare instead?"

"Raw beef? No, ma'am!" Cole tilted an imaginary cowboy hat at her and put on his strongest drawl. "A Southerner does not eat that sort of stuff from over there in Europe. A true Southerner eats honest-to-goodness barbecue. Then again—saying that—*true* Southern barbecue takes at least twelve hours, if not twenty-four, to cook."

"Like what you're making now?" Lina eyed the selection of chicken and vegetable skewers they'd bought, ready for the grill. "You plan to take twelve hours to cook this?"

"Let's just say you're not the only one who has changed." Cole turned back to the grill and made a stab at rearranging the coals now that they'd finally started glowing a bit. His father had lectured him on evening out the coals more times than he could remember. His father had lectured him about a lot of things. *Shake it off, man.* Maybe it was one of the plus sides of not seeing the parents anymore. No more lectures.

He cleared his throat and threw a question over his shoulder, in need of a distraction from the thorny trip down memory lane. "Now, apart from eating fish very quietly, I still don't have a good picture of you as a child. Any more nuggets you care to share?"

Lina looked at Cole's back, shoulders hunched after the talk of his father, and suddenly knew it was the same for him as it was for her. Complicated. Painful. Maybe it was the same for everyone—just the way things were when people's lives were intertwined. They became knotty and seemingly impossible to make right again.

A simple start. A couple fell in love, then life ensued and the twists and turns began—no family truly becoming the picture-perfect presentations everyone imagined others' lives to be. At the very least, Cole would surely miss his parents, being so far away. Like she missed hers.

"Pierogi!" Her voice was louder than she'd intended, but what the heck. Her mother's *pierogi* were worth a shout. Delicious little potato clouds with hidden treasures buried within their soft, fluffy—

Cole's face looked blank.

"You don't know *pierogi*? Oh…you are really missing something. Especially my mother's." Lina's legs floated up to the chair and she gave them a hug. "Everyone." She spoke seriously now. *"Everyone* brags about their mother's *pierogi*, but *my* mother's are actually, truly, the best in… definitely in the village I come from, if not the whole of Poland. She doesn't just make one type. No. She cooks with what is fresh. Just like you!" Lina pointed at the huge bundle of asparagus they'd picked up from the farmers' market on their giddy, kissing-break-filled journey back to Cole's place.

Cole had started smiling early in her narrative and didn't stop now. "You haven't tasted my cooking yet. I don't think it's quite time to put me on a par with your mother."

"Oh, when you taste my mother's *pierogi*…" Lina was off now, somewhere else. Poland, he guessed.

"Is she coming over?"

"No."

"You going home?"

"No."

Lina rose, silently gathering together the prosciutto, asparagus and a wooden cutting board before returning to the table and taking what looked to be an introspective sip of her wine.

"I have not seen my parents since my accident."

Cole already knew this from Madame, but stayed silent. She was finally ready to talk and he was all ears.

"When I learned I could no longer dance…" She stopped to pull a long strip of prosciutto from the butcher paper and painstakingly laid it out on the cutting board to receive some asparagus. As she began to roll, she gathered emotional momentum and began again. "When I learned I could no longer dance I felt so ashamed I could barely look at myself in the mirror. In fact, for a long time I don't think I even bothered. What was the point? All I would see if I looked at my reflection was the world's biggest failure." She waved away Cole's protest to the contrary. "No. For me—my whole life—*my* life was my family's life. My mother and father did everything for me." Another piece of asparagus disappeared into a nearly transparent slice of ham. "Everything was done in our house so Michalina could become a world-famous dancer. My father's work, my mother's meals…" She cocked an eyebrow at Cole. "*Pierogi* is not on the menu for a dancer. So she took extra jobs to afford the classes, the shoes. Oh, my goodness the *shoes*! I can't even think how many pairs I might have been through. Hundreds. At least."

She fastidiously stayed on task, but kept talking as if stopping would mean stopping forever and this was the time she needed to tell her story. "Their whole lives were my life and I worked so hard to make all my dreams come true for them—to make all the effort have been for something. And then…a bit of loose cartilage, a poorly executed plié and—poof—away it all went, down the drain or the gutter or wherever dreams go when they no longer hold you up."

"But you showed them you were made of stronger stuff than intangible dreams."

"Ah—you are partly right. Partly wrong. My dreams

did come true and I could finally relax and be happy that everything my parents had sacrificed had been worth it. I saved a little money so they have that. But I wasn't anywhere near being able to properly repay them for all they did for me."

"I don't think parents really expect that."

She presented Cole with a small pyramid of identically wrapped asparagus spears and shook her head until her smile was bright again. "Well. The girl I was—am—wanted to pay them back. And then, one day, this girl met a handsome doctor."

"Oh, he was handsome, was he?"

Cole drew her into his arms, his interest in the asparagus less important than taking a deep inhalation of Lina's summery, warm skin.

"Very."

"And what did he do?"

"He said get off your butt and do some work!" She poked him on the bottom for good measure.

Cole pressed his hips toward hers. "I'll bet you any amount of money he did not say that."

Lina giggled now, the weight of her story no longer pinning her to the ground as it had.

"He was very nice actually."

"Oh?"

"Yes, he offered me a job, which came with a puppy!"

"A puppy? Sounds like a strange man, offering a woman a puppy on the first day he meets her."

"Maybe he thinks they are both broken, perhaps they will see something in the other and get better. Or maybe the doctor is a mad scientist who can't help fixing broken things," she finished with a laugh.

"No." Cole gave her a quick kiss on the forehead and held her at arm's length. "I don't do that. I give advice, options. It's up to the person who hears it if they want to take it or not."

Lina's brow crinkled. His tone had been sharper than he'd intended. It was his sore spot and he hadn't responded well. But how could she understand what he had gone through? Effectively killing your fiancée…the one the whole town had wanted you to marry… Sure, it had been Katie's wish…well, part of one of her law classes: write your own will… They'd actually laughed at the time, neither of them having the slightest clue the price would be so dear.

Hadn't losing Katie been enough pain without both his and her families shutting him out?

Little creases appeared at the sides of Lina's eyes. As quickly as his hackles had risen, they went down again. It wasn't her fault he came with baggage. It was no one's fault. It was just life. And it was up to him to decide if he was going to drag it along after him the rest of his days, the people around him taking the unwitting fallout. Lina was important to him. He was as close to sure as a man could be that he loved her. He would have to try harder, more actively, to lay his demons to rest—or let her go.

He couldn't do that. Not yet.

He felt a sigh make him sag again. The thought of losing Lina was one too many for what was supposed to be a carefree afternoon. He took the well-practiced route of trash-compacting his past, choosing instead to soak up a nice drink of Lina. Her beauty knocked him for six, and her soul? Still waters were running much deeper than he'd thought.

"Hey, take a look at that broken puppy now!" He nodded toward Igor, who was happily throwing a stick for himself on the small patch of lawn. "I think you probably did more to fix him than I did."

"I had motivation," Lina countered.

"And what was that?"

"Ice cream." She smiled coquettishly and blew him a kiss as she skipped down the steps to join Igor on the lawn.

Yes. He smiled back. Ice cream did work wonders. Not to mention the positive affects of some seriously memorable—ahem—nighttime activities. He surprised himself by hoping there would be more of them. Being with Lina was about the most natural thing he'd ever experienced. But they each had rivers to cross. When and if they did, he hoped to heaven they ended up together.

CHAPTER NINE

"Right, Tilly! How are the knees today?" Cole gave the teen an encouraging smile. She was painfully shy and, according to her mother, dancing was the only thing that brought her out of her shell. A diagnosis of rheumatoid arthritis was exactly what she didn't need.

"They're okay. They hurt a bit," she replied, immediately contradicting herself.

"Let's see you walk round the office, shall we?" Cole swiftly began pushing aside chairs to make more room for her. He was walking on sunshine today and had to work hard to adjust his mood to match each of his patients. Waking up with Lina in his arms made the world a better place. But this was the workplace and he was her boss. Nice reality check. Not.

"I've been eating more fish and have totally given up burgers, which has just about ruined any social life I had left." Tilly play-moaned as she walked, with obvious discomfort, round the room. She was used to the routine. This was a been-there-done-that procedure for her and Cole felt for her.

"The changes in your diet could definitely help. Your mother tells me your kitchen is well stocked up with olive oil these days. How's your stomach dealing with the gluco-corticoids? Any nausea, muscle weakness, mood swings?"

"No," she snapped. That answered that, then.

"How's your blood pressure? You were just in with the nurse, right?"

"All right," she bit out, eyes fastidiously locked on the path she'd chosen to navigate round his office.

"Does all right really mean 'not so good'? C'mon, Tilly," he cajoled. "Talk to me. We can always give you an inhaler—or organize injections, if you'd prefer."

"I'd prefer to be at ballet class with the rest of my friends!" Tilly's voice cracked and Cole's heart went out to her. Ballet was most likely not on the cards for her anymore. Quite a few things were off her list of "normal girl" activities. Instead of giggling about boys with her friends or practicing her *pas de deux*, she was shuttled between appointments with him, a physio, a dietician, a pharmacist and a podiatrist, just to name just a few of the medical professionals she was required to see simply to keep the pain under control.

"I know, Tilly."

"How could you?" The teenager wheeled round on him. "How could you understand what it's like to know the only dream you had in life will never come true?"

Cole instinctively opened his arms wide and beckoned for her to come in for a hug. He knew it wasn't the British way, but he was an American and she was just a kid. A kid having a tough time. At the very least she deserved a hug.

He felt her shoulders begin to shake a bit as he folded his arm round her and it wasn't much of a leap to remember the day Lina had wept in his arms, tears flooding her eyes for all that she had lost.

Hugs he could give. Fulfilling dreams? Hell. What he would've given to feel his own mother's arms round him after Katie had died—or felt the familiar pat and clap to the shoulder his father had always given him when things had been tough. He'd had none of that. Not a single act of compassion. They had all but strung him up.

He pulled a box of tissues off the desk with his free arm and gave it a little wiggle in her eye line. Tilly pulled a couple from the box and allowed herself a heartfelt sob before she blew her nose and took a bit more time to snuffle and regroup.

When her breathing had steadied, he held her out at arm's length and gave her tearstained face a smile. "You know, I've been doing some reading and there is something that is meant to help."

Her eyes brightened and the hint of a smile began to tug at her lips. "This isn't another one of your hocus-pocus American things, is it, Dr. Manning?"

"A little bit." He grinned. "What do you know about swing dancing?"

"What?" She crossed her arms over her chest. "Like the cowboys do?"

"Kind of. Or, if that's not your scene, there is the Lindy Hop."

"Where the boys twirl you round nineteen-fifties style?" Tilly's smile was unabashed now.

"That's the one." Cole reached across his desk and grabbed a prescription sheet and started to scribble.

"More medicine?" Tilly pouted, immediately wiping the smile from her face.

"Something like that." Cole tore the sheet from the pad and handed it to her with a flourish.

"Go to Lindy Hop, ballroom or tango classes until something sticks. Go out with your pals. Have a burger every now and again. Get on with your life." Tilly read out loud, her voice growing increasingly disbelieving. "That's your prescription?"

"That's my prescription." Cole nodded, vividly aware,

as she left his office with a wave and a smile, that he could probably afford to follow his own advice.

"Ow-ww! Wugh!"

"Stop your wiggling!"

"Stop digging your elbow into my hip!"

Gemma began to cackle. She always did when Lina moaned. "This is peanuts compared to what you put yourself through at the ballet—so grow a spine!"

"I would if—" Lina began energetically, then stopped herself. No more excuses. She was on a path now—a good one—and Gemma was right. "What helped you?"

"Helped me what?" Gemma dug her thumbs deep into muscles Lina was sure she'd never forget she had now that she had become the massage therapist's official "hip guinea pig."

"Move on—after dance."

Gemma's hand movements became less tactical and more intuitive as her thoughts drifted off. Lina felt a sigh of relief work its way through her chest. Her new friend was a take-no-prisoners masseuse. She didn't do light and fluffy. She put muscles through their paces. It hadn't hurt this much before. Maybe so much sex after…quite an absence hadn't been such a wise move.

A little grin crept onto her lips without even taking a moment to reconsider. No doubt about it, she was on a fast track to the land of the love struck. Not that she could spin round and sing corny songs from musicals in the office. She and Cole had dealt with the working-together issue by ignoring it. Deeply mature and nigglingly not so fulfilling.

"I would say our cases are a bit different. I had an injury I could have recovered from—*did* recover from. And then was stupid enough to go back for more when they told me not to."

"I would have done the sa-*ame*! Ow! What are you doing with my poor glutimous maximus?"

"More like minimus. And it's *gluteus* maximus, you boob. Suck it up. Your booty is tiny, Keminsky. No pain, no gain. Didn't you do all the exercises you were given after your hip operation?"

Lina chewed on her lips in lieu of answering. *Gluteus maximus.* Latin was exactly the same Latin in Polish. She would have to revisit the anatomy coloring book she'd bought herself when she'd still been dancing. The knowledge was in there somewhere. She just had to tap into it.

"Aw—c'mon. Are you telling me all that famous ballerina discipline flew straight out the window?"

Giggling, she confessed, "The doctors were just as bossy as Madame and…" She sobered at the thoughts of the months she spent hiding away. "I'd just had enough. *Don't cross your legs… Do use ice… Don't lean forward while sitting… Do use heat… Don't try to pick up something on the floor when you are sitting or bend at the waist beyond ninety degrees.* My favorite was, *Don't turn your feet excessively inward or outward when you bend down*—the very thing I'd been trained to do again and again and again… *Out! Out! Wider! Out!* Pfft…" So much for her enviable turnout. Now it was the bane of her existence.

"Sounds pretty familiar." Gemma twirled her finger round and held the towel up for Lina to turn to the other side. "Bossy doctors, eh? You must be a glutton for punishment to come and work for Cole."

It was impossible to stop a flush of heat from coloring her cheeks.

"Ooh! Someone's still got it bad for Cole!"

Silence was the safest option here. So Lina chose it.

"Well, as I said, whatever that man does, he doesn't do

it in-house—so I wouldn't get your hopes up. He's prob-ably got a lady brain surgeon tucked away in his garret. Or a high-powered lawyer. Maybe a bored duchess or—"

"I get the picture." Lina hoped her dry response was enough to stop the speculation of who else might have also been sharing Cole's bed. It hadn't occurred to her for a second that she might not be the only one. The thought turned her stomach. For the past forty-eight hours she'd been quite merrily floating around on cloud nine. It was the only time in the past few months she'd let herself be-lieve she was enough for Cole. They'd been so...*whole* to-gether! The doubts began to tease away again. He was an amazing man. Intelligent, passionate, worldly...and what did she know about life-living? The insides of countless rehearsal studios and...erm...she could talk your ear off about tutus if that was your thing, but wasn't so sure it was Cole's.

"Don't let me put you off!" Gemma dug into Lina's good hip with the same verve as she had the other. "I al-ways say, 'Aim high!' and you're bound to catch some-thing on the way back down to earth."

"That's very Eastern European of you."

"No. That's the school of hard knocks talking, my friend."

"What do you mean?"

"I mean—and you probably already know this, so I don't know why I'm bothering to preach to the choir—life is tough! You can't always get you want and all that jazz. Just getting a social life together after my injury was hard enough. The other dancers in my troupe closed ranks as if my injury would infect them. Getting onto a whole new horse professionally was tear-inducing and it took ages, but it was a hundred thousand million times worth every frustrating minute."

"Better than dancing?" Lina allowed herself a glimmer of hope.

"Better for me. I can work when I like. As long as Cole's cool with it," she hastily added. "I discovered I love teaching massage as much as I love doing it, and most of all I get to help people. Don't get me wrong—dancing was amazing. It was the thing I'd thought set my soul alight—but it was a blinkered existence. Just listen to wise old me—shoot for the stars and you're bound to find something."

But "something" wasn't good enough. She felt it in her bones.

Tears pricked at Lina's eyes as reality set in. She'd been a fool to think her ridiculously perfect weekend with Cole had been anything more than a one-off. She had let a part of her heart believe otherwise and was regretting it now. It had seemed better than real—it had felt deeper than real. It had felt like...felt like kismet.

Silly girl, she chastised herself. *Away with the fairies as usual.* Had a couple of months working at a new job and meeting the most divinely kind, gorgeous and completely generous man she'd ever laid eyes on really turned her pumpkin into a carriage heading for the ball?

A lone tear snaked down her cheek and plopped onto the massage table, mercifully out of Gemma's sight. She needed to regroup. Floating on air was one thing—coming down for a landing was another. She'd already indulged in months of self-pity and a fat lot of good that had done her. Now was the time to get up and soar.

"I hope you're not looking up barbecue tips."

Lina practically jumped out of her skin, caught by surprise at the sound of Cole's low voice by her ear, his breath on her neck. It had been frantically busy all day and whenever their paths crossed at En Pointe, work was work and nothing more. But right now Cole's voice was much more after-hours than not and it sent a thrill of anticipation along her spine. Until she remembered what she'd been searching for on the internet. She grabbed the mouse and jabbed at it, frantically trying to shut down the page.

"Medical translator, eh?"

Obviously not fast enough, then.

"Oh, it's nothing."

"You seemed pretty captivated by it."

"I was just looking at it for a friend." *Who happens to look a lot like me.*

Cole did that leaning, crossed-arms, sexy thing against the wall that always made her lose focus. A stream of white lies wasn't going to help the situation. Best fess up.

"Remember when you saved Beatrycze at the Polish Centre?"

"I seem to recall you doing your part, as well," Cole brushed off his role in the incident.

"Well…this is sort of what I am looking up, but I think it's probably too much. I don't have the right background so…"

"So, what exactly are you saying? You're going to give up before you've started?"

"No, it's just…" *Sheesh…when you put it that way…* "I have a job already and this is full-time and so many of the places say a medical background is necessary."

Cole swiveled her chair round so she could no longer avoid the electric-blue gaze of his eyes. Looking into them was like looking into a truth factory. It was difficult to resist the urge to squirm. Feeling giggly and sexy was *so-o-o* much easier than laying the bare bones of your psyche on the line.

"You have a job you could quit."

His words felt like an icicle in her heart. He didn't want her here any more?

"No, I'm happy. This was just silly—something the doctor at the Polish clinic said. I was just daydreaming. Besides…" she put on her best employee face "…I haven't even finished my three-month trial. It would be a show of disrespect to my boss if I were to leave so soon."

Yes. She was testing the waters, but she had to. Didn't she?

"I think your boss would want you to be happy. And if that meant leaving En Pointe, he'd cope with it."

Oh.

"Go." She twisted her chair back round to face the reception area and flicked her fingers at him. She couldn't look into those eyes she loved so much anymore. Not without crying. "Shoo. Go away, bossman. You have a patient coming."

Cole glanced at his watch and the patient printout on Lina's desk.

"Yes, but not for a few moments." He felt the crease on his forehead take up position. It always settled in the dead center of his eyebrows when something weighed on him.

"Lina, you're not…?" He'd been going to ask if she was hanging around because of him but the arrogance of the suggestion made him back off. That and their "all work at work" rule. But he was the boss. He could break the rules, right? Or was he the one who needed to set an example?

"I'm not what?" There was a note of anxiety to her voice he didn't like to hear. He'd put it there and upsetting her was not on his agenda.

"You're not free for dinner tonight, are you?" *Just ask her directly, you goon.* Cole could've clunked himself on the head but opted for an expectant look.

Lina scanned the room. What was she doing? Checking for bugs from the other practitioners? Or finding an excuse to get out of it?

"I'd like to explain a few things."

He'd meant it as a good thing, but from the set of her lips he could see he hadn't chosen optimum boyfriend phrasing.

His eyes widened at the thought. Was he a *boyfriend*? The word sounded a bit more flimsy than what he was feeling for Lina—but it would do. For now.

She tipped her chin to the side but still wouldn't meet his eyes. Was each word he was saying just another shovelful out of the hole he was digging for himself?

Maybe it would be easier if she didn't work here. All he wanted right now was to pull her into her arms and tease the color back into those lips of hers with an endless flow of kisses. His fingers flexed in anticipation of caressing her. Lordy. He had it—and bad.

"Dinner? Ice cream? A walk? None of the above?"

"Maybe not tonight."

He was going to let her off the hook and then thought better of it. No way. What the two of them had was worth pursuing—and he wasn't going to squander it away on missed opportunities. What had his dad always said? *Opportunities rarely come to you, son, so you'd better make your own.*

"Unless you've got an appointment with the Bolshoi Ballet, I won't take no for an answer."

The silence between them was deafening. Cole couldn't believe he'd just stuck his foot in it—both feet in it—in such a massive way.

"I'm sorry, Lina, that wasn't what I—"

"I know. Don't worry. I've heard you say it to the others."

Brilliant. Not even an original ultimatum. Cole dropped down into a squat and turned her chair back to him.

"Now we definitely need to talk. And not here." From the look on her face it was going to take more than a table for two to set things right.

"Fine." It wasn't her happy voice.

"We'll sort this out." He gave her a pointed look. "Tonight."

For once Lina was grateful when the rest of the day passed in a swirling daze of calls, patients, mixed-up records, updated records, appointments to change, make and cancel. A series of tiny little things all rushing together to help take away the thoughts teasing at her conscience.

Was Cole trying to end things already?

They'd had just about the best forty-eight hours ever and now it was all coming to an incredibly abrupt halt. Was he suggesting she quit? Or was she just being crazy? Paranoid? Maybe all of it meant nothing. *Everything* and nothing. Just like her. She'd had everything and now…

Jasna cholera!

Why couldn't one teeny-tiny single thing go right for her?

She knew she was being melodramatic, but right now the despair she was experiencing felt like it would eat away at everything she'd left behind. The insecurity. The physical weakness. The pain.

She had felt so incredibly alive—not just over the past few days but the past few weeks. Especially when she was in Cole's arms. Her entire world had brightened.

The welcoming reception area suddenly felt suffocating. The plants, the beautiful soft furnishings, all the things designed to put people at ease had her on edge. She needed to get up—away from her chair, the room, the clinic.

Just *out.*

Get some air—some fresh air. Oh, how she longed

to let loose and run out into the fields behind her parents' house. Just run and run and run into the depths of the wildflower meadows and collapse in a sweaty heap by the river. It was a fail-safe cure-all. She pressed her fingertips into the edge of her desk and closed her eyes, forcing herself to steady her breathing. She wasn't going to let herself fall into that black hole of funk again. It was forgivable—sort of—after her accident. But now that she was back on her feet again? She'd have to see about closing ranks on her heartstrings a bit. But she could do it.

A cup of tea would have to stand in for the wildflower meadows of Poland for now.

Standing by the kettle, she closed her eyes again, slowly moving deep breaths in and out of her lungs. Ten, nine, eight…and one.

She was being foolish. Silly. Yo-yoing emotions were normal for a youngish woman in love. Right? She let the sound of the boiling water drown out her thoughts, just as she had that very first day she had walked into the clinic as the receptionist hopeful, and into Cole's life. She'd known he'd be something special from the moment she had laid eyes on him and she didn't want to let that go. Not now. Not when things had only just begun. She needed to show him she had resolve. Commitment. Tenacity. Whatever you wanted to call it. Cole had given her an opportunity—to work here at En Pointe and face her demons head on.

"Enough in the kettle for two?"

Gemma appeared at her side, mug in hand.

"Of course."

"You're the tops, Lina. What would we do without you?"

Lina poured the water for her, an ironic smile playing on her lips as Gemma left the kitchen, still dunking her herbal teabag in and out of the mug.

What indeed? She didn't have a clue if it would be the best thing or the worst thing to find out.

"I can't believe you found this place!" Lina's ear-to-ear grin was the perfect reward for ages trawling the internet to find just the right place. Chmurki—Little Clouds—was famed for its *pierogi*.

"We-ell, I don't know how close this will get you to memory lane as far as your mother's cooking will go, but…" Cole picked up his menu "…we'll give it a go, shall we?"

"There are so many amazing things…*i nie może odebrać.*"

Cole laughed. He had no idea what she'd just said, but it was nice to see Lina lost in the food of her homeland. By the third time the waiter came to see if they were ready, they had finally settled on their choices and ordered. Cole leaned back against the cushioned booth seat, grateful for the privacy it afforded. This was going to be harder than he'd thought.

"So, how are things going for you at the clinic?" By the sharp glance he received, the casual note he'd been hoping to hit hadn't worked.

"Is this my review? It's not quite three months."

"No. I just wanted to make sure you were happy in the job."

"It's great. Fine!" Her enthusiasm didn't quite reach her eyes.

"Hey, it's me you're talking to—not Dr. Manning. It's just Cole."

Her shoulders relaxed a bit, but the worry lines remained. "I am very happy at En Pointe. So grateful you gave me the chance."

"Hey," he quickly countered. "You're the one who got me out of a tight spot, remember?"

"Mmm… I'm not so sure that my spot wasn't a bit tighter than yours." The memory of the piles of unpaid bills, the cold air in the flat, the aching loneliness threatening to creep into the very marrow of her bones came to mind.

"Don't forget the help you gave me with Igor."

Lina felt her heartbeat quicken. What was this? Everything about it felt discordant. Even her skin felt clammy. Was this the Cole she had spent the weekend with? The warmhearted, laughing one who couldn't stop pulling her into his arms, nuzzling his head into the crook of her neck and whispering sweet nothings one after the other?

She couldn't help it. Her hackles rose. If he was going to break her heart he needed to speak to her like an adult, a woman. Not a broken little girl who needed a cuddle with a puppy.

"You know, I am not five years old. I used to dance until my feet bled—real blood. Real pain."

Now it was Cole's turn to look startled. "No, I know that. It wasn't my intention to—" He stopped, scrubbed a hand along his short shorn hair and turned the full beam of his eyes on her.

"Lina, I care about you. Probably a lot more than I should."

"What does that mean?"

If a heart could break into shards, she was quite sure this was what was happening to her right now. She needed this job—but she wanted Cole. Or was it the other way round?

A buzzing began in her ears and all she could do was stare as he pressed his fingers along the edges of the table until they were white with the pressure. Perhaps he thought without the heat of human blood running through them he would be better able to realign his thoughts.

Was he trying to tell her he'd overstepped the boss-employee boundary? It was just like the ballet—strictly unspoken but strictly adhered-to social rules... Date within your "class." Prima, Primo. Company, company. And she wasn't in Cole's class. That was becoming very, very clear.

"If you think I am not professional enough at work, I will improve. I can improve. This job is very important to me."

"Is it?"

"And here we have two *pierogi*—one with pork, one with vegetables." The smiley waiter slid the plates onto the table between them, either oblivious to or pretending not to notice the staring contest in progress.

"Bon appetit."

"Smacznego!" Lina grimaced a smile at him.

When the clinking of fork against plate became too much for her, Lina broke the silence. "What is it you want from me?"

Cole's gaze rose from his plate to meet Lina's after a moment's reflection. "I want you to do what you want to do."

"That's a bit loaded."

"Look, I've been making a complete mess of this by trying to beat around the bush. What I'm trying to figure out is why, after I've seen you check out those translator sites, you aren't going for it? Are you really happy at the clinic?"

"I don't know if there is a right answer to that." The few bites of dumpling she'd managed to eat sat leadenly in her tummy. She laid down her fork, giving up the charade of enjoying her meal.

"Do you want to do something else?" Cole persisted.

"I'm not in a position to do anything else." It took a lot of strength for her to admit it. Acknowledge that finances were still tight. It had, after all, only been just under three months since she had begun the job and there had been a lot of financial catch-up to do, even considering how generous the salary was. She folded her serviette, place it on the table and wove her fingers together on her lap, her posture returning to that of the days when she'd just received a rollicking good telling off from Madame. She knew how to take it on the chin.

"Can't you speak to your parents?"

"And become further indebted to them? I don't think so."

"But you have a good relationship with them, don't you? They support you."

"Is that how it is with your family? Support on tap?" The words had the desired effect and if she could have done anything to reverse what she'd said, she would have. Cole looked absolutely stricken. She'd never seen pain so vivid on a man's face before. Without another thought she was on his side of the booth, his head between her hands, forehead to forehead. "I'm so sorry. I'm so sorry. What have I said?"

Cole slid his hands up to cover hers, pulling them down from his face and holding them to his chest. "People who love each other sure know how to hurt each other, don't they?"

Lina's eyes widened, glassy with emotion.

Wait.

Had he just told her he loved her?

"Families," he clarified, instantly regretting it. Could this conversation go any more south than it already had?

He did love her. Whole heart. Whole soul. He'd shout

it to the hills if there were any! But he didn't seem to be able to tell her. *Why couldn't he just tell her he loved her?*

It was lay-the-cards-on-the-table time.

"Let's get out of here, shall we? Hampstead Heath?"

"A walk would probably be a good thing right now."

Finally. Something they were agreed on.

She surprised herself by giggling.

"What?" Cole's expression was suspect.

"Did you see the waiter? His face?"

"You mean the one who looked like he had the juiciest gossip in the world when we paid the bill after barely eating a thing?" Cole lifted a wry eyebrow.

Lina could only nod she was giggling so hard. Nerves? Most likely. Nothing about this day was what she had thought it would be and the careening emotional ride she'd been on didn't look as if it was near being over. Cole's face had already turned sober. As a counter, she could feel his fingers reaching for hers.

Had Cole just told her he loved her?

...when two people love each other...

"Turn left here."

The tree-lined avenue leading to the heath was a welcome visual antidote to the emotional rawness she felt. They'd touched on all her hot spots in a matter of minutes—seconds even—and it was hard to feel she'd risen to the occasion. Where had the single-minded girl she'd always been gone?

She chanced a glance at Cole. His blue eyes were doggedly focused on the path leading into the park. His grave expression was at odds with the gentle to-and-fro caresses his thumb was giving the back of her hand. Perhaps he wasn't even conscious of it. Perhaps it was his way of saying he was sorry.

She stopped herself. Cole didn't have anything to apologize for. He was the head of a clinic, her boss and her lover. Those were a lot of positions all rolled into one and if he saw that she was prevaricating—not showing commitment—all these questions were well deserved.

"Cole..." She wasn't quite brave enough to look at him as she spoke. "If this is about the job. I am there. One hundred percent I am there."

"Thank you, but it's not really about the job. Not right now. I need to tell you something. It might make it easier for you to understand what I'm about to do."

The tendrils of calm she had begun to feel evaporated instantly. She sat down rigidly on the bench he selected, away from the pathway where couples strolled, dogs were being led home after a walk or a swim in the ponds...where life was happening. They sat and watched other people's lives for a moment, Lina too frightened to say any more.

"Five years ago I was like you," Cole began. "Well, not like you—obviously I wasn't a prima ballerina but I was feeling at the top of my game. I lived in a great town, was number one son—well, the only son of a pair of ambitious parents who'd poured all their hopes and dreams into me, and then one day—" His voice caught and with it Lina felt her own lurch into her throat. He stared straight ahead. Not looking at her, not touching her. Was that what his childhood had been like? Bereft of emotion? Hers had been a walk in the park by comparison and it was painful to hear his voice flick into a virtual monotone. Survival skills, she supposed, for relaying the hardest memories. She knew the drill.

"Then one night my girlfriend—actually, she was my fiancée. I'd proposed a few weeks earlier, much to our parents' relief." Cole stopped and shook his head as if trying to get it all straight.

Lina's fingers wove together over her heart. It was already easy to tell this was going to be difficult to hear. As he continued, Lina's concerns were realized. It was painful to listen to. Heartbreaking to absorb.

"Katie, my fiancée, was the daughter of my parents' best friends. She and I always snuck off together during our parents' mandatory cocktail hours, dinner parties, picnics, country club dos…whatever. You name it and Katie and I were there. You know, playing board games, tennis…whatever. Our parents hung out together *a lot*. It was only natural—or inevitable—that we started dating."

"You said you were engaged." Lina's head shook in confusion.

"We did—we were." He gave one of those faraway laughs hinting at a time when life had been a bit more golden. "She'd known what I was going to do before I even started to bend my knee."

He looked at Lina blindly, the churn of emotions overriding anything else. It killed her to see this man—so very much in control of himself—completely at sea as he relived whatever it was he had gone through.

"Shortly after we got engaged—really soon—she asked me to sign a living will for her as part of an exercise she was doing at law school. For her, it had meant more than getting good marks. We'd had a close friend in high school whose parents had all but drowned in sorrow when their son had been injured in football practice and ended up on life support. Katie had been horrified when their grief ultimately led to an acrimonious divorce over whether or not to keep their son's life support going. It turned her into a vocal advocate of DNR if the victim had no brain activity. She insisted she never wanted me to have to go through anything like that. Not to mention the fact she couldn't bear the thought of a machine keeping her alive. So I thought nothing of it. I signed!"

He held his hands up as if being held at gunpoint. The expression on his face wasn't much different.

"We were young, invincible! Cole and Katie! Our parents had been friends forever and now we were set to be married. Just as our parents had half joked about—but not so secretly hoped for—for so many years."

Lina couldn't stop her nose from crinkling. Her childhood had involved so much choice! Again and again her mother and father had sought assurance that she was doing ballet because it was what she really loved. There had been absolutely no pressure from them. If anything, she would have bet money they wouldn't have minded an iota if their little girl had chosen a quiet life in the village where they lived. They had been happy. The three of them. It sounded nothing like the preprogrammed checklist of Cole's childhood. Her fingers curled round the edge of the wooden bench and squeezed. Hard. Hearing this story really made her miss her family.

"I know," Cole said, misinterpreting her expression. "It took me a while, but I finally stopped resisting."

"Resisting?"

"The inevitability of Katie and me getting married. And the smiles! They were so absolutely happy." Cole's face echoed his words as if reenacting a treasured moment. "I'd finally done the right thing. Their only child a doctor, their future daughter-in-law a fledgling lawyer—up and coming, but well on her way to a Supreme Court judgeship, they told everyone, voices brimming with pride. Sometimes I think they loved her more than me." He said the words without malice, but there was obviously a little boy somewhere inside the man sitting next to her still hoping for his parents' approval.

"Were you in love with her?" The words came out before Lina could stop them.

"I loved her," Cole acquiesced, scrubbing a hand across his head. "There weren't fireworks or anything. But she was a beautiful woman. Smart. Funny. We'd been all but promised to each other since birth."

"That must've been…" Lina sought for the right word and was poleaxed. "A bit weird?"

"Yes and no." His head tipped back and forth with the words. "We'd always been great friends and dating each other came naturally. We knew each other like… like family."

The sadness in his voice was almost more than Lina could bear and it wasn't even her story. She ached for Cole and couldn't think of a single thing to say that would help.

"So what happened?"

He cleared his throat, simultaneously pushing himself back against the bench as if seeking additional support. When he began to speak she barely recognized the voice as his own. Autopilot was more like it.

"I was at work one day, late shift at the hospital, and the ER paged me. The rest followed in a daze, really. The car accident had been extreme. Katie's vehicle had slid under a jackknifed lorry and the impact had resulted in massive brain trauma. Traffic was heavy, despite the hour, and it had taken some time—too much time—for the ambulance to arrive. Her doctor was taking me through her paperwork—the DNR—when her parents arrived and begged, pleaded with me to reconsider. As if I could!" He shot Lina a glance, eyes so full of emotion she was sure he was asking for her to agree with him. She nodded along, unable to begin to imagine what she would do if put in the same place. It was obvious he had loved Katie. Maybe not passionately, but she couldn't believe Cole would've asked her to marry him just to please his parents.

"My family, her family—they all swore she was responding. But in this case it was all false hopes. She'd been brain dead before she arrived at the hospital."

He paused for a moment as a family group wobbled past on shiny new bicycles, the youngest towed along in a bright red wagon looking as though he was having the time of his life.

Lina envied them the carefree evening they were having, then checked herself. They may have known hard times, too. They were as deserving of a fun night as the next person. Or—she crossed her fingers beneath her thigh, where her hands remained trapped—the person next to her. *How on earth did you give the go-ahead to end the life of a person you loved?*

Abruptly, Cole clapped his hands together. "And that was it for us as a family. They've not spoken to me since."

She heard the words but found it hard to register them. No matter how horrid she'd been to her parents, they had made it explicitly clear they would always, *always* be there for her.

"You mean your fiancée's family?"

"All of them. None of them." He looked her straight in the eye. "My parents haven't spoken to me since and with the loss of their support so too went the faith of my patients."

Lina's fingers flew to her lips in a combination of horror and disgust. Abandoning Cole like that when his grief had been as heavy as theirs? How could they have done that? He'd had to regroup on the edge of a coin.

"Don't." He shook his head at her. "Seriously. I get it. Intellectually, at least. My parents are a really smart pair, and that's how they deal with everything—clinically. It's just who they are. They'd become so attached to the idea of what my future had in store they just couldn't bear that the reality didn't match up. They were grieving the loss of the woman they'd hoped would be their daughter-in-law and wanted someone, *anyone* to blame. It was impossible for them to accept that the future they'd planned for me—us—boiled down to *paperwork*."

"But it was a car accident! You didn't have anything to do with that. And she wanted the DNR!" Lina couldn't help but jump to his defense. Cole wasn't the one in the wrong here.

Cole's head fell into his hands. Elbows on knees. Back hunched against the world. Lina resisted the urge to give it a rub. Console. Caress him. Everything about him screamed injured wild animal right now—one that would lash out if touched. She knew it wouldn't be personal. It would be that the pain was too unbearable.

He sat back, scrubbing away invisible tears. "Since then I've made it a practice not to pressure people into anything. Force them into doing something they don't want to. Doctors aren't gods. People need to make their own choices in life—that's what I've preached from the moment I left Maple Cove." He turned to face her, his eyes, his face still beautiful despite the sorrow etched into them. "Which is why I regret to inform you that while your services will be required for another week,

En Pointe will not be renewing your contract at the end of your three-month trial period."

"I'm sorry?"

"I'm firing you, Lina. You're fired."

CHAPTER TEN

"YOU'RE FIRED."

She blinked.

What?

He repeated it.

Shaking her head to make sure she'd heard him correctly, Lina looked at Cole again. His mouth was set. Hands folded together. Shoulders spread out broad, as if expecting to be challenged. His whole body was braced to defend himself.

She didn't need to hear him say it again. It was obvious what was happening here. He was finishing with her. Personally, professionally—what else was there?

Her first instinct was to protest. On a bare-bones practical level, she *needed* that job.

"You'll be given two months' pay to tide you over, as I realize this didn't come with much warning—"

"Are you *kidding* me?" Lina felt herself go into flight-or-fight mode and in that instant her proverbial dukes were up. She was ready to take him on. Or be blown away with the lightest breath of air.

Cole could have run her over with a steamroller and it would have felt better. Why tell her everything he had only to blow her off? Was it meant to lessen the pain? Because he'd hurt, too? She didn't even know where she stood on that front. Her lips parted, but nothing came out. An enormous "why" hung in the air between them.

Strangely, the world stilled when she thought it would race.

"I did it because you're afraid of being good at something else."

"What does that mean?" He'd officially just lost the right to pass judgment on her. "I haven't yet had a chance to become good at the job I had up until five seconds ago."

"Don't be ridiculous, Lina. You had that job nailed in minutes. You're kind, intelligent. Observant. It doesn't take a genius to do it. Madame knew you'd be fine."

"Madame? What's she got to do with it?"

"She—" He thudded his forehead with the ball of his hand. "You weren't meant to find out. She rang me and asked if I'd interview you for the job. I didn't want to." He stared at his hands. "I didn't think you could do it."

"Of course. What would make you think a lowly, broken ballerina could?" Lina couldn't help retorting, vividly remembering Cole's poor attempts at showing her how to work the phone system.

"Lina, please. This isn't meant to hurt you. I just think you're closing yourself off to what you really want to do because you're afraid to start over."

She stared at him, disbelief fueling the growing heat in her chest.

"The medical translator jobs?" he prompted. "You're interested in it, yes?"

"Yes, but—"

"But what? Why don't you go for it?"

"Because of the money. Because of the time. Because of the hours and hours and hours of my life it will eat up so that I will never be able to pay you back—pay back my parents. Do you want me to go on?"

"What do you mean *pay back*?"

For an intelligent man, Cole looked utterly flummoxed.

"I told you already." Lina sunk back into the bench. Bone tired wouldn't even begin to describe how she was feeling.

"Your parents? Paying things back? I thought you were over that."

"How can I get over that when I am also busy paying back debts to you? The cycle is endless—"

"You don't owe me anything!" Cole flung his hands out wide as if it would help make his point. "What I'm trying to talk to you about is moving on from that. If you see kindnesses as something that only builds up a list of debtors I—I really don't know what to say. Do you expect things from people when you are kind to them?"

"Of course not."

"Then why do you think anyone—your parents, me, especially me—would expect *payback*?"

Lina felt the prick of truth in his words but was too furious to give in.

"I thought you didn't like to make decisions for people."

"I thought you didn't like handouts." He regretted the words the moment they were out of his mouth because the truth was he was letting her go because he loved her. He loved Lina completely and believed with every pore in his body that if she stayed at En Pointe she would only grow to resent it—and then one awful day resent him. And he couldn't risk that. Right now he would live with her rage. Her anger. He'd said it before. Anger he could work with.

"Why are you punishing me for what happened to you?" Lina's voice was saturated with sorrow. It was impossible to know if he'd done the right thing.

"I had a lot of decisions made for me and I'm making

just one for you. One that—believe it or not—puts us on an even playing field."

"What? By *firing me* we're now suddenly equals?"

He stopped himself from reaching out to hold her hand. She was better than him. More open. More honest. "I suppose that's up to you."

She shook her head and rose to leave, one final green-eyed look of disbelief clouding her face as she turned to go.

His gut told him to chase after her. His heart told him it was pointless.

He huffed an unhappy laugh out into the cooling night air. Maybe he should have gone after her. Explained further.

Nah. Nope.

She had a lot of information to process and interfering more than he had? Making things worse would be pretty easy about now.

He'd done the right thing. Right?

History did have a cruel way of repeating itself.

"Budge over, Manning, I need a coffee."

Cole did his best not to flinch at the volume of Gemma's voice. Turned out no sleep and a night of emotional turmoil did not a charming Cole make.

"Blimey. Did you see Lina this morning? She's all smiley and everything, but her eyes…she's not *present*, you know? Like an alien crawled into her and ate the real Lina."

That was one way of putting it.

"What? We're playing the silent game this morning and no one told me?"

"Sorry, Gemma. Just a busy day ahead. A lot on my mind."

Gemma turned to face him. Recoiling would have been

too strong a word for her reaction—but he was guessing from her face he wasn't looking his best.

"Uh…boss? Everything okay?"

"Yeah, fine." Cole buried his real response behind his coffee mug before taking a much-needed gulp. Then another. "We're going to need to look for a new receptionist. Let me know if you know anyone who'd be a good contender."

He'd never seen anyone do an actual double take before. Wasn't his world just full of firsts this week?

"What about Lina?"

"I've decided not to offer her the full-time position." He drained his coffee, only just stopping himself from throwing the mug against the wall. *What a mess.* All the coffee in London wouldn't help him today.

"Any particular reason why you're not renewing the contract of one of our best receptionists, like, ever?"

"It just wasn't the right fit." Cole gave her his best this-conversation-is-over look.

"Don't you like her? I thought you two were thick as thieves!" Hands were on hips now. Gemma went in for the kill. "She's the reason your dog is well behaved."

He grimaced in response. Yes, that was true. And Igor would no doubt run away from home now. The potential disasters were piling up. Great. His first decision to interfere in someone's life in years and what do you know? First-rate disaster.

"And the filing system is now actually comprehensible to everyone who works here."

He drummed his fingers along the countertop and raised his eyebrows expectantly. It was torture listening to the wonders-of-Lina speech when all he wanted to do was agree.

"Not to mention the fact she is absolutely gorgeous.

That hair! I mean, have you ever seen anyone with hair like that? And those green, green eyes—a ridiculous shade of green! Who *looks* like that?"

His glare was entirely ineffective.

"And the patients love her." Gemma glared for added impact. *"Love. Her."*

"All right! All right. Enough. It just—" He scanned the room, searching for the right thing to say when there just really wasn't any right thing to say. "It simply isn't going to work out. Okay?" He gave what he hoped looked like a remorseful nod and left the room. If Lina wanted to be with him she would have to believe in herself before she could believe in him. How he hoped she would get there. Gemma's voice followed him down the corridor.

"Let it be heard that I think you're utterly mad, Cole Manning!"

On that, we can agree.

Returning to En Pointe the next day was a big enough hurdle. Sitting in her chair—correction, *the* chair—right at the heart of Reception, plugging in her headset as she pasted on a smile. Each moment was pure, unadulterated torture. But she had her pride, as if that were a mercy.

Cole had been pretty clear about seeing out the final week of her trial and, painful as it was, she knew if she could do it—face the man she loved in the wake of his rejection—she would be able to endure anything. She had once danced until her feet had bled, for crying out loud! Madame had taught her that. She'd just pretend it was class and then…she'd start over.

Just the idea of it made her shoulders sag.

The situation—her impending lack of an anchor—brought an added sharpness of focus to the day. Ironically, she'd seen life through a sort of hi-def filter when she'd

begun falling helplessly, hopelessly in love with Cole...
this was the same but with dark edges. Cole didn't love
her. Hadn't even wanted to hire her in the first place! She'd
been little more than a grudging *favor*.

How could she have been such an idiot? Just seeing
what she'd wanted to in lieu of the writing on the wall.
Cole didn't love her.

"Alyssa Thornton, to see Dr. Manning."

A young woman stood in front of the desk, tears swimming in her eyes, crutches just visible above the high reception desk.

"Yes, of course. Let me just get your records pulled
up here."

"He won't have any yet. This is a referral." The woman
didn't even bother to wipe away the tears beginning to
trickle down her cheeks.

"Oh, no! Let's get you some tissues. Come." Lina was
up and out of her chair in an instant. She knew that pain
and it was awful to see someone else going through it.
"Come sit over here and I will let Dr. Manning know
you are here."

"Is he a miracle worker?" The girl's dark brown eyes
pleaded with her for a positive response.

"Yes." She didn't even take a moment to consider it.
He might be many things she didn't like right now, but he
would always be a good doctor. "He will help you. It may
not be how you want to be helped, but he will help you."
Lina gave the girl's shoulder a quick rub before putting
her headset back on and ringing through to Cole's office.
The sound of his voice did its usual magic and she fought
the urge to pause and savor it, knowing this would be one
of the last times she would hear it.

"Alyssa Thornton for you."

"Thanks."

And the line went dead.

She ducked her head below the reception desk, actively stemming the threat of her own tears. She hadn't been able to think straight when she'd stormed into her flat the previous night, bag thrown to one corner, jacket thrown to another, shoes unceremoniously flicked who knew where. She'd just needed to sit, as she had so many times before, and stare at the wall as if it were some sort of magnolia-colored oracle. Three months ago it had been all she'd thought she had. But it hadn't been the wall that had helped her in the end. It had been Cole.

And what had her gut instinct been just now? To defend him. To acknowledge that sometimes the best advice wasn't the advice you liked—but it was what you needed to hear.

Had that been what he was trying to say to her?

"Alyssa?"

Lina swiped at her eyes before looking out into the reception area. Cole was helping the girl with her crutches, offering compliments from the get-go. "You're pretty quick on those things for a newbie!" And she may have just imagined it, but she was pretty sure he took an extra moment to look across at her—to meet her gaze—the crinkles round his eyes etching his face with more worry and concern than she thought he deserved. He deserved happiness, joy—and she'd just left him there alone, thinking only of her need to hide away and lick her wounds. Just as his family had after that awful, awful night with Katie.

It was all Lina could do to stay in her chair.

Her heart absolutely ached to be near him, with him. His pain was woven into her soul now and… *Urgh!* How had everything become so complicated? Was it all really very complicated in the end? She loved him and every-

thing he'd said to her was true. She was living her life
fearfully. Worried about paying back the impossible. The
only real way she could pay back her parents was to love
them. To be kind. And to acknowledge in her heart that
Cole didn't feel the same way she did.

She'd have to let him go.

"*Psst*, Lina—come with me."

Gemma crept up to the reception desk capering-thief
style, her hand cupped to the side of her mouth.

Lina shook her head, not trusting herself to speak.
Not just yet.

Gemma, never one to take no for an answer, jerked
her head melodramatically toward the kitchen. "*C'mon!*"
came the insistent stage whisper.

A line lit up on the telephone control system. Lina
pointed at it, and gave a "sorry...can't" shrug, grateful
for the reprieve. Her eyes traveled toward Cole's office
as she took the call and wondered how she'd do it. How
she'd ever fill the Cole-sized hole in her heart.

Eighteen cups of coffee wouldn't hurt him, would it? Not
just this once...

Taking advantage of the fact no one else was in the
kitchen, Cole reached for the sugar jar. He'd been coun-
seled, when he moved to England, that when one had had
a shock, a cup of tea with a spoonful of sugar did the trick.
Coffee was going to have stand in for tea today.

"Oh! Sorry." Lina, lunged for the corridor, looking
like a startled deer.

"No, don't go, Lina. I'm just on my way out." They did
one of those awkward doorway dances where no one was
going to come out the winner.

"Here, after you." He pulled the door wide open and
flourished a hand for her to enter. He still wasn't sure

whether making himself scarce or making himself available was the best way to go. Indecision seemed to be winning at this juncture.

"Thank you. Sorry. Thank you."

Nervous laughs filled the room but Cole didn't seem to be able to get himself to leave. There had been so much left unsaid when Lina had left the park. How deeply he felt about her, how being with her made everything better, how losing Katie had been heartbreaking but to not have had a lifetime with her hadn't been the biggest blow. He'd sat on the bench for another hour until the memory of Igor sitting alone had propelled him homeward. Home to a house that felt distinctly emptier without Lina in it.

"Cole." Her voice was a near whisper. "I just wanted to say I'm sorry."

"Sorry for what?" Cole shook his head. "You have nothing to be sorry for. I'm the one who should be saying—"

Their eyes met and the connection that had made so many moments between them ridiculously vital was back again.

"Sorry."

"Sorry."

Their voices wove together and they each laughed, Lina's fingers flying to cover up her lips as she did so. The emotion in the room was almost palpable.

"Lina! Finally!" Gemma virtually exploded into the room, not seeing Cole half-hidden behind the door. "I've been looking for you everywhere. I know it's none of my business, but I weaseled the news out of Cole that he's letting you go and I just wanted you to know how much of an idiot we all think he is. Blind!" She threw her hands up in the air as if it were the universal signal for blind and continued, hands on hips. "We all thought he was in love with you—but it shows you how much my radar is off in that department. Anyway..." she sucked in a quick breath "...I just wanted you to know how much we all value you here. How much we support you. So...I'm going to start a petition to keep you here."

Lina could feel Cole's eyes on her as she took in the rapid-fire volley of information Gemma was lobbing at her. She'd thought—no, hoped—that Cole was in love with her, too. But last night he'd told her the opposite... hadn't he? She caught a glimpse of him looking out from behind the door.

His face was impossible to read. Completely neutral. Her hopes soared, twirled round in midair, then abruptly plummeted back to earth. Cole had been clear. Was *being* clear. He didn't want her in his life. She should've done something she'd thought of at the beginning of the day, not skulked around. Well, no time like the present!

"Gemma, thank you so much. But please do not get any more signatures."

"Why not? You're not going to just lie down and take this nonsense, are you? Cole's gone absolutely mad!"

"No. But I must get back to my desk to write my resignation letter." She saw both of their eyes widen. "It is very nice that you want me to stay but, in fact, I think I will quit."

"What?" Cole stepped out from behind the door, much to Gemma's horror.

"Cole! Hey, didn't see you there. Sorry about the... uh...'idiot' thing. You know I love you, right?"

"'Course I do, Gemma." Cole's eyes remained locked with Lina's as he gave the frazzled physio a quick one-armed hug. "We're good."

Lina blinked. *Yup.* He was still looking at her. Blue, blue eyes swimming with questions she didn't know she had the answer to. All she knew was that she loved Cole and if launching herself at life with a renewed passion was what it took to open her heart enough to let him go, she was going to do it. Her way.

"Gemma." Cole moved into the corridor. "Will you excuse us? I think Lina and I need to have a chat."

"Comfy?"

Lina smiled at Cole's bemused expression. She'd just finished tucking her toes under her knees lotus style—her go-to position on his office couch. He was perched on the edge of his desk—not too far away—but she needed the distance.

"Very."

"Igor misses you."

"It's only been one day since I've seen him," she tutted, unable to hide the pleasure the news brought her.

"So…have you made plans already, then?" Cole skipped over the fact he was missing her, too, never mind the fact she hadn't even gone yet. But he wasn't going to push it. He'd already stuck his stick in her spokes and she'd gotten back on her bike. Just not in the direction he'd hoped.

"Yes, I would like to figure out how to go back to school. University," she quickly corrected.

He nodded, lips pressed together in a tight smile as she continued, "Learn to work with patients—translating, helping. I will be very busy. Too busy to finish my week here, I'm afraid."

A part of him enjoyed watching her give a nonchalant shrug. This was the Lina he'd fallen in love with. The one who he knew could really *own* her life. The one who shone under duress.

"We can call a temp agency to get a replacement in. No

problem there. Of course," he quickly interrupted himself, "whoever they send won't be a patch on you."

"Hmm," Lina muttered noncommittally, her lips pressing into one of those lovely rose-red moues.

"I'd like to make you another offer."

"Oh?" Her eyebrows rose in anticipation.

"How about we find you a corner here, with a computer, a desk. Give you a place to start researching. I think it's the least I can do."

"No. No, thank you. I think what I would really like right now...' Now it was Cole's turn to look expectant... "Is to go home. To Poland."

"Oh." He didn't have the heart for more. His "clever plan" had backfired.

"So that I can talk to my parents. Tell them everything."

The tightening in his heart loosened. Would she be coming back?

Needing to close the space between them, Cole crossed to the sofa, took each of her hands in his, his thumbs rubbing along the backs. They were so different—he and Lina. Considering where they'd each begun life, their paths they'd started, it was a wonder they had found each other at all.

It tore his heart to let her go—but he'd made his move and the outcome hadn't been what he had hoped for. So much for Project Interference. Life was not being terribly shy about showing him his mistakes.

"Would you mind if I were to leave a few things in a corner here, in the basement? I promise they won't take up any space."

Cole snapped to attention. Oh, this was bad. "You're giving up your flat?"

"Well, I think I will probably have to if I'm going

home. The rent will be money I can't afford and…well… seeing as I just quit my job I don't think my landlord will be very happy."

"Sure. Of course. Anything."

Lina tugged her hands out of his, pressing herself up and out of the sofa.

Was that it? Was she just going to leave now? Cole couldn't bear it—couldn't stop himself. He pulled her into his arms, and began to kiss her as if his very life depended on it. His hands cupped her beautiful heart-shaped face as his lips sought connection again and again with hers.

A soft cry escaped Lina's throat when Cole's arms slipped round her waist, hands shifting up her spine as he pulled her in closer to his chest.

Lina found it impossible not to respond. This would be the last time she ever felt him, tasted him. Just Cole and Lina in an office in the heart of Central London— blurring the lines of the busy day whirring past this sweet, soft bubble of perfection. She pulled back for a moment, her fingertips tracing along his face, then one by one his lips, lips teasingly trying to capture her fingers.

She didn't trust herself to brave the words aloud, making them real. *I love you.* She nodded and kissed him fervently, hoping it would be enough. Say enough. They obviously weren't meant to be and his kisses were so very bittersweet. Almost cruel.

Tears sprung to her eyes as she pulled herself out of his arms. "I must go."

Cole nodded. Said nothing to change her mind. Nothing to keep her with him.

She headed to the door without a backward glance. She was doing the right thing. When she returned home she knew she could begin to heal. It would be the first— the only—time she had seen her parents in years without having her name in lights, status, future roles for them to brag about—but she would have her head held high. When she was born she had just been Lina and they had loved her, and that was how she would return to them. A newcomer to a new way of being. Just Lina. As she closed the door to Cole's office, not daring to look behind her, she had to believe that that would be enough.

CHAPTER ELEVEN

COLE STARED AT the phone. He could feel Igor curling up beside his foot and was grateful for the support. He'd need it.

The only way he'd kept his pulse from jumping off the scale was a countless series of steadying breaths. He picked up the phone and stared at the numbers. He'd run through about a thousand different variations on how the conversation with his parents might go—how he'd even say hello—but knew the only way to find out would be to call them. It was late at night in London, but would be just after supper with his parents. They'd most likely be sitting on the porch, gabbing with some neighbors or wandering around his mother's cherished flower garden, pruning, fine-tuning, making sure it was still a contender for Maple Cove's Southern Bloom House Tours. Their house and garden, he imagined, had taken his place in their lives.

He reached down and gave Igor a scratch. The little guy had definitely pushed and prodded Cole's heart apart to accommodate a scruffy-pooch-sized place in it. It sat right next to the Lina-sized portion…a part of his heart he knew would be permanently dedicated to her, no matter what the outcome of her visit home. If that's what it was. He hadn't heard a bean since she'd left and the sheer emptiness he experienced each day without her was draining his energy stores.

He gave his shoulders a tight shrug. If he couldn't be with her, he could at least learn from her. He punched in the numbers that hadn't changed since he was a boy. The American ringtone sounded in his ear sooner than he expected and he almost hung up. Soon enough he heard the shuffle and clatter of his parents' old-time handset being picked up from the base.

"Hello?" It was his mother, her soft Southern accent shifting along the phone line straight into his soul. He'd missed her so much.

"Mama? It's Cole."

The silence that followed was as vast as the ocean that separated them.

"I'll get your father."

She put the receiver down before he could stop her—explain. Tell her how much he loved her. How broken he'd felt in the wake of Katie's death. It was so quiet it was hard to tell if she'd hung up entirely.

The sound of a second line being picked up straightened his spine. Mother and Father on the phone. Was it a sign they had forgiven him?

"Cole?"

"Hey, Dad. It's me."

"Found yourself a job?"

"Yes. Remember? I told you about it in an email. It's a specialist clinic in London. Mostly dancers."

"Oh, right!" His father's voice sounded tinny.

Cole had sent email after email at first. There had been no response to any of them. About a year ago he'd stopped trying altogether. The urge to go on the defensive had started teasing at him. The little boy in him had wanted to say, *What about me? What about my heart-*

ache? I know you lost a daughter-in-law and an idea of
what the future would be—but you gave up what was real.
What was living. You chose to give up your son. Your son
who did the right thing, the only thing, to do in that awful,
awful scenario.

Silence lay between them. So Cole told them about
the clinic, the famous dancers he had met and treated,
the innovations he was hoping En Pointe would make in
the future. All things that would've mysteriously found
their way into the *Maple Cove Gazette* if he'd idly dropped
them into conversation a few years earlier.

He could tell they were half listening, their responses
lacking the energy that would indicate true interest. He
couldn't really blame them. They hadn't spoken in years.
He had, perhaps, been too hopeful to think they would
treat his call as more than what it actually was—an unwelcome interruption to their evening.

"Mom?" There was silence. He tried again. "Mom?"

"Your mother's not up to it, son. She's not on the line
anymore."

"Do you think—"

His father jumped in, his rich voice weighted with
emotion, a weariness Cole had not ever heard before. "I
think perhaps it's best if you just leave it, son. It'd be for
the best."

"What if—"

Again he was interrupted.

"We're really pleased you're doing well over there in
England. I can't keep up with the politics over there. All
that shouting at each other in Parliament… Interesting.
And I catch your mother checking the weather over there
from time to time, so…" He let the implications drift in
and settle. They cared. They just couldn't let go of the po-

sition they'd chosen that would help them deal with their grief. Their disappointments with what would never be.

"All right, then, Dad. Nice to hear your voice."

"Okay, son."

"I love you." He didn't know if his father heard the words or not, the line cut out somewhere in there.

Cole tucked a hand under Igor's tummy and pulled him up into his lap. He'd grown a lot but was still puppyish enough that he could give the furry little beast a cuddle.

He remained dry-eyed. A bit numb. The call hadn't been satisfying in any way—but if he was honest, that had been the likeliest outcome. Falling in love had cranked up his capacity for believing in change. In forgiveness.

He spun the phone handset round a few times on the table, hardly able to bear the quietness when it rattled to a stop.

There was a way to feel better, to fill the hole in his heart. A hole he'd created his own damn self. He picked up the phone and scrolled through the directory, not allowing himself to overthink what he was about to do. He was at a crossroad.

It was decision-making time.

By the river was where Lina missed Cole most.

This river, her childhood river, was nothing like the Thames. No lights sparkling off it when the man you loved held you in his arms, kissing you again and again.

A growl began to form in her chest, manifesting itself into a scream. *"No-o-o-o-o!"*

Her cry bounced back against the sheer stone edges shooting up from the opposite side of the river. Thank heavens her parents lived in the middle of nowhere. Here she had countless places to sneak away to, private nooks and crannies in the wilderness she'd escaped to as a child to dance in. And now she had returned, a grown woman, grieving the loss of the man who had captured her heart.

In the end she'd decided to treat her trip home as coming home. She'd finally plucked up the courage to ring Gemma and ask for her final boxes to be shipped home. *Home.*

The word seemed even more weighted with meaning than ever before. Somehow, some way—in the space of three short months—home had become Cole Manning. His eyes, his smile, his skin, his touch. How a single thing in this small village in Poland could remind her of a doctor from America she didn't know. But it did.

The scent of the late summer flowers. Cole had given her flowers! Tucked one behind her ear the time he took her to Covent Garden. The coffee. Cole drank coffee! Thick and rich, just how she liked it. The *quiet*. The peaceful, sleepy quiet they enjoyed in his back garden that made the rest of London just slip away.

Really, she should be grateful. Grateful she'd only had three months' worth of her heart fall in love with him.

She threw three pebbles into the river. *Plop. Plop. Plop. Sink.*

Her shoulders slumped. Who was she kidding? Her whole entire heart was his and her body was here in Poland, doing what exactly? Standing around with a fish she'd caught over half an hour ago for— She checked her watch. *Niebiosa!* She couldn't believe she'd lost track of time. She'd been doing a lot of that lately. It was nearly time for supper and she had the main dish!

As she ran, she did her best to let gratitude flood her body that she had so much. The ability to run without pain, the *energy* to run. Parents so loving she hadn't felt the slightest bit of shame when she'd finally told them everything—she had only felt comforted, loved. Her old fishing bag slapped against her thigh as she ran. She'd caught a beauty today. Her parents were in fits of giggles each time she brought one home.

"We haven't eaten some of these dishes in years, Michalina!" her father had crowed as she'd insisted on revisiting each of her childhood favorites. "We're not bumpkins, you know. Your mother makes excellent *risotto* and her *paella*? You'd think she was Spanish!"

But Lina had teased and cajoled and gone fishing, for hours on end, soaking up the sun and the meadow-grass-perfumed breeze, huge stacks of medical books by her side. Studying was the only thing that— Nope. Not even studying pushed Cole into the further reaches of her mind. Nothing could.

She ran through the garden and straight into the kitchen, where she was met by the sound of laughter.

There—flanked by her parents, with a cup of her mother's thick, black coffee in his hand and looking as relaxed and as comfortable as if he'd been there a hundred times—was Cole. The pile of boxes she'd left behind at the clinic was stacked neatly by the door. But she'd asked Gemma to ship—

Cole!

Her eyes darted from one parent to the other, their faces wreathed in delighted smiles, and then and only then did she let herself meet those sky-blue eyes that sent her belly on a giddy flip-flop butterfly tour.

What was he doing here?

To press his point home? To get her out of his life completely? To tell her he'd made a terrible mistake?

She could hear her parents commenting on the traffic coming in from the airport, Cole's ability to travel light versus Lina's need for more, but none of it really registered. Her heart didn't even know what to do with the sheer volume of emotion she was experiencing.

Cole.

A warm heat spread through her chest. Watching his lips part into that knee-weakener of a smile felt like being warmed by a little slice of heaven.

She could hardly breathe.

In that moment Cole's eyes locked with hers. Anything that had felt incomplete in her life became whole. She loved him heart and soul. It was the most real thing she had ever felt.

"Earth to Lina." Cole's father waved a hand in front of her face. "Cole, you let this one run the front of your clinic? I am surprised given that she can't even offer you a kind greeting." Her father's voice was thick with pride.

"What are you doing here?" It was all she could manage. All she would allow herself.

"Lina!" her mother's tone was a chirpy chastisement. "Why, where are your manners?"

"Mamo, I'm not a little girl!" Lina was still staring into Cole's eyes, too focused to do little else. If he was here just to rub her face in— *Stop! Give the man a chance.* Her voice softened. "What are you doing here?"

"Come, Marja." Lina's father shooed his wife away from Cole so he could get out from behind the table. "We are cramping the style of the young lovers."

Lina threw a mortified look at her father. Dads, it appeared, could still be embarrassing even when you were twenty-seven.

Cole took Lina's hand in his, tingly sparkles setting her body alight. Wasn't she meant to despise him? Her body certainly didn't. Or her smile.

"Want to show me around town?"

Town was about a hundred meters of a high street,

if one were to call it that. It would only take about five minutes—if that. She tugged her hand free. It was still too much to process. She pulled her fishing tote off her shoulder and called to her mother, *"Mamo, będziemy mieć pierogi z rybą?"*

Cole's eyes ping-ponged between them, clearly hoping for a translation.

"I caught dinner!" She grinned, suddenly feeling as giddy as the teen she'd never really had the chance to be. "My mum is going to make my favorite dish from when I was a little girl."

Cole nodded, remembering. *"Pierogi."*

"Yes, good accent!" Lina's mother nodded, although it very clearly was not. How she could've doubted their kindness—their compassion—for even a second was beyond her. Lina pulled her mother into a quick squeeze before rejoining Cole at the door. "I love my mother." She beamed at her, dusty apron and all, from across the room. "You're a great mother, aren't you?" Her mother waved off the compliment, shooing them out the door as she did so.

Lina's mind did a quick recalculation. "Igor?" Her eyes shot to Cole, forehead raised in concern.

"Taken care of. Gemma has commandeered the full care and lavishing of affection he requires while I'm away."

"Is she the one...?"

"Who gave me your address? Yes."

"Go on." Lina's mother hustled them out of the kitchen, waving her kitchen towel at them to get out so she could have her domain left in peace.

Lina stood outside the house, looking around her. Were they having a joyful reunion or a horrid one? "Would you like to see the river?" If he was horrid, she could push him in. Just a little.

"I think somewhere private might be good." Cole gave her a wink.

"For what?"

"A talk." Cole looked serious and any giddy, excitement that had been playing round Lina's tummy collected in a dejected heap.

Ah.

They walked in silence until they reached the river's edge. She enjoyed his appreciative gaze as he took in what she thought was one of the most beautiful places in the world.

"You saved me, you know." He spoke the words to the river as if meeting her gaze would be too much.

"From what?" She sat on the sandy riverbank.

"Myself." He plunked himself down beside her, legs crossed, hands already busy pulling smooth river stones toward him.

"What do you mean?"

"I mean, you were there for me when I needed you." His gaze grew focused on the stones and he began to build a little tower.

"What are you talking about?" Lina drew back to inspect him. "I've been here."

"I rang my parents."

Lina's eyebrows shot up in surprise.

"I thought if you were brave enough to see your parents, I might follow suit."

"And?"

"Let's just say, I was wise to start with a phone call."

"Oh?"

"I won't be buying a ticket home—to North Carolina," he corrected, "for a while."

"I'm sorry." And she was. It had to have been a painful night and to have gone through it alone? It must've been awful.

He put on a brave face, picked up the stones one by one and flicked them across the river's smooth surface.

"Well, if I'm really honest. I can't say I expected anything less. So…after a bit of man time with Igor…"

Lina arched a curious eyebrow.

"I let him sleep on your pillow." Cole chuckled at the memory, the smile fading from his lips just as quickly. "Then I thought about everything else that was wrong with my life."

Lina folded her arms around her bent knees. She didn't know if she was ready to hear this. And how on earth had she saved him? And from what?

"All I wanted to do, Lina, was be with you."

Her eyes widened.

"I love you, Lina. I love you with all my heart. I think you're passionate. I think you're brave. I have hated every single moment you haven't been in London, in my—our—home, in my arms. I love you."

Lina blinked, staring into his eyes to see if what she saw there matched the words he'd just said. Was this really happening? He loved her?

"I can't believe you're here."

"I can't believe it took me this long."

They sat there a moment beside the river, each looking into the other's eyes until the tautness in their expressions softened. *They were together now.*

Lina scooped up handfuls of sand and scrubbed them along her bare feet, the intensity of emotion almost too much to bear.

"It's probably a good thing you decided to come out here instead of using the telephone." Lina's tone slipped into dry humor mode. "With my nonchangeable, nonrefundable ticket, having you here makes it much easier for me to get you to finally taste genuine Polish ice cream. It's beetroot season!"

Cole threw back his head and laughed. Laughed in way he hadn't since, well, since he and Lina had last been silly together. She had managed to bring that part of him back to life and he would be forever grateful to her.

"Marry me."

Her green eyes popped wide open, her mouth dropping into an astonished O.

"Study, work, whatever you want, but if you love me, please will you marry me? Come back to London. Come *home*," he said, only just resisting the urge to kiss her so that she could answer.

"Of course! Yes!" she answered, disbelief and happiness playing across her face. *"Yes!"* she shouted to the mountaintops soaring above them. *"Mam zamiar poślubić swoją miłość!"*

"What are you saying, you beautiful woman?" Cole drew a hand through her hair, fingers teasing at the nape of her neck to come in closer, receive the kisses he so plainly had to give her.

"I am saying you have made me the happiest woman in the world." As his lips touched hers, Lina couldn't begin to believe this was only the beginning. The beginning of so many new things—all of them with Cole by her side.

"Shall we go tell your parents?" Cole's lips tickled along hers as he spoke. She stole another kiss before answering.

"Not just yet," she whispered, her lips meeting his again and again. "Not just yet."

* * * * *

MILLS & BOON®

MEDICAL ROMANCE™

THE ULTIMATE IN ROMANTIC MEDICAL DRAMA

A sneak peek at next month's titles...

In stores from 24th March 2016:

- **Seduced by the Heart Surgeon** – Carol Marinelli *and* **Falling for the Single Dad** – Emily Forbes

- **The Fling That Changed Everything** – Alison Roberts *and* **A Child to Open Their Hearts** – Marion Lennox

- **The Greek Doctor's Secret Son** – Jennifer Taylor
- **Caught in a Storm of Passion** – Lucy Ryder

Available at WHSmith, Tesco, Asda, Eason, Amazon and Apple

Just can't wait?
Buy our books online a month before they hit the shops!
visit www.millsandboon.co.uk

These books are also available in eBook format!

MILLS & BOON®

Helen Bianchin v Regency Collection!

40% off both collections!

Discover our Helen Bianchin v Regency Collection, a blend of sexy and regal romances. Don't miss this great offer - buy one collection to get a free book but buy both collections to receive 40% off! This fabulous 10 book collection features stories from some of our talented writers.

Visit **www.millsandboon.co.uk** to order yours!

0316_MB520

MILLS & BOON®

Let us take you back in time with our Medieval Brides...

The Novice Bride – Carol Townend

The Dumont Bride – Terri Brisbin

The Lord's Forced Bride – Anne Herries

The Warrior's Princess Bride – Meriel Fuller

The Overlord's Bride – Margaret Moore

Templar Knight, Forbidden Bride – Lynna Banning

Order yours at
www.millsandboon.co.uk/medievalbrides

16_MB519

MILLS & BOON®

Why not subscribe?

Never miss a title and save money too!

Here's what's available to you if you join the exclusive **Mills & Boon® Book Club** today:

- ✦ *Titles up to a month ahead of the shops*
- ✦ *Amazing discounts*
- ✦ *Free P&P*
- ✦ *Earn Bonus Book points that can be redeemed against other titles and gifts*
- ✦ *Choose from monthly or pre-paid plans*

Still want more?

Well, if you join today, we'll even give you ***50% OFF your first parcel!***

So visit **www.millsandboon.co.uk/subs** to be a part of this exclusive Book Club!